Chance Hotel

by

Christopher Gorham Calvin

Chapter One
We Always Have Room

Jason Chance squinted through the sheets of rain that pelted his windshield as he coasted down an empty stretch of dark highway. His eyes burned at the edges and occasionally glossed over with tears, punishment for being on the road too long with too little rest. How many hours had it been? The fight had been the night before- the final fight as he now thought of it, by no means the first but with no uncertainty the last. Jason had spent the early morning hours packing a suitcase of necessities. He blew a silent kiss to his sleeping little girl, shared a regretful glance with his soon-to-be ex-wife, and said hello to the open road- miles and miles of opportunity, if only Jason could commit to a direction.

After dealing with a pressing business matter and putting a few personal affairs in order, Jason crossed state lines. The day was welcoming, with bright sun occasionally shaded by puffy white clouds. Traffic wasn't bad for a weekday, and Jason took advantage of it by rolling down his windows to enjoy the crisp air without being smothered by exhaust. He stopped at a diner for lunch, dodging what, in any other circumstance, would have been perceived as kind, small-talk questions from the waitress. From there he let his fluid levels dictate the next stops- gas when the car needed it, a new fountain drink or coffee when he needed it. The periodic stops gave Jason a chance to stretch his body, while the constant droning of audiobooks and rhythm of music through the car speakers gave Jason a way to occupy his mind.

Despite this, Jason found it impossible to completely clear his head. He would check his cell phone repeatedly to see if his wife had called. The phone wasn't in silent mode, but Jason found more comfort in seeing a lack of missed calls on the screen than he did in trusting his own ears that the phone hadn't rung. Yet in that comfort was also a strange mix of sadness and curiosity. Had he really expected his wife to call? Probably not, unless it was to chastise him for something else he did wrong on his way out the door that morning. Was he hoping she would call anyway? Absolutely, even at the cost of an ear-full of scolding. Jason knew he deserved it. And what about his daughter? She had run to her room crying over yet another screaming match between her parents. By the time the fight was over, she had fallen asleep. Didn't she wonder where her father had gone? Maybe not during the day, as she would assume he was working, but what about when he didn't show for dinner? Another round of tears swelled in Jason's eyes... only this time not from being tired. No, that wouldn't be too strange either, and so the phone continued to sit in silence.

Shortly after night set in, the rain began. It was light at first, but quickly grew heavy, so heavy that some cars had pulled to the side of the road to wait it out. Jason knew he should probably do the same, but he also knew he needed more than a quick pit stop. It was time to get a decent meal and take shelter for the rest of the night. Jason had seen little in the way of civilization for maybe fifty or sixty miles, so he assumed something had to be approaching soon. He pushed forward, rubbing at his eyes as furiously as the windshield wipers swept at the rain. Everything was dark ahead... and very blurry. The lines on the road had melted into puddles of reflective light. The passing trees had been swallowed by the surrounding darkness. The yellow flashing lights ahead were so big and bright-

"Oh shit!" Jason yelled as he slammed on his brakes and narrowly swerved around the stalled vehicle. His car lost traction, the tires squealing loudly as they glided across the wet road. Jason felt his body press against the seat as the car spun, at least once, perhaps twice, before coming to an abrupt halt. Jason grabbed at his chest with a trembling hand as if worried his heart would literally pop out of it. He sat there listening to his own broken breaths, a layer of sweat now readily forming over his entire body.

"I'm okay," Jason muttered to himself. "I'm okay, I'm okay, I'm okay." He repeated it as if trying to assure himself that he hadn't just died.

Jason took a minute, then another, for his body and mind to calm themselves. He quickly inspected himself to confirm he had not been injured. He then looked cautiously around the interior of the car. His messenger bag had flown off the passenger seat. His nearly empty fountain drink had sloshed slightly over the lip of the cup, but otherwise all appeared normal. Jason scanned the perimeter of the highway from his driver-side window. There was no sign of the stalled car, but then again, Jason had no idea how far his own car had spun, and it wasn't as if the rain allowed him to see into the distance anyway. Had he hit something? Jason leaned forward to see as much of the car's hood as possible. There was no sign of damage as far as he could tell. Jason tried to recall if he had heard anything, a thud perhaps, as he lost control of the car. No, he told himself; it was a clean spin-out. He just needed to be thankful it hadn't been worse.

After picking up his bag and cleaning the spilled drink, Jason closed his eyes and took a deep, relaxing breath. For a moment the thought of his daughter flashed across his mind, and Jason wondered whether he should turn around, go back home, try one last time to patch things up- no, there was no patching it up this time. Going home would result in nothing more than one more fight, and Jason didn't want that for anybody. He put the car in gear, ready to resume his journey, and the rain started to ease, as if validating his decision.

But then something caught Jason's eye. He hadn't noticed it in the downpour, but Jason's headlights were no longer shining far into the distance. Their beams were halted only ten feet ahead, obstructed by a fairly plain, slightly deteriorated roadside sign. But as Jason read the words on that sign, he felt a sudden epiphany, an odd sense of knowing, knowing exactly where his journey would take him next:

Chance Hotel

Just Ahead

We Always Have Room

Chapter Two
That's My Name Too

Jason's heartbeat had returned to normal. He was coasting smoothly down the highway, the rain all but stopped, the road clear of any other vehicles. It had only been a few minutes since his near-death experience, but Jason was feeling good, the knowledge that a warm bed and perhaps even some good food lay shortly ahead. And yet, something kept gnawing at him, a thought resurfacing over and over, vying for his attention.

We Always Have Room

What kind of bullshit was that? Jason had seen his fair share of misleading marketing, but clearly there was no way this absolute statement could be true. It was a hotel. It had a certain capacity. Capacity filled? No more room. But the sign claimed otherwise, and the funny thing was that, with no proof to back up the claim, Jason believed it. The hotel was in the middle of nowhere. Jason hadn't seen signs of life for miles and was pretty sure he wouldn't see signs of life for many more. So maybe this hotel truly was big enough to handle whatever load of guests that happened to pass through. Maybe...

Whatever the case, Jason would find out soon enough, for he had reached the hotel's highway exit. Trees flanked him on both sides as he followed a winding path into the unknown. A dot of warm lamplight was visible in the distance. Then several others, and shortly thereafter, the silhouette of a building. As Jason neared, he was able to better size up his destination. There was a main building, maybe twenty to twenty-five stories high. Attached were two smaller, oblong wings, one perhaps five stories high and the other existing at ground level only. The main building and larger wing were lined with rows of rectangular windows- guest rooms, Jason presumed. The smaller wing had large, evenly spaced, arched windows reminiscent of an event space. The structure as a whole had a modern rustic feel, built with a contemporary hotel layout, but adorned with flickering lanterns, natural wood beams, clay flower pots, and other decorations that seamlessly complemented the wilderness that served as the hotel's backdrop.

Jason's attention was drawn to the assortment of vehicles that sat idle in the hotel's parking lot. Some were modern like his own; others were older- much older, in fact, bordering on classic. And all of them shined under beads of water left by the rain. Either the storm had cleaned them well - and Jason supposed it had been strong enough to do so- or these vehicles were already spotless before the rain began. If so, maybe a good car scrubbing was a hotel perk. Jason made a mental reminder to ask later. He slowed his car as he approached the smiling valet waiting at the hotel's front door overhang.

"Good evening, sir," the valet said energetically as Jason rolled down the passenger window. "Checking in this evening?"

"Assuming you have room for me." Jason said dryly, making sure to suppress his sarcasm. "I don't have a reservation."

"Oh no worries, sir," the valet said, followed by an annoyingly chipper "we always have room."

"Right..." Jason was already feeling he would need a bottle of happy pills if he stayed here for any length of time. "I can park it myself if you could just point me to a spot."

The valet flashed his pearly whites. "Oh not a chance, sir. You get full service here. Just leave me the keys and head inside to get settled." He motioned toward Jason's messenger bag. "We'll make sure everything gets to your room safely. Just the one bag?"

Jason instinctively place a hand on the bag as if worried the valet would snatch it from him. It was a silly thought, he knew, but then again... "I'll take this one. I have a suitcase in the trunk."

"As you wish, sir."

Where was that hospitality when I *wished* to park my own car? Jason wondered silently. He was getting cranky, no, hangry, with a side of exhausted thrown in for good measure. Jason forced a smile and caved to the valet, relinquishing possession of the car, but not his messenger bag, and headed toward the revolving front door of the hotel.

"Oh, sir?" Jason spun upon hearing the valet's voice, wondering if there was a problem. In doing so, he felt a slight moment of dizziness. "One coat of wax or two?"

"I'm sorry?" Jason blinked his eyes hard to get the world to stabilize.

"Your car," the valet explained. "We offer a complimentary wash and wax for every guest. Would you like one coat or two?"

"Um-" Jason wasn't sure if he had ever made a decision about waxing his car in his life. "Whatever you think is best."

The valet gave a theatrical chuckle. "Of course, sir. I'll take care of it."

And with that, the valet was off. No, Jason thought, the valet was *off* well before he drove away with Jason's car. Left with nothing but the sound of nocturnal critters to keep him company outside, Jason turned once again and proceeded through the hotel's revolving front door. The lobby interior was mostly what he expected: a wide open space with a long check-in counter to one side, couches and wicker chairs forming a pseudo-great room around a large, stone fireplace to the other side, branching hallways angled toward the hotel's smaller wings, a bay of elevators, likely to the guest room floors, prominently on display dead ahead, and the soft, golden sheen of warm light emanating down from rustic chandeliers hanging overhead. Jason spotted another small offshoot just past the pseudo-great room as a family of four emerged from it. One of the kids was carrying a to-go container, and in the distance behind them, Jason spotted what appeared to be a restaurant dining table. Don't worry, he told his grumbling stomach, that's our next stop.

"Welcome to the Chance Hotel," a friendly voice said, startling Jason from his thoughts. "How may I help you?"

Jason turned to face the source of the voice. It was a sharply dressed young woman, flashing a smile only matched by the valet. Jason had seen her in his peripheral vision when he first walked in, only then she was standing near a small wooden podium talking with an equally sharp dressed, slightly older, man. Jason scanned for the podium again, finding it just in front of the elevator bay. The sharply dressed man was still standing there, staring back at him.

"I'm Leila," the young woman said, recapturing Jason's attention. "I'm one of the hotel's concierges. You look a little lost. Can I help with anything?"

"I just need to check in," Jason said blankly. His mind was detached from his words, distracted, but he didn't know why. "I assume-" He pointed to the long counter to the side.

"Yes, sir," Leila confirmed. "Our hotel manager will take good care of you. And if you need anything else," she placed a noticeable emphasis on the word *anything*, and Jason picked up on a shift in both her eyes and smile, an almost mischievous shift, he thought, "don't hesitate to ask."

As Leila turned away, Jason gazed past her at the wooden podium. The sharply dressed man, the other concierge Jason now pieced together, lifted his hand in a limp wave accompanied by a half-hearted smile. I guess he's the less friendly of the two, Jason thought bluntly. Then again, maybe she's a little too friendly... He let the thought go and proceeded to the check-in counter, where a single suited gentleman ruffled through loose papers.

"Hi there," Jason said, forcing every ounce of energy he had left into maintaining his social graces. "I'd like to see about getting a room, please."

"You'd like to see about getting a room," the hotel manager said smartly, "or you'd like to get a room?"

I'd like to punch you in the face, Jason almost mouthed back, but then the manager broke into playful laughter. "I'm just messing with you," he said sincerely. "You look a little on edge. You should speak with Leila and Richard when we get done here." He motioned toward the concierges. "They could set you up with a spa treatment, meditation session, hell, a good boxing workout, if that's what you need."

"I don't know if I'll be staying long enough for-"

"Oh, that's right," the manger said, shaking his head with inward disappointment. "I always get ahead of myself. First things first." He moved to a small computer and began typing. "How long are you staying and what kind of room are you interested in?"

Jason took a moment to think before answering. He didn't have a clear destination when he left his house that morning, and this place seemed as nice as any to hunker down in while he figured that destination out. But something about this place also gave him the creeps. Everyone was trying too hard to put on a friendly show... well, everyone except Richard, of course. Jason stammered, "I- I guess just one night... for now, anyway."

The manager smiled. "I'll put you down for three, just in case. Don't worry, there's no cancellation penalty." He typed a few keystrokes. "And the type of room?"

"Nothing fancy," Jason said honestly. He was a simple person when it came to amenities. A bed, toilet, shower, and maybe some air conditioning was all he really needed. "Standard room, or whatever you have closest to it."

"Don't worry, sir-" the manager began.

"You always have standard room?" Jason interrupted, stupidly pleased with himself for coming up with the quick play on words in his state of near delirium.

The manager pursed his lips curiously. "I was going to say we should have something to fit your needs." He typed again, then quietly added, "but what you said is true too."

Jason didn't have a response this time. After a moment, the manager tapped the keyboard in triumph and continued.

"Alright, we've got a room ready for you on the fifth floor of this building," he said. "I'll just need to collect some personal details, starting with your name."

"Coincidentally, it's Chance," Jason said, assuming the manager would make the connection. "Jason Chance." The manager's smile faltered. It only lasted a second, but there was no doubt in Jason's mind about having seen it. "Is something wrong?" Jason asked.

"No," the manger said, his original smile working extremely hard to hide some other emotion. Was it curiosity, concern, sadness, anger, fear? Jason wasn't sure. "No problem at all. It's just-" now it was the manager's turn to stammer. "It's just… that's my name too."

In that moment, Jason felt a sudden weight pressing down on him. Something wasn't right here. He knew that for certain. And this manager- was he being serious, or was this another friendly joke? And why were all eyes in the lobby now turned toward him? Or, not all eyes, Jason quickly realized, for there were guests roaming and lounging in the pseudo-great room that couldn't care less about this revelation. But the eyes of the manager and his hidden emotion, the eyes of the two concierges, both staring with fearful interest, the eyes of a maid Jason hadn't previously noticed, until she dropped her duster and bent to retrieve it with a shaky hand, and the eyes of a woman in a light grey suit, gripping a clipboard and pen so tightly Jason half expected one of them to crack. Hotel employees, Jason concluded, none of them in earshot, but all of them reacting as if his spoken name prophesied the end of the world... or their world anyway.

Jason inadvertently vocalized his inner thoughts. "What the hell is this place?"

Chapter Three
No Charges For The Chances

"Excuse me, sir?" The hotel manager asked as if he hadn't heard Jason's exclamation.

Jason was taken aback by the question. Had he just spoken out loud? Even though the words had left his lips mere moments earlier, he truly wasn't sure. Between the emotional fight the night before, the day-long drive through sun and rain, his near death experience with the stalled car, and the- to put it nicely- weirdness of this place, Jason's brain was on overload. He couldn't be certain of his own words... and if he wasn't sure about them, could he even be sure about everyone else's?

"You did just say," Jason began, hardly believing he was even asking the question, "that your name is Jason Chance too?"

The manager chuckled once more. "Oh no, sir," he said with a friendly shake of the head. "The name is Chance, but it's Marvin- Marvin Chance."

Marvin pointed to a nameplate pinned to his right breast pocket. Yup, Jason thought, that says Marvin. But had it been there the whole time? If it had, how hadn't he noticed it sooner? If it hadn't, when did the manager slip it on?

"Huh..." Jason was dumfounded, so he responded with the first bland thought that came to mind. "No relation, I presume?"

"You tell me!" Marvin bellowed with more laughter.

Laughter and smiles, Jason thought; they were becoming a trend around here. Well at least now he knew where he could

16

score some of those happy pills he might need. "So, uh, you own the hotel?" He asked.

"I'm afraid not, sir," Marvin said a bit more calmly. "This hotel was around long before I was a part of this world. Probably be around long after I leave it too."

"Family business?" Jason pressed.

"Not that I'm aware," Marvin replied.

There was something odd about his responses to the family oriented questions, Jason noticed, as if he were both answering them and dodging them at the same time. "So just a coincidence then that the hotel bears your surname?" He asked.

"As far as I know."

There it was again, a non-answer answer. "And a coincidence that the hotel bears my surname too?" Jason followed.

"Well," Marvin started as if he would provide more concrete information this time, "we do share the same surname, Mr. Chance." His voice wasn't confrontational, but it did come across as challenging. "Of course," Marvin added, "we aren't the only two people to step foot in this hotel with the name Chance. I guess it's more common than you might think!"

"If you say so..." Jason acquiesced. He quickly scanned the lobby, wondering if the hotel employees were still eyeing him as if he were the spawn of Satan. But both the guests and employees were going about their individual business, seemingly oblivious or uncaring about Jason's conversation with Marvin. Had they been this way the entire time? Surely Jason hadn't imagined the frightened stares, the shaky hands, the- he suddenly felt dizzy again.

"Whoa, now," Marvin told him, noticing the visible unsteadiness in Jason's posture. "It looks like we need to speed this up so you can get some rest." He typed a few more keystrokes into his computer. "Okay, so as I was saying, we have you for three nights, suite on the twenty-first floor-"

"What happened to the fifth floor?" Jason interjected while simultaneously questioning his own mental recollection of whether Marvin had previously mentioned the fifth floor. "Standard room?" Had Marvin said that either?

"Complimentary upgrade," Marvin responded with a smile. "For someone who bears the hotel's namesake."

"It's really not necessary."

"It's really not a problem," Marvin retorted. "Your suitcase should already be there-"

"You just assigned the room!" Jason said wildly.

Another smile. "We move fast around here when we need to." Marvin tapped his keyboard in triumph, just as he had when booking the original standard room. "Okie-dokie. You're all set." He grabbed a magnetic keycard from a nearby drawer and handed it to Jason. "Room 2101. Take the main elevators and turn left when you reach your floor."

Jason eyed the keycard suspiciously. "Don't you want a credit card or something to cover incidentals or make sure I don't stiff you?"

"Not necessary, Mr. Chance," Marvin said. "Have a good evening... and do get some rest."

The hotel manager quickly stepped away as if he had something more important to deal with. Perplexed, Jason followed after him, catching him at the podium where the two concierges still stood.

"Why not?" Jason asked loudly.

"I'm sorry?"

"Why don't you need my credit card?" Jason clarified. "Every hotel I've ever stayed in has asked to keep a form of payment on file." Jason caught the male concierge, Richard, share what appeared to be a nervous glance with Leila. "What makes this place so different?"

"Well, it's hotel policy, Mr. Chance," Marvin said as if Jason

18

should have known better. "There are no charges for the Chances."

"That's the stupidest thing I've ever heard." It wasn't until after the words had already escaped his mouth that Jason realized he had said them. He tried to backpedal, but now his words failed him altogether. "I mean, I-"

"It's okay, Mr. Chance," Marvin said reassuringly. "Stupid or not, it is hotel policy, and as manager, I'm obliged to enforce that policy."

Jason continued to find himself at a loss for words. These people were crazy. Heck, this whole place seemed a little crazy. But then again, Jason hadn't felt like he was in his right mind since arriving either. He tapped the keycard against his palm. "I think- I'm going to go to my room now," was all he could manage to say.

Jason vaguely heard Marvin praising his decision as he strolled past the podium toward the elevator bays. He pushed the call button and waited, watching the old-fashioned analogue arrow above the sliding doors slowly arch across decreasing numbers.

"Might I make a suggestion?"

Leila's soothing voice was so close to Jason's ear that he could feel the short bursts of her warm breath. Jason turned to her, half expecting to see the entire podium trio standing there with butcher knives or chloroform towels or alien heads- any of the three wouldn't be that out of line with the direction this insane movie of a night had taken. But it was just Leila standing there, with no weapon and definitely no alien head, and instead with a much needed expression of compassion.

"I know you're exhausted," she continued, "but you should probably get a bite to eat before heading to bed." She motioned toward the corridor through which Jason had earlier spotted a dining table. "Our in-house restaurant is the best. Our chef is so good that he'll make you want to stay here forever. Well, that or take him home with you." She smiled welcomingly. "Either way, you get the point."

"Thanks," Jason said sincerely, though he wasn't sure if it came across that way in his current mental state. He thought about the promise he had made to his stomach. Then he thought about laying his head on a soft pillow and saying goodnight to this overbearing day. Promises were made to be broken after all. "I may just wait until breakfast."

Leila looked as though she was genuinely disappointed with his response. "Well if you change your mind, let me know on your way to the restaurant." Her eyes met his. "I can head up to your room, turn down your sheets, prepare a warm bath and some relaxing music..." She let that last suggestion linger between them for more than a passing moment. "While you eat, of course."

Any meaningful words escaped Jason again, so all he said was: "of course."

The elevator chimed, signaling that the car had arrived. Jason waited for a handful of other guests to disembark before stepping inside. Leila was right; he was exhausted. She was also right that he should probably try to eat. But Jason was worried that any attempt at getting through a meal would end with his face substituting his plate of food for the pillow it longingly needed. Jason reached for the button to the twenty-first floor, then hesitated. An upper floor suite would be one of the most expensive rooms in the hotel. You don't just give those out for free to a one-off guest, especially for a policy that sounded so ridiculous it had to be imaginary. Jason marched off the elevator and returned to the podium.

"I'd like to see it," Jason told Marvin, interrupting an ongoing conversation between the manager and Richard. Both men eyed him curiously. "I'd like to see the policy. You must have a hotel handbook or something official you could show me."

The two men pressed their lips together as if trying to stifle laughter, but then the laughter broke through anyway. It wasn't menacing laughter, as Jason had expected, but friendly laughter shared by two people who were privy to a common joke. Jason glanced at Leila, who rolled her eyes playfully at her coworkers' antics.

"There is no policy," Jason accused. "You're messing with me again." His words incited even louder laughter now, angering Jason, who felt that, despite receiving what was otherwise five-star service, he was being taken for a fool. "Is it also policy to make fun of your guests like this?"

"No, sir," Marvin choked through the laughter before settling himself down. "No. I'm sorry, Mr. Chance. We're just laughing because there is no handbook to show you."

"Because there is no policy," Jason accused once more.

"Oh, no," Marvin replied matter-of-factly. "There is a policy. It's just- well, this hotel's so old that they put policies of that importance in much more obvious places."

He gestured past Jason, back toward the elevator bay, but with his hand angled upward, not quite on a trajectory for the ceiling, but close enough. Jason followed with his gaze until his eyes landed on a series of metallic gold, capital letters that someone had once painstakingly centered near the top of the elevator bay wall- a permanent, decorative fixture that blended into its surroundings, but was on display for those who wished to take notice:

NO CHARGES FOR THE CHANCES

"Well I'll be damned," Jason muttered in disbelief.

He wasn't sure how long he stood there repeatedly reading that phrase, but he guessed it must have been at least a minute or two. Jason was eventually snapped out of his trance by Leila, who quietly took him by the arm and led him away from the elevator bays. As he passed the podium, Jason heard himself utter a weak thank you or two to Marvin and Richard, and when Leila stopped him, Jason found himself just outside the dining room hallway.

"Enjoy your dinner, Mr. Chance," she said warmly.

Jason debated reiterating his original intent, to break the promise to his belly and skip his meal, to head straight to bed, but then the aromas of freshly baked bread and warm olive oil and sizzling meats and sugary desserts all began to waft past him. At that moment, Jason realized his decision had already been made for him. He looked at Leila gratefully. "I will."

Chapter Four
It's What You Really Want

The hotel restaurant was much larger than Jason had expected based on his initial glance. He estimated it held maybe fifty or so tables, all evenly spaced across elegant carpet, each with a dark tablecloth and large burning candle in the center. The candles provided the primary source of light for the space, the overhead chandeliers purposefully dimmed, the windows of the exterior facing walls displaying only the darkness of the surrounding woods. Decorative, open-flame fire pits strategically placed among the tables gave the room a cozy feel, and a live pianist filled the air with a low-key, relaxing tune. A glossy, dark wood bar spanned one of the longer walls of the restaurant. Smaller, shot glass candles were spaced equally along it, one for each barstool, and an extensive selection of liquors lined row after row of glass shelving that nearly ran nearly the length of the bar itself. At the entrance to the restaurant was a wooden podium, much like the concierge podium in the lobby, and standing behind it with shoulders straight was another sharply dressed woman patiently awaiting Jason's arrival.

"Good evening, Mr. Chance," she said. "My name's Marie. I'll be your hostess this evening."

Jason glanced at the nameplate pinned to her right breast pocket. Yup, he thought in a slight moment of déjà vu; that says Marie. "Hi Marie."

"Would you like table seating or bar seating this evening?"

She asked.

Jason perused his options. Hotel guests were spaced sporadically among the tables such that none were too close to each other, but also such that no one open table was very secluded. The bar, on the other hand, had a pair of businessmen nursing drinks at one end, but was otherwise wide open. That option seemed much more comfortable in Jason's unsteady state. He relayed his choice to Marie.

"Sure thing," she said with a pep in her step. "Follow me."

Marie led Jason to an area of the bar about a third of the way down from where it began. It couldn't have been a more perfect spot- not at the front end where Jason would be cramped, not at the far end where Jason would have to listen to the businessmen drone on about whatever money they were making or losing today, and about as far away as one could get from the nearest populated table. It was Jason's own personal dining space.

"I'll have a waiter bring some ice water shortly," Marie told him before motioning toward his messenger bag. "Would you like me to hold that up front while you eat? We have a secure coat closet."

"No thank you." Jason slipped the messenger bag from around his arm and placed it on a neighboring barstool, giving it a slight pat with his hand. "I'd like a little company with my meal," he joked lightly.

"Of course, Mr. Chance."

Marie then left him to get settled. A few moments later, a waiter delivered a tall glass of ice water as promised. Strangely, the waiter didn't ask whether Jason wanted something else to drink, but Jason didn't mind. In fact, some ice water was exactly what he needed to rehydrate and perhaps clear his head. More strange was that the waiter didn't take Jason's order either, and neither the waiter nor Marie had left him with a menu. Uh oh, Jason thought stupidly, the five-star service is wavering already.

He chuckled to himself.

"Something funny?" A deep male voice asked. Jason looked up from his glass of water to find a hulking, dark-skinned body enveloped in a bright white coat standing behind the bar. The chef, Jason presumed, only this chef looked like he had been more than a chef at one point in time. Ex-military perhaps. "I like a good joke," the chef said with absolutely no humor in his voice.

"I'm honestly just laughing at myself," Jason replied timidly. "It's been a long day."

"I bet." The chef glared at him with an oddly knowing eye. "The name's Terrance, and I will be the preparer of your food this fine evening. What would you like?"

Jason shrugged. "I uh- I haven't seen a menu yet."

Terrance raised his eyebrows and leaned toward Jason, his mass intimidating as it stretched across the bar top. "And?"

Jason's words were slow with confusion. "And I don't know what you've got?" It was a half statement, half question kind of response.

"And that somehow changes what you want?"

Terrance was giving Jason a look that said *you're going to be eating out of the vending machine if you keep this up*, so Jason tried a different approach. "May I please see a menu?" He added for good measure: "Sir?" Jason spoke as if he was a child who had done something wrong.

Terrance grunted, maybe even growled, as he stood back and reached under the bar. He removed a large, glossy bi-fold from some unseen hiding spot and held it at Jason's eye level. "Does this help?" The chef said sarcastically.

The front of the menu was black, with the name Chance Hotel centered in gold lettering. The food options were on the interior, but Jason thought if he tried to grab the menu, his hand might become the hotel's newest special of the day. He stared, unmoving, awaiting further instructions, when a child's voice rang out behind him.

"Bye, Chef!" The voice said gleefully. "Thanks for another amazing meal!"

Terrance's intimidating scowl transformed in a flash. The beast of a man was beaming, his body loose as he tossed a wave to the child Jason was too afraid to look for, as it would require him turning his back to Terrance. "No problem, Pete!" The chef yelled. "Score one for me at your game tomorrow!"

"I'll do my best!"

The child's voice was more distant with that final response, and a moment later Terrance turned his attention back to Jason, his body rigid once more, the scowl back in full force. Jason tried to speak, but he couldn't think of anything safe to say. Maybe he should tell the chef he had a little league game tomorrow too? "Look man- sir, Chef- Chef Terrance-" Jason saw the hulking man noticeably roll his eyes. "I don't know what you want from me."

"I want," Terrance said in a slow, stern voice, "you to tell me what you would like for dinner." Jason's eyes instinctually focused on the menu in Terrance's hand. "Oh good God, man!" Terrance exclaimed. "Look," he waved the menu within Jason's grasp, "I could give you this and you could pick from the limited selection on it and whatever you picked would be delicious." He slammed the menu down. "But it wouldn't be what you want." Terrance slid the menu in Jason's direction, as if tempting him to pick it up. "You're the guest. You worry about making your request. I'm the chef. Let me worry about how I'll actually get it to you."

Jason still wanted to see the menu, but now the challenge had been established. Chef Terrance wanted to know what Jason wanted, absent any restrictions whatsoever? Jason would gladly tell him. "I would like a poached lobster tail with a hint of garlic, a golden brown crostini with melted cheese on top, and a side of heavily buttered, heavily seasoned, slightly charred broccoli florets. I'm not picky about the cheese or seasoning."

Jason had purposely chosen seafood since a hotel this far in the middle of nowhere probably wouldn't keep a large quantity of it on-hand. He specified a crostini over cheesy garlic bread because it was the less likely of the two to be in the restaurant's kitchen. And he chose the broccoli- well, because he liked broccoli and was curious what Chef Terrance would do with the flexibility in his instructions. Jason watched as his opponent eyed him with a *challenge accepted* kind of stare.

"Coming right up, Mr. Chance."

Chef Terrance took the unused menu with him and returned to the kitchen. In the silence that followed, several questions arose in Jason's mind: Why the hell had Chef Terrance been so confrontational with him? The man obviously had a soft side, but maybe it was only reserved for children? And when did Chef Terrance learn his name? Jason didn't remember offering it, but he supposed Marie could have shared the intel behind closed doors. But then, how did Marie get his name? And speaking of doors- did Marie really offer to put his bag in a *secure* coat closet? Why did a coat closet need security? Better yet, why had she assumed his bag needed security? Before Jason could address a single thought, Chef Terrance returned and aggressively set a plate in front of him.

"What the hell is this?" Jason asked as he observed the lightly toasted peanut butter and jelly sandwich sitting before him.

"It's your dinner, Mr. Chance," Terrance replied as if nothing was wrong.

"It's not what I ordered."

"It's not what you ordered," Terrance said, once again leaning in to ensure he had Jason's undivided attention, "but it's what you really want."

So this was how Terrance was going to play it, huh? Jason was starting to get a feel for how this man thought, how he used his physical presence to push his own agenda, to mess with others just to see if they would cave in or fight back. Jason locked eyes with the chef and slid the plate back towards him. "I would like," he said with conviction, "a poached lobster tail with a hint of garlic, a golden brown crostini with melted cheese on top, and a side of heavily buttered, heavily seasoned, slightly charred broccoli florets." He then repeated with emphasis: "I'm not picky about the cheese or seasoning."

Terrance nodded respectfully, and for a moment Jason even thought he saw one edge of the hulking man's lips curl upward. "Very well," Terrance told him.

He took the plate and returned to the kitchen once more. Jason slumped on his bar stool, relief washing over him that Chef Terrance hadn't tried to knock his head off for his insubordination. Then, as he waited for his new meal, Jason pondered what Chef Terrance would present next. The peanut butter and jelly sandwich was the easy way out, something simple that anyone without a peanut allergy might acquiesce to. But if Chef Terrance couldn't produce Jason's exact order- and Jason was feeling fairly confident he couldn't- then the chef would next need to produce something equally or even more satisfying to stop Jason from pushing back. Jason nursed his glass of ice water as he watched an analogue clock on the wall. Five minutes passed, then five more. Chef Terrance emerged from the kitchen with a plate in hand, but brought it to another waiting guest. On his way back to the kitchen, he gave Jason a wag of his finger. What the hell was that supposed to mean? Jason wondered. A few more minutes passed, then Chef Terrance appeared again, this time headed in Jason's direction.

"Your order," the chef said with more than a hint of disdain in his voice. "Be careful. The plate's hot."

Jason looked at the meal- his meal, the *exact* meal he ordered, right down to the lightly charred broccoli tips. "How did you-"

But Chef Terrance was gone, probably back to the kitchen to sulk in his defeat. The aroma from Jason's plate activated his salivary glands. He grabbed his utensils and dove in, first trying the lobster, then the broccoli. They were amazing, a unique burst of flavor with each bite. Jason tried the crostini- absolutely scrumptious. He took a sip of water and went in for a second bite... then stopped and stared at the sizable chunk of lobster glistening at the end of his fork. It truly was the best poached lobster he had ever eaten; it looked amazing, smelled amazing, and more importantly, tasted amazing. So why then didn't he want another bite? Jason's stomach pleaded with him to satiate it, and it was then that Jason realized as good as this dish was, it wasn't going to get that job done.

"Pssst," Chef Terrance hissed quietly. Jason looked up from his dinner to find the hulking man standing in front of him once more, another plate in his hand, and on the plate a lightly toasted peanut butter and jelly sandwich. "I made you a fresh one. The other one sat too long. Bread got mushy." The chef extended his free hand toward Jason's meal. "May I?" Jason nodded and silently surrendered his fork. Chef Terrance swapped the lobster dinner with the sandwich. "Enjoy," the hulking man said with uncharacteristic sincerity.

And then he was gone again. Jason stared at the sandwich, confused even by his own actions. Then the first wave of that lightly toasted bread filled his nasal cavities. It was soon accompanied by the sweetness and nuttiness of its contents, a harmony of flavors that longed to be consumed. Jason took a bite, then another, and another after that. A couple of minutes later only crumbs remained to evidence the sandwich massacre that had just taken place. But Jason was happy, and his stomach was even happier, for that was the best damn peanut butter and jelly sandwich he had ever had.

Chapter Five
L

When his meal was over, Jason tried to pass his credit card to Marie, offering to pay for the peanut butter and jelly sandwich he ate, the one he didn't, and the lobster dish he assumed went to waste, but secretly thought might have been eaten by Chef Terrance.

"Not necessary, Mr. Chance," Marie had said when she refused his payment. "There are no charges for the Chances."

Slightly annoyed and determined to pay for something before he checked out of this hotel, Jason dropped a couple of folded dollar bills in the pianist's tip jar. He then left the restaurant, noticing that the lobby was much emptier and quieter than when he first checked in, and returned to the elevator bays Leila had cleverly deterred him from earlier. Speaking of Leila- she was nowhere to be seen following Jason's dinner. Neither was Marvin nor Richard, or any of the other hotel employees Jason had seen in the lobby earlier that night. In fact, there were no hotel employees present at all, leaving Jason to wonder what would happen if another guest arrived. Oh well, he thought, not my problem. He called the elevator and proceeded to the twenty-first floor.

The elevator doors opened to a carpeted foyer where two recliners flanked a window to the woods and a heavy wooden desk sat opposite the elevator bays. Atop the desk was a potted plant, a chessboard, and what Jason assumed was a service phone to the front desk. Jason passed through the foyer to an adjacent hallway lined with guest room doors. The doors were spaced much farther apart than he was used to in other hotels, likely because he didn't stay in suites at other hotels, and there were a total only four or five of them- Jason couldn't be sure given the dim lighting at the far end of the hall. He found the door to his room, buzzed himself in with the magnetic keycard Marvin had given him, and flipped on the lights.

The guest suite did not disappoint. Designed with an open floor plan in mind, the door opened to a spacious living area with a couch, coffee table, and wall-mounted television. To the left was a large kitchenette- though after his meal that night Jason wondered why anyone would even use it- with a full size fridge, gas cooktop, built-in oven and microwave, and island seating. Jason whistled in awe as he set his messenger bag on the island counter. The living area alone was bigger than most hotel rooms Jason had previously stayed in, and he wondered what this would have cost him had he not had the lucky disposition of being born a Chance.

To the right of the entrance, through a set of open double doors, was the bedroom, which Jason estimated had a footprint equal to the living area and kitchenette combined. The bedroom was populated with a king sized bed, a cushy recliner, a dresser, and another wall-mounted television. The bed sheets were turned down and a stack of fluffy pillows had been propped to one side. On the nightstand next to the pillows was an ice bucket, filled, with the top of a small glass bottle protruding from the frozen lumps it contained. Milk? Jason thought as he lifted the frosty bottle and examined the white liquid sloshing inside. There was a folded note hanging from the neck of the bottle by red ribbon:

I thought you might like this to chase down the peanut butter. -L

Jason smiled. Did Leila treat all the hotel guests this well? Probably, Jason admitted, though he still held on to the slight chance that he was receiving extra special treatment. A small object carefully placed at the base of the pillows grabbed his attention next. It was a paperback novel- horror or science fiction by the looks of it, with a partially shadowed, tentacled creature on the cover. When Jason picked it up to get a closer look, another folded note fell from its pages:

Just in case you know how to read. -R

Well, Jason told himself after taking a moment to absorb the peculiar message, I guess it's the thought that counts. He set the book on the nightstand and proceeded to a closed door leading to an adjacent room. The bathroom, Jason assumed, or rather hoped, otherwise he might have just discovered the true purpose of the kitchenette. As Jason approached the door, he heard a relaxing melody playing within. She didn't... he wondered, already knowing the answer. A plume of steam rolled over Jason's body as he opened the bathroom door. Inside the large, tile-lined space, a warm bath had already been drawn. Thick terrycloth towels hung from what appeared to be a built-in towel warmer, and a small, old-fashioned radio- the source of the relaxing music- glowed on the corner of the double vanity.

Jason returned to the bedroom and downed a glass of milk. He then stripped his clothes, grabbed the novel and his cell phone and immersed himself in the warm water of the tub. Jason allowed himself a few minutes of pure relaxation, time for the water to soften his skin, the steam to open his pores, time to simply zone out and let go of the stresses of the day. When time was up, he reached for his phone and checked again for missed calls, but there were none. Jason glanced at the clock. His wife and little girl would be getting ready for bed about now. Maybe he should call them, not to talk or fight or rehash what had already been said and done, but to simply say goodnight. Jason found his wife's name in the recent call list. No, he then told himself. His daughter didn't know he was gone for good yet; no sense in upsetting her right before bed. Jason put the phone to sleep and set it aside.

He reached for a towel to dry his hands and grabbed the novel. Jason knew he should let his eyes rest, but he also knew that if he didn't occupy his mind, he would end up dwelling on his family feud from the night before. He flipped open the cover of the book and lazily skimmed the first page. The main character was a fisherman named Hap, and he apparently had a history with some sea monster, but the townsfolk accused him of going crazy on the open water.

Let me guess, Jason thought, the sea monster is real and a lot of townsfolk are going to die before they accept that Hap is completely sane...

A few pages later, the first of the townsfolk met his demise, and the rest chalked it up to a freak accident. "That figures," Jason muttered under his breath before wondering why Richard left him such a ridiculous book. Nonetheless, he kept reading. The bath had somehow stayed warm- Jason suspected it had heaters beneath the ceramic- and as dumb as the novel was, it was succeeding at distracting him from his thoughts. A few deaths later and, surprise surprise, the townsfolk were turning to Hap to help save the day. By page sixty, he was assembling a ragtag crew of fisherman who, despite being totally unqualified, Jason suspected would hunt the sea monster down in honor of all those lives that had been lost.

The air suddenly cracked so loudly that it pierced the bedroom walls and startled Jason in the tub. Thunder? Jason wondered as he set the novel down. The air cracked again, and this time Jason was pretty sure it wasn't thunder. It was higher pitched and more forceful than that. Jason climbed out of the tub and wrapped a towel around himself. He pulled back the edge of the curtain on the bedroom window and stared out into the night, steeling himself for the next crack. Jason wasn't prepared enough, though, when it blasted his ears only moments later, sending a nerve-racking jolt through his body. After composing himself, Jason looked into the darkness once more. There had been no flash of light, no visual indication that a storm was nearing. In fact, Jason then realized, the sound hadn't come from the sky at all. It had come from-

Crack! The noise blasted him again, not from above, but from below. Jason looked down, where twenty-one stories beneath him a dimly lit cement path wound from the hotel's main building, through landscaping, and to the building Jason had guessed was an event space. There was a flashing, no flickering, of blue-ish light just outside of Jason's view. *Crack!* That was the source, Jason was sure of it.

A tall, blonde man ran onto the path yelling something Jason couldn't make out from this height. He seemed frantic, repeatedly looking back as he tripped over his own feet. *Crack!* Jason flinched once more at the noise. He could only imagine how loud it must be at ground level, and knew it was at least loud enough to bring the blonde man quivering to his knees. Jason watched as the man's gaze shifted upward from the blue-ish light, as if looking at something tall that Jason couldn't see from his angle. An instant later, a large, fleshy tentacle shot out of the dark, a miniature tidal wave of foamy water following as it cracked like a thunderous whip and wrapped around the blonde man. The tentacle retreated as fast as it had emerged, taking the man with it and sending smaller waves of froth into the landscaping.

Jason stumbled back from the window, terrified. He tripped on the towel he had wrapped around his waist and crashed sideways into the nightstand, knocking his head against the heavy ice bucket. The bedroom grew dark...

When Jason opened his eyes, he was back in the bathroom, soaking in warm water and still listening to the relaxing sounds of the radio. He looked at the waterlogged novel struggling to stay afloat in the tub and wondered how long he had been asleep. A half hour or so, Jason ultimately determined after checking the time on his phone. The side of his head throbbed, no doubt from slamming it against the ceramic tub in his sleep. It was probably what woke him, he surmised. Jason grabbed a towel- the same towel he had dreamed of grabbing already- and wrapped it around himself as he stepped out of the tub. He drained the water, tossed the ruined book in the bathroom trash can, turned off the radio, and walked back into the silent bedroom.

Everything was as he left it. There was no sign that he tripped into the nightstand, no disturbance in the ice bucket or the neighboring glass he had used to grab a swallow of milk before his bath. Well yeah, Jason reprimanded himself, why would there be? He got dressed and sat on the edge of the bed, checking his phone one last time for a missed call he knew wouldn't be there. He then lay back against the stack of pillows, sinking softly into a comforting embrace. Though his body was pleased, Jason's mind couldn't settle down. Deep down he knew it had just been a dream, yet Jason needed something more concrete to put his mind at ease, a confirmation that he hadn't truly witnessed a giant tentacle monster murdering another hotel guest. He stood back up and strolled to the bedroom window. Just one look, he told himself before pulling back the curtain, one look to confirm nothing's out there. Then, after a calming breath, Jason peered out.

It was just as he remembered from his dream. Mostly darkness, with the only light coming from the ground below, where a winding path did indeed bridge the gap between the hotel's main building and one of its wings. But there was no blonde man, there was no tentacle, nor loud cracking, nor flickering blue-ish light. All was normal, at least insofar as anything was normal at the Chance Hotel, and Jason was about to let the curtain fall back into place when one thing that differed from his dream caught his eye. A yellow object- no, two yellow objects- on the winding path. Even from this distance, Jason could make out enough of their distinct shapes to conclude what they were: wet floor signs. A man in janitorial garb walked onto the path with a mop and bucket in tow. He slapped the threads of the mop across the pavement, which Jason now realized was already dark with moisture. After a few passes, the janitor wrung out his mop and wiped a hand over his forehead, looking up as if to take a breath of fresh air. Jason couldn't be certain, but he thought the janitor was looking at him. A moment later, his suspicion was confirmed as the janitor lifted a limp hand and gave him a half-hearted wave.

Jason recognized the weak attempt at a silent greeting immediately. "Richard?!"

Chapter Six
Quality Control

After hastily getting dressed, Jason proceeded back to the elevator that had deposited him on the twenty-first floor a little over an hour earlier. He honestly didn't know what he was planning to do when he went back downstairs, but he had to do something- something to make sense out of this crazy night. He watched the numbers tick down on a digital display inside the elevator: nineteen, eighteen, seventeen. It was odd, Jason thought, that the inside of the elevator was adorned with a modern readout while the exteriors used old-fashioned analogue floor indicators. Then, as the elevator lights flickered, Jason's thoughts shifted to how it would be just his luck if the elevator broke down with him on it. No, he told himself, it would actually be quite fitting, all things considered. But the elevator didn't break down. Its lights stopped flickering, and it successfully landed on the first floor as instructed.

Jason stepped out of the elevator and observed the lobby cautiously. It was completely empty now, devoid of both hotel staff and guests, and someone had even dimmed most of the lights. It was as if the hotel had been put to bed for the night, as silly as Jason thought that sounded. He scouted around slowly, not because he was afraid- okay, maybe a little afraid- but also because he was having trouble gathering his bearings. Jason tried to imagine what direction he would face when the elevator dropped him off on the twenty-first floor. He then tried to follow his imagination through the foyer, then the hallway, into his room, then his bedroom, and to the window-

Awesome, Jason thought dryly as he came face to face with a solid wall. He didn't have a good sense of direction, and he knew it. Jason returned to the elevator bays and tried again, this time shortening the walk down the imaginary hallway and turning a little later toward the imaginary bedroom. Nope, he thought as he stared at another slab of painted sheetrock; that's a wall too. Jason tried three more times before he finally found what he was looking for: a single glass door leading to the courtyard that stood between the main building and the event building. Like a frightened child, Jason approached the door from the side and peeked out for a mere second before pulling his head back. Idiot, he scolded himself, the second-long glance not enough to ascertain anything that might be waiting in the dimly lit night. Jason peeked out again, slowly, but with more conviction.

Soft garden lights lined the winding path. Jason saw that the landscaping surrounding the path was much fuller and taller than it had appeared from his bedroom window. He saw the first of the wet floor signs- he assumed the other was past the first curve of the path- but he didn't see Richard, nor the mop and bucket. More importantly, he didn't see a giant, brooding monster, nor the remnants of what used to be a human body. Jason took a deep breath, opened the courtyard door, and stepped into the night. The air was sticky, humid from the earlier rain-

Jason stopped after one step onto the concrete walkway. "You dumbass," he whispered to himself. "The rain..."

Of course the pavement would be wet. Jason had driven through one hell of a storm to get to the Chance Hotel and had even seen beads of rain on the cars in the hotel parking lot. But that was hours ago, right? Jason had since checked in, had dinner, taken a bath, fallen asleep during that bath... the ground would have dried by now, right? Or wouldn't it have? Jason began down the path toward the event space. The ground wasn't just wet with soaked-in moisture; there were still fairly prominent puddles standing here and there. But again, Jason supposed as he passed the second wet floor sign, it could have been the rain.

Jason reached the other end of the walkway, where the landscaping opened to reveal a large patio that was staged for social engagements, with numerous umbrellaed tables, a stone island that Jason assumed was the hosting point for banquets, and a wooden platform with lights strung overhead nested into the woods- a dance floor, most likely. Of course, none of it was actively set up- the lights were off, umbrellas closed, island empty- but Jason could picture it being quite the party spot when in use. The patio sat adjacent to the event hall, and Jason was pretty certain now that it was indeed the purpose of the single-story building. He spotted a door and Jason wondered whether it would be unlocked, curiosity getting the better of him. But as Jason moved toward the door, something else much more relevant diverted his attention: the patio was dry.

Jason touched the ground to be certain, and sure enough, it was bone dry. He looked up to ensure there wasn't a canopy or some other protection from the weather mounted overhead- there wasn't. Jason then retraced his steps, back toward the walkway and landscaping, only then realizing that not even all of the walkway was wet. It was dry for the first few feet on the patio end, and it wasn't until a few feet into the damp area that Jason passed the second wet floor sign once more. He paused, trying to remember his dream... if it was a dream. Was this where the blonde man had been standing? If so, it would explain the water. It would also mean that giant supernatural sea creatures were real... or that Jason was in the middle of a psychotic break. The latter was much more likely, Jason thought as he tried to position himself to mimic his dream victim. The blonde man had been staring at something; what was it? Jason arranged his feet into what he recalled to be the blonde man's final stance and looked up, only to see the side of the Chance Hotel, a series of decorative windows giving view of the lobby.

Well that was a big help, Jason thought as he let his shoulders slump. But he also knew it was better than the alternative...

It was then that Jason noticed movement in his peripheral vision. His eyes darted to the source of the movement, beyond the decorative windows, where a partially shadowed figure watched him from the hotel's lobby. Jason immediately turned down the path, headed toward the glass door that would take him back into the hotel, and as he moved, so did the spying figure, as if on a course to beat him there. Jason's heart pounded. Was it one of the hotel staff? Another guest? Something else? He heard his breathing turn audible. Was it trying to check on him? Lock him out? Hell- eat him? Jason reached the door first and yanked it open, nearly breaking the hinges. The woman on the other side screamed in surprise, causing Jason to let out his own startled scream as he stumbled backwards.

"I'm sorry," the woman said as she clutched at her chest. "I'm so sorry, Mr. Chance. I didn't mean to frighten you."

Jason found his balance and steadied his nerve before taking a good look at the woman who nearly scared him to death. He didn't immediately recognize her, but he definitely recognized the clipboard in her hand, the one he thought she might break if she gripped it any tighter when he first checked in.

"I'm Katherine," the woman said with a nervous smile. "Katie- you can call me Katie." She showed Jason her clipboard, where a partially completed checklist was on display. "I'm the hotel's head of quality control."

Jason laughed, the absurdity of his fear and even his trip to the courtyard finally clear to him. "I thought you were- I thought-" Jason shook his head as he let the thought go and tried to stifle his outburst. "Hi Katie," he eventually said. "Nice to meet you."

"Likewise, Mr. Chance." Katie stepped aside so he could return inside. "I saw you while making my final rounds for the day. Is everything to your satisfaction so far?"

That's a loaded question, Jason thought. Then, for simplicity, he opted for a more traditional response: "Sure," he said. "Yes. I am satisfied."

Katie nodded. "Glad to hear it." She walked with Jason as he started back toward the elevator bays. "I hope you're not down here because the transformers woke you. They are the noisiest things..."

"Transformers?" Jason asked.

"A whole slew of them nearby," Katie explained. "Some critical juncture for the power gird. The problem is they're continuously overloading. Creates quite the ruckus."

Jason recalled the cracking sound from his dream. "Now that you mention it, I did hear something earlier."

"We're quite sorry about that," Katie told him. "But don't you worry. The hotel has its own generators. Even if we get cut off from the power grid, we keep operating."

"That's good," Jason said, unsure how else to respond to her random factoid. They arrived at the elevator bays. "I guess I'll head back to my room now."

"Right so, Mr. Chance."

Katie was friendly enough, Jason thought, but there was something else to her. There was a nervousness, a fear almost, similar to what he thought he saw when he checked in, but more subdued, as if she was attempting to hide it. The elevator car arrived, but Jason didn't get on, a new thought popping into his head.

"Katie, you said that you're the head of quality control, right?" Jason asked rhetorically. "I noticed the path outside was pretty wet."

Katie nodded. "We had quite the storm come through before you arrived tonight."

"Yeah, but it's just the walkway," Jason countered. "The rest of the ground is dry."

"Hmm," Katie pondered for a moment. "Oh, you know what?" she then said. "We have sprinklers in the landscaping out there. You probably just saw the runoff."

"You run the sprinklers even after a heavy rain?" Jason asked, noting the contradiction in her explanations.

"They're on a timer," Katie replied quickly.

She replied too quickly, Jason observed, and with increased nervousness. He pressed her harder. "But only a portion of the path was wet. The landscaping runs the entire length."

Katie didn't have an immediate comeback this time, and Jason thought he saw her gulp apprehensively. "Let me check-" she said anxiously as she flipped through some pages on her clipboard. "Ah, here it is," she then said with a forced smile. "Broken sprinkler head at the start of the path. There's an order in to our maintenance crew to fix it."

Jason leaned in to see the order, but Katie let the clipboard papers fall back into place before he could get a good look. She then stared at him with eyes that almost screamed *please just accept what I'm saying*. Was Katie hiding something? Or was she simply nervous by nature and not comfortable with confrontations? Jason didn't want to come across as a complete asshole, so he let her off the hook.

"That makes sense," he said, hoping to relieve her of her stress. Jason called the elevator again, and this time stepped on. "Katie," he then said, one last curious thought coming to him, "is it normal for Richard to do janitorial work for the hotel?"

"Richard?" Katie exclaimed. "Oh dear no. I can't get that man to lift a finger to clean anything."

"Oh." The candidness of her response surprised Jason. "I thought I saw him mopping some water-"

"Benji," Katie replied quickly. "You probably saw Benji. He's the head of our janitorial staff. Usually works the night shift alone."

Jason peered at her suspiciously. "It really looked like Richard."

"Nope," Katie said with that nervous smile of hers, "definitely Benji."

A moment ago it was *probably* and now it was *definitely*- quite a hasty escalation. But before Jason could inquire further, the elevator doors began to close.

"Goodnight, Mr. Chance."

And then he was alone. As the elevator ascended, Jason wondered just how much truth there had been to Katie's many convenient answers. They were all plausible answers, quite reasonable answers really, and yet Jason suspected they weren't the truth. Well, except for the comment about Richard. Then again, Jason suspected the sudden existence of a tentacled creature from beyond the deep wasn't exactly the truth either. The elevator lights flickered, and Jason hoped if Katie had been truthful about anything, that it was about those generators. A few moments later, the digital readout displayed a bright twenty-one, and the elevator dinged as its doors opened once more. Jason returned to his room, stripped his clothes, and headed into the bathroom to use the toilet before going to bed. It was there that he saw the novel Richard had left him slowly drying out in the bathroom trashcan. Jason stared at the creature on the cover, the instigator of tonight's anxiety, and realized his curiosity was far from satisfied. Jason wanted the truth, no matter what that truth might be, and he was going to get it.

Tomorrow, he then thought as a yawn overpowered him. Tonight, he needed to sleep.

Chapter Seven
Maybe Tomorrow

Jason awoke to sunlight shining brightly from behind his closed bedroom curtain. He checked his phone and saw that it was almost eleven. He never slept that late at home, but the previous day's events had clearly taken their toll on him. Jason scolded himself inwardly for not setting an alarm, for he had planned on calling his daughter that morning to let her know he was okay. Now she would already be at daycare and he would have to wait until evening. With no other reason to call his wife- she hadn't bothered calling him- Jason climbed out of bed, dressed, and headed for the door. He stopped as he passed his messenger bag, guessing that a maid would probably stop by to tidy up, and decided to take it with him.

At ground level, Jason stepped off the elevator to a much livelier lobby than he had seen the night before. Guests were bustling to and fro. Marvin had a line at the check-in counter and Katie was walking that line with her clipboard. Probably making sure they're satisfied with their wait, Jason thought smartly. Richard was actually tending to a couple's needs- or at least appeared to be- pointing excitedly at a colorful brochure as they nodded along. Leila was kneeling next to a sad-looking child as if giving him a pep talk, the child's parents smiling on in approval. There was a doorman Jason hadn't met yet escorting guests as they entered through the revolving front doors, and there was a steady stream of guests headed to the restaurant for what Jason could only assume was brunch at this point. Good luck giving all of them what they want, Jason thought comically as the image of Chef Terrance trying to serve a hundred people at once flashed through his mind.

Jason sat in an empty chair in the pseudo-great room, his eyes drawn back to Leila. Another unknown hotel employee brought her a red balloon, which she then tied around the sad boy's wrist. Wait, Jason told himself, he's not a sad boy anymore. The boy wrapped his arms around Leila's neck, and peering past his shoulder, Leila caught Jason's watchful eyes. Jason instinctively adverted his attention elsewhere like a schoolboy that had just been caught looking down a girl's shirt. Yeah, he told himself sardonically, that's the image you want to portray. Mustering up a slightly higher level of maturity, Jason looked back toward Leila, who flashed him a knowing smile.

"I take it the rest of your night was peaceful, Mr. Chance?"

Katie's voice snapped Jason from his gaze. He found the head of quality control standing only a foot away, clipboard still in hand and pen at the ready. "It was," Jason told her honestly. "Slept like a log."

Katie smiled, a genuinely happy smile, rather than the nervous smiles she forced the night before. "So glad to hear it." She made a mark on the top sheet of her clipboard, as if inquiring about Jason's restfulness was one of her to-dos for the day. She then flipped a few pages deep. "By the way, I spoke to our maintenance crew this morning. They said that they're really busy, but will try their hardest to repair that broken sprinkler head before end of day."

Did Katie actually think Jason cared that much about the wet pathway through the courtyard? Well, Jason considered, he did grill her about it a bit excessively yesterday. "Thanks for letting me know," he said, feigning appreciation.

"Certainly."

And with that, Katie was off. Not *off* like the valet had been *off*, Jason chuckled to himself, but definitely still *off*. Jason noticed Richard had shaken himself of the brochure couple and now stood alone at the podium. He thought of the commitment to getting answers he had made to himself before going to bed; what better place to start than the source? Jason rose from his chair and meandered toward the podium. As he neared, Richard casually looked away... then took a step away. Was he really trying to run? Jason wondered as the concierge took a few more steps toward the nearby hallway.

"Richard?" Jason called out, stopping him in his tracks. "Can I ask you something?"

Richard spun to face Jason, a sly smile plastered across his lips. "Why of course, Mr. Chance."

"Were you-" Jason paused. Did he want to ask about the book or the courtyard first? Which was less suspicious? Which was less confrontational? Maybe he should've thought this through a bit more before acting. "I wanted to thank you," he said, deciding to pivot to a less aggressive tactic, "for leaving me with some light reading material last night."

"Oh you're quite welcome, Mr. Chance." Richard turned as if their conversation was over.

"I stayed up reading for a while," Jason said louder than necessary to let the concierge know they weren't done. "And at one point I looked out of my window and thought I saw you mopping up a spill or something outside." Passive aggressive, Jason thought, this should be a nice middle ground.

Richard pressed his lips together doubtfully. "No sir, wasn't me."

"But it *really* looked like you."

"Hmm..." Richard hummed thoughtfully. He then stepped closer to Jason, leaning in as if about to share a secret as he pointed a single finger at the lettering pinned to his chest. "Did he have a name badge that said 'Richard' on it?"

Yeah, you son of a bitch, Jason thought. He had a name tag that was legible from the twenty-first floor. "I can't say that he did."

"Well there you have it!" Richard exclaimed as if the mystery had been solved. "Wasn't me. Besides, I had a poker game with some of the staff last night. Got cleaned out pretty good, too. Not my finest three hours."

Jason could see this was getting him nowhere. "Thanks," he said, when he really wanted to say thanks for nothing.

"Anytime," Richard replied before quickly continuing his retreat.

Why couldn't anything be straightforward in this place? Jason asked himself as he leaned against the podium and observed the lobby once more. It was beginning to settle down, the declining number of guests no longer moving about so frantically. Jason tried to spot Leila, the one member of the hotel staff that made him feel truly welcome, but she was gone, probably to get milk and a warm bath ready for the next customer. Jason sighed and turned his sights to the check-in counter, where Marvin was organizing his workspace after just clearing out his line. Maybe a little small talk with the boss would get him somewhere.

"Busy morning," Jason said, opening the conversation.

"Ah, Mr. Chance," Marvin greeted as he lowered some papers to give Jason his undivided attention. "You caught us at prime check-out time. How was your first evening at the Chance Hotel?"

"It was- interesting," Jason said, a not entirely untruthful response.

"I bet it was!" Marvin commented a little too enthusiastically.

His words suggested he knew what Jason had been through the previous night... or perhaps he simply felt the Chance Hotel was an interesting place. Ambiguity on top of ambiguity...

"Did you get some breakfast this morning?" Marvin asked, keeping the small talk alive.

"Nah, overslept," Jason told him. "Long day yesterday."

"Of course," Marvin replied. "Well, just remember that breakfast is the most important meal of the day. Skip it and you never know when you'll get a chance to eat again."

"Uh-huh," Jason muttered as he wondered when Marvin had become his mother. "I'll probably grab lunch in a bit to make up for it."

"Lunch," Marvin repeated back to him, a perceivably darker tone underlying his otherwise jolly voice, "right."

So the small talk wasn't working out so well either, Jason told himself. Better to end it and get on with his day. "Okay," he said abruptly. "I guess I'll let you be."

Before he could walk away, Marvin continued. "Are you still planning on ch-"

The manager's words were cut short by a man in white athletic gear who eagerly pushed past Jason and likely would have shoved the check-in counter aside had it not been nailed to the floor. "Mr. Chance!" The man said happily.

Jason was taken aback by the salutation, momentarily forgetting that he and Marvin shared the same last name. He then scanned the man who had interrupted their conversation, a slender man, muscular in a tennis player sort of way, and tall-tall and... blonde? Jason felt his pulse race. He had seen this man before, or at least dreamt of him.

"I wanted to thank you so much for what you did for us," the man told Marvin, his face glowing. "Sarah and I will never forget it."

Jason saw an athletic-looking woman standing a few feet back, babysitting a matching set of rolling luggage. Sarah, he presumed, likely a girlfriend or fiancé or wife- Jason couldn't get a look at her ring finger to tell for sure. She was glowing too, as if riding on top of the world. Maybe Jason should find out where they had scored their happy pills...

"It really was our pleasure," Marvin said, sharing credit for whatever the man was so excited about with the rest of the hotel staff. "You two have a safe trip home."

Marvin extended his hand, and the athletic man shook it vigorously. "Will do, Mr. Chance. Will do!"

Jason watched as the athletic man returned to Sarah and the two joined one set of hands while pulling their matching luggage with the others. How cute, Jason thought to himself as a bit of vomit tried to rise up to say hello.

"My sincerest apologies for that," Marvin told him. "We do aim to please our guests and, well, sometimes they're quite grateful for it." He shuffled the papers he had previously put down. "Where were we? Oh right- are you still planning on checking out today, Mr. Chance?"

Jason heard Marvin's words, but they were distant, far from the trance he found himself in as he watched the athletic couple leave. It wasn't the couple's physical appearance that had his attention, nor was it their nauseating love for one another or the medicated euphoria Jason was jonesing to get his own hands on. No, it was their luggage, or rather, it was the water drizzling out of the corners of their luggage, leaving thin rivers running the length of the lobby floor.

As soon as the couple had exited through the hotel's front doors, Jason saw Katie march to the nearest river and snap her fingers authoritatively at a janitor across the room. It wasn't the Richard-like janitor, but some other janitor Jason hadn't seen before. He grabbed a mop and bucket in response to Katie's command and immediately went to work on the slipping hazard. Then, apparently sensing she was being watched, Katie turned to look at Jason. He knew his face must have been portraying a mix of confusion, suspicion, and anger, but he didn't care. He wanted to see how Katie would react, what convenient explanation she would have for this. But Katie didn't approach him and didn't try to explain. Instead, she gave him one of her awkward, nervous smiles and accompanied it with a shrug that said *well, that just happened.*

"No," Jason said confidently in response to Marvin's distant question as he watched the janitor sweep the head of his mop back and forth over the glistening lobby floor. Then, with notably less confidence, he said: "Maybe tomorrow."

Chapter Eight
Left, Right, Left, Middle

Jason stood in front of the first floor elevator bays, staring at the call button. It beckoned to be pressed, yet Jason couldn't bring himself to do it. He wanted to confront Katie about the athletic couple's wet luggage. He wanted to drag Richard along for the conversation to watch the concierge squirm as she futilely tried to conceal the truth. But what exactly was that truth? That Jason hadn't been dreaming when he saw a giant sea monster murder the athletic blonde man? Certainly no one would question his sanity over that claim... and of course it didn't help his case that the supposed victim was alive and happier than a fly on fresh horse shit, nor that the hotel's main building and courtyard showed no evidence of structural damage that a giant sea monster would have obviously created. It also didn't help his case that Jason had been reading a book about a giant sea monster in an exhausted state- a prime setup for a bad dream- and that he himself recalled waking up from that dream, still in the bathtub where he had fallen asleep to begin with. When he really thought about it, Jason's only evidence that anything was amiss was some wet pavement and the dripping luggage the athletic couple had rolled through the hotel lobby only minutes earlier. The former Katie claimed to have a work order for, but it was the latter Jason just couldn't let go.

Why were the couple's belongings so wet? Why couldn't they simply put the offending clothes or other articles in plastic bags?

Was everything in the suitcases wet? Was it in plastic bags but they weren't watertight or had perhaps sprung a leak? Jason stewed in his own head, going round and round until reaching a discouraging conclusion: that the only people who would likely give him the truth were the two people who had just left the hotel, wet luggage in tow, and who he would likely never see again. Jason pressed the elevator call button and stepped on as soon as the car arrived.

As the elevator rose, Jason tried to think of creative ways he could get in touch with the athletic couple. He could tell Marvin he ran into the couple at dinner the night before and wanted to follow up with them about a conversation they were having. No, Marvin would see right through that lame story. Also, both Chef Terrance and Marie could easily disprove his false narrative. The elevator lights flickered as Jason tried to think of a new scheme. What was with that? He then wondered briefly as the flickering ended as quickly as it had begun. Jason shook his head and refocused on the task at hand. Maybe he could hack into the hotel's computer system and retrieve the couple's contact information from there. Oh wait, he had about zero hacking skills. Well that's not going to work, Jason silently admitted.

The elevator dropped him off on the twenty-first floor. Jason began walking toward his room when he realized that, behind his quest to solve the sea monster riddle, another mystery was poking at his brain. That flickering light in the elevator- Jason couldn't recall whether he saw it on his first trip up after eating dinner the night before, but he was pretty certain he had seen it on every trip since. And while at first the flickering seemed random, Jason's brain was telling him it wasn't... there was something almost systematic to it, but what? Jason returned to the foyer and recalled the elevator. He scanned the interior of the car for any abnormalities, but seeing none, he stepped on.

Jason pressed the button for the lobby and waited. The

digital floor readout decreased steadily: seventeen, sixteen, fifteen... Jason turned his head from side to side, his eyes sweeping back and forth between the overhead lights, and suddenly there it was. The lights flickered erratically, emitting electrical popping noises that were so soft Jason might not have noticed if he hadn't been looking for them. And then, just as before, the flickering stopped. The elevator car continued its descent and its doors opened to the lobby. Jason waited, as if half-expecting the elevator to provide him with some sudden revelation, but all that happened was the doors slid shut as programmed to do.

Jason pressed the button for the twenty-first floor and the elevator began to rise. He watched the lights more closely this time, and when the flickering began he tried to mentally log which bulbs flickered, in which order, and how many times. It was too much information to capture on a single trip, so when Jason reached his floor, he waited for the elevator doors to shut and pressed the button for the lobby once more. The left light was the first to flicker, then the right, the left again... or was it the middle next? When Jason reached the lobby, he restarted his ascent. It was the left again, he confirmed. Left, right, left, then middle, and then right again. The elevator reached the twenty-first floor and Jason immediately jammed the button for the lobby repeatedly, wanting to see the pattern again before he lost track.

"Left, right, left, middle, right, middle, middle," Jason whispered to himself. The flickering stopped, but he continued his mantra. "Left, right, left, middle, right, middle, middle." He hit the ground floor and instructed the elevator to ascend again. "Left, right, left, middle, right, middle, middle," he said again as the flickering started once more. "Left, right, left, right, right, middle-"

Wait, Jason told himself, that wasn't correct. The pattern

had changed on him. Or had he gotten it wrong this time? Jason descended again and watched ever closely. Left, left, right, middle, middle- it was completely different from either of the prior two trips. What the hell? Jason made another round trip to confirm. Yup, the pattern- if there had even been a pattern in the first place- was officially broken. The lights were flickering and, as far as he could tell, it was in a totally random order.

But Jason wasn't ready to give up. The conspiracy theorist in him now fully awakened, he searched for the next best thing to latch onto: the electrical pops. He'd been so busy counting flashes of light that he had all but ignored the small noises that occurred during the flickering. Jason pressed the button for the twenty-first floor and began ascending again. This time he closed his eyes to ignore the flickering itself and instead focused his efforts into his ears. Small pop, break, small pop, break, two quick pops... for whatever reason, Jason found keeping track of these significantly easier than keeping track of the flashing lights. He reached his floor, pretty sure he knew the popping pattern already, and instructed the elevator to turn around so he could check himself. Small pop, break, small pop, larger pop... damn, it wasn't the same. As with the lights, Jason took one more round trip to confirm the disappointing observation.

He exited the elevator and stood back to take in the view of the ground floor elevator bays in their entirety. Aside from the hotel's 'no charges' rule plastered above them, there was nothing wrong with the appearance of the elevators. Jason had been hoping for an epiphany; what he received was self-doubt. Did he really think the elevators held some deep secret only he could discover? Did he really think that secret was embedded in flickering lights and the sounds of loose electrical wiring? Maybe he needed more sleep.

An elderly gentleman in a tweed brown jacket stepped past Jason and pressed the elevator call button. Jason opened his mouth to warn the gentleman- then stopped. Warn him of what? Jason asked himself. Of the deadly flickering lights? Ooooh, scary. The elevator doors opened and the elderly gentleman stepped into the car. If Jason was going to act, he needed to do it now.

"Excuse me, sir?" He said, placing a hand to block the elevator doors from closing. "Um... have you noticed anything strange when riding the elevator?" Oh yeah, Jason thought, he's lost his mind now.

The gentleman put a cupped hand to his ear. "What's that?" He spoke far louder than necessary, as if he didn't have control over his own volume slider. "You're going to have to speak up!"

"Have you noticed anything strange-" Jason hollered briefly before stopping himself. He was drawing stares from some of the nearby guests. "You know what? Never mind."

He spoke those last words in his normal tone of voice, and the gentlemen smiled and nodded in response. Had he heard what Jason said? Probably not. Did it matter? Definitely not. Jason moved his hand, and the gentleman was on his way. Jason then turned and perused the lobby for his newfound nemesis, Katie. If broken sprinkler heads and a little spilled water qualified as quality control issues, then surely bad electrical wiring would count as well. Much to Jason's dismay, and similarly delight, Katie was gone, no doubt having run off in search of another poor sap to snap her fingers at. Oh well, he'd report it to her later. Or not. He'd think about it.

Done feeling like a dumbass for the time being, Jason returned to the elevator bays and pressed the call button. He gave himself fifty-fifty odds that the elderly gentleman would still be in the elevator car when the doors opened, unable to find his way back to his room. But just like Katie, the gentleman had vanished. Like magic! Jason thought, eliciting laughter from no one but himself. Yeah, he definitely needed more sleep. Jason stepped into the elevator and, for about the hundredth time that day, pressed the button for his floor. He watched the digital floor counter tick higher. He knew the flickering lights would begin soon, but he honestly didn't care anymore. Jason's brain only had capacity for so many battles at once, and he didn't rank the shorted-out lights high enough to warrant further processing power. Nine, ten, eleven... the flickering began, and the floor counter hung extra long onto the number twelve before jumping straight to fourteen. So many hotels were superstitious about having a thirteenth floor- why should the Chance Hotel be any different? The flickering stopped by the time the digital readout showed fifteen, and soon Jason was back on his floor, looking out at the empty foyer that awaited him there.

The Chance Hotel *was* different, though, Jason reminded himself without leaving the elevator car. Everything he had experienced since arrival led him to believe that. It was quirky, and weird, and secretive, and maybe even dangerous. If any hotel had a thirteenth floor, it would be this one. Jason knew he should let it go. He knew he should just get out of that elevator, return to his room, and take a nap despite waking up only a little earlier. But his curiosity got the best of him, and he punched the button for the lobby once more.

Sixteen, fifteen, fourteen... the flickering kicked in, and this time the floor counter stayed on the number fourteen a little too long before jumping to twelve. The numbers might have been skipping thirteen, but Jason had a strong suspicion that something was physically there. By floor eleven, the flickering had stopped, and now Jason knew why his brain had picked up on a pattern in the phenomenon. He arrived at the ground floor and pressed the button labeled "twenty-one" again. One more ride was all it would take to confirm what he had already convinced himself was true, and as the elevator doors slid shut, Jason caught a glimpse of Marvin, still alone at the check-in counter, waving and smiling at him as if to say *goodbye, it's been nice knowing you.*

Then Jason was alone, and the ascent began. Three, four, five, six... he watched in anticipation. Nine, ten, eleven... Jason braced himself for the flickering that soon began. He saw the digital floor reader hang on the number twelve as expected. He waited, expecting it to make the leap to fourteen at any moment- but then the elevator ground to a sudden halt, jolting Jason off his feet. The once-flickering lights went dark and the digital floor reader swapped its traditional numerical display for the letters 'ER.'

As in 'error,' Jason quickly surmised, his eyes naturally darting to the only source of light left in the enclosed car. His mind drifted to his previous night's thoughts about the elevator breaking down, and for a moment, Jason wondered if he had jinxed himself. Then he considered the repeated trips he had made in the elevator that day. Up and down, up and down, lobby to twenty-one, over and over in an old elevator that clearly had an electrical problem. At that point Jason realized he hadn't jinxed himself- he had done this to himself.

He let his head fall back against the elevator floor and stared despairingly into the darkness overhead. "You've got to be shitting me."

Chapter Nine
In Case Of Emergency

Jason lay on the elevator car floor, motionless, repeatedly asking himself how he could have been so stupid. His mind then drifted to thoughts about the car floor, about the waves of guests that tromped their shoes on it daily- shoes with grime and dirt and discs of flattened chewing gum, shoes that had passed over filthy pavement, stepped in muddy puddles, trekked through dog shit- Jason leaped to his feet with a shudder and the sudden desire to take a really hot shower. It was too dark in the elevator to see what nastiness he had been rubbing his body against, so his mind imagined the worst. Jason shuddered again and tried to shake the thought.

"Okay," he said aloud, as if vocalizing the words would spring him to action, "time to get out of here."

Jason looked at the elevator's digital readout, which continued to display an error code, and wondered whether the mechanical lift had automatically triggered an alert to the front desk or perhaps a third-party monitoring service. If so, all Jason had to do was sit and wait to be rescued. Well, maybe not sit... But what if it hadn't triggered an alert? Eventually someone would report the elevator being out of service, but how long would that take? This wasn't the only elevator car. Assuming the others were still operational and could handle the capacity of guests currently registered, it could take weeks for someone to notice there was an issue.

Jason scanned the elevator control panel, which was dimly lit by the digital readout just above it. There was nothing special about the control panel: buttons for each floor arranged in a tidy grid, a 'hold the door open' button that people rarely used, a 'close the door now' button that people frequently used but that rarely did what it claimed to do, and a keyhole for manual control of the elevator during servicing. None of the buttons glowed as they normally would have when receiving power, but Jason pressed a few of them anyway on the off chance they might do something. They didn't.

Jason looked around the rest of the elevator, but quickly determined it was too dark to trust his eyes to locate anything that might be of assistance. He felt around the control panel for any other buttons he might have missed, but didn't find any. He then started down one of the elevator's side walls, moving his hands from top to bottom as if practicing his mime-in-an-invisible-box routine. When finished examining the first side wall, Jason moved to the rear wall, but he continued to come up empty. He moved to the second side wall, and finally to the partial wall on the opposite side of the elevator door from the control panel.

Bingo, Jason thought, as he felt his palm run across a vertical seam in the otherwise smooth metal. Jason focused both hands on the area around the seam and soon located a corner which led to a shorter, horizontal seam. Another corner and another vertical seam followed. Then another corner- a box, Jason deduced with excitement as his fingers followed a second horizontal seam until they ran into what Jason believed to be a pull-tab. He applied pressure and the rectangle of metal swung down on bottom hinges, revealing a red telephone and a glowing sign that read:

USE IN CASE OF EMERGENCY

Jason smiled in the darkness, the thought of imminent

rescue already calming his nerves. He picked up the phone, momentarily fearing it might not be operational, but quickly overcoming that fear upon hearing an automatic ringing through the earpiece. The phone rang once, twice, three times… as it droned in Jason's ear, he wondered who he was calling and, more importantly, would they be around to answer? It was just about lunchtime, after all. Six, seven, eight… counting the number of rings was even more nerve-racking than counting the flickering lights that had gotten Jason into this mess to begin with. Eleven, twelve…

Jason felt his stomach grumble. Marvin had warned him that skipping breakfast was a mistake, and now Jason was feeling the effects of that mistake in full force. Nineteen, twenty… Jason questioned why he was even counting the rings. It's not like he was going to hang up, even if he hit ring one-thousand. He was trapped, and the phone was his only lifeline. Even if it took a million rings, Jason would hang on until someone finally greeted him from the other end. Twenty-three, twenty-four… Jason's mind turned back to Marvin. Marvin, Marvin, Marvin… Marvin Chance, so friendly and yet somehow so suspicious, the hotel manager who loves the fact that you share his last name so much that he gives you free room and board. The hotel manager who tries to be your mother and tell you when you should be eating. The hotel manager that waves *adios, asshole* when you get onto an elevator that's about to break, leaving you to die a slow, starving death while the emergency phone laughs in your ear with its never-ending ringing. Thirty-six, thirty-seven…

Jason dropped the phone, letting it dangle from its expandable cord as it continued to ring. He slid down the adjacent elevator wall, landing his butt close enough to the dangling receiver that he could continue to count its repetitive sounds. Forty-one, forty-two…

Jason swung his mind away from Marvin and instead to

Katie and her checklist. Surely mopping the elevator floor was one of her daily quality control checks, right? If so, Jason had been laying- and was now sitting- in only a handful of guests' shoe shit. That wasn't nearly as bad as the hundreds it could have been. Whew, Jason thought as he considered the common saying 'the enemy of my enemy is my friend;' Katie might actually be an ally in his current war against the elevator germs. Nah, Jason then countered, Katie was still his enemy, and that clipboard of hers probably contained her secret battle plans. Fifty-seven, fifty-eight...

Though he hadn't been trapped in the elevator all that long, Jason could tell the dark confinement was already getting to him. He was going loopy, his mind lashing out at the supervillain team-up of evil doctor Marvin and his dastardly sidekick Katie and their elaborate elevator death trap. Jason's eyes darted back and forth, trying to spot invisible forces he was certain were scurrying about in the surrounding darkness. His ears began hearing imaginary voices repeatedly calling 'hello' as if trying to get his attention-

Wait! Jason snapped out of his delusion and looked at the emergency phone. There was someone trying to get his attention! "Hello?" He sputtered as he put the receiver back to his ear.

"Yeah," a heavily accented, aggravated voice responded, "who is this?"

"It's Jason Chance. I'm one of the hotel guests. I'm stuck in an elevator in the main building." The voice on the other end didn't respond immediately, and Jason was pretty sure he heard an unintelligible whispered exchange taking place. "Uh, hello?"

"Yeah, give me a minute," the voice then told him gruffly. More whispered exchanges, then: "Alright, you say you're stuck in an elevator? How'd that happen, anyway?"

Jason really didn't feel like getting into it. "Can you please just send someone to help?"

The voice ignored his request. "My system here shows the elevator made repeated trips between the ground and twenty-first floor. Real fishy stuff. What the hell were you doing in there?"

"I was just trying to figure out-" Jason stopped, already mentally exhausted by the series of events. "Look, does it really matter?"

"It matters why you broke my elevator," the voice said accusingly. "Do you know how old those things are? How hard it is to get good parts?"

"Listen, I'm sorry," Jason said, rubbing his eyes and trying to keep his cool, his brain reminding him that the voice on the other end of this phone was his only way out of the elevator car. "I thought the elevator had an electrical problem and was trying to be certain before bothering anyone about it."

"So you made your point by breaking it?" The voice asked rhetorically. "That's commitment."

No kidding, Jason thought, though for the sake of keeping the peace, he didn't vocalize it.

"All right," the voice said. "What floor did you get stuck on?"

"I'm not entirely sure," Jason replied as he once again glanced at the 'ER' displayed on the digital floor readout. "I think I'm right around the thirteenth floor."

"The what?" The voice asked as if he hadn't understood Jason.

"The thirteenth floor," Jason repeated with greater articulation.

"You say you're between floors?"

"No," Jason told him, his irritation beginning to show. "I'm somewhere around the thirteenth floor. You know, one-three?"

Silence. For a moment Jason thought the voice had hung up on him, but then it returned, not pushy this time, but as if honestly trying to assist him. "Mr. Chance, I'm afraid I can't help you if you can't tell me where you are."

Jason bit his lip to refrain from saying anything he might regret. Whoever this person was, he had a system that told him what Jason had been doing in the elevator. Did the system not also show where the elevator had gotten stuck? Jason decided to try a different approach. "I'm somewhere above the twelfth floor, but below the fourteenth floor." He hoped he didn't sound too condescending.

"Oh," the voice replied. "Well okay then. So you're between floors!"

Jason slapped his forehead in frustration. "Sure," he said, caving to the voice's asinine view, "I'm between floors. Can you help me now?"

"Certainly, Mr. Chance. I'll send someone immediately."

Before Jason could get another word in, the voice disconnected, leaving him listening to a monotonous dial tone. Jason placed the receiver back in its cradle and shut the emergency panel. It wouldn't be long now, he told himself hopefully. Yet at the same time, a doubtful voice in Jason's head pondered whether that was true. It pondered whether the accented savior on the other end of the phone was sincere about sending someone to rescue him. It pondered who that savior was, and whether sending help was simply a matter of shouting to someone down the hall, placing a call that would hopefully get answered, or sending an email that may or may not get read. It pondered whether the call had even taken place, or if Jason had imagined the entire thing in his loopy state.

As Jason stood waiting in the silent darkness, another question came to mind. Clearly, the voice on the emergency phone hadn't been aware of an elevator problem, suggesting the other elevator cars were likely still in operation. But if they were, then why hadn't Jason heard their motors humming and gears turning as other hotel guests used them? Had the elevator cars been soundproofed that well? If so, what was the point? If not, why had Jason heard nothing but silence before and after his emergency phone call? Curious, and already feeling filthy anyway, Jason placed his bare ear against one of the elevator's side walls. He waited patiently to hear the sound of reverberations bouncing through the adjacent elevator shafts, but there were none. Jason tried the other side wall, but came away with the same result. Maybe no one was coming and going right now. At lunchtime? Highly unlikely, Jason concluded.

Jason revisited his idea of soundproofing. There could be layers of it behind each of the elevator's walls, but it would be extremely difficult to soundproof the door, especially given it had a split in the middle by design. The door faced outward, toward the guest floors, not toward the adjacent elevator shafts, but maybe the ascent and descent of the other cars were loud enough to reach it anyway. Jason found the center seam, placed his ear against it, and waited. The first thing he noticed was a faint, electrical hum, and then behind that hum the sound of light wisps of air. No, not wisps, he determined, whispers. Unintelligible whispers like those he thought he heard during his phone conversation. Maybe he hadn't heard them on the phone at all; maybe he'd been hearing this sound, the sound from outside the elevator car, the entire time. Jason repositioned his ear to hear better. The electrical hum intensified, making the whispers harder to hear. There was an echo of a distant clicking noise, then the sound of a churning gear. The hum quieted again, and within the whispers, Jason now heard an eerily familiar word. It hissed softly from beyond the elevator door, reaching out from the unseen darkness to gently touch the tip of his ear: *Jason...*

Jason yanked himself away from the elevator door, his brain telling him from behind wide eyes that it must have been his imagination. A moment later, the elevator buzzed back to life, its buttons illuminating and the overhead lights momentarily blinding its passenger. When his vision returned, Jason saw the digital floor reader counting up: eighteen, nineteen, twenty... and a moment later the door opened to the twenty-first floor. Jason darted out of the elevator and into the sanctuary of the waiting foyer. He then watched as the elevator door closed and the analogue dial above the bay swung into the teens and continue toward the single digits. Jason breathed a sigh of relief.

It was then that his stomach gurgled at him as if to say *great job, genius, but you still haven't taken care of me yet...* Jason's brain sided with his stomach, reminding Jason of the coziness of the hotel restaurant, projecting imaginations of Chef Terrance handing him a plate of food that would most certainly satiate his needs, of biting into what was guaranteed to be one of the most succulent- Jason broke from his thoughts and eyed the elevator call button. Hell no, he told his stomach and brain defiantly. Jason removed himself from the foyer to avoid any further temptation to take another journey downstairs and located a sign that said 'vending machine' with a small arrow next to it. Yup, Jason thought to the dissatisfaction of his internal organs, that'll do just fine.

Chapter Ten
Out Of Order

Jason felt the crisp potato chip crack between his teeth. It was salty, oily- not the least bit healthy- but it sure tasted good after having gone so long without food. Jason chomped on another, and then a third. His taste buds were delighted with his choice of junk food, even if his stomach probably wouldn't be. Don't worry, stomach, Jason said inwardly as he eyed the assortment of unopened potato chips, chocolate bars, nuts, mini-donuts, beef jerky, and candy that he had lazily piled on the coffee table in his guest suite, there's plenty more where that came from.

Jason hadn't intended to raid the vending machine like a stoned teenager trying to satiate a drug-induced case of the munchies. In fact, all he planned to grab was the bag of potato chips he was now halfway through and a soda. But despite the tag below the chips that read '$1.50,' when Jason entered the chip's slot number into the vending machine keypad, the neighboring digital reader flashed at him a very familiar 'no charges' message before dispensing the chips and spitting his money back at him. Bewildered that the vending machine was programmed to give out free items, and even more bewildered that it knew he was the one requesting the items, Jason punched the number for a roll of mini-donuts. Again, the vending machine flashed its 'no charges' message and gave the snack food over willingly.

Wanting to push the machine a little harder, Jason had next

chosen the most expensive item in the case, the beef jerky, priced at eight dollars. Same result. Jason examined the vending machine for a camera, or perhaps something that would indicate the presence of a fingerprint sensor, but he found nothing obvious. Then again, even if he had found one of these devices, it's not like the hotel had collected his biometric data upon check-in... at least not with his consent. Jason tried another item, which again he received free of charge. Maybe the vending machine was simply programmed to give everything away for free, a perk of the twenty-first floor suites, perhaps?

Jason returned to the twenty-first floor foyer, this newest hotel mystery challenging him to tempt fate by taking another ride in a metal box of death. Surprisingly, the elevator doors Jason had so eagerly departed only a few minutes earlier were now blocked off by a strip of yellow caution tape. Hanging from the tape was a sign that communicated, in no uncertain terms:

OUT OF ORDER

The blood-red letters stood out boldly from their white background, and Jason wondered when someone had snuck onto the floor to put it there. Regardless, the sign was enough of a reminder of Jason's near-traumatic experience that he opted to ignore the other available elevator cars and instead seek out a stairwell. He found it at the opposite end of the hallway from his suite. Jason worried the stairwell was for emergencies only, that an alarm would blare in his ears the moment he pushed open the door, but he saw no signs indicating that would be the case, so he forged ahead.

The stairwell was as one would expect: plain, with no attractive decor to hide the concrete walls and floors, cold, fluorescent lighting that contrasted with the warm lighting covering the guest-facing areas of the hotel, and each floor marked by a number on a simple plaque next to the door leading to that floor's hallway. Jason made his first stop on the twentieth floor, but he quickly noticed that the guest room doors were arranged similarly to the doors on his floor, suggesting they might also be suites. He returned to the stairwell and dropped to floor nineteen. There, the doors were more tightly grouped- regular rooms, Jason surmised- so he strolled down their hallway until he found a vending machine. It appeared identical to his own- same items, same prices, same model machine. There was no reason for Jason to expect a different outcome, yet he placed his bet on a cylindric bag of peanuts...

"Son of a bitch," he whispered under his breath as the machine mimicked the behavior of its twenty-first floor brethren.

Okay, so maybe free snacks weren't just a perk of the twenty-first floor; maybe they were a perk of the entire hotel. There was only one way for Jason to find out. He returned to the stairwell and descended farther, popping his head onto each floor until he found exactly what he was looking for: a trio of young teenagers loitering on their phones on floor sixteen. They would be perfect. Jason meandered past the group of teens and found that floor's vending machine. He went through the motions of making a purchase without actually engaging the machine at all. He then made an audible groan loud enough for the teens to hear, not that he could guarantee they were listening. For added effect, he hit the side of the machine in false frustration.

"Hey, kids!" Jason called down the hallway, drawing the teens' eyes away from their electronics. "The vending machine's not working. Think you could give me a hand?"

The kids looked at each other as if Jason had asked them to strip their clothes and do a magic rain dance, then returned to their phones without further acknowledgment. Jason sighed. Of course it was too much to ask a teenager to do a good deed. That, or he was giving off some seriously creepy pervert vibes. Fifty-fifty, Jason thought.

"Fine," he called out, "help me with the machine, and I'll buy each of you whatever you want."

Yup, Jason told himself, definitely leaning into creepy pervert territory now. But it worked. Free junk food was enough of an enticement to pull the teenagers from their electronics. They rallied around Jason, their hands outstretched as if to say *pay me in advance, creepy dude.*

"Here," Jason told them as he passed a couple of dollar bills to each teen. "If you can get it working, you can keep whatever comes out."

Jason took a few steps back to both give the teenagers some space and have an unobstructed line of sight to the vending machine display. The first teen put his money into the machine, pressed the key combination for a pack of gum, and retrieved his snack from the delivery door below. The vending machine returned appropriate change, which the teen handed over to Jason as he made room for his friends.

"Looks like it's working just fine," the teen said with attitude.

"Yeah," Jason replied, mystified by what anyone else would have perceived as a completely normal transaction. "I guess it was user error."

"We still get our turns, right?" The next teenager up- the only girl in the group- asked.

"Yeah, go ahead," Jason told her, his brain elsewhere as it churned hard to come up with an explanation for the divergent behavior of the vending machine.

The girl put her money in, chose a bag of pretzels, and joined her bumble gum associate in the hallway. Once again, the vending machine charged her appropriately, this time not returning change as she had given it the even two dollars required. The third teenager followed suit, also purchasing a bag of pretzels, with the same outcome.

"Thanks for your help," Jason told the trio when they

finished.

"Yeah," the first teen responded with even more attitude than before, "anytime."

The teenagers shoved and giggled their way back to their starting positions and immediately returned to their phones. Jason set his eyes upon the vending machine, certain he was overlooking something, but baffled what it could be. After a few moments of contemplation, however, it hit him. Jason hadn't actually tried using this vending machine himself. He had used the ones on the twenty-first and nineteenth floors, but had only pretended to use this one to catch the attention of the teens. Maybe it, unlike its peers, was an honest-to-goodness, capitalism-driven, money-charging machine.

Jason had only one dollar bill and the change from the bubble gum kid left in his pocket. He put the money into the machine and looked for an item worth that exact amount. Ah ha! A bag of chocolate candies would do the trick. Jason punched its number into the vending machine keypad. The machine whirred and squealed as it processed the transaction and deposited the bag of chocolates into the delivery bin below. Jason waited, certain that an act of mysticism would soon follow, and was more disappointed than relieved when it didn't. Just like with the kids, the vending machine had taken his money, an even exchange for the snack food it had given him in return.

"Humph," Jason grunted. "That was anti-climatic."

His mission had been successful; a rare win against the mysteries of the Chance Hotel. Well, sort of, anyway. There was still the question of why the other two vending machines had given away their goods for free, but now at least Jason knew it had nothing to do with him. His stomach seconded that thought as it encouraged Jason to return to his room and dig in to his collection of treats. Jason leaned down to grab the bag of chocolates, and as he did so, a flashing message caught his eye:

'no charges.' It was blinking rhythmically on the vending machine's digital readout, contradicting the machine's own actions. Jason stared at it curiously, and a moment later the machine began dispensing dollar bills at him. Six of them in total, followed by four quarters clinking into the coin tray below- the total amount of Jason's money that had been put into the machine.

"Son of a bitch!" Jason yelled as he hit the machine again, this time with true frustration. He looked around wildly for the other-worldly entity that was egging him on. "I'm not taking it back," Jason then stated defiantly as he swiped the bag of chocolates from the delivery bin. "I paid for these. I'm taking these."

In an act that may as well have been the equivalent of spitting in Jason's face, the vending machine's money dispenser made one short whirring sound and released the six dollar bills that had been hanging there. Jason watched them flutter to the ground, making no attempt to grab them. He then titled his chin upward proudly, as if to tell the vending machine *ha, I showed you.* Leaving his money behind, he then returned to the stairwell, catching a glimpse of the teenage trio rounding up his loose cash in his wake.

Once back on the twenty-first floor, Jason marched angrily to his room, passing his own floor's vending machine along the way. It was the original culprit, the instigator of the unhinged emotions he now felt. It deserved to be punished for its wrongdoings. And what better way was there to punish a service machine than by taking away its ability to serve? Jason stopped at the machine at began punching buttons, instructing it to dispense item after item into the delivery bin below, all the while the message 'no charges' flashed across its digital display. When the bin was full, Jason bundled the items in his arms and brought them to his room, where he dumped them on the coffee table. He then returned to the machine and repeated his actions. Rinse and repeat, five more times, until all that remained in the vending machine was one sleeve of peanut butter crackers. Then Jason took that, too.

Jason smiled at the memory as he finished off the bag of potato chips. Part of him felt just a little guilty about raiding the vending machine, but a much larger part of him felt gratified by his actions. Still hungry, Jason set the empty chip bag aside and perused his stash of sweet and salty treats. What the hell, he thought as he tore open a sleeve of powdered donuts. The empty carbs weren't going to do much from a hunger perspective, but they were going to make him feel good... at least until the unavoidable sugar crash a few hours later.

As Jason bit into the first one, he heard a soft noise coming from beyond the door to his room. Jason froze and listened closer, thinking maybe it was his imagination, but soon he heard another noise from the same direction, this one almost like a set of items trembling on an uneven surface. Uh oh, Jason thought, the vending machine has come for revenge. He set the donuts aside and crept toward the door. Jason heard a dull clang followed by the shuffling of feet. He glanced around for something, anything, that he could use as a weapon, but saw nothing. More shuffling, a heavy step, and then silence. Jason neared the door...

Boom! Boom! Boom!

The powerful knocks startled Jason so much that the hairs on his skin went rigid. Those clearly weren't in his imagination, and Jason's mind quickly ran through the list of likely suspects that could be waiting for him to answer. There was, of course, the vending machine, but it would've probably broken the door down instead of taking the time to knock. There was also Leila, who had already shown her willingness to enter Jason's room, but probably would've knocked a bit friendlier. Then there was

Marvin, who might be a little peeved that his free-riding guest had turned into a junk food thief. There was Richard- nah, Richard wouldn't care enough. And then there was Katie, good ol' clipboard-carrying, policy-enforcing Katie. Yup, she would be just the type to ferociously beat down his door upon finding the vending machine in a state that was bound to fail her quality control check.

Before Jason garnered the nerve to find out, he heard more footsteps, still heavy but moving away, until they were gone. Well, Jason thought, that rules out Katie; she wouldn't have quit so easily. Jason quietly cracked open the door and peered down both directions of the hallway, which were empty. He then looked down and found a room service tray awaiting him. Jason hadn't ordered room service- he didn't even know whether the hotel offered it- but here it was nonetheless. Jason saw a tented card next to the covered platter and napkin-wrapped silverware. Cautiously, he bent to retrieve the card and flipped it open:

Junk food is NOT a substitute for a good meal. -T

Jason froze again, not out of fear, but definitely out of shock. How had Chef Terrance known Jason had raided the vending machine? Why had he brought Jason a meal instead of beating down the door and giving the freeloader an ass-whooping? Why had he brought the meal himself instead of sending a waiter or concierge or dedicated room service staff member? Jason carried the tray into his room and set it on the kitchen island. Underneath the stainless steel cover, he found a glistening steak, a pile of grilled mushrooms, and a handful of broccoli florets- slightly charred, and with visible seasoning and butter. Jason took particular note that the dish contained no empty carbs; he supposed Chef Terrance felt he had enough of those already. Jason unwrapped the silverware and dug in. He already knew the meal would hit the spot, and yet was still taken by just how wonderful it was. As he chewed the perfectly cooked steak,

75

Jason concluded he no longer needed his treasure trove of junk food. He would return it, as embarrassing as that might be. Maybe when he finished his meal. No, Jason thought, his eyes falling upon the messenger bag he had placed on one of the island chairs after his midday excursion, maybe a little later. Right now, he had something more pressing to attend to.

Chapter Eleven
Naughty, Naughty

When Jason finished his meal, he rinsed his plate and utensils in the kitchenette sink and reassembled the room service tray, which he would bring back to the restaurant on his way out. Jason figured that was the least he could do given Chef Terrance's hospitality, even if that hospitality had been a not-so-subtle way to scold Jason for his dietary choices. He freshened up and retrieved his cell phone from the bedside nightstand, where he had placed it to charge. As had been the case since beginning his journey the day before, there were still no missed calls. Jason opened his map app and performed a search for 'Mackey and Sons,' the regional bank he and his wife used for all of their important accounts. The app simply hung as if it were thinking, and after a few moments, Jason force-closed it and tried again. Again, the app hung and returned no results.

Jason opened his web browser and tried the search there. The browser's loading bar filled halfway and stopped, leaving Jason staring at a blank window for nearly a minute before the words 'no data connection' appeared. Odd, Jason thought, as he confirmed he had a full five bars of service. He tried rebooting the phone, but that didn't alleviate the issue. Oh well, Jason then told himself, that's what concierges are for. He slid his cell phone into his pocket, gave himself a once-over in the mirror, grabbed his messenger bag and the room service tray, and headed out the door.

Jason looked back and forth, debating between the elevator and stairwell ends of the hallway, the former of which was partially blocked by a housekeeping cart. Can't go that way, Jason lied to himself. It was justification for an irrational decision to trek twenty-one floors worth of steps instead of catching a quick elevator ride to the lobby. No, Jason corrected himself, a potentially life-ending elevator ride to the lobby. Nothing irrational about that. He started toward the stairwell door, but stopped when someone called out to him after only a few strides.

"Mr. Chance?" The voice had a chipper European accent- overly friendly yet fun to listen to. "Woohoo, Mr. Chance?"

Jason turned to find a uniformed housekeeper chasing after him. She was tall and muscular- definitely the type of woman who could handle changing the sheets on her own- and she wore a jolly grin beneath her rosy cheeks. For a moment, Jason thought she might run him over, that Chef Terrance had delivered him his last meal in anticipation of his trampling death under the heels of Mrs. Clause. Luckily, the housekeeper slowed as she neared, and Jason had once again avoided an untimely demise at the hands of the Chance Hotel. Whew.

"That's not for you to take, Mr. Chance," the housekeeper said as she snatched the room service tray from his hands. "That's my job. You just leave it in your room."

The housekeeper removed a master keycard from her hip pocket and started back toward Jason's door. Not wanting her to discover his vending machine loot, Jason followed on her heels.

"That's okay," Jason said, his mind racing to think of quick excuses. "I don't mind bringing it down, Miss…"

"You can call me Olga," the housekeeper told him as she neared the door. "And that's nonsense. The guests don't do the work."

"It's no work," Jason retorted as Olga raised her keycard to the electronic lock on his door. "I wanted to thank the chef anyway." She wasn't listening, so Jason changed tactics as the lock clicked. "I'd prefer you not go in there! It's- uh, a germaphobe thing!"

Olga laughed heartedly. "That's baloney," she then chanted in her chipper accent as she pointed toward the empty space around Jason's door handle. "Germaphobes hang their 'do not disturb' sign on the door."

Crap, she had him there. Why hadn't Jason thought to hang the sign when he left? It didn't matter now, for Olga had already pushed the door open. She stood in silence, staring into Jason's room, where he was certain the evidence of his shameful deed was fully visible. Jason hid his face behind a hand and closed his eyes, trying hard to will Olga's presence out of existence. It didn't work.

"You've been naughty, naughty, Mr. Chance," the housekeeper said with several clicks of her tongue, her eyes clearly fixated on the mess on Jason's coffee table. "Naughty, naughty indeed." Her jolly tone had devolved into one of serpentine accusation.

"I was going to return it," Jason replied timidly. "I just- I had something else to do first."

Despite it being the truth, his statement came across like a falsehood, his voice inadvertently rising to make a question out of his claim. Olga's gaze turned to Jason, her eyes narrow and smile wicked. Jason felt she was passing judgment on him, as if deciding whether to believe him or have him thrown in the hotel's brig, and it left Jason wondering just how many years it had been since Olga ditched her life as an international assassin to join the housekeeping staff of the Chance Hotel. He half-expected her to smother him with a chloroform rag and torture him until he divulged the reason for his vending machine assault. But instead the housekeeper kept her cool and made no aggressions toward Jason.

"You leave this to me, Mr. Chance," she said slowly, with an almost too-serious undertone. "Olga knows how to clean a mess."

Of that, Jason had no doubt. "Thank you," he said with a relieved gulp.

And just like that, Olga's demeanor flipped back to its jolly default. "Now scoot!" She ordered. "Leave Olga to do her job."

Yes, ma'am, Jason thought with obedience. He made his way to the stairwell and began his descent. The trek was a monotonous one- down fourteen steps, turn, down fourteen more, turn, down fourteen more- and with every one, Jason could hear the echo of his movements reverberating throughout the hollow cement column. Even though Jason had gravity on his side, the muscles in his legs started to burn a little over halfway down. He told his body to suck it up, that this was nothing compared to what the return trip would be like, but deep down he suspected he might not actually have the willpower to make a return trip.

Jason hadn't bothered counting the floors as he descended. He had started so high up he knew counting would be more discouraging than anything else. But he was counting now, with only five floors left and sweat seeping from his pores to cool his warm body. Four, three, two... the end was in sight; Jason just needed to push a little harder. Half a minute later he was there, at the door to the ground floor, twenty-one stories of muscular misery behind him. Jason noticed that the stairwell actually continued farther, probably to a basement of some sort, but he had no interest in exploring that right now. He was a man on a mission, a sweaty, irrational, but well-intended mission.

Jason entered the ground floor and tried to get his bearings. He was at the end of a slender hallway that he hadn't previously seen. At the end of the hallway was a bend, and beyond the bend was the lobby's pseudo-great room. Jason emerged into the great room and scanned for familiar faces. Marvin was, as usual, helping guests at the check-in counter, leading Jason to wonder why the manager hadn't hired someone else to do that job. The maid Jason had briefly spotted during his own check-in was dusting fixtures around the great room. Katie and her servant janitor were nowhere to be seen, but Jason took note that the lobby floor was shiny and dry in their absence- he would be sure to let Katie know later. Then there was Leila, chatting happily with what appeared to be newlyweds at the concierge podium. A smile formed on Jason's face as he took a step in her direction.

But then he stopped, feeling the layer of sweat that had beaded on his forehead and in his hair and that was certainly noticeable to anyone he neared. There had to be a public restroom near the restaurant which Jason could use to make himself more presentable. He wound his way around the great room, casually hiding behind furniture and walking parallel to other guests to avoid being spotted by Leila. Jason then entered the restaurant hallway, where he located the door to the men's room just in time to slip in before Marie returned from showing a family of four to their table.

Inside the restroom, Jason splashed cold water on his face and dabbed his body dry with paper towels. He straightened his clothes, touched-up his hair, and checked his breath. Not wonderful, but passable. He then exited the restroom and checked the concierge podium. Leila was still there, the newlywed couple walking away, and no other guests vying for her attention. Perfect, Jason thought as he resumed his steps toward her.

"Can I help you with anything, Mr. Chance?"

"Shit," Jason muttered to himself upon hearing Richard's voice. He turned to find the other concierge standing barely two feet from him, most definitely encroaching on Jason's personal space as he bent his body forward. "I, uh-" Jason tried to think of something to say as he took a step back, leaving some room for God between him and his friendly-but-not-really host.

"You…?" Richard asked with a patronizing smile.

Jason's day had barely begun and already his brain was exhausted. He wanted to pretend Richard hadn't intercepted him. He wanted to speak with Leila, the employee nice enough to draw him a warm bath and leave him an ice cold bottle of milk. He also really wanted a breath of fresh air, and some time away from the confines of the Chance Hotel, during which he could clear his mind before returning fresh to tackle another mystery that would most certainly await him. Jason took a deep breath and told himself to play nice.

"Yes," he then said through gritted teeth, "I could use your help."

Jason recounted his phone search for Mackey and Sons and the technological issues that plagued it. Richard brushed off the data connection error as a byproduct of the electrical grid disturbances from the night before. He then told Jason to give him a couple of minutes as he retreated to the concierge podium, where he flipped through some documents before placing a brief phone call. Leila had left the podium by then, and though Jason assumed she couldn't have been gone long, he couldn't find her anywhere in the lobby. A moment later, Richard returned.

"All right, Mr. Chance," he said in the most professional tone Jason had heard from him since arriving at the hotel, "today's your lucky day."

Maybe by his count, Jason thought sarcastically.

Richard continued. "There's a branch of Mackey and Sons about four miles from here. They're open until five o'clock, and we've already got your car and directions waiting out front." The concierge looked at Jason as though he had just hit his quota for a good day's work. "Is there anything else I can do for you right now?"

"No," Jason replied, surprised at himself for the words that followed, "you've been a big help."

Richard gave him an uncaring shrug. "That's my job," he said plainly before departing.

Wouldn't know it, Jason thought to himself. He then proceeded to the hotel's revolving front door, where the doorman Jason hadn't met yet flashed him a warm smile and wished him a pleasant journey. As Jason passed through the doors, he glanced back, hoping to catch sight of Leila in the lobby, but she had yet to return. Then Jason was outside. He walked to the edge of the parking lot, where two vehicles awaited. One belonged to another guest who was currently being assisted by the same valet that had assisted Jason the prior evening. The other was a black sedan, a chauffeured vehicle by the looks of it, no doubt at the ready for one of the Chance Hotel's more prestigious guests.

What Jason didn't see, however, was his own car. He strolled down the sidewalk, then strolled back in the other direction, and by then he came to the conclusion that Richard's newfound professionalism was likely just another ruse to get under Jason's skin. His car clearly hadn't been retrieved from whatever distant corner of the parking lot in which it now sat. Jason thought about returning inside to file a formal complaint against Richard, but quickly decided against it; one, because he doubted his complaint would actually accomplish anything, and two, because he just didn't care enough to go through with it. Jason felt confident he could find his own car, but he would need his keys if he was going to take it anywhere.

"Is there something wrong, Mr. Chance?" The valet asked with his obnoxiously pearly grin as Jason approached.

"I just need my car keys," Jason told him, not bothering to

relay his exchange with Richard.

The valet shot Jason what he was sure was a rare frown. "Is there something wrong with your car?" He looked like he might cry.

"No," Jason assured him, "I just have an errand to run."

The valet's frown immediately transformed into a sympathetic smile. "But, Mr. Chance," he said, motioning his hand toward the black sedan, "we have a car for you right here."

"This?" Jason asked incredulously. "No, I just need *my* car. I can drive myself."

"Absolutely not, sir," the valet said with a laugh. "What kind of hotel would we be if we made you drive yourself around town?"

A normal one, Jason said inwardly. Then, to the valet: "I don't really like attention."

"Don't worry, Mr. Chance," the valet replied as he opened the sedan's rear passenger door, "our driver will be discrete."

Jason glanced inside the vehicle. It was normal enough, with only a few minor luxuries such as plush leather seats and extra legroom. The driver, an older gentleman, gave Jason a welcoming nod, as if to tell him he would be okay, that the car wouldn't bite. Accepting his gesture, Jason threw his messenger bag onto the far seat and climbed in. The valet shut the vehicle door behind him and motioned for the driver to roll down Jason's window.

"Giles is at your disposal for the afternoon," the valet told Jason. "He'll take you to Mackey and Sons, but don't hesitate to have him make any other stops you need."

"Thanks," Jason responded sincerely while also wondering why the hotel was giving him such royal treatment. The slogan was 'no charges for the Chances,' not 'free chauffeurs for the Chances.' Oh well, he'd take it anyway.

"It's no trouble at all, Mr. Chance," the valet said. "And when

84

you're done, Giles will make sure you get right on back here lickety-split."

The valet flashed his pearly whites once more as the tinted window slid shut, leaving Jason alone with his thoughts in the air-conditioned shade of the sedan, his driver, Giles, giving full attention to the road as the vehicle kicked into gear. Jason watched the Chance Hotel shrink away as the sedan pulled onto an adjacent tree-lined street. He had gotten away, all limbs still attached and fresh blood still pumping through his veins. Pretty soon Jason would be out of sight of Marvin and Richard and Katie, of the sea creature that killed-but-didn't-kill the athletic guest, of the elevator that had tried to starve him to death as it sat frozen on a thirteenth floor that apparently didn't exist...

Jason chuckled and told himself he should be relieved. He was getting his breath of fresh air, even if filtered by the vehicle's air conditioning unit. He was getting a chance to unburden himself of hotel-induced stress, and to clear his mind... yet he didn't feel relaxed, and he felt in no way relieved. Jason couldn't figure out why, until the last words of the valet replayed themselves in his mind:

And when you're done, Giles will make sure you get right on back here lickety-split.

It was at that moment when Jason realized why he couldn't feel good about his escape from the weirdness and danger that had repeatedly interfered with the past twenty hours of his life. He may have left the Chance Hotel, but he wasn't free of it. He was trapped in this black sedan, the hotel's sedan, driven by the hotel's chauffeur, his own car and keys- heck, even his personal belongings- secure in the hotel's custody. The Chance Hotel's royal treatment of Jason- if that's what one could really call it- wasn't royal at all. He was a prisoner, and though he may have been let out for yard time, his guard would escort him back to his cell soon enough.

"Shit," Jason muttered to himself again.

Chapter Twelve
It's Not My Money

"Pardon me?" Giles asked from the front seat of the sedan. His question was non-accusatory, an innocent inquiry from someone who hadn't quite heard Jason's profane utterance. "Did you say something, Mr. Chance?"

Jason looked to the car's rearview mirror, where the reflection of Giles' eyes looked back at him. The eyes were old and worn, and behind them was the soul of someone kind, a dutiful servant who had met the needs of hotel guests for who knows how many years. Jason saw no need to burden the driver with his own despairing thoughts. "No," he said, "sorry."

Jason stared lazily at the passing trees as the sedan pressed farther from the oddities of the Chance Hotel. He thought of his daughter, and how her last memory of him was one in which he was exchanging shouts of hostility with her mother. Her mother... Jason repeated inwardly, not his wife. Jason glanced down at his empty ring finger and felt a wave of shame wash over him. He had worn his wedding ring faithfully since the day he said 'I do.' But on the night of *the fight*, when his wife told him to get out once and for all, he pulled the ring off and threw it across the room in anger. At the time, he did it in symbolic recognition that their marriage was officially over, even if not on paper. Now he realized how childish an act it had been and wished he could take it back, not because he had hope of salvaging his relationship, but because there was more symbolism in that ring than just his wedding vows. There were memories- memories of better times with his wife, memories of a love that would never truly be lost despite their separation, memories of the daughter they brought into the world together...

Jason told himself he couldn't make any excuses tonight. He needed to call his daughter to ensure she wouldn't worry about him. He would use the opportunity to also have a peaceful exchange with his wife, for no other reason than to set the mending process in motion. After all, they would need to be on civil terms to continue parenting together. The tree line broke and a ray of warm sunlight bright enough to pierce the sedan's tinted windows blasted Jason's face. His eyes took a moment to adjust, and when they did, Jason saw buildings and cars and people- civilization beyond the confines of the Chance Hotel, where normal people went about normal business as they led normal lives.

It's a miracle! Jason wisecracked to himself, having half-expected his little road trip to be as much of a ruse as everything else the Chance Hotel had thrown at him. But as the familiar signage for Mackey and Sons entered his view, Jason accepted that there was no funny business about this trip; he had made a request of the staff of the Chance Hotel and they had delivered with top-notch service. Giles pulled the sedan into the parking lot of Mackey and Sons and parked in the outer row of spaces.

"I'd drop you off at the door," Giles said, "but I heard you don't really like attention."

"No," Jason replied. "This is perfect."

He grabbed his messenger bag and stepped out of the vehicle. The warm sun felt great as it fell over the rest of his body. Jason took in a deep breath of air. It wasn't the freshest, not even close to as fresh as that surrounding the Chance Hotel, but it represented freedom. Jason wasn't on yard time anymore. He was back in society- a smelly, hustling and bustling society, but society nonetheless. He thought about running. How far could he get before Giles ran him down in the sedan? Or would Giles simply call in the dogs to go after him? Dogs named Richard and Katie and their keeper, Marvin. Jason chuckled at the thought of Richard's head on a dog's body, his tongue flapping wildly as he bounced down the street with Marvin in tow.

"Okay, now you're just being silly," Jason said quietly to himself. He realized he must have looked odd just standing there lost in his own imagination and gave Giles a thankful wave before starting across the parking lot. He was glad Giles hadn't brought him to the door like some celebrity in need of an indentured servant; it wasn't a look Jason cared for. But how had Giles known that? Jason told the valet he didn't want attention, but wasn't that before they approached Giles' sedan? Or was it after and Jason's memory was hazy? Or had Giles simply heard them talking through the sedan's closed doors and windows, even though their soundproofing seemed pretty good during the drive? Jason shook off the questions as he approached the door of Mackey and Sons. He had something more important to focus on now.

The interior of the bank reminded Jason of his local branch back home: a few offices off to one side, some customer seating and a coffee machine to the other, a rope line straight ahead, and beyond it, a counter of teller stations. Just your average regional bank, and luckily not too busy at this time of day. Jason wound his way through the rope line and waited to be acknowledged by the next open teller.

"How can I help you, sir?" She asked as Jason approached and set his messenger bag on the sliver of counter space allotted for customers.

"I'd like to make a deposit." Jason handed her his ATM card and ID so she could locate his accounts. "Seventy-thousand dollars, all to the high-yield savings account."

The teller paused for a moment, as if she wasn't sure she had heard him correctly. Then she froze altogether as Jason removed stack after stack of banded hundred-dollar bills from his messenger bag and stacked them in front of her. Jason gave her an *is there a problem?* look, prompting her to resume his account look-up.

"I'd also like to speak to someone about taking out a fifty-thousand dollar loan," Jason added, "to be deposited into the same account."

Jason noticed the teller twist her face at the curious request. But instead of questioning him, she responded with dedicated customer service. "I can certainly help you with that, Mr. Chance."

Yes, please do, Jason thought as he continued to haphazardly pile the stacks of bills, drawing the attention of several other eyes in the building. The teller typed at her computer, paused with confusion, typed a little more, and then politely excused herself in the *there's a problem, but I'm going to let someone else deal with it* sort of way. Jason watched her scan her security badge and exit through a locked door behind the counter. She reappeared seconds later in the lobby, where she proceeded to one of the offices Jason had passed on his way in. The teller directed the eyes of the man in the office- the manager on duty, Jason presumed- to his computer screen and pointed out multiple secret details while explaining her concerns. It was moments like these that Jason wished he could read lips. The teller and the manager both looked at Jason. Then the teller stepped aside as the manager stood from his desk and straightened his tie and jacket. Uh oh, Jason thought, she's bringing back the big guns.

"Mr. Chance," the manager said with honest but somewhat condescending politeness as he stood just outside his office door, "I can help you complete your transactions in here."

Jason locked eyes with the manager, then deliberately shifted his vision to his mostly empty messenger bag and the stack of money on the teller counter, then looked back at the manager challengingly. In response, the manager gave him a shit-eating *any day now* kind of smile. Perturbed, Jason grabbed each stack of hundred-dollar bills and one-by-one returned them to his messenger bag with more force than necessary. The teller had disappeared into her hidden employees-only area by then, and it wasn't until Jason was clear of the counter that she reappeared at her post- a typical move to avoid confrontation.

"I'm sorry to pull you aside like this, Mr. Chance," the manager said as he escorted Jason to a chair across from his own. "The name's Bob. I'm the manager on duty this afternoon."

Nailed it, Jason thought, hoping for a prize for his ingenuity.

"I called you in here because we have a bit of a unique situation," Bob continued. "Unfortunately, there's no easy way to tell you this, so I'll just say it. Your wife has revoked your access to your accounts."

Though not surprised she would try, Jason was surprised the bank complied. "But they're joint accounts. Don't you need my permission to make changes like that?"

"Actually," Bob clarified, "they're not. Your wife, being the primary source of income for your family, opened the accounts in her name and added you as a secondary user. She has the right to revoke that usage at any time."

Yup, Jason thought, that sounds like my wife. "Okay, but I'm not trying to take anything out of the accounts. I just want to put this money in." He patted the messenger bag. "There's got to be a way to do that, right? I mean, there's no harm-"

Bob cut him off. "Your wife had her branch add explicit notes forbidding you from transacting in the accounts in *any* manner... deposits included." Bob let Jason stew on that for a moment before pitching an alternate idea. "You could, of course, open a checking or savings account in your own name if you want a safe place to store your money."

"It's not my money," Jason mumbled. He then thought about Bob's proposition and countered with his own modification. "Let's say I deposit the money into a new account. Could you do one of those electronic transfers or something to then move the money into my wife's account? That way it's coming from the bank inst-" He stopped when he saw Bob shaking his head.

"I'm afraid it's still your transaction," Bob told him. "In which case, we're still bound by your wife's request."

Jason was beginning to grasp the bigger picture. "So I suppose that loan I wanted to discuss..."

"Would be subject to the same restrictions," Bob told him. "Unfortunately, your money-"

"It's not my money!" Jason repeated, this time loud enough and with enough frustration that he drew the attention of the bank's security guards. Jason closed his eyes and composed himself. "I'm sorry," he then told Bob. "Clearly you understand what I'm trying to do. Is there any way, any way at all, to make it happen?"

Bob frowned genuinely. "Not as things currently stand. You could give the money directly to your wife for her to deposit, or you could ask her to lift the restriction on the account you want to deposit it to. Short of that..." His voice trailed off.

Short of that, Jason was shit-out-of-luck. He pulled his cell phone from his pocket and scrolled to his wife's contact card. A simple call is all it would take. But it wasn't so simple, was it? Even if he told his wife exactly what he intended to do, she wouldn't believe him, not with how they left things. She would tell him to go screw himself and likely call the bank to double-down on her restrictions. Jason turned the phone off and looked at Bob.

"I appreciate your time," he told the bank manager as he stood to leave.

Bob extended a friendly hand. "I'm sorry we couldn't do what you wanted. If you change your mind about opening an account in your own name, we'd be happy to have your business."

Jason considered the offer as he shook Bob's hand. He wanted to protect the money, especially given the questionable safety of the Chance Hotel, but he also considered how it would look if he deposited the money in an account solely in his name. If his wife found out... and more importantly, if the subsequent judge and jury that would surely be convened found out... it wasn't great optics. Jason would have to take his chances until he could deliver the money to his wife in person.

Bob was kind enough to walk Jason to the front door. Or maybe he was still hoping Jason would change his mind about opening a new account. Either way, it was nice to have the company. As they approached the door, Jason spotted another customer seated in the waiting area looking agitated as he tapped at his cell phone. It reminded Jason of his own experience before leaving the Chance Hotel.

"Hey Bob," Jason asked, "have you been having any issues with your cell service today?"

Bob's face spoiled the answer. "Data connection's been on the fritz since late last night. The towers around here are really unreliable. You too?"

"Yeah," Jason told him, actually feeling relieved to discover the cellular interference wasn't a manifestation of the Chance Hotel. "Well, thanks again."

Jason and Bob shook hands once more and Jason stepped back into welcoming sunlight. Under any other circumstances, the warm blanket of light would have comforted Jason as it thawed his skin from the chill of the bank's air conditioning. But right now Jason felt defeated, having failed at the one goal he set out to achieve with his time away from the Chance Hotel. Giles must have sensed his defeated attitude too, for the older driver looked at him empathetically through the rearview mirror as Jason climbed back into the waiting sedan.

"You know, Mr. Chance," Giles said with a kind voice, "my bank is just a few minutes up the road if you want me to take you there instead."

Jason considered the idea. Maybe he could open a new account at a different bank, then initiate a funds transfer back to the account at Mackey and Sons. No, Jason told himself, that probably wouldn't work either. Even coming from a different bank, his name would still be attached to the initiating account, and Mackey and Sons would reject the transfer all the same. Jason frowned as his eyes fell upon his messenger bag and his brain pondered over the seventy-thousand dollars still tucked safely within it.

"No," he eventually told Giles. "You can just take me back to my cell."

"I'm sorry, sir?" Giles asked.

Oh shit, had Jason just said that? He backpedaled quickly to avoid further questions. "You can just take me back to the hotel." Real smooth...

Giles didn't press him, and Jason didn't try to provide additional explanation. Jason watched as Mackey and Sons and the rest of civilization fell behind them, eventually disappearing altogether as the tree-lined road to the Chance Hotel engulfed the sedan on its return trip. Jason may have felt like a prisoner of the hotel, but at least he felt wanted by it, which is more than he could say about his own family or just about anything else right now. In fact, Jason realized with a notable degree of shock, he was almost glad to be going back.

Almost.

Chapter Thirteen
Jason Chance, Amateur Detective

Upon his arrival back at the Chance Hotel, Jason expressed his sincere thanks to Giles for taking him to Mackey and Sons and for respecting Jason's wishes along the way. Jason felt as though the elderly driver might just be his newest best friend- well, second best behind Leila anyway. Jason was then greeted by the valet, who was so delighted to see Jason that he questioned whether the valet had accidentally over-medicated himself in Jason's absence. The unnamed doorman gave Jason a similar greeting, welcoming him back as though welcoming someone to their long-lost home. And just like a long-lost home, the ground floor of the hotel didn't look much different from the way Jason left it, except for being just a tad less busy.

Jason headed directly for the elevator bays, eager to get back to his room and straighten out his messenger bag. He would probably count the money while he was at it, if only to put his mind at ease that he hadn't lost any in transit. But standing between Jason and the elevator bays was the concierge booth, and leaning lazily against it was Richard, who had already seen Jason coming and would now be impossible to avoid.

"Did you have a good trip, Mr. Chance?" Richard asked in an ambiguously interested voice.

"The ride was fine, thanks," Jason replied, hoping to break off the conversation.

Richard didn't catch on. "The ride was fine..." He eyed the

lumpy state of Jason's messenger bag. "...but the destination was unsatisfactory?"

Jason suspected Richard was smart enough to guess what he had stashed in his messenger bag. After all, Richard had been the one to look up the local Mackey and Sons branch on Jason's behalf, and there are only so many reasons for someone to visit a bank. Jason gripped the bag a little tighter, almost defensively, as if Richard had suddenly become a predator and Jason's greenbacks were its preferred food.

"Yes," Jason admitted. "It was..." He used Richard's phrasing back at him. "...less than satisfactory."

"That sucks," Richard replied bluntly. The concierge then instantly switched gears, as if that had been the extent of his interest in Jason's venture. "Well, if we can do anything else for you- back massage, golf lessons, poker game, whatever- just let us know."

Jason couldn't help but notice that one of those options was intended to ease him of his monetary burden. "Yeah, sure," he said suspiciously.

Their conversation over, Jason proceeded to the elevator bays. He had thought about taking the stairs, but it had been hard enough coming down and the idea of trekking back up held no appeal, even at the risk of death. Besides, guests had been using the elevators while he was away; if there was any further danger, surely they would have reported it already, right? Jason pressed the call button and noticed that the doors to the elevator car he had gotten stuck in earlier were free of any signage. Had the hotel's maintenance crew really inspected and fixed the problem that quickly?

Ding.

Jason supposed he was about to find out, for just his luck, those were the doors that opened to his command. Jason hesitated, asking himself whether he was really willing to put his faith in the absence of a warning sign as his only confirmation that this particular elevator car was fit for use. He turned away, a nagging voice in his head trying to convince him that the walk back up the stairs wouldn't be as bad as he imagined. But then Jason spotted Richard staring at him, watching as if watching a horse race, eagerly waiting to find out if his bet would pay out or not. Would Richard have bet for or against Jason? Definitely against, Jason told himself, and that was enough motivation for him to resist the urge to run away. He stepped boldly into the elevator car and stared Richard down in defiance as the doors slid shut. Then regret set in.

What now, dumbass? Jason asked himself, fearful of pushing the button for the twenty-first floor, but damn certain he wasn't going to get back off at ground level. To accept Richard's unspoken challenge and then back out was far worse than having not accepted the challenge in the first place. Maybe he could take the elevator partway up, to floor ten or eleven perhaps, and then take the stairs from there. No, Jason thought, Richard's going to be watching the whole way. It won't be enough to have seen Jason get on the elevator; he'll have someone watching for Jason to get off too.

Jason considered using the stairwell as an interlude- taking the elevator to floor eleven, walking the stairs to floor fifteen, and then taking the elevator the rest of the way, skipping the problematic section of the ride, but giving the appearance that he had gone the distance. No, Jason shot himself down again, the analogue floor dials above each elevator bay would spoil that plan. There was also no guarantee that Jason would be greeted by the same elevator car that he was now on when he recalled it at floor fifteen.

As Jason tried to think of another alternative, he pictured Richard still watching from the concierge podium. Just as the analogue floor dials would expose his plans to avoid the potential elevator malfunction around the thirteenth floor, they were currently exposing Jason's inability to muster the courage to push an innocuous round button. How long had he been standing there debating what to do? One minute? Two? Five? Richard was probably salivating with victory, waiting for Jason to run screaming from the elevator car with his tail tucked between his legs, waiting to feast on the hundred-dollar bills that would fly cartoonishly free from Jason's messenger bag as he ran. Jason wouldn't give Richard the pleasure, so he gritted his teeth and pounded the button for his floor.

The elevator rose... duh, what else had Jason expected it to do? He leaned back against the rear car wall and watched the numbers on the digital readout increase. Six, seven, eight... boy this brought back memories. Jason held his breath when the readout reached twelve, and without fail the elevator lights began to flicker, Jason's ears now attuned to the small, electrical popping noises that accompanied them. So much for the hotel's maintenance crew...

Jason didn't breathe again until the digital readout flipped to fourteen and the flickering stopped. Even then, he didn't breathe easy, for he really just wanted off of this defective death trap as soon as possible. Seventeen, eighteen... just a few more floors. Jason closed his eyes and told himself it would be okay. He was past the mechanical failure point. Heck, he was nearly to his floor. Surely he would make it there in one piece.

Ding.

The elevator stopped at the twenty-first floor and its doors slid open, revealing the foyer Jason had lovingly come to associate with extensions of his lifespan. He jumped off the elevator before it could ensnare him once more and quickly peered down the adjacent hallway to spot whomever Richard may have sent to observe his arrival at the finish line. But there was no one in sight, guest or hotel staff alike. Maybe the contest had been in Jason's head. Maybe Richard hadn't been silently daring him to ride that elevator, and was instead just spacing out in Jason's direction. Nah, Jason thought, that would be too coincidental.

Jason considered looking around for signs that someone had been in the area, even if they were gone now. But how exactly would he do that? Perform forensics on footprint fibers in the carpet? Dust for fingerprints on the elevator buttons? That idea was just about the dumbest he had had since arriving at the Chance Hotel, and there had been a few stinkers already. Ending his amateur detective career before it had really even begun, Jason decided to head back to his room. He had only gone a few steps down the hallway, however, when something struck his sensory perception. Jason didn't need a portable forensic kit and sterile gloves to examine the foyer; he only needed his eyes, eyes which told him something was definitely different from when he last walked through there.

Jason backed up to the foyer and immediately looked at the desk that sat across from the elevator bays. The objects that had been there when Jason first checked in to the Chance Hotel were still there: a potted plant, chessboard, and service phone. The phone appeared undisturbed. The soil in the plant appeared moist, but not freshly wet, as if maybe Olga had watered it when making her rounds earlier that day. The chessboard, on the other hand- as far as Jason could recall, the chessboard had been hosting all pieces in starting positions each time he had passed it. But that had changed. Now, a white pawn had been advanced two spaces, an opening move, awaiting an opponent's response. Jason looked around as if he suddenly expected to see another guest lingering nearby. After all, he probably wasn't the only person staying on the twenty-first floor. Maybe one of the other patrons had begun a game, but then abandoned it to use the bathroom or grab some food or-

Face it, Jason told himself, you don't really believe any of that. But if it hadn't been a guest, and instead had been one of the hotel staff spying on behalf of Richard, why would he or she have left proof of their presence? And why play only an opening move? Jason had given the mystery person more than enough time to get further into a game while pussyfooting around his decision to ride the elevator. Maybe the move hadn't been made by Richard's spy at all, but by someone quietly sending a message into space, hoping on a whim that someone else would see the message and have enough decency to respond.

Jason glanced around one more time to ensure he was alone. He then casually approached the chess board, grabbed a black pawn, and moved it two spaces forward to defend what he assumed was the white player's next target square. Jason then waited for something both mysterious and mystifying to happen. He waited for the next white piece to magically move itself, as if guided by the invisible hand of a hotel spirit. He waited for the board to upend itself, throwing its pieces across the room after being violated by Jason's unworthy touch. He even waited for angels to rain down from the heavens, as if moving the chess piece had inadvertently disturbed the delicate balance between good and evil in the world. But none of that happened. In fact, nothing happened.

"Hmph," Jason grunted. "Well that's that I suppose."

He plopped down in one of the foyer recliners and stared at the chessboard in deep thought. Someone wanted to play a game, a game likely intended for him, but who could it be? Jason tapped his fingers rhythmically, his curiosity rising to the top of his mind's emotional heap. There was work to be done, Jason's curiosity told him. A mystery demands an investigation, and an investigation requires someone with the deductive reasoning and persistence to see it through to the end. Who better than he, Jason Chance, Amateur Detective, to face off against this mystery, the mystery of the Chance Hotel's phantom chess player?

Jason felt a fresh determination overtake him. He stood confidently and gave the chess board one more hard stare, as if to tell both it and his mystery opponent *game on.* He then turned his gaze to the analogue floor counter above his favorite elevator bay, to the small, nearly unnoticeable gap of blank space between the numbers twelve and fourteen. Jason would solve the chess board mystery, eventually... of that he was almost certain. But first, he had a much larger, much more intriguing- and if Jason was being honest, probably more deadly- mystery to investigate. He was going to solve the mystery of the thirteenth floor. That, or he was going to die trying.

Chapter Fourteen
Operation Cash Stash

The cleanliness of Jason's suite caught him off-guard when he returned from his excursion to Mackey and Sons. All furniture had been reset to starting positions, the physical layout of the suite looking the way Jason remembered it looking when he first arrived the night before. The curtains of each window were drawn back to allow the afternoon sun a chance to say hello. The carpeted areas of the suite were plush with fresh vacuum trails, and the non-carpeted areas sparkled as if mopped and then lightly waxed. Jason also noticed a fresh scent in the air- not quite natural, but not overtly chemical either... rather pleasing, in fact. Most importantly, the pile of junk food Jason had left on the coffee table was gone. Jason set his messenger bag down and rummaged through each cabinet in the kitchenette, wondering if Olga had simply relocated the junk food to a more fitting and organized spot, but it was nowhere to be found. As promised, she had cleaned his mess. Probably disposed of the dead bodies and sanitized his room of forensic evidence while she was at it.

Jason grabbed his messenger bag and dumped its contents where the junk food pile once stood. He arranged the bundles of cash into stacks of ten, completing seven in total as expected, a small swell of relief settling over him. Jason then began placing the money back in his bag, taking more care than he had at the teller's counter at Mackey and Sons. He quickly stopped, though, the thought of Richard's predatory eyes giving him sudden reservation. Jason had no substantiated reason to think Richard was a thief, but he had no reason to trust the concierge either, and Richard clearly suspected Jason's bag held a large sum of money. Maybe it wasn't the best idea to leave the money in it. In fact, Jason then thought, it was probably a stupid idea to leave the money in it. He had been toting the messenger bag all over the hotel as if strolling through a friendly neighborhood where crime was unheard of. But as friendly of a neighborhood as the Chance Hotel appeared to be, Jason had an inkling that it was also the kind of neighborhood where the little girl playing hopscotch would pull a knife on you when your back was turned.

Jason scolded himself for not depositing the money at Mackey and Sons when he had the opportunity. So what if his wife found out the money was in an account with his name on it? He would just explain the situation and- nope, Jason cut himself off, that was the problem right there. His wife no longer cared about his explanations, or, as she often called them, his excuses. She would assume the money being deposited into an account to which Jason had sole access was exactly what it looked like, and then she would rain down the fires of hell and damnation upon him. Yup, Jason reassured himself, he had *definitely* done the right thing by bringing the money back to the hotel. But he still needed to protect it.

Jason hadn't seen a programmable safe in the room when he first checked in, so he scouted around for one but came up empty. He then thought about Marie's offer to store his bag in the secure coat closet by the restaurant. Jason still wasn't sure what a secure coat closet even was, but if Marie had access to it, then other employees likely did too, so that wouldn't do. The same held true for any master safe the hotel might have, though its access would probably be a bit more restrictive. Nonetheless, any of those options required Jason to trust at least one staff member with the money, and trust was hard to come by at the

Chance Hotel.

Jason looked around his guest suite, considering a not-so-secure, but definitively more private, option. The suite was spacious, with numerous amenities Jason hadn't needed, but had been happy to indulge in anyway. It wasn't the pleasantries of the amenities Jason was focused on right now, though; it was the variety of nooks and crannies they provided. Nooks and crannies in which someone could stash their valuables from interested parties. Would it be smart to hide the money behind the disguise of an unassuming room rather than behind the lock and key of a safe or bank account? Nope, but it was the best option available in light of other considerations.

Jason returned to the coffee table where the stacks of cash still sat. He split each stack in two, creating fourteen piles, five-thousand dollar each, and dispersed them among his hiding spots. At first it was easy, with Jason placing one stack in the indentation where the water line connected to the rear exterior panel of the refrigerator, another in the far recesses of a high corner cabinet that required standing on a chair to reach, a third underneath his mattress, a fourth in the pillowcase of the rearmost pillow atop the mattress, a fifth and sixth carefully propped behind the wall-mounted televisions in each room... Jason was initially surprised at his own ingenuity. He continued to place stacks of cash around the guest suite with little effort until, when he had four stacks remaining, he almost doubled up on a previously used hiding spot.

Whoops, Jason thought as he scanned the room for alternate locations for the remaining money. Unfortunately, as far as he could tell, he had used all the good hiding locations the guest suite had to offer. Jason considered purposely doubling up four locations, but that went against his idea of spreading the bounty around to prevent large losses in the event of any one discovery. So instead Jason settled for some lesser hiding spots: on the windowsill behind his bedroom curtain, on the edge of the tub tucked behind the shower curtain, in the microwave, and under his mattress, but on the opposite side from the first stack he hid under there. Okay, Jason admitted, that last one was a cheat, but he convinced himself that a king-size bed was large enough to count as two separate locations.

Jason considered the list of suspects who could potentially find the money in his room and evaluated the level of threat they each presented. There was Leila, who had already entered the room in his absence to draw Jason a bath. The gesture was meant to comfort him upon his initial arrival, and now that he was a seasoned guest of the hotel, Jason doubted Leila would visit his room much more. Even if she did, Jason felt her threat level was relatively low, that her kind demeanor was an honest projection of her inner personality. Then there was Richard, who had also entered Jason's room in his absence to bring him the sea monster book. Jason's inner alarms blared at the thought of Richard's threat level, but Jason told himself that Richard had no further reason to visit the room, and if he ever had a reason, Leila would probably accompany him and keep Richard in check.

Last, there was Olga... Olga, Olga, Olga. There was no way Jason was going to convince himself that Olga wouldn't find the money during her next cleaning. Heck, she would probably launder the money for him- in more ways than one- and then return it neatly where she found it. Did that make her a threat? Jason supposed not. Olga was someone who knew how to keep secrets, and Jason trusted she would keep his. What he didn't trust was his own memory. So, before setting out on his investigation of the thirteenth floor, Jason noted the placement of each stack of cash in an electronic document on his phone. He titled the document 'Fixer Uppers' to deter interest should anyone maliciously intrude into his device later. Jason also didn't trust that a random maid, or maintenance worker, or perhaps even Marvin wouldn't unexpectedly visit his room for official or unofficial purposes, so he hung his 'do not disturb' sign on the outer door handle as a final precautionary measure. Just like the germaphobes, Jason thought with a proud smile.

He took one last inventory of how his suite looked, ensuring no money was visible and nothing appeared out of the ordinary. Jason then stuffed a towel into his messenger bag to give it the appearance of still being full and slung it over his shoulder. He figured if people saw him lugging the bag around- scratch that, if Richard saw him lugging the bag around- it would divert the concierge's attention from seeking the contents of the bag in Jason's room. Confident that he had done all he could reasonably do to protect the money, Jason then exited the room, ready to set out on his mission to uncover what he had now convinced himself was the hotel's dirtiest secret.

But as he stood in the hallway, swinging his eyes from elevator end to stairwell end in repeated succession, Jason realized he hadn't put much thought into exactly how he would solve the mystery of the Chance Hotel's thirteenth floor. Sure, he could try getting himself stuck on the elevator between the twelfth and fourteenth floors again, but that didn't work out so well last time; and heaven help Jason if he had to place another call to his gruff rescuer using the emergency phone. On the other hand, instead of getting himself stuck passing the thirteenth floor, Jason could just go straight to the source of the mystery. Did the elevator control panel have a button for the thirteenth floor? Jason tried to picture it in his mind, but the trauma of his confinement made the memory hazy. What about the stairwell? Had Jason passed a door to the thirteenth floor on his way down earlier that day? Again, the memory was hazy.

It's a crapshoot, Jason told himself. And if he was truly going to pursue this clandestine endeavor, then he may as well be prepared to go all-in. He proceeded to the foyer, ready to face the elevator bays that awaited him there. But the chessboard that adorned the foyer desk instantly diverted Jason's attention. On it, a white knight had been advanced from its starting position. Second move, Jason deduced, his invisible opponent apparently having accepted Jason's challenge while he was conducting Operation Cash Stash. Jason considered the emerging attack pattern from the white end of the board and moved another black pawn in what he believed, or at least hoped, was an optimal response. How long had he spent hiding bundles of money around his room? Jason wondered. Who had known he'd be gone long enough to slip in a play? Also, why the hell was there so much secrecy over a board game?

Jason shook away the questions like a dog might shake away water after a bath. The chess opponent mystery was secondary to his primary mission. Jason would continue the game, but he wouldn't let it distract him from the investigation at hand. He turned and stoically faced the elevator bays as he pressed the familiar call button. Jason then closed his eyes in an attempt to calm the anxiety tightening his chest. He breathed deeply and slowly, telling himself that his investigation would be worth it, that beneath the facade of a traditional hotel, this building held secrets beyond his wildest dreams, secrets worth discovering, secrets worth risking his life over. It was the machinations of a lunatic for sure, and yet Jason kept reassuring himself that he was still just as sane now as he had been before his arrival at the Chance Hotel. Then again, he couldn't really be sure how low of a benchmark that established.

Ding.

The elevator doors opened. They were the same doors that always opened for Jason, the same elevator car that always greeted him waiting silently on the other side, a mechanical coffin ready to host Jason as its next cadaver. Jason steeled his nerves, once again telling himself that the truth would be worth it- lying to himself really, but unable to admit it as he took a step forward, embracing whatever fate he would face within the confines of his boxy metal friend. Jason turned and took one last look at the twenty-first floor foyer, at the chessboard and the game underway upon it, and he made a quiet wish to survive long enough to play his next move. Then the doors slid shut.

Chapter Fifteen
Stupid Superstitions

Confined once again to the death trap elevator car, Jason felt a newfound sense of self-confidence and commitment to the investigation at hand. He immediately scanned the elevator control panel, or more specifically, the seven-by-three grid of floor buttons nestled within the panel. Twenty-one in total, Jason's elementary mental math confirmed, one for each floor all the way from the ground level to his room at the top. Jason's eyes stared at the button for the first floor and traced over each consecutively numbered button, confirming no gaps in the sequence, until they reached the button for floor twelve at the end of the fourth row and swiveled to the beginning of the fifth row, where an unlabeled button sat dimly among its glowing peers.

So, Jason told himself, there's a button for the thirteenth floor; it just isn't marked. Stupid superstitions. Jason reached for the button and then paused. What if there was more to the thirteenth floor than superstition? What if there was a reason elevator passengers were discouraged from going there? Obviously someone thought it was a bad idea if they had gone through the effort to replace the preprinted elevator button with a generic placeholder. Jason recalled the strange whispers he had heard when trapped in the elevator earlier that day. He told himself they could have been mechanical noises. He told himself they could have been the creaks and groans of an aging building long overdue for a makeover. Hell, he even admitted they could have been in his head, nothing more than paranoia manifested from his fear in the stalled elevator car. But the whispers had said his name... or at least, Jason thought they had. He saw his extended index finger, now just inches from the unlabeled button, tremble involuntarily.

Something wasn't right. Jason's brain knew it, and clearly his body did too. He felt a ghostly chill spreading over his skin, creeping its way down his spine and through his appendages, prompting Jason to withdraw his finger without pushing the unlabeled button. Jason sighed in relief, and only then did he realize just how hard his heart had been pumping in his chest. But a moment later, the elevator descended anyway, as if it didn't care that Jason had chickened out at the last moment. It knew his intent, and it was going to force him to follow through. Jason felt a lump in his throat and pressed his back against the rear wall of the elevator car as he watched its digital floor reader steadily decrease the display from twenty to nineteen, then nineteen to eighteen... Jason shivered, not from the chill that had spread throughout his body, but from the fear that fueled it. Fifteen, fourteen- the elevator stopped, and the doors opened, revealing the trio of teenagers Jason had met earlier, waiting for their ride with their eyes glued to their phones.

"Oh look," the girl of the group said when she noticed the elevator car had arrived, "it's the vending machine guy."

Yup, that's me, Jason thought, just your average run-of-the-mill vending machine pervert. He was so glad to see the teenagers that he didn't mind the predatory title and even thought of offering them more candy if they would just take a ride with him. Check that, if they would just accompany him down the elevator shaft in a very non-sexual kind of way. Jason gave the trio a brief and unavoidably awkward greeting, then retreated to a corner of the elevator to put as much space as possible between himself and them as they piled in. Jason wiped fresh beads of sweat from his forehead as he watched the pretzel boy of the group press the button for the ground floor, and it was then that Jason realized his friendly metal death trap hadn't grown a mind of its own after all. It had simply been summoned to the fourteenth floor by his adolescent acquaintances, acquaintances who didn't seem remotely fazed by the flickering lights and electrical pops as the car made the leap from floor fourteen to floor twelve. Were they so entranced by their phones that they hadn't noticed? Or did they notice but simply didn't care? Or, worse, were the flickering lights and electrical pops also in Jason's head, where normal people- if that's what these teenagers were- obviously wouldn't react to them?

The bubble gum bandit of the group blew a large pink bubble, popped it, then loudly chomped it back into his mouth. Jason drifted from his inner questions about the thirteenth floor elevator oddities and instead wondered whether that was the same piece of gum the boy had started on earlier that day or a fresher one he had opened later. Either way, it made him the smart one of the group, his free snack lasting far longer than those of his companions. The boy must have sensed Jason's curious stare, for he turned to Jason with suspicious eyes that Jason immediately avoided with his own. Luckily, the tension didn't last much longer, as the elevator dinged upon reaching the ground floor.

"See ya later, vending machine guy," the girl told Jason as she and her companions filed off.

Jason watched them stroll through the lobby, magically navigating around the other guests without taking their eyes off of their screens. Teenage sonar at its finest, he told himself. The elevator doors then slid closed again, returning Jason to his solitary confinement. He took a moment to consider how scared he had felt when the elevator first started moving, and how foolish he must have looked jammed up against the rear wall like cornered prey waiting to be eaten when the teenagers boarded. Stupid superstitions, Jason reiterated to himself. He steeled his nerves again and reached for the unlabeled button on the elevator control panel. Despite a voice within him screaming *no, don't do it!* Jason jammed the button so hard he almost tore the ligament in his index finger.

And then nothing happened.

Jason pressed the button again, but with the same result. He then continued to press it over and over again, sometimes with excessive force, sometimes with the gentle touch of a feather, sometimes holding the button down for a few seconds, and other times pressing so rapidly he was sure only every other press would even register. Yet, no matter what he tried, the elevator was unresponsive. As far as Jason could tell, the dim, unlabeled button was exactly what it appeared to be: an inactive placeholder for a floor that presumably didn't exist.

Damn, Jason thought, so much for the direct approach.

He pressed the 'open door' button at the base of the control panel and exited onto the ground floor, where his first sight was that of Richard leaning against the concierge podium with such boredom that Jason half-expected both to tip over at any moment. Jason ignored the concierge- and Richard returned the favor- as he proceeded into the lobby. What now? Jason then asked himself as he glanced around for ideas. He could ask the hotel staff about the thirteenth floor, but he suspected they would play dumb just as the voice on the other end of the elevator's emergency phone had done earlier that day. He could start querying the guests to see if any of them were currently staying or had previously stayed on the thirteenth floor, but Jason had already established a creepy vibe with the teenage trio and didn't fancy extending that vibe to the rest of the hotel populace. That left the stairwell option. The elevator's digital readout always hung on floor twelve or floor fourteen, depending on the direction of travel, as if physically bypassing a space between them, but the closed doors prevented Jason from verifying what was really happening outside of his metal container. The stairwell wouldn't have that luxury. Either it would wind past an extra floor or it wouldn't, and there was really only one way for Jason to find out.

He started toward the hallway that led to the stairwell door, but then Jason's common sense made a rare appearance and steered him back to the elevator bays. Jason only needed to verify the existence of the thirteenth floor, not the twelve that came before it, so he could save his leg muscles and bypass those. He stepped onto the elevator car, which somehow hadn't been called away to serve another guest yet, and pressed the button for the twelfth floor. A few moments later he was there, stepping out into a foyer that reminded Jason of his own, only without the added amenities of chairs, and a desk, and, lest he not forget, a phantom chess player. Jason left the foyer and followed the twelfth floor hallway to its stairwell entrance. So far, so good.

Jason entered the stairwell and began climbing through the hollow column of cool concrete. He recalled from his trek down earlier that day that each floor was separated by two sets of stairs facing alternating directions. Jason reached the top of the first set of stairs, made an about-face, and started up the second set. This was the set that would lead him to the thirteenth floor, if there was a thirteenth floor, and Jason could feel the exhilaration pulsing throughout his body as he closed the gap between himself and the next stairwell landing. A moment later he was there, having finally traversed a path that led to his intended destination, but what Jason found there was more perplexing than he expected.

As Jason had already surmised when taking more elevator

joyrides than he cared to admit, a space for the thirteenth floor did indeed exist. By space, though, Jason simply meant that there was extra distance between the twelfth and fourteenth floors. Whether that distance comprised true space, as in empty space that could be divided into hallways and rooms, was still a mystery, for at the landing for the thirteenth floor Jason found nothing more than a concrete wall where the stairwell exit should have been. He had no way of knowing whether there was a traditional hotel floor on the other side of that wall, or whether solid concrete stretched from one end of the hotel to the other.

Jason knocked on the wall, his knuckles making a dull thud against the cold surface. Well, it's not hollow, Jason thought. Or did concrete work differently than wood in that respect? Jason wasn't sure; he had failed construction class in school. He tried pushing on the wall, wondering if it was just a facade that hid the true entrance to the thirteenth floor behind it. Nope, it was pretty solid. Jason then rubbed his palms along the concrete surface, much like he did in the dark of the elevator car that had trapped him. Maybe there was a seam for a hidden door, or a panel, or-

A stifled cough echoed down from overhead, alerting Jason that he wasn't alone. "Hello?" Jason asked aloud, only to be met with the response of silence. He tried to peer around the next set of stairs, but the arrangement of steps made seeing the next landing nearly impossible. "Who's there?" Jason asked, again receiving the same silent response.

Jason instinctively reached for his messenger bag as if he needed something to defend himself with. He then remembered his final act of Operation Cash Stash and realized he was unlikely to towel someone to death before they did him harm, so he let the bag fall back into place at his side. Jason took a cautious step up the next flight of stairs, that same voice from before repeating its mantra: *no, don't do it.* Jason took another step, and then a third, keeping his eyes peeled for any threat that might be lurking above. The mystery visitor sneezed and, apparently realizing that he had given himself away, took off running, his shoes rapidly ascending the floors above. The secrets of the thirteenth floor no longer his most immediate concern, Jason quickly pursued.

Chapter Sixteen
There Is No Thirteenth Floor

Jason ran past the fourteenth floor landing in hot pursuit of whomever had been spying on him. He proceeded up the set of stairs to the fifteenth floor landing, forcefully hiking up one leg after the other as if he were doing a military tire drill, a burning sensation in his calves quickly setting in. Soon he was on the sixteenth floor, then seventeenth, and with each floor, Jason closed a bit more of the gap between him and his target. Jason's lungs begged him for more air and his ascent slowed by necessity, but so did that of the unidentified person he was chasing. Eighteen. Jason heard the leading footsteps stop on the next landing and the sound of a stairwell door being yanked opened. Jason launched his body forward and glimpsed a lanky male dashing into the nineteenth floor hallway. The glimpse immediately triggered recognition in Jason's mind, for it wasn't just any male than had lunged through that door. It was Richard, and he had apparently ditched his concierge dress for something more casual- a lame attempt to disguise himself should Jason discover him.

Jason quickly climbed the final set of stairs to the nineteenth floor landing and swung the stairwell door open, but Richard was gone and the hallway was silent. He considered continuing the chase, but Jason was pretty certain Richard couldn't have spanned the distance to the elevator foyer at the far end of the hallway in the short time it took Jason to climb those final few steps. Jason also hadn't heard the familiar ding of the elevator's arrival, which meant Richard must have ducked into hiding somewhere, perhaps in the vending machine nook or into a guest room or some well-disguised storage closet. It didn't matter, Jason decided, because he was going to make it known that he had caught Richard in the act.

Jason retreated into the stairwell and quickly descended the steps he had just climbed. Going nineteen floors down after racing six floors up was going to be a bitch, but Jason wasn't going to let a little muscle burn derail him from outing Richard's sneaky behavior. He knew he couldn't outrun the elevator's descent once Richard initiated it, but Jason also knew that Richard would be cautious about coming out of hiding and would need additional time to change back into his normal employee garb, which should give Jason just enough time to beat the concierge back to his podium.

Around the tenth floor, Jason began skipping every other step and even used the stairwell rails to propel himself past the last few steps before each landing. It was a surefire way to break an ankle, but Jason didn't care. He made it to the ground level in record time- not that there had been much haste to his previous Olympic heat- and flung open the stairwell door. Jason then raced down the inconspicuous hallway that exited directly into the lobby, his eyes darting immediately to the concierge podium- where Richard was still lazily propped, somehow looking even more bored than before as he barely attempted to stifle a yawn. Jason staggered over to the podium, blissfully ignorant of the *is that man okay?* looks he was getting from the other hotel guests he passed.

"How'd you do it?" Jason wheezed in disbelief as he neared Richard. "How-" He broke into a coughing fit, bending in half as his lungs finally told him enough was enough.

"Mr. Chance," Richard said nonchalantly. "Are you all right?

117

Can I get you some water?"

Jason waved him off, but Richard signaled to another hotel employee who promptly delivered a glass of ice water. Jason gulped the water between gasps of air and slowly returned his body to an upright position.

"How did you do it?" Jason repeated, his mental and physical state in no mood to beat around the bush. "How did you get down here before me? How did you have time to change your clothes?"

Richard smiled awkwardly. "I'm afraid I don't know what you're talking about, Mr. Chance." He motioned his hand toward a nearby chair on the edge of the pseudo-great room. "You look a little unwell," Richard then said with a semi-accusatory tone. "Maybe you should sit."

"Don't patronize me," Jason snapped. "You were in the stairwell with me just minutes ago. How'd you beat me back here? And why the hell aren't you more tired?"

"I really don't know what you're talking about," Richard reiterated with what seemed to be sincere conviction. "I'm been here almost the entire day. Ask anyone. Heck, ask yourself. You've seen me multiple times with your own eyes, Mr. Chance."

He had a point there, Jason considered, his breathing finally coming back under control. "So that wasn't you in the stairwell?" Jason had been so certain.

"Afraid not."

Jason studied Richard's face for a tell, a twitch, anything that would indicate the concierge was lying to him, but there was nothing. "I supposed it was Benji, then?" Jason asked sarcastically as he recalled the bullshit name Katie had fed him during his previous claim of mistaken identity.

Richard thought about Jason's suggestion for a moment, then said, "yeah, probably."

Well, at least they're all crapping the same bullshit around here, Jason thought. He was about to press Richard further, but then Marvin joined them at the podium, a look of grave concern plastered across his face.

"Mr. Chance," he addressed Jason with a sense of friendly urgency, "are you quite all right? You look terrible." He motioned to the same chair Richard had motioned to moments earlier. "Perhaps you should have a seat."

"I tried to tell him-" Richard started.

"I'm fine," Jason cut the concierge off. "Actually, I'm glad you're here," he then told Marvin. "Maybe you can help clear the air."

"I'm at your service, Mr. Chance," Marvin said, his usual jolliness replacing the urgency in his voice so quickly that Jason questioned how legitimate it had been in the first place.

"I was in the stairwell a few minutes ago checking out the thirteenth floor," Jason explained, "when I thought I saw Richard spying on me. I chased him to the nineteenth floor where he escaped me, so I returned down here to confront him about it and now he's denying it ever happened." Jason knew he sounded like a first-grader tattling on the class bully, so he countered by presenting Marvin with his best no-nonsense face. "Can you tell me whether Richard left this podium in the past ten to fifteen minutes?" There he was, Jason Chance, Amateur Detective, at his prime.

Marvin stared intently at Jason as if processing the story with utmost seriousness. For a moment, Jason thought the manager might actually sell out his employee by admitting Richard had snuck away from the podium. But that moment ended as soon as Marvin broke into heavy laughter, with Richard joining in on the amusement shortly thereafter. Well aren't they a couple of yucksters? Jason thought as he remembered the two of them laughing at him in similar fashion the night before, when he had questioned the hotel's 'no charges for the Chances' policy.

"I can't tell you how glad I am to be the butt of your jokes," Jason told them dryly. "Again."

"I'm so sorry, Mr. Chance," Marvin said through his over-emotive grin. "It's just- I can't get Richard to move above a snail's pace when the building's on fire."

"It's true," Richard added with a nod. "Been there, done that."

"I just can't picture him running," Marvin continued, "especially not up multiple flights of stairs. He'd probably bribe someone to give him a piggyback ride before attempting a single step on his own!"

"Also true," Richard admitted without shame.

Marvin's laughter began to subside. "Besides, we don't have a thirteenth floor."

Not this again, Jason thought. He wondered whether Marvin's humorous exchange had been a tactic to distract him from revoking Richard's spy of the year award. He wondered now if Marvin would try to bog him down in wordplay about the thirteenth floor like the respondent to the elevator's one-eight-hundred hotline had done. Well, Jason decided, if Marvin's plan was to aggravate Jason into submission, he had another thing coming.

"Actually, you do have a thirteenth floor," Jason corrected bluntly and clearly, ensuring Marvin couldn't play the deaf card on him. "I was there, in the stairwell, just a bit ago."

"Well sure," Marvin then admitted, "we have a thirteenth level that sits between floors twelve and fourteen, but it was never hollowed out for use. Bad luck and all that jazz. The concrete slab was added for upper level structural support during an expansion years ago. But that's all it is: a concrete slab." Marvin gave Jason's shoulder a gentle squeeze. "Rest assured, Mr. Chance, there is no thirteenth floor in this hotel."

There's going to be one less hand in this hotel if Marvin doesn't move it soon, Jason thought inwardly. Unfortunately, though the manager's explanation was one of technicalities, that didn't make it any less valid. In fact, it made perfect sense. More importantly, it also aligned with what Jason had already convinced himself to be true, that the concrete he encountered on the thirteenth floor stairwell landing was solid through and through. It wasn't the exciting climax Jason had hoped for when his investigation first began, but then again, real life was almost always more disappointing than fiction.

"Boy, I feel silly," Jason said with an embarrassed laugh. He then looked at Richard for one last confirmation. "And that really wasn't you in the stairwell?"

"It really wasn't," Richard said without a hint of dishonesty. "Sorry."

"It was probably just some kid," Marvin offered as a way to ease Jason's mind. "We've had a band of teenagers roaming from floor to floor, causing mischief. They even vandalized the vending machine on your floor, Mr. Chance." Jason could feel his cheeks turning red, but Marvin gave no indication that he noticed. "My guess is one of them was going to play a prank on you, but got scared at the last minute."

"Maybe so," Jason falsely acquiesced so Marvin would stop wasting everyone's time with speculation. "Sorry to have bothered you both."

Marvin assured Jason that he was no bother before returning to the check-in counter. Richard gave Jason a disingenuous smile accompanied by a *ta-ta, bitch* kind of wave, then returned to his prior position of laziness. Having struck out on one mystery, Jason turned to the elevator bays, intent on solving his other one, that of his phantom chess opponent. To his delight, however, Jason spotted Leila stepping into his usual elevator car with a small vase of yellow flowers in her hands. Her eyes locked with his for just a moment, and she gave Jason a warm smile as the elevator doors slid shut. Damn, Jason thought as he tried to tame the butterflies in his stomach, if he had just given up his arguments a minute sooner...

He strolled to the elevator bays and pressed the call button. At least with Leila stealing his regular car, Jason might have a chance to test out the other death traps the hotel had in service. So you know, yay to that. Jason waited for nearly two minutes, then pressed the call button again, thinking maybe his first press hadn't registered. Another minute passed, and still no other car came to claim him. At this rate, Jason supposed he was going to be hitching a ride in his regular car after all.

He looked at the analogue dial above his usual set of elevator doors to see whether it was on its way back from Leila's destination, and at that moment it was as if time had stopped dead in its tracks. Jason's heart raced and the butterflies in his stomach returned in full force, not because he was about to see Leila again, but because, despite the warmth and kindness she had previously shown him, her true nature had just been revealed. Jason felt his blood erupt into a full-fledged boil as he double- and triple-checked what his eyes had communicated and his subconscious had already processed, that the arrow on the analogue floor dial wasn't pointed at a specific number. No, it had stopped between two numbers, at the nearly imperceptible space between twelve and fourteen, to be exact. Jason clenched his hands into shaky fists as he forced his brain to accept that which it didn't want to accept, that which meant he had been betrayed by the one person who had made him feel welcome in this insane asylum, that Leila, innocent, unassuming Leila, had just gone to the thirteenth floor.

Chapter Seventeen
Olga Doesn't Forget Anything

Jason tore his enraged eyes from the analogue floor dial and spun around to face the lobby. He didn't know what he wanted more: to knock Richard and Marvin's blocks off or to drag both men to the elevator to give them one futile opportunity to weasel their ways out of admitting the existence of the thirteenth floor once more. But like a couple of Houdinis, Richard and Marvin were suddenly gone, their respective posts empty. In fact, Jason realized, all the hotel staff were gone, leaving no one but other guests for Jason to unload his anger upon. Way to play dirty, Jason thought. But his anger was far more focused than the hotel staff gave him credit for, and Jason knew exactly where he could let it loose.

He ran back to the stairwell hallway, through the stairwell door, and up the thirteen flights that stood between him and Leila. Jason's legs were ablaze by the time he got there, but he barely noticed, their fire nothing compared to the emotional fire that burned within him. Jason approached the concrete wall where the door to the thirteenth floor should have been erected and pounded so fiercely that he was pretty sure he would break his hand if he didn't ease up soon.

"Leila!" Jason hollered loudly. "Leila, I know you're in there!" There was no response, so Jason pounded harder. "Leila!"

Again, nothing. Jason paused and considered what he must

look like to any guests who happened to be traversing the stairwell right now. He had gone from vending machine pervert to verbally abusive customer in the course of a single day... some really proud accomplishments there. But then again, what did it matter? The only other person he had ever seen in the stairwell was not-Richard, and not-Richard was just as complacent in turning Jason into the ass he was currently being as anyone.

"Leila!" Jason yelled as he resumed his pounding. "Leila, you can't hide in there forever!"

Jason hit the wall a few more times, then stopped to assess the state of his opponent's defenses. Yup, the concrete was just as solid as ever, and Jason's hand throbbed terribly. This was going to take a while. Dejected, Jason let his forehead rest against his enemy's cool surface. Maybe he should've put a little more thought into this battle before sending in the troops. Had he really expected Leila to hear him through who-knows-how-thick a layer of solid concrete? Could he even be certain Leila was on the other side of that wall? Maybe there was another explanation for the elevator floor dial pointing to the space where the number thirteen had been conveniently omitted. Maybe-

Of course! Jason told himself. That's probably what the floor dial looked like when he was trapped in the elevator car earlier that day. Maybe Leila was trapped too. Maybe she was flailing blindly in the dark, unable to find the emergency phone that could get her rescued. Maybe- no, Jason admitted. He was deceiving himself into finding an excuse for Leila. He wanted to give her an out, if only because he didn't want to believe she was like the other hotel staff. But he knew that any excuse he allowed would be a betrayal of his own instincts, instincts that told him Leila was on the other side of this wall, on the supposedly non-existent thirteenth floor that had so far eluded Jason's investigatory prowess. He stood tall and resumed his pounding once more.

"Leila! I know you're in there! I-"

Something cracked in Jason's hand, eliciting a loud yelp as he fell back against the nearest stairwell railing for support. Damn, Jason thought, that's going to need some time to heal. He tested his hand by trying to make a fist, but the pain was too great. Jason dropped onto his butt, cradling the injured hand with his other as he debated his next move. Maybe this wasn't worth it, Jason considered. Maybe he should just return to his room like a normal guest and focus on putting his life back in order. Maybe he should see a doctor...

Jason rotated onto his knees and propped his weight on his good hand to push himself up, and that's when he saw it. It was so carefully disguised, so flush with the rest of the concrete that surrounded it, intentionally painted, pocked, and scuffed to match its surroundings perfectly- but it was there: two long, horizontal seams connected by two shorter, vertical seams. A box, just like the emergency phone box in the elevator car, only smaller and rotated ninety degrees, with its pull tab nestled deep within a pockmark, where the casual eye would never see it.

"Son of a bitch," Jason whispered.

The box was low to the ground on the wall adjacent to the one Jason had been pounding. Jason squeezed the pull tab, and the box swung open to reveal a digital keycard reader, the same type of reader Jason had seen on every guest room door, including his own. Now that he knew what he was looking for, Jason examined the adjacent wall carefully, and it didn't take him long before he found the door seam, disguised as a natural concrete crack, the door it belonged to covered in a concrete veneer that concealed it from all but the most curious of observers. Jason considered trying brute force to pry open the hidden door, but the continued stinging in his hand smartly swayed him away from that approach. Instead, Jason dug in his pocket for the keycard to his room. He knew it was a long shot, but he waved it in front of the reader hopefully, anyway. A single, rejecting buzz confirmed what Jason had already expected: if he wanted through this door, he was going to need higher access. He was going to need staff access, and he knew exactly where he could get it.

Jason climbed to the fourteenth floor and peered down the hallway. Empty. He then climbed to the fifteenth, with the same result. But on floor sixteen, Jason found exactly what he was looking for, a housekeeping cart, sitting idle outside of a guest room that was currently being serviced. Jason emerged from the stairwell quietly and tiptoed toward the cart. He could hear the brushing of a hand coming from the room's open door as the housekeeper inside attempted to de-wrinkle bed sheets. Then he could hear the thumps of pillows being fluffed.

Jason reached the cart and scanned for the housekeeper's keycard, hoping on a whim that he or she didn't carry it in their pocket. He saw stacks of fresh towels and washcloths, sealed bars of soap and other toiletries, new ice bucket bags, fresh bedding supplies, and just about everything else a housekeeper would need... except for a master keycard. Jason shifted his position to check the other side of the cart, where he then saw a lanyard peeking out from beneath a clipboard similar to the one Katie always carried with her. Just maybe, Jason thought as he reached for the lanyard with his good hand...

"Naughty naughty, Mr. Chance..."

Jason froze mid-theft, the familiar European accent sending chills down his spine. He saw Olga standing in the doorway of the room being serviced and slowly retracted his hand, his mind racing to think of excuses before she carried out what was certain to be her own special brand of corporal punishment for Jason's obvious guilt. Unfortunately, Jason's brain had formed a recent habit of failing him when he needed it most, and this was no exception.

"What do you need that I didn't already leave in your room?" Olga asked with glaringly suspicious eyes. "Olga doesn't forget anything."

Jason was sure she didn't. Come on, brain, he encouraged inwardly, all the while gazing at Olga with what he could only imagine was an unintentionally dumbfounded expression. Ten seconds passed, ten seconds that felt like an eternity under the heat of Olga's stare. Then ten more passed, and at that point Jason realized silence wouldn't get him anywhere. Olga was going to force an answer out of him, and if passive aggressive tension didn't get the job done, Jason suspected she had more forceful and effective ways to proceed. Suddenly, by some miracle, Jason's brain actually provided him with the get-out-of-jail free card he needed.

"N-No," Jason stammered, "you didn't forget anything. I was walking by and accidentally bumped your cart. I thought I saw the stack of washcloths falling."

Okay, it wasn't the best excuse, Jason admitted to himself, but it was better than standing there with his thumb up his ass. Olga bent slowly to her left to get a better view of the washcloths. Then she bent slowly to her right, squinting her eyes as she analyzed the terrycloth stack. Curious, Jason bent over as well, not to look at the washcloths, but to make sure Olga's eyes hadn't started glowing red, the first warning sign in any good killer cyborg movie that the bots were about to turn on the humans. Jason knew he shouldn't have looked; he just couldn't help himself. He also instantly regretted it the moment Olga's eyes locked onto his. Luckily, they were still human eyes.

"Washcloths seem fine to me," she said flatly. "What were you doing on this floor, anyway?"

Seriously? Who was the amateur detective here? Of course, the key word was amateur, and Jason knew that was him, because Olga was clearly a professional. Come on, brain, Jason encouraged again, desperately in need of another unexpected save. He could feel perspiration beginning to trickle down his face. Part of it was from nervous sweat, born from the fear of bodily harm Olga might inflict upon him, but part of it was left over from his stairwell excursions, and that gave Jason what he felt was an absolutely brilliant idea.

"I was just taking a walk," he said. "Trying to get some exercise. Twenty-one floors of torture is a great cardio workout."

Jason froze again. He had heard the mistake as it left his lips, but had committed to finishing the sentence. Torture? Really, dumbass? Had he seriously used the word 'torture' out loud with Olga? Torture was probably her middle name. Even if it wasn't, Jason didn't need to be putting the thought in her mind. Despite that faux pas, though, he had just given Olga the perfect excuse. With all of his running around the stairwell, Jason looked, and probably smelled, like a hot mess, which meant his physical appearance matched his lie. Olga studied him as if trying to decide whether to send him to the gallows or to congratulate him on his efforts to be healthy. Jason hoped it was the latter.

"Mr. Chance," Olga said with slow and deliberate disapproval, "we have an exercise room for that. You go there next time." It was an order, not a suggestion.

"Yes, ma'am," Jason said obediently.

He didn't wait to be shooed off by Olga this time, and instead bee-lined it straight for the stairwell, doing his best mall walker impersonation along the way. Once out of Olga's sight, Jason took a minute to recompose himself and examine his injured hand, which had turned slightly blue and puffy on one side. He also took a minute to think for a change. Jason still needed a staff member's master keycard if he was going to gain entrance to the thirteenth floor, but his experience with Olga had now dissuaded him from trying to lift one from the housekeeping staff. He needed a new set of targets, and, as fortune would have it, he knew of a spot where those targets commonly gathered.

Jason descended one floor to avoid passing Olga again, then exited the stairwell and went straight for the elevator bays, having no intention of putting on his exercise facade for another fifteen flights. He pressed the elevator call button, and within thirty seconds, his usual car arrived to pick him up. Oh, so it does still work, Jason thought smartly. He stepped onto the elevator car without his usual worrisome debate about mortality and pressed the button for the ground floor. Then, as the elevator doors slid shut, he wondered why he hadn't stopped at the nearest vending machine to grab some popcorn and a soda along the way, for the thirteenth floor light and sound show was about to begin.

Chapter Eighteen
Don't Worry, You're Next

Jason stepped off his usual elevator car after a thankfully uneventful descent from the fifteenth floor. Well, uneventful if he ignored the electrical malfunctions that manifested as he passed the thirteenth floor, anyway. Jason passed the still-empty concierge podium and proceeded straight to the hotel lobby, where the first staff member he saw was the maid he had noticed a couple of times already since checking in, but hadn't met personally yet. She was wiping down the check-in counter with spray cleaner, probably taking advantage of Marvin's convenient absence to give it a good cleaning.

The maid's master keycard was openly visible, dangling from a retractable cord secured to her waist, just waiting to be snatched and grabbed, should Jason be so emboldened. There were two problems Jason saw with that idea, however. First, the keycard was dangling awfully close to an area that, should Jason miscalculate his grab in the slightest, would result in him earning that pervert title he had previously bestowed upon himself in jest. Second, a snatch and grab wasn't exactly discrete, and right now Jason needed discretion if he was going to break onto the thirteenth floor without interference. He ruled out the maid as a potential target and scanned for the next.

There was the doorman Jason also hadn't met, but who had greeted him warmly upon his return from Mackey and Sons and seemed like a nice enough guy. Jason hated to take advantage of the doorman's kindness, but he was desperate and willing to do just about anything to prove the thirteenth floor's existence. That didn't matter, though, for the doorman's keycard was nowhere in sight, probably tucked away safely in a jacket pocket, which made him a dead-end as well. Jason scanned the lobby for any other staff members and, not finding any, considered his options.

The housekeepers and maids wouldn't make suitable targets because they used their keycards frequently and therefore kept them securely guarded on their bodies at all times. The doorman, valet, and higher ranked staff such as Marvin, Leila, Richard, and Katie wouldn't make suitable targets because they used their keycards less frequently and wore outfits in which the keycards could be tucked out of sight when not in use as not to disrupt their professional appearances. Jason needed a middle ground. He needed to find a staff member who was unlikely to keep their keycard constantly dangling on their body, but who also might set their keycard down because it didn't suit their daily wardrobe or job to keep it at the ready. He needed a staff member who didn't have pockets, or at least one with a job that required setting personal belongings aside when getting to work, perhaps because the job was too messy or, just the opposite, demanded extreme cleanliness...

Jason's eyes fell on the hallway leading to the hotel restaurant. Bingo. Jason walked casually to the entrance of the hallway and waited patiently until another guest requested Marie's attention. He then raced past her hostess station and straight through a set of swinging doors next to the bar that he assumed led into the kitchen. Jason had to shield his eyes for a moment as they adjusted to the brightness of the open work area, which was loaded with stainless steel tables and cooking equipment, multiple stoves and ovens, at least two sets of heavy-duty doors to what Jason presumed were industrial freezers, a dishwashing station far to the back, and what Jason guessed was a final plating counter where an army's worth of dishware and utensils lay in waiting.

Jason wasn't sure what he had expected from the kitchen based on the one meal he had eaten at the bar the night before, but it definitely wasn't this. The work space was nearly the size of the restaurant itself, and its bright fluorescent lighting reflected off of every steel surface and wall in an almost sterilizing manner. It was spotless as far as Jason could see, almost as if it had never been used. But it had been used, Jason knew from his own meal the night before, and it was currently being used, or so the barrage of succulent smells wafting off of meals being prepared told him.

Jason didn't see any kitchen employees, but he heard something sizzling in the distance, so he followed his ears and his nose until the flames of a stove topped with multiple pots and pans came into view. Chef Terrance was on the other side of the stove, his back turned to Jason as he fiddled with something Jason couldn't see on one of the stainless steel prep tables. Jason stepped cautiously toward Chef Terrance, his eyes scanning for the hulking man's personal items. The kitchen was so large, there was no telling where the chef kept his stuff while cooking. For all Jason knew, maybe Chef Terrance kept everything in his pants pockets beneath his chef's coat, or in a locker on the other side of the workspace, or in the bowl of one of the seven or eight unused stand mixers Jason had already seen. Heck, for all Jason knew, Chef Terrance's personal items didn't even include a master keycard. After all, what did the chef really need one for?

Jason had gone about as far as he could without risking being seen should Chef Terrance turn around. This was the moment of truth: proceed and potentially get caught, or turn around and find another victi- volunteer, Jason quickly corrected his thoughts. He had nearly decided on the latter when he glimpsed something black and rectangular resting on the seat of a chair about ten feet from the active stove. Jason took a step to his right to get a better view of the object, which he now identified as a phone. Chef Terrance's phone, he assumed, sitting right next to Chef Terrance's wristwatch and master keycard.

Jason crept toward the chair ever so slowly as not to make noise or accidentally bump into something. He was in the open now, so much so that there would be no hiding or disguising himself if Chef Terrance turned even the slightest. Jason looked at the pots and pans on the active stove. He couldn't see all of their contents, but the ones he could see contained simmering broth and sautéing vegetables. The broth wasn't an issue, but those vegetables would need tossing soon. Jason picked up the pace as Chef Terrance's handling of whatever was on that prep table became more forceful. Jason neared the chair and stopped, realizing that he would enter Chef Terrance's peripheral vision if he stepped any closer. Instead, he leaned down and stretched his good hand toward the master keycard. His arm was fully extended, but his fingertips fell just short of the coveted object. Jason tried leaning a bit more, his body straining against the pull of gravity not to topple over-

Thwack!

Jason's heart leaped as the loud noise shot across the open space of the kitchen. He lost his balance but dropped his good hand to the ground just in time to prevent himself from crashing down. Jason's eyes darted to the source of the noise: a thick wooden cutting board, above it, a glistening cleaver in the tight grip of Chef Terrance's hand, and resting next to it on the cold steel of the prep table, a large, severed fish head.

Thwack!

Check that. Two severed fish heads, their dead eyes staring at

Jason as if to tell him *don't worry, you're next*. Nope, Jason thought as he gulped down a lump in his throat, not worth it. He remained close to the ground as he retreated the way he had come, still without a master keycard, the prized object reminding him of the bitchy hot girl in his high school chemistry class. You could look at her, but don't even think about touching her. In hindsight, Jason was pretty sure he deserved the low grade he received in that class.

He reached the swinging doors and passed through to the dining area. Jason then acted as relaxed as he could manage with the images of Chef Terrance's slaughterhouse burned into his mind's eye, and strolled out of the restaurant with his head partially turned away from the hostess stand to avoid drawing Marie's attention. Like most of his efforts since checking in to the Chance Hotel, however, it didn't work.

"Mr. Chance?" Marie called out, not in the suspicious manner Jason had expected, but with the charm befitting a restaurant hostess. "Mr. Chance, one moment please."

Jason paused as he waited for Marie to catch up to him. Keep acting casual, he reminded himself; there's no way Marie knows what you're up to. Marie reached him, and Jason flashed her the type of *I'm not doing anything wrong* grin that only a guilty person could muster. Marie did a subtle double-take as if unsure of what to make of his gesture, then proceeded as if nothing unusual had occurred.

"Mr. Chance, I just wanted to remind you about your dinner reservation tonight."

"Reservation?" Jason asked. He didn't recall making any such reservation, but then again he was relying on the same hunk of gray matter that had him seeing giant sea monsters, playing chess with ghosts, and trying to break into a floor that multiple sources with better information than him insisted didn't exist. What was a forgotten restaurant reservation?

"Yes, sir," Marie confirmed. "I tried calling your room several times to remind you, but well-" She bobbed her head playfully. "You're obviously not there."

"Riiiiiight," Jason said, unintentionally drawing out the word as his brain struggled to get up to speed. "What time did I make my reservation for again?"

"Oh anytime," Marie replied. "We'll have a seat at the bar reserved for whenever you get hungry. And you didn't make it; Chef Terrance did. He said something about making sure you eat a proper meal..." Marie shook her head. "I don't know."

Whew, Jason thought. He was only ninety-eight percent crazy instead of ninety-nine percent; that was a relief. What wasn't a relief was that the Butcher of Fish Head Bay had taken it upon himself to start policing Jason's meals. First, it was supervised recreation time, now supervised meal time. Pretty soon, Jason was going to have to start petitioning to go pee by himself.

"Thanks for letting me know," he said to Marie, feigning gratitude as he reminded himself that she was only the messenger.

Marie excused herself to tend to a family that had arrived at the hostess stand in her absence. Jason continued on to the lobby, but stopped short of revealing his presence when he spotted Richard back at the concierge podium. Richard looked slightly less bored than usual as he watched a pair of kids graffiti the lobby floor with a game of tic-tac-toe. Katie's not going to be too happy about that, Jason thought. Oh, and there she was. The quality control queen emerged from her ice layer, clipboard at the ready to smack the kids upside their heads. Run, kids! Jason thought gleefully. Run while you still have a chance!

It was too late. Katie had reached them and opened fire with a wag of her finger and a mouthful of scolding words. The kids ran away laughing before she could finish her tirade, which meant they were either really inconsiderate or really smart... Jason suspected it was both. Katie snapped her sorceress fingers, conjuring a member of the janitorial staff out of thin air and putting him to work on removing the offending x's and o's. Inspired, Jason held his good hand in front of him and thought hard about a master keycard before snapping his own fingers. Sadly, his magical powers were about as effective as his common sense.

He spotted Katie redirect her angry gaze to Richard, apparently aware of his complacency in the defacement of hotel property. Richard pretended not to see her, but he couldn't pretend not to hear that snap as she physically demanded his attention. Richard slunk his way to Katie with a *who me?* sway to his step. Then the scolding session continued. Jason couldn't hear Katie's words but, given who she directed them toward, he eagerly wanted to. He hugged the far wall and made his way closer to Richard and Katie, going as far as the concierge podium before her voice became barely audible to his ears.

"... and every time we go through this!" Uh oh, Katie was using her mad voice. "Do you have any idea how much floor cleaner we've wasted for your entertainment? We're going to end up scrubbing the varnish off one day!"

Richard mumbled something in reply, but Jason couldn't understand it. He leaned against the concierge podium and turned his ear toward the arguing pair, but it wasn't enough. Getting any closer would require strolling out in the open, but it was worth it for a front-row seat to Richard's ass spanking. Besides, what did Jason have to hide? He was a guest of the hotel, simply taking in the sights. He was allowed to roam the lobby like anyone else. He-

Jason's thoughts ceased instantly as his eyes fell to the top of the concierge podium, where Richard's master keycard sat unattended, just inches from Jason's fingers. No, Jason told himself, it couldn't be that easy. But it was, for the keycard wasn't an optical illusion. It was real and abandoned and a moment later in the grips of Jason's hand. Jason considered that this could be a setup, that Richard could have planted the tic-tac-toe kids while Marie ran interference, that Katie could have reenacted her janitorial snapping act for no one's benefit except Jason's, that Richard purposely left the keycard behind when walking away from the podium, that despite all their efforts to divert him, the hotel staff actually wanted Jason to discover the thirteenth floor. It was all possible, but frankly, it sounded a little crazy.

Jason stared at the keycard clenched between his thumb and forefinger. Crazy was relative in the Chance Hotel, and this little piece of plastic was Jason's first-class ticket to crazy town. With Katie still berating Richard for his failure to meet her unattainable standards, Jason quietly stepped away from the lobby, returned to the elevator bays, pressed the call button, and instructed the arriving car to take him to the twelfth floor, from which he would transfer to the stairwell on his way to his final destination. All aboard, Jason thought as the elevator doors shut. Choo choo!

Chapter Nineteen
Shut Up, Subconscious

Ding.

The elevator doors opened to the twelfth floor foyer. Jason stepped out cautiously, his muscles tense and at the ready should any of the hotel staff be waiting to run interference on his journey. But the foyer was empty and, aside from an elderly couple arguing over whether they should bring an umbrella on whatever outing they had planned for the day, so was the twelfth floor hallway. Jason made quick work of the distance between him and the far stairwell door. He entered the stairwell as quietly as he could, then ascended with soft steps, constantly peering toward the thirteenth floor landing, trying to identify any signs of resistance before they were close enough to stop him. Again, though, there were none.

Jason arrived at the landing and opened the access panel to the hidden digital keycard reader. He gripped Richard's master keycard tight, moved it toward the reader, then hesitated, that voice in his head once again saying *don't do it, Jason*, followed by *no good can come of this*. The voice wasn't screaming at him as it had done on the elevator when he had tempted fate with the thirteenth floor once before. This time it was speaking calmly, aware that the mind it was trying to sway had already cracked and needed to be brought down from the ledge before being reprimanded. What if the voice was right? Jason thought. It was his own subconscious, after all; perhaps it sensed danger that his surface-level senses didn't.

But what could be dangerous about a simple floor of guest rooms in the middle of an ordinary hotel? Correction: a *secret* floor of guest rooms in the middle of an *otherwise not-so-ordinary* hotel. Nope, double correction, Jason told himself: a secret floor of guest rooms in the middle of an otherwise not-so-ordinary hotel *that was home to a potentially dangerous sea monster, a chess playing ghost, and a really stupid name-based pricing policy.* Seriously, what business sense did that policy make? Jason shook the question off. The accounting of the Chance Hotel was a mystery to be tackled another day.

Jason heard the voice in his head warning him again. *Walk away, Jason*, it said. *Walk away while your body is mostly intact.* Jason looked at the deep bruising that had spread across his one hand. Surely if the chess playing ghost lived on the thirteenth floor, it wouldn't cause him further harm. How would Jason continue his game with it? In fact, if the ghost did live on the thirteenth floor, maybe it had been the source of the whispers Jason had heard when trapped in the elevator! Maybe it had been trying to give him advice on how to step up his chess game. Or, Jason considered with a shudder, maybe the ghost was inviting him to join it for a game of a more *permanent* nature...

Then there was the other alternative. The sea monster, if it really existed- which was definitely a point up for debate given Jason's mental state- needed to live somewhere. What if it was beyond the hidden doorway Jason was about to carelessly open? Would its fleshy tentacle whip out to grab him with a thunderous crack, as it had the athletic blonde man? What then? Would Jason simply awake the next day and check out of the hotel with a sopping wet suitcase and hot new lady friend in tow, or would the sea monster ensure he checked out of life altogether? Maybe that voice in Jason's head was on to something...

"Screw it," Jason said aloud.

He waved Richard's master keycard in front of the digital reader before he could second-guess himself further. Unlike when he presented his own keycard to the reader, Jason heard a positive digital beep in response to Richard's, the sound of unmistakable acceptance. There was a noise like a gear turning, followed by an unusually loud deadbolt thud, from behind the concrete facade that camouflaged the thirteenth floor landing door. Then the door partially opened, swinging inward on hinges that were so massive they had to be installed on the inside of the door to avoid giving away its existence. Clever, Jason thought as he stood and pushed the door the rest of the way open.

Beyond the doorway was a dark hall that made a quick ninety-degree turn. It had to, Jason realized, for the hidden door had been installed perpendicular to the flow of the building. Jason took his first step into the hall. *Please don't do this*, the voice in his head pleaded in one last attempt to save him from whatever might be waiting around the blind corner ahead. But Jason wasn't interested in listening to his inner conscience. The staff of the Chance Hotel had spied on him and lied to him to keep him away from this floor; no matter the danger, Jason wanted to know why. He stepped farther into the hallway, and, as soon as he cleared the swing of the stairwell door, it shut itself with a solid thump, plunging Jason into blackness. Shit, Jason thought as he stood there in the dark, unsure of what he should do next. But when his eyes adjusted a moment later, Jason saw with relief that he wasn't in total blackness, for there was a glow of soft, warm light barely visible from the turn up ahead.

Jason used the glow as a guiding star, reaching the end of the brief perpendicular hallway and taking a deep, shaky breath before rounding the corner to the thirteenth floor. What Jason saw next was both familiar and yet oddly perplexing. The thirteenth floor hallway reminded him of all the others he had passed through. It was carpeted and long enough that Jason couldn't see all the way to the other end, and both sides were lined with guest room doors secured by digital locks, with lanterns mounted between them to light the way. But unlike the other floors Jason had seen during his brief time at the Chance Hotel, the guest room doors on the thirteenth floor were spaced extra close together. Like really close together, Jason determined upon closer examination, so close that he wondered if there was anything more than an oversized bathroom behind each one. Weird.

The lighting on the thirteenth floor was also pretty terrible, the lanterns providing only a fraction of the light they provided on other floors, severely limiting how much detail Jason could see without being right next to something. Speaking of detail, Jason also noticed that whomever installed the lanterns had done a pretty shitty job, as barely any of them were level and a few were notably damaged. Most also flickered erratically, making Jason wonder if they were on the same electrical circuit as his favorite elevator car.

Jason proceeded down the hallway in slow and deliberate fashion. Something about this place made him feel uneasy, even though, as far as he could tell, it held no immediate threat to his safety. The passageway to the secret stairwell door soon fell into darkness, Jason having gone far enough down the hallway that his usable light could no longer reach it. Until that point, the hallway had been eerily silent, but now Jason heard a faint whirring, followed by a click, and then a buzz. He froze, his first thought that one of the digital door locks had just been disengaged. Jason's heart pounded so forcefully that he could feel his shirt bounce away from his chest with each beat. He waited, his mind ablaze with images of the potential horrid creatures that could emerge from any one of these doors, only to discover that a late afternoon snack named Jason Chance had been tricked into delivering himself to their doorsteps. Talk about five-star room service!

Jason eyed every door he could see in both directions, but none had opened. He eyed the darkness past the visible doors, his body rigid as it prepared for an attack. Then Jason heard the noise again. A whir, followed by a click, and then a buzz. This time, he nailed the direction of the sound. It came from ahead, farther into the hallway and away from the only viable exit of which Jason was aware. At least, he assumed it was a viable exit. Caught up in the moment, Jason had forgotten to check whether the stairwell door had a handle, digital card reader, or any other mechanism by which he could open it from the inside. Awesome.

Jason took a step forward as the series of noises repeated once more. He no longer believed them to be coming from a door lock, for he had heard no other sounds, such as the movement of feet or rubbing of clothing, and had seen no movement other than his own- though admittedly that would be difficult with the constant shifting of shadows on the surrounding walls. More comforting was that Jason had concluded the noises were coming in fixed intervals, a mechanical repetition rather than the result of living activity. They grew louder as he traveled deeper into the thirteenth floor, and soon Jason identified the general area from which they emanated. It was a small side room with no door and the glow of dim fluorescent lighting within. As Jason neared, he recognized the room, having spent quite some time ripping off the vending machine in its twenty-first floor counterpart.

Unlike his own, the vending machine in this room was empty and had cobwebs spanning across its interior cavity as if it hadn't been used in years. There was a large crack in the display case glass, and the fluorescent bulbs meant to showcase the junk food that would normally be inside the machine were just as unreliable as the rest of the lighting on this floor. Jason traced the repetitive noises to the general vicinity of the vending machine's keypad. He waited patiently, his eyes alert to catch the source of the sounds in action during their next interval. Then there they were- whir, click, buzz- all in succession. The whir came from the dollar bill intake as it yearned to be fed with phantom money. The click came from somewhere within the payment mechanism, for Jason heard it reverberate out of the coin return tray. The buzz came from the machine's digital readout, as it blinked 'no charges,' half the letters obscured by broken LEDs. Creepy, Jason thought as he waited for the cycle to repeat once more. Then, after confirming that the vending machine was indeed the sole source of the repetitive noise he had been hearing, Jason returned to the adjacent hallway.

He continued forward, partly relieved that, so far anyway, the thirteenth floor had proven to be a rather benign place. And yet, Jason couldn't shake the feeling that he shouldn't be here, that his very presence was a violation of the natural order that would ultimately result in dire consequences should he not turn back immediately. Maybe there was something to the feeling, or maybe it was the effect that the thirteen floor's run-down ambience was having on his already delusional mind. Jason couldn't be sure either way. He passed door after door, their tight, equal placement on each side of the hallway so meticulous that it stood in stark contrast to the haphazard care with which the interlaced lanterns had been installed. It was unsettling, suggesting that perhaps, a long time ago, this had been a fully functioning floor, and that some unseen force had twisted its intricate design to better suit a more perverse purpose.

Jason...

Shut up, subconscious, Jason told himself. He had come this

143

far; there was no way he was going to turn back now. Besides, he had gone far enough that he was probably closer to the elevator foyer than the stairwell passageway. Given it was his experiences in the elevator car that first drew Jason's interest to the thirteenth floor, he couldn't declare this investigation a success until he uncovered whatever might await him there.

Jason...

This time, he instantly froze, an uncontrollable chill shooting through his spine. That wasn't Jason's subconscious trying to talk to him- that was the whisper. It was the same whisper he had heard when trapped in the elevator car, only there was nothing unintelligible about it now. It had said his name. Twice. Of that, Jason was absolutely certain, and, despite what he had just told himself, it was enough to warrant a retreat.

"Okay," Jason said with a quivering voice to ensure it was himself doing the talking. "Now it's time to get the hell out of here."

It was perhaps the wisest the decision he had made yet. The only problem was, he wasn't sure if he could.

Chapter Twenty
There Are No Coincidences

Jason looked back toward the stairwell end of the hallway, but darkness cut his vision short of the stairwell passageway. In fact, he could barely see past the dim glow of the vending machine side room, which itself had been a decent distance from where he first began this procession into the unknown. Jason peered ahead, hoping to see a similar glow that could guide him to the elevator foyer instead, but no such glow broke through the distant blackness. Forward or back? Jason tossed in his head. Forward was the closest exit at this point, but that was assuming Jason could figure out how to access the elevator, which he presumed would require more effort than pushing the call button given the secretive nature of the thirteenth floor. Going backwards was a longer trek, but at least the destination was familiar, even if Jason didn't know for sure he could get out the same way he had gotten in.

"Good enough," Jason said softly, again speaking aloud to assure himself that it was he, and not the whisper, guiding his actions.

Jason began to turn around, a small part of him berating the act as that befitting a coward. Better to be chickenshit than a chicken filet, Jason considered in defiance. But even as he made the mental decision to stick to his guns, Jason paused, for something caught his eye just ahead, at the edge of the visible spectrum of his current surrounding light. It was small, maybe the size of a large kitten or puppy, and it was sitting still on the hallway floor right in front of an approaching door. Jason couldn't make out what the object was, or even if it was animate, without getting closer. Oh well, he told himself as he continued his turn and took a few steps toward the stairwell end of the hall.

But his curiosity had the better of him. There had been no other obstructions in the thirteenth floor hallway prior to this point, nothing to indicate use of the floor by guests or any other sign of life. What if this object, whatever it was, broke that trend? What if it gave Jason insight into the purpose of this floor? Richard was eventually bound to notice his master keycard was missing, and, given Jason's prior activity regarding the thirteenth floor, he was sure to be suspect number one. He may never have another chance to learn its secrets.

"You're such a dumbass," Jason told himself quietly as he felt his feet make another one-eighty and resume their forward procession. Maybe he would make smarter decisions in his next life, he thought inwardly, because this one was about to come to an abrupt end.

It didn't take long for the mystery object to come into clearer view, and once it did, Jason felt a momentary sense of relief. The object was a vase of flowers, yellow flowers, Jason determined once he was close enough that their color was no longer distorted by the flickering lamplight and shadows. Jason had seen these flowers before. They were in Leila's hands when she hopped aboard the elevator in the inciting incident that set Jason's current course of action into motion. So this was her great sin? She had taken the elevator to the thirteenth floor to deliver flowers to the room in front of which he now stood? It wasn't exactly the betrayal Jason had in mind when he first learned of her destination. But, Jason then considered, if Leila was delivering flowers to this room, that must mean a guest is staying there...

Jason checked the room number: 1301. He was staying in 2101. Did that mean this room was vertically aligned with his own? Probably not, given the vast difference in room spacing on this floor versus the twenty-first, and yet, Jason felt as though he were standing in an equivalent location of the thirteenth floor hallway as he would have been when entering his own room. Was there something to that, or was it mere coincidence?

"There are no coincidences at the Chance Hotel," Jason told himself resolutely.

He had encountered so much randomness and chance since his arrival. From the sharing of names, to the sea monster both on page and in real life, to the sentient vending machines and seemingly mass awareness of his activities, to the multiple Richards- only one of which was supposedly the real Richard- to the push and pull of the thirteenth floor, which the hotel staff had tried to keep hidden, but the hotel itself tried to reveal, and to which Jason gained access through nothing more than sheer luck. At some point, he had to accept that the degrees of randomness and chance were too great to be true. Jason had to admit that there was likely a grander plan unfolding, a plan in which he was both a willing, in some cases, and unwilling, in most others, participant.

Jason, the keycard...

It was the whisper again, and this time it came from a specific direction. It came from behind the door to room 1301. Jason felt for Richard's master keycard in his pocket. He had been so concerned with gaining access to the thirteenth floor that he hadn't considered it had additional uses, namely the ability to access any guest room he wished. Jason removed the keycard from his pocket and eyed the digital card reader affixed to the door before him. It was then that Jason noticed the popping sounds- electrical pops, like those he heard in the elevator whenever he passed the thirteenth floor. Was this their source, or had he been oblivious to them the entire time he had been on this floor? The pops grew louder as Jason moved the keycard closer to the reader. The flickering of the lights along the wall became more erratic, as if the hotel had joined Jason's subconscious in sounding alarm bells.

Jason... the whisper said again. *Do it.*

Jason couldn't tell whether the whisper was friendly or malevolent. At first it had scared him, but now it beckoned him, guided him as if trying to help him solve the mystery with which he was so obsessed. Jason inched the keycard closer to the reader. Any moment now it would be in range, and the door to 1301 would unlock, and then Jason's questions would be answered. The source of the whisper would be revealed, and with it, the secrets of the Chance Hotel would be spilled. The pops grew so loud that they began to hurt Jason's ears. The lights at each end of the hallway grew totally dark as if all of their energy were being sucked toward one central location, the location where Jason now stood, just outside of room 1301.

Do it!

Jason was so entranced by the whisper that he hadn't noticed the ding of the arriving elevator, nor the panicked approach of someone racing toward him from the darkness. The person emerged into what was left of the hallway's lamplight and launched themself toward Jason's outstretched arm, knocking it away just before Richard's keycard could establish communication with the digital reader for room 1301. The next thing Jason knew, he had landed hard on his side, unsure of who or what had run into him, knowing only that whatever it was, it had landed nearby. The electrical pops subsided as the hallway lighting returned to its original decrepit state.

"Give me that!" Jason heard Marvin holler angrily as he felt the manager's weight press against his body. Marvin was swiping wildly at Jason's hand, the hand that was somehow still holding on to Richard's keycard.

"No," Jason said firmly.

He shuffled out from under Marvin and pushed himself up, taking several steps back as Marvin lost his balance and face-planted against the carpet. There was little doubt in Jason's mind that he was the one in the wrong here, that Marvin's assault was justified by Jason's own wrongdoings, but in the heat of the moment, Jason didn't care. Marvin was the hotel manager, which meant he was the mastermind behind the secrecy of the thirteenth floor. Jason wasn't about to capitulate to him now.

"You want it?" Jason asked as Marvin rose from the carpet. "Come and get it."

Jason took off running toward the stairwell passageway. He was younger than Marvin, and guessed that if he could make it to the end of the hallway and find a way out quick enough, the older manager would be no match in a stairway competition. What Jason had forgotten was that he had already exhausted his leg muscles during his earlier stairwell excursions, and so he was just short of his destination when Marvin slammed into him from behind, sending both men crashing into a nearby door.

Jason heard a sharp crack as his body sandwiched between the door and the hotel manager. He wasn't sure what in his body had broken, but for the moment all appendages seemed to be in working order, so he shoved Marvin off of him, lowered his shoulder, and rammed the hotel manager into the opposite wall. Marvin fell to his knees, choking for air, as Jason entered the dark passageway that would take him to the hidden thirteen floor door.

"Wait!" Marvin wheezed. "I'm trying to help you, you idiot!"

Jason paused in the shadows of the passageway. Was it possible that Marvin was telling the truth for a change? Had he really tackled Jason in an effort to help him? Jason recalled the way the whisper's words had sent a feeling of dread through his body when first speaking his name. Had Marvin not intervened, Jason would have met the source of the whisper, the source of cold, unyielding dread, face-to-face. In hindsight, he really was an idiot.

Jason pocketed Richard's keycard, returned to the hallway, and extended his good hand to Marvin. "Come on," he said, then set his feet as Marvin leveraged Jason's weight to pull himself up.

"Thank you, Mr. Chance," Marvin said, his professional demeanor resuming now that their scuffle had ended. "Please follow me."

Marvin led Jason through the dark passageway and to the hidden stairwell door. He held his own master keycard against a digital reader Jason hadn't noticed on his way in, and after the secret door's lock disengaged with the same heavy thud Jason had heard earlier, it swung open, allowing the two men passage back into the stairwell. Once they were both clear on the thirteenth floor landing, Jason watched as the hidden door swung itself shut, still amazed by how well concealed it was against the surrounding concrete.

"What were you thinking, Mr. Chance?" Marvin asked in a manner similar to how a parent might question the poor choices of their child. "You stole one of my concierge's keycards. You broke into a secure floor that we had explicitly steered you away from..."

"Explicitly?" Jason countered. "What exactly was explicit about it? You didn't tell me to stay away from the thirteenth floor. You told me it didn't exist. The only thing explicit about that was your bullshit."

"You're correct," Marvin surprisingly admitted. "We did lie to you, but it was for your own good. You were getting too curious, and we were afraid you might hurt yourself."

"How?" Jason asked with more than a little aggression behind the one word question. "Who or what is staying on that floor and why are you concerned that it would hurt me?"

"There's no one staying on the floor-"

"Then why didn't you want me opening that room?" Jason cut in.

Marvin closed his eyes and placed the tips of his fingers against his forehead as if willing the frustration away. He breathed calmly, then opened his eyes and explained softly and slowly. "You saw the state of that floor. It's been shut down for years. There have been accidents... people have been hurt by the deplorable conditions. That room you were about to walk into-" Marvin shook his head. "It may as well be a giant death trap."

It's not the only one, Jason thought silently as the vision of his favorite elevator car flashed in his mind. "Let me get this straight," he then said aloud to Marvin, "you're telling me that there's nothing unusual about the thirteenth floor except that you've let it go to shit and therefore it's a safety hazard?"

"I wouldn't use your choice phrasing myself," Marvin replied, "but, essentially, yes."

"Then why not just say that?" Jason asked, utterly bewildered at the chain of events that had led him to this moment. "Why all the secrecy? Why the lies?"

Marvin shrugged. "We have a reputation to uphold." He said it lightly, as if he believed the ends justified the means. "You know how superstitious people can get about the number thirteen. The last thing we need is for potential guests to think there's something... abnormal about the Chance Hotel."

Jason was flabbergasted. He turned and waved his arms at the concrete facade that stood between them and the thirteenth floor. "This is abnormal, Marvin!"

"This," Marvin snapped back at him, "is here to keep people like you safe, Mr. Chance." He held out a rigid, open palm.

"Richard's keycard," Marvin demanded. Then, as an afterthought: "Please."

Jason stared hard at Marvin. He didn't know whether to believe the manager; but he did know he'd been caught, and that he should probably feel grateful if the worst Marvin did to him was to take back the keycard that didn't belong to Jason in the first place. He dug the object from his pocket and passed it to Marvin reluctantly. Marvin eyed the card briefly, then bent down and opened the hatch to the hidden digital card reader, which gave him a rejecting buzz in response to a quick scan.

Damn, Jason thought as Marvin closed the hatch and returned upright to face him. "I had to try," he said with a devilishly innocent smile.

Marvin wasn't amused. He held out Jason's room keycard and monitored carefully as Jason swapped it with the master keycard he had stolen from Richard. Without a word, Marvin then pocketed the master keycard and began descending the stairs to the twelfth floor landing. Jason's investigation of the thirteenth floor had officially reached its end. And yet Jason still had questions, with one particular question bothering him above all others.

"Just so you know," he said loudly in Marvin's direction, "your death trap of a room was calling my name before you showed up. And I don't mean that figuratively."

Marvin paused as he made the turn to the next set of stairs. "That's impossible."

Jason shrugged. "Impossible if what you've told me is the truth." He let the passive aggressive accusation linger for a moment before continuing. "But it did happen."

Marvin didn't look at him. Jason wondered whether it was because the manager was deep in thought, questioning Jason's sanity, or simply trying to keep his continued lies intact by not flashing a revealing tell. Whatever the case, Marvin wouldn't divulge it, and instead silently resumed his descent.

"Have a good evening, Mr. Chance," Marvin called out after he disappeared below the angle of the next set of steps. "And do try to stay out of trouble."

Just like that, Marvin was gone, the sound of the twelfth floor landing door shutting behind him as he exited the stairwell. Jason, on the other hand, was right back where he had started, on the thirteenth floor landing, without access and with barely any additional answers than he had before. Maybe he wasn't cut out for this detective gig after all. Or maybe the mysteries of the Chance Hotel were just too difficult for him to crack. Either way, he supposed it was time to move on.

Chapter Twenty-One
Why Does A Hotel Need A Doctor

Ding.

The elevator doors opened to the twenty-first floor foyer after a brief ascent from the fourteenth floor, where Jason had caught a ride to save his legs from further stairwell torture. Jason stepped out and his eyes immediately honed in on the chessboard, where his ghostly opponent had already played its next move. Jason considered playing a responding move, but he was already down from his experience on the thirteenth floor and didn't feel like setting himself up for additional disappointment. He bypassed the board without playing and sulked back to his room instead.

Once inside, Jason performed a haphazard audit of Operation Cash Stash, confirming that a handful of his bundled bills remained undisturbed in their original hiding spots. He had no reason to believe someone would have entered his room and taken the money in his absence, but at this point he also trusted the staff of the Chance Hotel about as much as a pet bird might trust a house cat not to eat it while the owner is away. Comfortable that no theft had occurred, however, Jason then plopped down on the living area couch and considered his options.

He was certain that, despite Marvin's uncharacteristic directness about the thirteenth floor, there were more mysteries to be uncovered there. Jason was also certain that the hotel staff

154

would keep such close eyes on him going forward that successfully uncovering those mysteries would be near impossible. Then there was the phantom chess player... another mystery waiting to be solved, and possibly one that was still achievable, but far less intriguing if Jason was being completely honest with himself. There was also the baffling hotel accounting policy... on second thought, that wasn't as much a mystery as it was an utterly stupid business decision. Jason could let that one go.

He noticed that the sunlight streaming into his room had taken on a deeper orange hue, signifying the approaching end to the afternoon and nearing transition to evening. Jason had started this day promising that he would call his daughter to let her know he was all right; with nothing else demanding his immediate attention, now was a perfect opportunity. He grabbed his phone, confirmed that he still had no missed calls, and selected his wife's name from his contact list. The other end of the line began to ring. Once, twice- and then it suddenly cut off in the middle of the third. Jason's immediate thought was that his wife had ignored his call and sent him straight to voicemail, but her familiar voicemail message never came. Jason disconnected and selected his wife's name from the contact list again. This time he could hear the open connection, but the ringing never started.

What the hell? Jason thought. He checked the battery indicator in the upper portion of the screen: one percent. Maybe the phone was too weak to establish a proper connection with the nearest cell tower. But why was the battery so low already? Jason had charged it earlier that day, and he had barely used it since then. Then again, he had spent a lot of time in the hotel's elevator and stairwell, places where the phone would struggle to find a signal. Maybe the signal searching drained it, even in its idle state. Whatever the case, the screen went dark a moment later, the battery now completely dead. Still determined to call his daughter, Jason quickly rose to return the phone to its charging cable on the bedroom nightstand.

His journey was interrupted by a rhythmic knocking on his hotel room door. Was Chef Terrance doing another meal drive-by? Nah, Jason told himself, it was too early for that. Besides, Marie had already made it clear that Chef Terrance expected Jason to attend dinner in person tonight. Maybe it was Richard doing a drive-by in the more traditional sense, sort of a *take this, bitch* for stealing his keycard. Jason instinctively looked around his room for somewhere to hide.

The knocking repeated. Hmm, Jason thought, it didn't seem to be a drive-by of any sort. Someone actually wanted his attention. Jason supposed it could still be Richard coming to let him have it, but then again, the knocking had no aggression behind it, and Richard would have more than likely let himself in now that he had his access back. Jason stopped his ridiculous search for a hiding place and answered the door just as a third round of knocks had begun.

"Can I help you?" Jason asked the stooped, elderly man standing outside his door.

"Jason Chance?" The man asked in a thick German accent.

"Depends on who's asking," Jason replied. He immediately regretted the defensive response, for the time-worn gentleman standing before him was in no way threatening and had done nothing to deserve Jason's ire. "Sorry, yes, that's me."

"Good." The man pushed his way past Jason without waiting for an invitation, showing a surprising amount of strength for such a fragile build. "My name is Heinrich Scholz," he said as he sat a large, black leather bag on the kitchenette island. The bag was nearly as wrinkled as Heinrich's face. "I'm the hotel's resident physician."

"Physician?" Jason asked as he reluctantly closed the door to the hallway. "As in, a doctor? Why does a hotel need a doctor?"

Heinrich began removing various medical instruments from his bag and lining them on the island top. "Because accidents happen, Mr. Chance. Of course, there's a fine line between an accident and an act of stupidity." He motioned to the nearest island chair. "Sit."

Jason wasn't sure what to make of the hunched German man, but he was pretty sure he didn't care for the way Heinrich had insinuated that Jason was on the 'act of stupidity' side of that line. That being said, Jason had to give the doctor credit for his assertiveness, even if it carried with it an air of rudeness. He sat in the indicated chair.

"Give me your hand," Heinrich ordered. Jason complied, and seconds later, he felt a sharp sting as Heinrich slapped the offered hand with a tongue depressor. "Give me your injured hand, you bumbling idiot!"

Jason swapped the offered hand with his deeply bruised one. Despite it being consistent with his smart-ass nature, he hadn't actually given Heinrich the wrong hand on purpose. Either Jason really was that much of an idiot, or his subconscious had initiated the insolent gesture autonomously. Jason preferred to think it was the latter, and to that he had to say *bravo*.

"Hmmm," Heinrich vocalized as he examined the damage to Jason's hand. "You did quite the number on this one." He sighed with the type of disappointment only a doctor could have. "It won't require surgery, but you will need to take better care of it for at least a couple of weeks."

Jason watched as Heinrich constructed a makeshift splint out of tongue depressors, gauze, and medical tape. It reminded Jason of movies and television shows where medics in the field would jerry-rig tools out of whatever materials they had on hand to service victims' wounds. "You've been doing this for a while, haven't you?" Jason asked curiously.

Heinrich huffed as he wound medical tape around Jason's wrist. "For a long, long time."

"Long time at the Chance Hotel... or a long time before that?"

"A long time is a long time, no matter where it's spent," Heinrich grunted.

Confucius couldn't have said it better, Jason thought. But it wasn't a straight answer, and Jason wasn't ready to let Heinrich off the hook completely yet. "And in your time at the Chance Hotel, have you handled a lot of injuries?"

Heinrich paused his work and stared at Jason, clearly annoyed by the inquiry.

"I mean," Jason explained innocently, "I just haven't heard of a hotel with a resident physician before. It's hard to imagine the cost of keeping you on call is..." He drifted off, not sure how to finish that sentence without blatantly insulting Heinrich.

"As I said," Heinrich replied with the expression of someone who had completed the sentence on their own, "accidents happen." He pulled tight on the roll of medical tape still attached to Jason's hand, sending a yelp-inducing pain straight to Jason's nerve center.

Jason got the message loud and clear and switched topics. "If you don't mind me asking, how did you know I needed your services?"

"Front desk called."

Jason was hoping for something a little more specific. "Front desk... as in Marvin? Or Leila? Maybe even Richard?" Heinrich paused and stared at Jason again. Jason knew what came next if he pushed the inquiry further. "Never mind," he said. "Front desk. Got it."

Heinrich returned to work on Jason's hand and finished the makeshift splint a moment later. He then removed an emergency ice pack from his bag, cracked it to begin the chemical reaction within, and slapped it down on Jason's bruises with the tender loving care of a sadist. "Keep that on until it's no longer cold," Heinrich ordered. "Keep the splint clean and ice it three times per day for the next week. I'll perform a check-up after that."

"Um, I think there's been a mistake," Jason said as Heinrich began packing his bag. "I won't be here in a week. I may not even be here another day."

Heinrich huffed again. "Think what you want, Mr. Chance."

What the hell was that supposed to mean? Was it a threat of some sort? Jason had been suspecting he was the hotel's prisoner, but he also knew he had the free will to check out at any time. Surely no one could stop him from doing that...

"No, really," Jason emphasized as Heinrich closed his bag and marched toward the door, "I told Marvin that I only needed one night."

"Check-out was this morning," Heinrich said without looking back, "and yet you are still here."

"Well, Marvin put me down for three nights," Jason explained.

Heinrich didn't give him a chance to finish. "Have him put you down for six more and I'll see you in a week." The doctor opened the door and stepped into the hallway before turning to look at Jason. "Unless... you don't want to stay?"

"No, I don't want- I mean, I like the hotel, but I-" Jason rubbed his head in frustration, unable to get the right words out.

Heinrich must have sensed Jason's anguish, for his next words came without the doctor's typical gruff. "Would you like a piece of advice from an old man?"

Defeated, Jason looked curiously at the worn face and sunken eyes before him. "Sure."

"Ask yourself what matters most to you," Heinrich told him. "For some men, it's their families. For others, it's their jobs. Others: fame, fortune, power, respect..." He paused while Jason processed his words, then asked: "Do you know what doesn't matter to most men?"

"What?" Jason asked, genuinely intrigued by Heinrich's forthcoming words of wisdom.

"Banging one's hand against a concrete wall to the point of self-injury, as if one can overcome the laws of physics through sheer will alone!" Heinrich's voice was contemptuous, as if the act of self-mutilation went against everything for which he stood. "If that's what matters to you, then you have a priority problem, and that's something only you can fix." Heinrich turned away and stormed toward the elevator foyer. "I'll see you in a week," he called back before rounding the corner to the elevator bays and disappearing from Jason's sight.

Dumbfounded, Jason stood in the doorway to his room, frozen save for the blinking of his eyes. He wasn't sure if he should be insulted by the doctor's departing words, or thankful that they had been said. Jason looked at his bruised hand and asked himself whether the injury had been worth it. He had nothing to show for his adventures on the thirteenth floor. The only thing he had gained was knowledge that the thirteenth floor was in a deplorable condition, that someone or something was being hidden there, and that the staff of the Chance Hotel was just as dishonest as Jason had already suspected they might be. In sum, he had gained nothing of value... and certainly nothing that mattered to his life.

Jason stepped back into his room and shut the door. His daughter- that's what mattered most to him. Jason's failure to recognize that had led him to this hotel, and his continued failure to recognize it had kept him a prisoner within it. But not for much longer. Jason continued the journey he had started before Heinrich showed up at his door. He plugged in his cell phone using the charging cable he had left on the bedside nightstand and waited for the screen to light up. He then scrolled to his contact list-

And found that it was a jumbled mess of broken characters. Had the internal storage been damaged when the phone's battery ran dead? It didn't matter. Jason knew his wife's phone number by memory, so he closed his contacts and opened the phone dialer. Unfortunately, the dialer had been scrambled as well, and though Jason tried entering his wife's phone number as if the digital number pad were intact, the dialer refused to recognize his touches. Jason tried rebooting the phone, but it was no use. For all intents and purposes, the device was fried.

Jason tossed the phone on the nightstand and sunk his face into his palms. The sight of the Chance Hotel had been such a relief after his long day of driving and near-miss car crash, but his time in the hotel had been fraught with aggravation, frustration, and increasing levels of despair. Heinrich had told Jason to ask himself what mattered most. Jason knew the answer; now he just had to fix it. He grabbed his messenger bag, removed the hotel towel, and began retrieving the money he had hidden away during Operation Cash Stash. When he was finished with that, he would pack his suitcase, perform one last sweep to ensure he left nothing behind, and head downstairs with all belongings in hand. Marvin expected Jason to stay two more nights. Heinrich planned to see him in a week. But Jason was in control of his own destiny. Another night at the Chance Hotel meant another night away from his daughter, and that was no longer acceptable. Jason was going to check out of this hellhole... he just needed to do it before the hotel found a way to shackle him in for good.

Chapter Twenty-Two
What's The Harm

Jason sealed his suitcase's zipper, stood it on its hind wheels, and rolled it to his hotel room door. His messenger bag and the seventy thousand dollars it contained were already slung over his shoulder. Jason took a brief glance around the empty guest suite in the dimming evening light, then opened the door and carried his belongings into the hallway. In retrospect, room 2101 had been the nicest hotel room in which Jason had ever stayed, so nice that a part of him had already become attached to it. The room had become his vacation home in the absence of having a proper home, a place for him to relax, to soak in a warm bath and fall asleep to relaxing music. A place to gorge on junk food in defiance of personal health. A place to be pampered while others cleaned his mess. A place to dream about giant sea creatures violently murdering other hotel guests...

Okay, Jason thought, maybe that last part wasn't very nice, but the rest of it had been great. If only the Chance Hotel at large had been the same, he might not be so eager to leave yet. Jason took a hard glance at his suitcase. It would only take a few minutes to unpack it. A few minutes and then he'd be settled back in, ready to embrace whatever other creature comforts his guest suite had to offer. Jason felt the keycard in his pocket press against his thigh, as if reminding him *hey, I'm still here* in hopes that Jason would take it out and reverse his current course of action. No, Jason told himself. He had made his mind up. It was time to get back to his daughter, so he shut the guest suite door and turned away, forcing himself not to look back.

As he strolled down the twenty-first floor hallway, Jason wondered how his wife would handle him showing back up at their doorstep unexpectedly. She'd probably have a cow, so between now and then, Jason needed to think of a way to smooth over his unwanted reappearance. The first thing he would do was make it clear he didn't return to fight; the second would be to make it clear he didn't return for her either. He was going back to be a proper father- no more, no less, and his wife was going to have to find a way to deal with that. She could kick him out of her life, but she couldn't remove him from their daughter's, no matter how much she might want to.

Jason turned the corner to the twenty-first floor foyer. As if guided by an unseen force, his eyes instantly looked to the chessboard, the pieces upon it unchanged since he last passed it. Jason considered playing one last move before checking out, but what was the point? Why continue playing a game he wouldn't finish? Surely someone else would come along and pick up where he left off. Then again, as far as Jason knew, no one had touched that chessboard since the game began except for him and his ghostly opponent.

"Sorry, pal," Jason said as if the competitive apparition could hear him. "I guess I forfeit."

Jason pressed the elevator call button. It was silly, but he actually felt bad for abandoning the game in mid-play. He told himself he was playing against a ghost of the hotel, but he supposed in reality he was playing against some lonely soul with nothing better to do, or maybe against a little kid who was getting a thrill out of thinking Jason was the friendly specter shuffling pieces around behind the scenes. As Jason continued to stand waiting for the elevator to arrive, the chess board beckoned to him.

Come on, just one more move... what's the harm?

It wasn't an audible voice like the whisper that had said Jason's name on the thirteenth floor. It was just Jason's inner desires, tempting him to prolong his stay at the Chance Hotel in the name of friendly competition, much the way they had tempted him not to depart that wonderful guest suite in the interest of bodily pleasures. Feeling the pressure, Jason told himself to be strong and to not give in.

But really, what's the harm?

Jason took a step toward the chessboard. He had seen his ghostly opponent's move earlier, and in the back of his mind had already considered several responses, though he hadn't exerted the mental effort to isolate which was best. Maybe if he just looked at the physical board for a couple of minutes he could- no, Jason stopped himself again. He couldn't let himself get derailed from his departure. It was what the hotel wanted, but it wasn't what was best for him. Jason turned his back to the chessboard, fighting the temptation to play. Luckily, the elevator arrived to relieve him of his temptation shortly thereafter.

"Why hello, old friend," Jason said to the familiar car that opened to receive him.

He stepped in, unafraid of the trip that lay ahead. Jason silently applauded himself, realizing that his lack of fear wasn't driven by ignorance, as it had been during his first few trips on the elevator, but by confidence. Jason was confident that, despite still not fully understanding the mysteries of the thirteenth floor and their connection to this elevator car, they would do him no harm- at least as long as he left the door to room 1301 shut, anyway.

Jason pressed the button for the ground floor and watched the digital floor readout tick down as the elevator descended. Like clockwork, he was treated to a matinee performance of Breakin' 2: Electric Boogaloo from the moment he passed the fourteenth floor until just before reaching the twelfth floor. It was a short movie, but Jason felt he understood the gist of it. He still wondered about those flickering lights, though. Not the ones in the elevator- he was over them- but the ones on the thirteenth floor. They had flickered just the way the lights on the elevator did, but had also shown off some really impressive voodoo when Jason almost opened the door to room 1301. What the hell was in there, anyway? And why bother whispering Jason's name? Why not just shout to Leila or Olga or Marvin or just about anyone with more knowledge and authority than him to get on the thirteenth floor and open that door?

Jason may not have had all the answers he wanted, but he did have that last one. It was because the staff knew better than to open that door. It's why Marvin intercepted Jason before he could release... whatever was waiting behind it. Oddly enough, despite the red flags and feelings of dread, Jason was still curious what would have happened if- no, Jason told himself for yet a third time, don't even think about it. The only question he needed to be asking himself right now was whether he was going to pick up a fast food burger or chicken tenders for the drive home. He supposed it was really a question of whether he wanted to stain his shirt with mayonnaise or barbecue sauce, and which one would bother him more for the duration of the ride. The elevator dinged and opened its doors for Jason to exit.

Jason patted the car wall on his way out. "I'd tell you I'm going to miss you," he whispered with a smile, "but we both know the truth."

Jason rolled his suitcase into the lobby, which he found full of familiar and unfamiliar faces alike. The unfamiliar faces mostly belonged to other guests, many of whom were filing down the restaurant corridor, presumably because it was time for dinner. The familiar faces were mostly hotel staff, though Jason noted some guests with who he had become acquainted

165

during his brief stay as well. The first familiar face he saw, or rather tried not to see, was Richard's. Jason passed the concierge at the podium outside the elevator bays, avoiding eye contact while hoping to avert an awkward conversation about felony larceny and trespassing. In avoiding Richard, Jason then spotted Marvin, who was helping a family of guests at the check-in counter, but looked as though he would be free to check Jason out after that.

Jason also spotted the trio of teenagers, surprisingly not on their phones, and instead playing some card game Jason didn't recognize, but that seemed to be worthy of some good laughter. Near the teenagers, Jason saw Katie walking with the pair of janitors she seemed to keep on retainer in the event that someone left an errant strand of hair where it didn't belong. Her clipboard serving as her compass, she was leading them toward a branching hallway that Jason assumed led to the guest room wing of the hotel.

Jason's eyes fell on the doorman he hadn't met. The doorman was making conversation with the happy-go-lucky valet that always seemed to be on duty. Jason never did find out who the valet's happy pill dealer was; he made a mental note to ask on his way out. Off to the side of the door, at the edge of the pseudo-great room, Jason saw the elderly gentleman with the hearing problem he had briefly interrogated that morning. Not only did the gentleman make it off the elevator earlier that day, but he had even managed to get back to the lobby this evening. Impressive. The gentleman was still wearing that brown tweed jacket and, as far as Jason could tell, still couldn't hear a damn thing. Leila had a hand on his shoulder and was already on her third repetition of trying to explain to him to follow the rest of the crowd if he wanted something to eat.

Oh, Leila... the hotel had saved its final temptation for last. Technically *temptations*, with an 's,' Jason thought. There was the obvious one: the spark that could potentially ignite between a soon-to-be-single male drifter and an attractive, warm-spirited female professional. Talk about a prime setup for a dirty movie. But there was also the more confrontational one: the desire to approach Leila about her trip to the thirteenth floor, about the vase of flowers she had left outside of room 1301, about which aspects of her personality were real and which were a fabrication in service of the Chance Hotel. As much as Jason might want a starring role in The Concierge Comes At Night, he wanted answers even more.

Marvin finished assisting the family at the check-in counter. Jason noticed, but kept his attention focused on Leila, who had finally gotten her message across to the deaf gentleman and sent him on his way. As if aware of being watched, Leila looked up, and then looked in Jason's direction. She made eye contact, a sorrowful expression on her face- Jason quickly turned his gaze away. The path to Leila was the path back into the clutches of the Chance Hotel and the unsolvable mysteries it held. The path to Marvin was the path to checking out and seeing his daughter again. As hard as it was to reject that fourth and final temptation, for the second time that day, Jason actually made the wiser choice.

Chapter Twenty-Three
Management Does Have Some Discretion

"Hi," Jason said to Marvin as he halted his suitcase next to the check-in counter. Despite the actual note he was leaving on, Jason tried to maintain as friendly of a tone as he could muster. "I'm going to go ahead and check out." He placed his keycard on the counter, his official act of surrender.

Marvin eyed the card, then Jason, curiously. "Is there something wrong with your accommodations? We can move you to a different room if you'd like..."

He's not really trying to play dumb, is he? Jason thought before forcing a smile. "I think we both know why I'm leaving. And we both know it's for the best."

Marvin looked genuinely upset as he picked up Jason's keycard and placed it behind the counter. "I'm sorry to hear it's come to this," he said, keeping his eyes low as if trying to hide his emotions. "Give me a minute to print your invoice."

Invoice? Jason wondered. Wasn't the stay supposed to be charge-free? Maybe Marvin was using the word 'invoice' loosely to refer to Jason's checkout paperwork. He supposed he would find out soon enough. In the meantime, as Marvin typed away at his computer, Jason scanned the lobby to keep his mind occupied. Many of the familiar faces he had just seen were still there, though Katie, the janitors, and the deaf gentleman had all departed for their respective destinations. Notably, Leila had departed too, or, Jason quickly realized, was in the process of departing. She was walking briskly toward an open elevator, and Jason could have sworn he saw tears rolling down her cheeks as the elevator doors closed with her inside. Did that have something to do with him?

"Here you go, Mr. Chance," Marvin said behind him. "Just a quick payment and signature, and you can be on your way."

Jason let go of his thoughts of Leila and turned his attention back to Marvin, uncertain whether he had heard correctly. "I'm sorry?" He looked at the freshly printed paper laying on the counter before him. It was an invoice all right, with a lengthy and descriptive itemization of numerous charges. Jason didn't bother reading the details, and instead honed in on the bottom line, which stated that there was an amount due of twenty-six thousand, five hundred, seventy-four dollars and twenty-three cents. "What the hell is this?"

"It's your final bill," Marvin explained, clearly back for an encore performance of his 'playing dumb' routine. "We take cash or credit, whichever you'd prefer."

"I'm not paying this," Jason told him.

"Then you're not checking out," Marvin replied matter-of-factly.

Jason scanned the itemized items. The bulk of the charge was for his guest suite, which had been billed at twenty-thousand dollars for his single night of stay. An additional twenty-five percent had been tacked on for a late check-out. The rest of charges included his multiple dinners from the previous night, room service that afternoon, housekeeping and concierge fees, valet service, chauffeur service, gasoline surcharges, a cancellation fee for the dinner reservation he hadn't even made for himself, and a line labeled 'miscellaneous' to which four hundred dollars had been attributed.

"What happened to 'no charges for the Chances?'" Jason asked, his blood boiling.

"You didn't abide by your end of the commitment," Marvin answered plainly, "so we're not bound to abide by ours."

"What-" Jason flailed his arms in frustration. "What are you talking about?!"

"You agreed to a three-night reservation," Marvin stated as if laying out objective facts before a judge and jury. "Only one night has passed; ergo, you didn't hold up your end of the agreement."

"I only asked for one night," Jason said angrily, his teeth clenched so tightly they hurt. "You put me down for three!"

"Nonetheless," Marvin retorted, "the reservation says three. You broke your commitment; therefore, we don't have to keep ours."

Jason could feel his body beginning to tremble with rage. "I suppose that's embossed on a wall around here too, huh?"

Marvin smirked. "Management does have some discretion, Mr. Chance."

Jason glanced at the invoice again. "You told me there were no cancellation penalties. It's the only reason I let you keep the three-night reservation in the system in the first place."

Marvin spun the invoice to face him. "I don't see any cancellation penalties on this bill. Just the charges you racked up." He rotated the invoice back to Jason. "Unless you're referring to the fifty-dollar fee for tonight's dinner reservation. In which case, you're free to file a formal charge dispute with Katie. Though... her backlog of cases is quite lengthy right now."

Sure, Jason thought, he would file a formal charge dispute with Katie, right after he filed a lawsuit for fraudulent business practices and a restraining order against every last staff member of this damned hotel. Of course, first he had to get out of the hotel and, as absurd as it sounded, that was proving exceptionally difficult. It wasn't as though Jason could dine-and-dash, so to speak, because the hotel had possession of his car. He couldn't call for a ride either, because he didn't have a working phone, and he assumed no member of the staff would assist him with an alternate means of communication. Jason could simply walk out, make the trek back to the highway and attempt to hitchhike, but that probably wasn't the smartest option, given what he was carrying around his shoulder. Maybe a guest would help him out if he just explained-

"I'll take that payment whenever you're ready," Marvin said, interrupting Jason's thoughts.

Perhaps that's the easiest option, Jason admitted to himself. Pay the bill, get his car, and get as far away as possible. It was a costly option, because there was no guarantee Jason would ever recover that money, lawsuit or not. There was also no guarantee that Marvin would actually let him leave once he paid the bill. The hotel manager hadn't exactly established a precedent for honest business dealings. Besides, Jason wasn't even sure he could pay the bill. According to Mackey and Sons, his wife had cut him off from their joint bank accounts. Jason didn't have any accounts of his own, and he was pretty certain he didn't have enough headroom on his credit card to cover twenty-six thousand dollars and change. There was more than enough money in the messenger bag to cover the bill, but Jason wasn't about to touch that.

"What if I can't pay it?" He asked. "This is a lot of money. Maybe we could work out a payment plan of some kind? How about... five hundred now and the rest spread over a year or two?"

Jason didn't want to give Marvin so much as a penny. But he felt five hundred dollars was a fair price for one night's stay and the services he received. He also had no intention of making good on the remaining balance once he was gone.

Marvin released a heavy sigh and looked at Jason with displeasure. "Now Mr. Chance, let's not pretend we don't know how that would play out." He then eyed the invoice as if contemplating a compromise. "I'll tell you what- I won't make you go through the hassle of dealing with Katie. I'll remove the fifty dollars as long as you pay the rest of the debt you rightfully owe." Marvin's eyes flicked to Jason's messenger bag for the briefest second. "I'm sure there's... some way you could think to pay." He smiled with one of those *I'm a really shitty person* kind of smiles.

Now Jason understood the scam. Richard must have told Marvin about the trip to Mackey and Sons. Though neither of them knew just how much money Jason was carrying, they must have guessed it was at least enough to cover this bogus bill. Jason thought about trying to explain to Marvin how the money wasn't his to spend, but he assumed the manager wouldn't care. Jason needed a way out of this mess. He stared blankly at the invoice as the rusty gears in his head attempted to churn out a solution. So far, the best idea he had was to get the assistance of a good-natured guest. But would Marvin even let him get close to another guest at this point? Could Jason be sure that the other guests weren't in on the scam? Paranoia feeds paranoia, Jason's inner voice told him unhelpfully. Then Jason's eyes spotted something. It was a line of fine print accompanying the signature line at the bottom of the invoice, and it gave Jason an ingenious idea.

"You said I broke my commitment," Jason established as if ready to present his defense to the court. "By checking out early?"

"That's right," Marvin confirmed.

"But I can't break the commitment until I actually check out," Jason then followed. "And according to this," he pointed at the fine print, "I haven't fully completed the check-out process until I sign this document."

"Yes, that's true," Marvin also confirmed.

"So if I don't sign it, and I stay two more nights," Jason asked with caution in his voice, "and then I check out on-time the day after... then I'll have upheld my agreement?"

"Yes."

"And there'll be no charges?"

"That's correct."

"No charges of any kind?" Jason reiterated with emphasis on the *any*.

"You'll receive a zero dollar invoice to sign," Marvin said, putting Jason's concern to rest.

Jason slid the invoice back toward Marvin, who promptly removed it from the countertop and replaced it with Jason's keycard. Jason eyed the keycard with disdain. He didn't want to take it, because taking it meant accepting the prison sentence the Chance Hotel had unlawfully imposed upon him. But two more days in jail was better than the twenty-six thousand dollar alternative. Besides, Jason had won a small victory just now; he simply had to play the game the way the Chance Hotel wanted him to play it. He grabbed the keycard and shoved it into his pocket before turning his conquering eyes toward Marvin.

"You realize this is crazy, right?" Jason asked rhetorically. "At twenty thousand dollars a night you could let me walk away, give the room to someone else, and make bank. But you'd rather have me stay, occupying what I can only assume is the most expensive room in the hotel, eating your food, using your services, and not make a dime for it. Why? What am I missing, Marvin?"

"I don't make the rules, Mr. Chance," Marvin said with sincerity. "I only enforce them."

"I think you're full of shit," Jason accused with an angry whisper.

Jason wasn't sure why, but Marvin couldn't look him in the eyes any longer. "That's your prerogative, Mr. Chance." The manager reached into a drawer below the counter and removed a small envelope. "By the way, someone dropped this off for you about an hour ago. They didn't leave their name and, before you ask, I wasn't here to see who they were and I don't know which member of the staff they gave it to either."

That was a mighty specific way to deter him from inquiring about the source of the envelope, Jason thought. He hesitated before taking the item from Marvin. Who knew he was staying at the Chance Hotel? Better yet, who had even heard of the Chance Hotel? And who would be looking for him even if they knew he was there? Jason analyzed the nondescript envelope, but it contained no clues. He then started to open it, but paused, aware that Marvin was watching closely. Unwilling to appease the manager's curiosity, Jason then pocketed the envelope without checking its contents.

"Two more nights," he said softly. "Then I'm gone."

He didn't give Marvin a chance to reply, and instead walked away while he could still revel in the victorious outcome of this little skirmish. Unfortunately, deep down, Jason knew that, despite his newfound success, the Chance Hotel was still winning the war at large. It hadn't stripped him of what little money he had to his name, but it hadn't granted him his freedom either. In hindsight, Jason kicked himself for not just giving in to one of the many temptations the hotel had presented him with on his way to check out. At least those would have been more interesting, and possibly even more pleasurable, restraints to shackle around his ankles. Oh well, Jason thought as he pressed the call button on the elevator bays, what's done is done. As he waited for his usual elevator car to arrive- at this point he made no presumption that another would ever take its place- Jason felt the envelope crinkle in his pocket. He wanted to know what was in it, but, after all he had been through, was also in a state of heightened alert. He would wait until he got back to his room to open the puzzling object. And then, well, who knew? Maybe the biggest mysteries of the Chance Hotel were still to come.

Chapter Twenty-Four
It's Your Move

Jason opened the door to his guest suite and flicked on the light. It was just as he had left it about twenty minutes earlier, in the same default state that Jason had seen the first time he entered the suite the night before. This time was slightly different, however, for Jason felt a sense of welcoming return, as if the prodigal son was back where he belonged. Jason propped his suitcase near the entrance, shut the door, and opened the flap to his messenger bag. Time for Operation Cash Stash Part Two, Jason told himself.

He reused all the good hiding spots from his original mission- the nook behind the fridge, the high cabinet, the backs of the televisions, and so on. But with Marvin now aware of and, more importantly, set on obtaining the money, Jason opted not to use the lesser refuges and instead to double-up the amount of cash in the best of them. When he finished, Jason tried to adjust the inaptly named 'Fixer Uppers' list on his phone, but found it was just as scrambled as the rest of the device.

Oh well, Jason told himself as he retrieved the wrinkled hotel towel that had served as his secret acquaintance on his many adventures in the Chance Hotel. He would have to hope his memory was more reliable than his electronics. Jason crammed the towel back into his messenger bag to again portray it as being full to the growing number of parties interested in its contents. He then unpacked a handful of necessities and one change of clothes from his suitcase to reinforce the appearance of his reluctant willingness to serve out the remainder of his prison sentence, should anyone come prying into the matter.

When he finished those tasks, Jason plopped down on the living room couch. Once again, he was back where he had started. Only this time, he had something to show for it. Jason pulled the mysterious envelope Marvin had given him from his pocket. It was thin, likely containing no more than a single sheet of paper, which had Jason all the more baffled about its purpose. Now comforted by the privacy of his room, Jason removed the contents of the envelope. As suspected, it was just one sheet of standard white printer paper, tri-folded to fit in its delivery vehicle. Please let it be a pardon, Jason thought hopefully as he unfolded the paper; with credit for time served, he then added to his wish. To Jason's disappointment, it was neither. In fact, it wasn't much of anything, for the paper only contained three words, printed in black ink in the dead center:

It's your move.

Jason stared at the words for nearly a minute, unsure whether he should treat them as ominous or informative. Was this some unspoken challenge by one of the hotel staff? Was it a way to goad him into getting himself into further trouble? Maybe there was a clause in his reservation agreement that the 'no charges' rule could be invalidated if he didn't keep his nose clean. After all, Marvin had already shown a willingness to ignore the supposedly iron-clad hotel motto should the right circumstances present themself. Or just maybe...

"No way," Jason muttered to his empty room.

He dropped the note, grabbed his messenger bag, and darted out the door, jogging down the hallway to the elevator foyer, where the chessboard still sat waiting, its pieces frozen in time as it longed for the return of its missing player.

"It's your move," Jason said under his breath as he slowly

approached the board. He analyzed the position of each of the pieces, considered the responding moves he had already narrowed down, and then shifted one of his knights along its permitted L-shaped path. Jason was pleased with his decision to move the knight. It put him in a defensively powerful position that would be difficult for his ghostly opponent to overcome.

"It's your move now," Jason said with a smile to the opposing army of inanimate pieces. He then sat in one of the foyer recliners and watched through the neighboring window as nighttime settled over the woods outside. As he listened to the buzzing and chirping of small nocturnal creatures waking from their daytime slumber, Jason wondered how long it would take for his opponent to show him- or herself. Surely if the mysterious challenger wanted a true game- and the anonymous taunt suggested they did- they wouldn't keep ducking Jason's presence and instead sit to take him on face-to-face. But, a half hour later, as Jason continued his lonely wait in the elevator foyer and the chessboard remained untouched, he questioned the accuracy of his assumption.

Jason stood and stretched, only then realizing that his foot had fallen asleep, an uncomfortable bed of tingling needles pressing into its sole with each shift in body weight. Jason tried to keep his weight on just the toes of the foot as he hobbled into the adjacent hallway and paced back and forth between the foyer and his room to wake his foot up. It took about four laps, but the tingling eventually subsided. Upon Jason's return to the foyer, however, a new tingle, one that made the hairs on his arms stand on end, instantly shot through him. His opponent had made a move.

Jason's eyes shot to the analogue floor dials above each elevator. They showed no cars were near his floor. Not surprising, Jason thought, for he hadn't heard the familiar ding of an elevator's arrival. Jason then looked down the twenty-first floor hallway, toward the stairwell door that he knew provided access at the distant end. There was no movement, but then again, of course there wasn't. Jason had been pacing in that very hallway. There was no way someone could have snuck past him...

And yet, clearly someone had. Jason didn't know how, but his ghostly opponent had taken advantage of Jason's temporary absence from the foyer to play what Jason now realized was a very strong responding move. Jason analyzed the position of each piece on the board and considered his options. One choice was safe, keeping his own pieces out of harm's way, but doing nothing to advance his long-term attack plan. The other choice was risky, leaving a pawn vulnerable, but with the potential to pay off later. Never one to shy away from risk, Jason chose the latter of the two moves.

"Okay," he said aloud. "Let's see what you've got now." Jason returned to the recliner and resumed his stare into the darkened woods. He didn't care how long it took this time; he was going to wait until his opponent showed to continue their game. Besides, it wasn't like Jason had anything better to do. He was contractually obligated to stay put in this hotel, and staying put was exactly what this little mystery required. Though, in hindsight, Jason had wished he had grabbed some snacks from the vending machine and maybe even Richard's book from his bathroom trash before planting himself so resolutely in his current spot.

Jason stewed over the note that had prompted him to set the abandoned chess game back into motion. Marvin had told Jason that someone left the envelope that contained the note for him, but Jason supposed that could have been the latest in one of Marvin's many lies. No, Jason reminded himself, Marvin seemed just as interested in the contents of the envelope as Jason. That suggested the manager didn't already know what the envelope contained. But he seemed so direct in deterring Jason from inquiring about the envelope's source. Was he protecting one of the staff? Why?

Jason considered whether he had looked at the note closely enough. Maybe it contained a clue he didn't see at first glance. Unfortunately, Jason had dropped the note on the coffee table in his room before racing down to the chessboard. To examine it more closely, he would have to abandon his post. You know what's going to happen if leave for even a moment, Jason told himself. But what difference did it make? His ghostly adversary would make another move, and then Jason would respond, and at that point he could make his stand- or sit- as he awaited his challenger's comeback.

Yup, that's an option, Jason decided. He stood- his foot luckily already awake this time- and headed into the hallway. On a whim, Jason double-backed after only a few steps and peeked his head into the foyer, but it was just as empty as he had left it. Okay, Jason told himself, do this quickly. He broke into a run, dashing toward the door to his room as his good hand fumbled for his keycard. Too much time! Jason scolded himself as he struggled to remove the keycard from his pocket while in motion. Abort, abort!

Jason spun on his heels and raced back to the foyer, huffing and puffing as his eyes swung to the chessboard to catch his opponent in the act. But the opponent wasn't there, and the pieces hadn't moved. Jason took a moment to catch his breath. He then removed the keycard from his pocket and positioned it between his fingers in such a way that he could trigger the lock on his room door as efficiently as possible upon approach. Okay, Jason then said silently, attempt number two. He checked the analogue floor dials above the elevators, confirming the cars were far from his floor, and then darted again.

This time, Jason extended the keycard toward the door lock

while still in motion. He yanked the door's handle as his body weight nearly took it off its hinges. Jason then stumbled across the entryway, grabbed the note and envelope from the coffee table, and raced back to the foyer, slamming his room's door loudly behind him. He might get a guest complaint about that one later...

As expected, though Jason couldn't have made the trip any faster, it was still too much time. His ghostly opponent had arrived, made a move, and disappeared once more.

"Well, shit," Jason said as he eyed the black pawn that had been removed from the board. He was playing at a disadvantage now, both on the board and in real life. Jason had already contemplated what he would do if his opponent took the pawn, so he wasted no time carrying out his next move. Then, before he could return to the foyer recliner, Jason had an epiphany. Well, more of an e*piss*any, Jason thought as he chuckled inwardly, because he had suddenly realized that he needed to pee.

Jason considered trying to hold it, but he knew that wouldn't last long. Oh well, what harm was one more freebie for his ghostly challenger? Jason returned to his room, walking instead of running this time, set his stuff aside, and used the bathroom. He took his time cleaning up, even giving his face a quick cold water scrub to help him stay alert. Jason then grabbed his belongings and returned to the foyer once more, where a new move unsurprisingly awaited him.

Jason analyzed the chessboard. The move his opponent had made in his absence was not one Jason anticipated. In fact, as far as Jason could tell, it appeared to be a mistake, for it left one of the white bishops exposed. Jason considered for a moment that it might be a trap, but he could think of no way that capturing the white bishop would put him at a greater disadvantage than he was already in, so he decided to capitalize on the mistake.

Okay, Jason affirmed, now it was time-

Jason sighed. He had forgotten to grab some snacks. He knew he shouldn't bother going for them. For one, it would give his opponent another opportunity to perform a clandestine strike. For another, it was really going to piss Chef Terrance off, especially considering Jason was already planning to play hooky on his dinner reservation. But then again, what was Chef Terrance going to do? Kick him out?

Jason decided to take his chances. He returned to the hallway and began the trek to the vending machine, hoping deep down that Olga had bothered to restock it after his previous naughtiness with the mechanical foe. Jason made a silent promise that he would behave this time and take his free goodies without complaint if she had. But when he was only a few feet from the vending machine enclave, a familiar noise grabbed Jason's attention.

Ding.

Someone had just arrived back at the elevator foyer. Jason immediately abandoned his quest for snacks and ran down the hallway. No one had emerged from the foyer to head toward a guest room, and no second elevator ding had followed, which meant whomever had arrived on the twenty-first floor was still there, likely kicking off the next phase of their friendly little competition. Jason rounded the corner to the foyer, expecting to find it empty despite evidence to the contrary, and was startled to discover Leila standing there, hovering over the chessboard with a gaze of curiosity. Had he caught her in the act? Was she his ghostly opponent? Jason's eyes fell to the pieces on the board, which were unchanged. Had Leila realized her error on the previous play? Had Jason's responding move caught her by surprise, and now she didn't know how to salvage her attack?

Before Jason could reach a determination, Leila looked up at him, her face solemn and her eyes apologetic. She had a frown across her lips, which then opened to speak to Jason with Leila's forever heartwarming voice. "Can we talk?"

Chapter Twenty-Five
Grandmaster Chance

Jason could feel the sincerity of Leila's request radiating toward him just as the warmth of the sun had done during his excursion earlier that day. Nothing about her or the words she spoke indicated she was his adversary, not in the otherworldly chess game, nor in his stay at the Chance Hotel. And yet, Jason couldn't shake the thought of her betrayal, the image of her getting onto that elevator and riding it to a floor the hotel staff had insisted didn't exist. Was Leila one of those lying staff members? Jason honestly couldn't remember now, but he was leery of letting down his guard.

"I'm not sure we have anything to talk about," he said.

Leila frowned again, a frown that melted right through Jason's stubborn defenses. "Mr. Chance-"

"Um," Jason cut her off, "I'd prefer it if you referred to me as Grandmaster Chance."

He motioned to the chessboard and flashed Leila a half-smile to show he was willing to make peace. It was enough to dissolve her frown, and Leila then gave back a little by eyeing him with playful suspicion before turning her attention to the chess pieces. She made exaggerated leans from one side of the board to the other, her mouth puckered in contemplation, then looked back at Jason with a half-smile of her own.

"A real grandmaster would've known better than to take that bishop," Leila said with confidence. "You'll be lucky to survive another five moves."

Bullshit, Jason thought. He joined Leila at the chessboard and re-analyzed his previous decision. It was rock solid, or so he had thought before Leila challenged that belief. He considered one possible counterattack his opponent could make, then another, then-

"Son of a bitch," Jason muttered as the flaw in his move became clear.

Leila smiled triumphantly. "See? Five moves, tops. Then you're a goner."

She was right, contingent on Jason's opponent not making an equally stupid mistake between now and then. Jason glanced at Leila, his pulse quickened by their physical closeness. "So... you're pretty good at chess, huh?" Maybe Jason should have asked her to call him Smooth Talker Chance- it would have been equally untrue.

Leila shrugged coyly. "I play from time to time."

Jason studied her face, how her smooth skin barely curled as she spoke. For whatever reason, he found it fascinating. "Are you playing a game right now?" He asked, hoping he could get her to confess to being his ghostly opponent.

"I suppose that depends on whether you're asking about chess... or something else."

A moment of curious tension lingered between them. Out-Of-His-League Chance... that's what Jason decided his true title should be. Luckily for him, just before the tension reached the point of being uncomfortable, Leila released a friendly cackle and backed away, dropping loosely into the closest recliner. Jason felt the tightness in his body ease.

"If you're asking whether I'm your secret opponent," Leila then said with a grin, "I am not."

"But you do know that I have a secret opponent?" Jason fished.

185

Leila's grin morphed into a *come on now, Mr. Chance* kind of smirk. Of course she knew he had a secret opponent. The entire staff likely knew, because the chess game was probably just the latest in a series of manufactured events designed to keep Jason in the hotel. It was no different than the broken sprinkler, sentient vending machine, or hidden thirteenth floor. But why? Jason wondered. Why did they care so much about keeping him around?

"So, who is my secret opponent?" Jason asked. It wasn't the highest priority question on the tree, but maybe it could be the first chip into its trunk.

"Don't know," Leila said with a shake of her head.

"Don't know or won't tell me?" Jason pressed.

Leila shrugged nonchalantly. "The outcome's the same either way."

She was right about that, but it still didn't answer Jason's question. He tried a different approach. "Well, if you're not here to play chess or tell me who is, then what are you doing here?"

Leila straightened her posture. "I came to make sure you don't miss your dinner reservation," she said in her most professional tone. She then followed with a much more natural, borderline pathetic, voice: "And I was wondering if you wanted some company. I haven't eaten since breakfast."

"I'm surprised Chef Terrance lets you get away with that."

Leila rolled her eyes. "He's a big softie once you get to know him. You'll see."

"I probably won't be around long enough for that to happen," Jason countered.

Leila didn't acknowledge him. Jason thought he saw something in her face, however- a twitch, perhaps- some subtle reaction to his words, even if she didn't vocalize it. Instead, Leila stood and pressed the elevator call button. The doors to Jason's favorite death trap opened instantly, apparently having never left after dropping Leila off a few minutes earlier. Leila stepped into the awaiting elevator car and shot Jason an irresistible smile.

"Shall we?"

A few minutes later, Marie sat the pair at a private section of the restaurant bar. She told Jason to enjoy his meal, then gave Leila a sly wink that Jason was pretty sure he wasn't supposed to see, for it was one of those *just between us* kind of winks that girlfriends sometimes share. The restaurant was fairly empty, the rush of the dinner crowd long over. But just like the night before, the pianist was still going, and the candles were still flickering, producing an atmosphere of calm and relaxation... and possibly even a bit of romance? Or maybe that was in Jason's head.

"Well, well, well," Chef Terrance's voice boomed into Jason's ears as he approached. "I see you decided to join us this evening. All hail the vending machine hero!"

Jason lowered his head as he felt his face flush with embarrassment. Clearly, Chef Terrance had decided not to exercise discretion regarding Jason's earlier sustenance transgressions. He peeked at Leila, wondering whether she was in the circle of knowledge. Yup, Jason confirmed, she knew. Though, to her credit, she looked away respectfully while trying to stifle a chuckle.

"So," Chef Terrance said, throwing the weight of his body behind his voice like an animal trying to display its dominance, "what would you like this evening?"

As Jason's color returned to normal, he spotted something reflecting nearby candlelight out of the corner of his eye. He looked up to find that Chef Terrance had set a menu in front of him. Jason stared at its glossy cover for longer than he probably should have, but he just didn't know what to make of it. Was it a peace offering or a challenge? Or was it a Trojan Horse whose wrath would be unleashed should Jason dare to open it? Jason looked into Chef Terrance's eyes for some sort of hint, but the man was stoic. Jason then realized that he didn't actually need a hint, because he hadn't come to the restaurant tonight intending to see a menu. The only reason he was in this position of uncertainty was because Chef Terrance had unexpectedly offered the menu. To remove the uncertainty, Jason simply had to remove the instigating force.

"I'll have whatever you bring me," Jason said as he slid the menu toward Chef Terrance.

Chef Terrance smiled. No, really, Jason had to convince himself. Chef Terrance smiled! A genuine, overtly pleased smile, directed at none other than Jason himself. Hallelujah!

Chef Terrance turned his attention to Leila while jabbing a thumb in Jason's direction. "He's a fast learner."

"That he is," Leila said.

That I am, Jason thought stupidly.

Chef Terrance proceeded to ask Leila what she wanted for dinner, but she deferred to having whatever Jason was having. What... no *but it's not what you really want* nonsense? Jason asked inwardly upon noticing Chef Terrance didn't give Leila any flak for her answer. Oh well, Jason was more than happy to let it go if it meant keeping the Butcher of Fish Head Bay and his kitchen of sharp tools pleased.

"So you had a busy day?" Jason asked Leila after Chef Terrance had departed. He was working really hard for that Smooth Talker Chance nickname to make a comeback.

Leila didn't seem to mind his awkwardness. "It wasn't too bad. Why do you ask?"

"Oh-" Jason replied, thinking the reason for the question had been obvious, "you had said that you hadn't eaten since breakfast."

"I just had some personal stuff to take care of this

188

afternoon," Leila responded with what Jason suspected was a hint of discomfort.

Jason thought back on his day and the various times which he had spotted Leila while traversing the hotel. She always seemed to be working, except perhaps- "The flowers," Jason said, recalling the yellow floral arrangement Leila had taken to the thirteenth floor. "The flowers weren't work related, were they?"

Apparently too uncomfortable to speak, Leila looked at him and shook her head.

Jason added this new nugget of information to the part of his brain that had been storing knowledge about the thirteen floor. He immediately made a connection. "Marvin... he said that there had been accidents on the thirteenth floor. Someone you knew-"

Leila closed her eyes tight as she turned her head away, the attempt to hide her tears confirming Jason's hypothesis. All this time, Jason had been thinking Leila was just another liar trying to deter him from discovering some dark secret about the hotel. But in reality, she was a mourner, and her trip to the thirteenth floor had been nothing more than a payment of respect to someone she had cared deeply about, but who had been taken from her prematurely.

"I'm sorry," Jason said. "I shouldn't have- I'll stop asking questions."

He scolded himself for ruining what otherwise could have been an enjoyable evening. Jason supposed he deserved it for being so aggressive in solving hotel mysteries he had no proof were actual mysteries in the first place. In fact, taking a step back to look at things objectively, he concluded that he might have been a bit of a jerk. There were far more mature ways he could have satisfied his curiosities. Case in point: this dinner.

"I'm really sorry," Jason repeated. "I'm going to head back to my room so you can eat in peace."

Jason grabbed his messenger bag from a nearby stool and began to stand, but Leila seized his hand firmly. She was looking at Jason again, her eyes glistening, but with no new tears falling.

"No, stay," Leila told him, her words pleading rather than filled with anger or hurt. "I asked if we could talk, and you're talking. You haven't done anything wrong."

Jason set the messenger bag down and retook his seat. "I wouldn't have asked if I had known-"

"I know," Leila assured him. "And it's okay to ask. It's just hard for me to talk about it. You see, I had a friend- more of a mother figure, really- and I lost her up there." Leila shut her eyes once more, and Jason could see her chest rise and fall with deep, calming breaths. "Hardly a day goes by that I don't think about her."

Jason wasn't sure if he should keep this particular conversation going, but he didn't want Leila to think he wasn't sympathetic to her feelings, either. "What happened to her?" It was a risky question, and Jason told himself he would drop it if Leila didn't want to discuss it.

"I can't-" Leila sighed, and Jason could sense an emotional battle waging beneath her surface. "I can't tell you that." She looked at him and bit her lip. "There are plenty of things about this hotel I can't tell you. But I don't want to lie to you either."

This was the true Leila speaking to Jason now; he was certain of it. She wasn't acting on behalf of the hotel or fulfilling some over-the-top concierge duty; she was being herself... and she was being honest. Leila knew that Jason had figured out something was right about the Chance Hotel, and she was willing to acknowledge it, even if she couldn't give him all the answers he sought. As he had once believed, and now knew to be accurate, Jason had a genuine friend in this crazy place.

"I'll make a deal with you," he said. "You don't lie to me, and I won't press you on anything you tell me you can't talk about."

He held his good hand out to her.

Leila took the hand and shook it, a smile arising as the battle within her subsided. "That sounds like a good deal."

Chef Terrance emerged from the kitchen with a plate in each hand. On each plate was a quarter-pound burger, dressed, on a perfectly toasted bun. A waiter followed behind the chef with a large plate of freshly cut fries and two dipping bowls of ketchup. Chef Terrance sat Jason and Leila's burgers in front of them, then arranged the fries and dipping bowls between them as the waiter retrieved two glasses of iced tea.

"I figured you two could share these," Chef Terrance said, pointing to the fries. "Don't want to fill you up too much." He then focused on Leila's face, specifically on the redness around her eyes.

"It's okay," Leila said, raising a hand to proactively tame Chef Terrance. "Really."

The chef eyed her doubtfully, then turned and wagged a finger at Jason as if to say *hurt her, and your head will be the next on my table.* He then walked away slowly, shooting Jason one last threatening stare before passing through the kitchen door.

"Oh yeah," Jason said, "he's a softie all right."

Leila laughed audibly, instantly easing whatever remaining tension had been hanging in the air between them. She then took a large bite out of her burger, which left a thin trail of mustard on her lower chin. "Oh my God, that's so good!"

"Even better when it's free," Jason replied as he took an equally large bite. "I don't suppose there's a 'no charges for the staff' policy around here?"

Leila shook her head and swallowed. "Not that I'm aware of."

"I also don't suppose you could explain that one to me," Jason said before taking a sip of what turned out to be some really remarkable tea. "The whole 'no charges' thing? It honestly doesn't make a lick of sense."

Leila nodded in agreement as she chewed on a second bite. "Actually," she said once her mouth was empty enough to speak, "that one I could tell you about."

"Oh yeah?"

"Yeah." She tossed a fry playfully into her mouth. "But I'm not gonna."

"Because...?"

Leila smiled at him. "Because like Chef said, you're a fast learner. And it'll be better when you figure it out on your own." She winked as she tossed another fry into her mouth. "Trust me."

Jason wasn't sure what she meant by that, or how figuring out a matter of accounting could be anything remotely exciting or satisfying. But in that moment, he did trust Leila, and he was simply happy to have her there to share in his meal. Jason pondered over that as he bit into his burger once more and felt the heat of ground meat, the cold of condiments, and the buttery goodness of a toasted bun blend together in his mouth. An excellent meal and even better company... right now, they were both exactly what Jason wanted.

Chapter Twenty-Six
Tit For Tat, Mr. Chance

"No, really!" Leila exclaimed as Jason eyed her dubiously. "I was there." She wiped a smear of condiments from her plate using her final piece of burger before plucking it into her mouth. "I'm telling you, Richard didn't leave the table for nearly three hours. He kept thinking his luck would return, but his luck took off with every last cent he brought to the game."

"But it looked just like him!"

Jason and Leila had been at their conversation for nearly thirty minutes. Jason held Leila to her promise not to lie to him, picking her brain about some of the lighter aspects of the Chance Hotel instead of pressing her on the issues he assumed she wouldn't be able to discuss. Leila had confirmed Katie was the pill she appeared to be, that the maintenance crew wasn't always the most responsive group and that Jason was lucky they had answered his emergency call from the stuck elevator car, that yes, the other elevators did work despite never picking Jason up, and that no, there was no giant sea monster currently terrorizing the hotel- though Leila refused to answer whether there ever had been at one point in time. Now Jason was asking about spotting not-Richard mopping the sidewalk in the hotel courtyard shortly after his sea monster dream. He thought for sure Leila would finally clear the air on the issue, but, like the other members of the staff, she insisted he couldn't have seen Richard.

"Maybe it was Benji," Leila suggested.

"That's what everyone keeps telling me," Jason replied, finally accepting defeat on the matter. "At least confirm this for me: does Benji actually exist?"

Leila laughed playfully. "Yes, Benji exists. He works the

overnight shift. The only guests that tend to meet him are the ones that sleepwalk." Leila shot Jason a sly smile. "Or the ones who go walking when they're supposed to be asleep."

Jason caught the knock against his nocturnal hotel activities. "Maybe I wouldn't have gone walking if it wasn't for that stupid book Richard left me." Leila gave him an *oh really* look that made Jason quickly reconsidered that claim. "Well... and falling asleep in the tub, and having that ridiculous dream, and the transformers shorting out, and Rich- Benji waving to me. Okay, so there were a lot of reasons I went roaming last night."

"And here I thought one of them would have been to find me," Leila said, feigning hurt.

Jason was at a loss for words. Was she suggesting... nah, he was probably reading too much into it. Yet here they were, having dinner together as if on some kind of getting-to-know-you date. Jason thought back to the night before, when he first met Leila, and that mischievous smile she had given him. He thought of her soothing voice in his ear, the way she had cared for him by steering him to the restaurant and prepping his room for his arrival. Jason had felt something in those interactions, a connection perhaps, or maybe just a testosterone spike, an evolutionary response to encountering a woman who was equally attractive and intriguing, and not too distant from his own age. Whatever the feeling, Jason wasn't sure whether or how he should act on it.

"I- uh..." He shook his head in disbelief and how out of practice he was. He had been married for years, and despite the many problems between Jason and his soon-to-be-ex-wife, infidelity had never been one of them. "I've got nothing."

Leila grinned fiercely, as if throwing Jason off his game had been her plan all along. She reached for one of the final few fries from their common plate just as he did the same and, for a lingering moment, their fingers brushed against one another.

Jason withdrew his hand slowly, surrendering the target fry to Leila. Leila stared longingly at him, the unexpected touch clearly not a part of her game.

"You can have it," Jason said. "The fry, I mean."

"Thanks," Leila responded, her eyes remaining glued to Jason's for another second or two before breaking away. Leila downed the fry and chased it with the last sip of iced tea in her glass. Jason watched in silence, trying to think of something else to say, but Leila beat him to it. "So," she said with an inflection that indicated she was changing subjects, "I've answered some of your questions. It's your turn to share."

Jason cocked his head curiously. "Was that part of the deal?"

Leila thought for a moment and shrugged. "I guess not... but it's only fair, don't you think?"

"I guess so," Jason agreed hesitantly. "What do you want to know?"

"I don't know," Leila said with a giggle. It was largely an innocent giggle, and yet behind it was that same mischievousness Jason had noted the night before. "Make it something good."

"Well," Jason started, "My first name is Jason. You can start calling me that, by the way. I grew up in a podunk Midwestern town you've probably never heard of."

"Fryersburg," Leila chimed in.

"Right," Jason confirmed, his brain delayed in processing the infinitely low odds that she would know that. "Wait. How did you-"

Leila grinned playfully once more. "I already know the basics, *Mr. Chance*." She said his formal name with emphasis, as if it were against her professional duty to refer to him otherwise. "I want you to tell me something interesting. Something the average person doesn't already know."

The average person has no idea where I'm from, Jason

thought suspiciously. Heck, the average person doesn't know a thing about me, much less *the basics*, whatever those were. Jason tried to get a read on Leila's face, but all he saw was that hybrid innocent-mischievous inquisitiveness. He didn't see a single sign of malice.

Leila must have felt Jason analyzing her. "Don't get weirded out on me now," she said in a deescalating tone. "We do our homework on our guests, especially those who stay free of charge. We already know your full name, where you're from, and your current address. It's not exactly hard information to come by these days." The mischievousness in Leila's smile took a front seat to the innocence. "I want you to tell me something I can't find by typing your name into the search bar of a web browser. Tit for tat, Mr. Chance."

Anything not publicly available about Jason was probably something he didn't want other people to know. Especially not Leila, with whom he felt such an instantaneous and powerful connection. Not that Jason had anything egregious to hide. He just didn't want to be judged for the multitude of embarrassingly poor decisions he had made in life.

"I don't know what to say," Jason replied in a weak attempt to escape the corner into which Leila had put him. He knew that wouldn't be good enough, so he followed with a compromise. "Is there something particular you want to know about me?"

Leila frowned. She was obviously disappointed by his failure to be forthcoming. Her next words also made it clear that she had been ready to pounce if Jason went down this very road. "Sure, let's start with something difficult," she said it as if the words had been cocked and loaded for a while already. "What's with the seventy thousand dollars?"

Jason nearly choked on the sip of tea he was drinking. "Excuse me?!"

"Come on, Mr. Chance," Leila said with an oddly friendly *let's cut the bullshit* tone. She pointed to his messenger bag. "You're not fooling anyone with the towel you've got stuffed in there. Also, it's got to be killing your shoulder lugging that thing around this place. Down twenty-one floors, up to the thirteenth floor, back down to the lobby, up again... it's hurting my shoulder just thinking about it."

Jason stared at her, once again at a loss for words.

"You know," Leila then told him, "the staff actually have a pool going trying to guess how much money you've got stashed around here. Something tells me I'm going to win, though," she said with a wink.

Still shellshocked, Jason's mind raced with questions. Should he be angry? Hurt? Upset at Leila for taking part in the contest? Upset at himself for his naivety? Jason had already surmised that Marvin, Richard, and Giles had figured out his messenger bag contained a boatload of money. But he had no idea the rest of the staff was in on it, nor that they had deduced he was no longer carrying the money on him, nor that he had become the subject of the hotel sportsbook! Jason suddenly felt nauseous as the world began to spin.

"Whoa there," Leila said as she placed a steadying hand on his back. "Stay with me."

Leila's hand was warm and her touch friendly. It helped Jason regain control of his equilibrium, and a few moments later, his queasiness passed. He looked into Leila's eyes, silently conveying the concern her revelation had caused.

"Don't worry," Leila said with that soothing voice of hers, "no one's going to take your money. We're just having some innocent fun at your expense. Besides," she said in a firm, yet still playful, voice, "it's your own fault being so damn secretive about it!" Leila must have noticed Jason's stare turn incredulous, for she backed down immediately. "Okay, maybe we're a little hypocritical in that respect."

At least she could admit it, Jason thought as he continued to process everything Leila had just told him. His body was weak, his head like a bowling ball suspended from his shoulders, his stomach in knots, undoubtedly questioning whether to keep digesting the burger and fries Jason had just sent its way.

"You mentioned seventy thousand," Jason said once he finally mustered enough energy to speak. "How-"

"Don't tell anyone, but I might have cheated a little," Leila confessed quietly. "I thought the guys were being jerks by setting up the pool, so I had Olga go find the money and count it. Don't worry, though, Olga knows how to keep a secret."

Yeah, Jason had already determined that.

"Besides," Leila continued, "she was pretty impressed by your creativity. She almost gave up after finding the first sixty-eight thousand, but she thought that was an odd amount, so she persisted until she found the final two. What was it she said to me?" Leila put on her best European accent as she quoted her colleague. "He's clever, clever, that Mr. Chance."

Yup, Jason thought. Terrible impression aside, that sounded like Olga.

"So," Leila then said in her normal, playful voice, "I'm going to win the pool and take the boys' money; personally, I think they deserve it." She dropped the playfulness and looked at Jason with sincerity. "But since you and I are being so honest with each other, I'd like to know: why does a man show up at a hotel late at night, with no reservation, carrying seventy thousand dollars in cash, which he then brings to a bank, but doesn't deposit, nor is he willing to spend?" Leila let the question linger so Jason could realize just how odd that appeared from her perspective. Then she made her ultimate point. "For all the mysteries you think this hotel holds, honestly, from my point of view, that's the greatest mystery of all."

Chapter Twenty-Seven
Until You Didn't

Jason felt the heat of Leila's watchful eye as he debated how forthright to be with her. On the one hand, there was no point in denying the existence of the seventy thousand dollars. Olga had seen it with her own eyes and reported the amount back to Leila. And even though Leila hadn't shared that information with the rest of the staff, clearly they must have suspected they would find out eventually. After all, how else would they determine the winner of their pool? On the other hand, Jason despised himself for even having the money in the first place. So much so that he wished he could reverse time, if only by a week, to undo the chain of events that had brought it into his possession. Now Leila wanted to know about that chain of events, and if Jason told her the truth, there was a very strong possibility she might start despising him too. On his short list of things he didn't want, that one was second only to the money.

"I don't suppose you'd drop it if I told you it's not my money?" Jason asked, hoping Leila would give him an out.

"Is that true?" She questioned.

"Yes."

"Well then, not a chance!" Leila exclaimed. "That just makes it even more interesting."

Jason sighed and shut his eyes so he could focus on his thoughts. Leila had agreed not to lie to him and, as far as Jason could tell, had lived up to that agreement. It was only fair for Jason to be honest in return. But how could he admit to someone he liked, someone he viewed as a rare friend in a building full of enemies, someone he could see being more than friends, that he was a sorry excuse for a human being? As if reading his thoughts, Leila placed a comforting hand on Jason's arm.

"Hey," she said softly, "you don't have to tell me. I can see it's not something you're ready to share. Just know that if you ever want to get it off your chest, there's no judgement here. Good or bad, I'm happy to listen."

Jason expected himself to take advantage of Leila's offer not to share. But then he realized that the secret of the money had been slowly eating away at him, contributing to both his frustration at Mackey and Sons and his aggravation over not being able to get in touch with his daughter. Jason *wanted* to share the story of the money. He wanted to confess what he had done; only he didn't have anyone to safely confess to... until now.

"It's my daughter's money," Jason blurted out to prevent himself from avoiding the topic any longer. "It's her college savings, to be more accurate. Her grandfather left it to her as her inheritance when he passed away, and decent market returns have grown it substantially since then."

A look of confusion washed over Leila's face. "Well, there's nothing bad about that."

Jason released a deep, stuttered breath, dreading what would leave his mouth next. "There is when you know it was almost two hundred thousand dollars just a week ago... and that I'm the reason it's not anymore."

Well there it was. Jason hadn't given Leila the details, but his secret was out. He had squandered more than half of his daughter's college education fund, a fund that he and his wife couldn't afford to replenish without moving into a house with a significantly lower mortgage and taking a hacksaw to all but the most necessary of expenses. And that didn't even take into account the financial fallout of their splitting up. Even if their paychecks remained the same, now Jason and his forthcoming ex-wife would incur double the living expenses, double the utility bills, and so on as they each proceeded on their own trajectory in life.

"You want to tell me what happened?" Leila asked.

I most certainly do not, Jason thought to himself. But Leila's question wasn't demanding in any way, and Jason was pretty sure that she would let him off the hook without additional inquiry if he told her that. And yet, crazy as it might have felt, admitting what he had done to Leila actually gave Jason a sense of relief, as if the burden of his secret was being lifted from him despite having done nothing to actually atone for his wrongdoings.

"I used to get involved in a lot of shady business deals," Jason told her. "Back when I was younger. I'd say back when I was dumber, but-" He shrugged in acknowledgment that he couldn't support that claim. "Anyway, one time I got in way over my head, went into debt with the kind of people you don't want to be indebted to, and nearly bankrupted my family in the process. My father-in-law bailed us out and made it clear that he'd have me thrown in jail and lawyer up to ensure I never saw my daughter- my wife was pregnant at the time- if I ever got involved in that stuff again."

"Was this the grandfather that left your daughter the money?" Leila asked.

"Sure was," Jason replied. "In his will, he stipulated that the money couldn't be used for any purpose other than education prior to my daughter's eighteenth birthday. At that time, if she decided not to go to college, she could withdraw the money to use as she saw fit." Jason frowned as he remembered the will reading; it had just been him, his wife, and an unemotional lawyer seated at an otherwise empty conference table on the upper floor of some big time law office. "No one ever said it out loud, but the stipulation was aimed at me. My father-in-law's lawyer stared right at me when he read it, and when I didn't acknowledge him, he shared a knowing glance with my wife. She didn't think I saw it, but I did."

"Was there reason..." Lela trailed off, as if she was unsure how to ask what she wanted to know. "I mean, were you still-"

"Involved in those shady business deals?" Jason helped her complete the thought. "At the time, no. My brush with fiscal and family catastrophe sent me walking down a straight and narrow path. Unfortunately, the path was so straight and narrow that there wasn't much room for financial growth. At the same, with a new kid in the house and the expenses that came along with her... I kept thinking that if only I could make one good investment, one rockstar return on a significant amount of money, that my financial worries would be over; I could instead focus on simply being the greatest dad I could be. I fought the urge to do it for so long."

"Until you didn't," Leila stated.

"Until I didn't," Jason confirmed. "A week ago, an old associate called me with an investment opportunity. Minimal risk, high potential for return. But there was a minimum investment threshold, and I didn't have the free cash to meet it."

"So you withdrew your daughter's savings," Leila followed.

"Correct," Jason replied, unable to look Leila in the eye. "I knew it was wrong, but I also knew the money came from a man who hated me, who considered me unworthy of his daughter and his family legacy. I wanted to use the money- his money- to prove that I was capable of turning it into something more... that I could support my family. I did it out of spite, and somehow I let that blind me to the damage I was potentially causing." Jason lowered his head, the weight of his shame pressing down on him like an invisible shoe stepping on the lowly bug that he was. "My wife found out, and that was the straw that broke the backbone of our marriage." Jason sighed heavily. "And so I left."

Leila nodded as she took in the story. "That's how you wound up here."

"Yup," Jason told her. "I stopped by my colleague on the way out of town and demanded my daughter's money back. I figured at worst it was still sitting there stagnant; at best, maybe it earned a few bucks in the short time it had been invested. Boy, I couldn't have been more wrong." Jason bit his lip as he stared blankly at his empty plate. "I didn't believe him when he told me most of the money was gone, but he logged into his brokerage account and showed me the portfolio. My body turned to mush; I thought for sure I was going to have a heart attack right there in his apartment." Jason's voice trembled. "When that feeling passed, I wanted to hurt him. Hell, I wanted to kill him... but deep down, I knew I had no one to blame but myself. I insisted he return whatever money was left- it was about seventy-eight thousand then- but he made excuses about transaction restrictions and falling below the investment threshold and a few other bullshit things to try to keep me vested. I knew he probably had some other sucker's cash on-hand somewhere in his apartment, so then I demanded he give me as much as he physically had in his possession, figuring he could work out the nuances later."

"That's where the seventy thousand dollars came from," Leila deduced.

"You got it," Jason replied with a weak smile. "I wasn't in a good mental condition to return home, nor to face the wrath of my wife when she learned how little of the money was left. So I started driving, intending on depositing the money in my wife's bank account once I stopped and got settled. Only by then she'd cut off my access. Ironic, huh?" Jason chuckled half-heartedly. "Anyway, now I'm stuck sneaking around with a boatload of cash that doesn't belong to me and my wife and kid have no clue I even tried to get the money back."

"You haven't called them?" Leila asked, her tone indicating

surprise.

"Yesterday I was being a stubborn ass, waiting for them to call me," Jason explained. "Today my phone broke. And given how things were going around here... let's just say I didn't think any of you would be willing to put me in touch with the outside world."

Leila frowned. Jason couldn't tell if she was saddened by his feelings, disappointed at his assumption, or a little of both. Their waiter emerged from the kitchen and came to collect their plates. Jason remained quiet, his head once again lowered in shame, not wanting to continue their conversation until he and Leila were alone again. Not five seconds after the plates had been cleared, however, something heavy and metallic slammed down on the counter before Jason. He looked up to see Chef Terrance's meaty hand resting atop an old-fashioned rotary phone.

"Your little girl needs to know her daddy hasn't abandoned her," the chef said sternly.

Jason's eyes darted from the phone to Chef Terrance, to Leila, and back to the phone again. He had all but given up hope of speaking to his daughter while still captive in the Chance Hotel. But now hope was sitting just inches away from him, ready to be embraced. Jason wanted to tell Chef Terrance thank you, but his throat had closed off his ability to speak. Instead, he just nodded in agreement from behind glistening eyes.

"We'll give you some privacy," Leila said with a gentle squeeze to Jason's shoulder.

She and Chef Terrance retreated to the far end of the bar, where they kicked up a quiet conversation. Jason suspected it was about him, but he didn't care. He took several steadying breaths, then picked up the old-fashioned receiver and turned the number dial, listening to the archaic tick-tick-tick-tick of electronic pulses between each digit he entered. Jason then held his breath as the phone made its long distance connection, as the ringing began, and after only four of them, his daughter's sweet and innocent voice answered on the other end.

"Hello?"

Chapter Twenty-Eight
Goodnight, Mr. Chance

"Baby girl?" Jason asked, unsure of whether the voice he heard on the other end of that old phone was real or simply his imagination placating his desires. "It's daddy."

The voice on the other end lit up like a firework on the fourth of July. "Daddy?!" The excitement was real... far too real to be his imagination, Jason decided. "Daddy, daddy, where you been?"

"I had to take a trip, sweetheart," Jason told her. There was no need to get into the specifics with a four-year-old. She wouldn't understand them, anyway. "I'm sorry I didn't say goodbye. You were sleeping when I left."

"I woke up, and you were gone," his daughter stated with a hint of youthful accusation. "Yeah, I went looking for you, but you weren't there. Mommy said you left and you were gonna be gone a long time. I asked her why you left but she wouldn't tell me. Why'd you leave, daddy? Did you go to do work? I think you went to do work, but I think it's time for you to come home again. Are you going to bring me a present when you come home? I like when you bring me presents."

Jason felt a comforting blanket of happiness wrap around him as his daughter rambled on in the same manner he recalled her doing on so many prior occasions. The ramblings were a joyful reminder of home, of the life Jason felt like he had walked away from an eternity ago, even though it had only been one day. Unfortunately, the blanket that enveloped Jason wasn't immune to being pierced by the bleak chill of sadness he felt upon realizing he didn't have any answers to give his little girl. He had assumed his wife would have turned her against him by now, more than likely by mentioning that Jason had left because he had done something bad- a real no no, as his daughter would put it. It wasn't as though Jason believed his wife was vindictive. He just knew how hurt she was and figured she would have, at a minimum, inadvertently badmouthed him in front of his little girl. But now it seemed she hadn't, and that may have actually been worse, for it left Jason holding the bag to explain his actions.

"No," he told his daughter, "it wasn't work. Daddy just had to take a trip, but it'll be over soon and then I'll come see you."

"And then you'll come home?"

"Well…" Jason didn't want to lie to her, but he also didn't want to tell a four-year-old that her daddy and mommy were splitting up over the phone. "I'll definitely see you."

"Yay!" His daughter exclaimed. "You'll come home and you'll bring me presents and then you'll stay forever and ever!"

Jason told himself not to correct her now. Let her be happy; it'll tide her over until he gets back to town to sit her down for a longer conversation. He changed subjects. "Have you been being good for mommy?"

"Um, yeah, but…" The little girl hesitated, then spilled her confession. "I broke my lamp."

"Your bedroom lamp?"

"Yeah, I broke it," Jason's daughter said in a self-scolding tone. "I did a real no no and now it's gone forever. Mommy told me it was okay since she broke hers first."

"Mommy broke her bedroom lamp?" Jason asked.

"Yeah… she told me not to tell anyone. It broke the wall too."

"Mommy broke the wall, or the lamp broke the wall?" Jason asked for clarification, something he was used to doing when trying to get the facts straight from a toddler.

"Yeah," his daughter said in an unclear response. "There were a lot of pieces. Mommy told me to stay away so I wouldn't get hurt. Getting hurt needs a bandage. Daddy puts my bandages on, but he isn't here."

"I'll be there in a couple of days," Jason reminded her.

"Yeah, he's not here right now. I want him to come home, but he went to do work. I hope he brings me a present when he comes home."

Jason wasn't sure why she was suddenly talking so strangely. "Baby, I'm here. Daddy's right here. I'll come home soon. I promise."

"But... I don't know when he's coming back."

"I'm coming in a few days!"

"I hope he brings me a present. I like presents."

"I know you do. I-"

Jason suddenly heard his wife's voice in the background, and based on the words he could make out, apparently she hadn't known their daughter had answered her phone. "Who are you talking to?" The voice was getting louder and clearer, as if his wife was nearing the receiver. "I told you not to answer mommy's phone without permission."

"It's okay mommy," their daughter said, "I was just pretendin'."

Jason heard the scuffle of the phone on the other end changing hands.

"Who is this?" His wife then demanded.

It occurred to Jason that the hotel's phone number obviously wasn't in her caller ID, so he swallowed his pride and responded. "It's me."

"Hello?" His wife asked, her voice suddenly garbled with electrical interference. "I want to know who this is."

"It's me," Jason tried telling her again. "I'm calling from a hotel phone."

"Hello?" His wife asked once more. Jason considered for a moment that she might be playing dumb and purposely not acknowledging him. But her tone sounded genuine. "Whoever this is, don't call this number again."

Now her voice was so garbled that Jason could barely make out the words. The next thing he heard was an empty dial tone, the line having disconnected. Jason debated calling back, but he already knew it was no use. His wife would have immediately blocked the unknown number, and even if she hadn't, she certainly wouldn't answer another call from it. Jason hung up his own receiver as Leila and Chef Terrance returned.

"Well?" The chef asked in a friendly, *are you satisfied* kind of way.

"I don't suppose you have another phone around here?" Jason asked hopefully.

"We have other phones," Chef Terrance told him, "but they all share the same line. Why? Did you get to talk with your daughter?"

"Yes. Thank you."

Despite the short length and abrupt end to the conversation with his little girl, Jason was grateful for what Chef Terrance had done. Maybe Leila was right about him after all. He was gruff and intimidating and definitely the type of person who would put you on his butcher block if you crossed him the wrong way, but deep down there was a certain softness to him, even if he did his best to hide it. As if aware of what Jason was thinking, Chef Terrance gave him a respectful nod and then returned to the kitchen, phone in hand.

"Want to get out of here?" Leila asked, motioning toward the restaurant entrance.

If Jason hadn't been in such an emotional state over his daughter, his libido would have screamed *hell yes*, though there was a good chance it would have been misreading the situation. Instead, a much tamer Jason agreed to follow Leila out of the restaurant. They stopped to share a few parting words with Marie, who kept glancing from Leila to Jason and back as if she believed the force of her gaze would magically push them closer together. Leila and Jason then proceeded to the hotel lobby, which was largely empty by that point, and ambled toward the main elevator bays.

"So," Leila said as they walked, "what are you going to do now?"

"Well," Jason replied, "I'm going to make things right for my daughter. I don't know how yet... but I owe it to her to try. I suppose I- hey, what's going on there?"

Two hotel workers Jason hadn't seen before were carrying a lighting truss through the lobby. The truss was lined with colored spotlights, some of which appeared to be attached to mechanical mounts that Jason guessed allowed them to be remotely repositioned. Something about the setup poked at Jason's brain, but he couldn't finger why. It didn't matter, though, for a moment later the workers were gone, having turned the corner to the courtyard door Jason discovered the night before.

"Is someone having a party?" Jason asked, remembering the entertainment patio he had seen at the far end of the courtyard pathway.

"Tomorrow night," Leila told him. "It's just a small gathering of hotel staff and friends."

"It looked a little more impressive than that," Jason noted.

"Marvin tends to go overkill on these things."

"Right..." Leila's mention of Marvin's name triggered an unpleasant memory for Jason. "Speaking of Marvin-"

"He's not going to take your daughter's money," Leila said quickly. "That's what you want to know, right? Just finish out your reservation and you're free to go. The real question is: what are you going to do once you leave? You were saying something about making things right. Are you going to return home to your wife and daughter?"

"To my daughter, yes," Jason replied with emphasis on his omission. "And then I need to figure out a way to get the rest of her money back."

"Would you like some friendly advice?" Leila asked as she and Jason reached the elevator bays and stopped.

"Sure."

"Get a new job. Hell, get two new jobs. Whatever it takes to stop getting wrapped up in... how did you put it?" Leila attempted her best impression of Jason. "Shady business deals."

Jason smiled weakly. "I really do suck, don't I?"

"Yeah," Leila said straight-faced. She held it for a moment, then let a playful grin crack. "When it comes to chess, anyway. You don't suck at life. You just did something really, *really* stupid." She stressed the second 'really' so much that the word was like a verbal gut punch to Jason. "But you did it with good intentions, and for that, maybe you deserve a second chance to make it right."

"To be honest," Jason said hesitantly, "I think I'm probably on my thirteenth or fourteenth chance already." He closed his eyes and grimaced. "God, I'm such a screw-up."

Leila clasped Jason's hands tightly, the warmth of her skin soaking into his. "You're not a screw-up," she said sternly. "You're an idiot... but that's forgivable." Leila eased her grip, but kept Jason's hands in hers. "You want to feel better about yourself? You need to let go of your regret and do your damnedest to fix your mistakes. And who cares if you're on your thirteenth or fourteenth chance already? We can accommodate."

Jason looked at her quizzically.

"This is the Chance Hotel," Leila explained as if Jason should have seen her response coming. "Remember, there are no charges for the chances here."

Nice one, Jason thought to himself, admiring Leila's play on words. His usual elevator dinged as it arrived to pick him up, but

Jason was so taken by Leila that he couldn't remember either of them pushing the call button. He stared into her eyes, and she received his stare without the nervousness or tension that might cause someone to look away.

"I guess you've got a chess game to get back to," Leila said softly.

"Something else I'm apparently going to need a second chance at," Jason chuckled. "I don't suppose you want to come up and be my coach?"

"That would be cheating," Leila replied with words that Jason was pretty sure carried more than one connotation. "Besides, I need to get back to work. Richard hasn't eaten dinner yet, and I'm guessing he's about ready to kill me by now."

"Fair enough," Jason said, trying to mask his disappointment as he stepped into the awaiting elevator car. "Well, I really appreciated your company this evening. Maybe we could do it again sometime?"

"I thought you weren't going to be around long enough for that," Leila picked playfully.

Jason shrugged. "I've still got one night left on my reservation."

"Yes, you do," Leila agreed, her soft voice and piercing eyes sending Jason's heartbeat into instant overdrive. "Goodnight, Mr. Chance."

And with that, the elevator doors ended their conversation.

Chapter Twenty-Nine
Or Something

Jason's heart was still racing when the elevator dropped him off on the twenty-first floor, and he had barely a care in the world as he played another chess move in response to the one his phantom opponent had played while he was at dinner. Two thoughts then occurred to Jason at that moment. One, the absentee move was pretty solid evidence Leila had been truthful when claiming she wasn't Jason's chess opponent; and two, Jason's responding move brought him one step closer to an inevitable, and almost certainly unfavorable, endgame.

Jason didn't bother waiting around for his mystery competitor to show for the next exchange. Instead, he headed straight for his room, where he tossed his useless decoy messenger bag aside, cleaned up, stripped his clothes, and wasted no time climbing into bed. Jason thought of his daughter, and her need to have her daddy back. He also thought of Leila, and his conflicting desire to see her again the next night and, if possible, for many nights beyond. Jason's conflict soon gave way to deep slumber and a nonsensical amalgamation of random thoughts colliding with coherence and incoherence alike. He saw visions of his daughter running down the thirteenth floor hallway, of her entering an unlabeled room beyond which Richard smiled as he presented Jason with a cake, while behind Richard Leila fed a bite of that same cake to a creature Jason couldn't see clearly, except for its flapping, fleshy tentacles. Jason's daughter called to him from a nearby beach, where Jason could hear ocean waves lapping against the shore as his daughter giggled and skipped in the sun. Jason felt the sand beneath his shoeless feet, yet was still surrounded by the golden glow and rustic decor of the Chance Hotel.

From somewhere in the distance, he heard indistinct shouting. It was one man and one woman, unintelligible with their words but obviously frantic. Jason heard a loud pounding and saw the wall nearest to him buckle as if hit by an unseen force. *Come on, daddy*, his daughter's voice echoed from afar. Jason felt the tide reach his feet, causing them to sink ever so slightly into the sand. More pounding, and more commotion as the panicked voices passed Jason by, their owners as ghostly as Jason's chess opponent. Jason saw his daughter in the distance, where a lone guest room door stood in the sand of the beach. *Bye-bye*, Jason's daughter said without moving her lips. She gave her daddy and wave and opened the door, which led to a sea of infinite blackness. Jason tried to go after her, but his feet were now trapped, the wet sand now sludgy and up to his ankles. More pounding and more buckling as Jason tried to pry himself free, as his daughter stepped into that endless blackness, as Jason screamed for her not to go-

And then he woke. Surrounded by darkness himself, Jason sat up quickly, unsure of where he was. Then reality set back in, and Jason remembered he was safe and sound in his room at the Chance Hotel. Well... he was in his room, anyway; the safe and sound parts were both debatable. Jason leaned his head back against the wall and took several deep breaths to calm his nerves and clear the memories of that nightmarish journey from his mind. Then he heard it- the same pounding from his dream, only much more distant, and between pounds the same indistinct voices yelling excitedly.

The first thought Jason had was that the hotel staff making party preparations in the courtyard were being inconsiderate of their guests' sleeping schedules. He checked the time and saw that it was nearly five o'clock, late enough that the early birds might be awake, but early enough to piss everyone else off. Jason peered out of his bedroom window, but didn't see any party activity in the courtyard below. He didn't see Leila feeding cake to a fleshy sea monster either, so that was a relief.

Boom. Boom. Boom.

The pounding and voices were closer now, so Jason threw on some clothes and turned on a handful of lights around his room. The voices were becoming clearer, and Jason was pretty sure he heard the name 'Marcus' uttered between other unintelligible words. Jason looked around for something he could use to defend himself from Marcus or whoever else was pounding on the walls if necessary. Unfortunately, Jason's room was far from being a proper armory, and unless he planned to beat someone to death with a pillow or toothbrush, Jason was mostly shit-out-of-luck.

Boom. Boom. Boom.

The pounding had reached Jason's door. He heard the frantic male voice call out a questioning greeting, as if unsure whether Jason's room was occupied. Jason then heard the even more frantic female voice emit something along the lines of a plea for help. Jason quietly approached his door so he could better assess the commotion, but he made no move to open it. The last thing Jason wanted to do right now was get involved in someone else's drama. He had finally come to terms with his temporary imprisonment in the Chance Hotel. He had a plan- or at least the start of a plan- for how to rectify his personal life once that imprisonment ended. He didn't need anything derailing that course of action now.

"Please!" The female voice pleaded. "We're looking for our son. If you can help us at all…"

She didn't finish the thought. Jason heard the male voice mumble, and then he heard the footsteps of the panicked couple continue down the hallway as they made their way to the next room and banged once more. Jason told himself to turn off the light and return to bed, that he had no business inserting himself into this couple's troubles. Besides, it wasn't like Jason had seen their son, but therein lied the crux of the matter. The couple had lost their kid, and if there was anything Jason could relate to, it was that.

You never learn, Jason told himself as he unlocked his door. Chef Terrance would be so disappointed. Jason swung the door open and stepped into the hallway, his presence immediately drawing the attention of the couple. Unless they were planning to join their son at a raging pajama party, something was definitely wrong.

"Oh thank God," the woman said as she closed the gap between herself and Jason. "We were starting to think no one was staying on this floor. I'm Judy, Judy Roberts." She motioned to the panicked man who had followed behind her. "This is my husband, Marcus. We're looking for our son."

"He's missing?" Jason asked as if it wasn't already obvious. "I mean... why do you think he's here?"

"We're staying one floor down," Marcus explained. "But no one on our floor has seen him, so we figured we'd try the ones nearby. He's a good kid; he wouldn't have just run off. He probably got hungry and went scouting vending machines or something."

There it was: *or something*. The *or somethings* were the things that always led to unexpected trouble. Burned out, secretly sex deprived co-workers? Maybe they could grab a drink... *or something*. Old college buddies running into each other at the bar? Maybe they could shoot the shit... *or something*. A born-again gambler, a three-time-sober alcoholic, and a fresh-out-of-rehab drug addict meeting up for a bite to eat? Maybe they could check out the casino buffet... *or*- actually, that one sounded like the setup for a really bad joke. Jason tucked it away for later. The point was, he was all too familiar with the *or somethings*, and he didn't like them.

216

"The vending machines around here are a little finicky," Jason told Judy and Marcus without going into detail. "Maybe he went to the restaurant?"

"The restaurant can't possibly be open this early, can it?" Judy asked rhetorically.

Don't do it, Jason told himself. Don't volunteer to get caught up in this family's drama. And yet, he just couldn't help himself. "I'm acquaintances with the chef," Jason blurted out. He knew 'acquaintances' was probably too strong of a word, but it was easier than trying to explain that he and Chef Terrance shared a quasi-friendly, quasi-adversarial, customer-employee, father knows best, son's a piece of shit with redeeming qualities type of relationship. "I could take a trip down there while you keep looking up here."

"Would you please?" Marcus asked. "My boy's name is also Marcus. Marcus Jr."

What the hell have you gotten yourself into? Jason asked himself as he feigned a smile. "Sure."

He shut the door to his room and hurried to the elevator foyer as the pajama squad continued beating other guests' doors down. Based on their response rate, it really did seem Jason was the only active reservation on the twenty-first floor. That, or he was the only one stupid enough to open his door to a pair of frantic strangers at the ass-crack of dawn. He reached the elevators and pressed the call button. As he waited, Jason found himself sneaking a peek at the chessboard. Sure, he was supposed to be focused on finding the couple's missing boy, but he also had his own pending execution to stave off. If Jason was going to sacrifice sleep to join Judy and Marcus on their wild goose chase, the least he could do was contemplate his next move while he ran around. That way, his early morning adventures wouldn't be a total waste of time.

Oddly, though, the chessboard was no different than Jason

had left it before turning in for bed. Had his ghostly opposition opted to get some sleep too? Did ghosts even need sleep? Jason suspected he would still want sleep even if he was dead, but maybe that was him applying notions of the physical body to a post-physical world. But what if- Jason shook his head to clear it of its paranormal thoughts, and refocused on the situation at hand. There was another, much more grounded, and much more likely, possibility at hand: what if Marcus Jr. was Jason's chess opponent? It would make sense given the abrupt stoppage in play. It also created a moral dilemma for Jason, for Marcus Jr. may have snuck away from his parents to make his next move, and doing so might have put the kid in whatever danger he could be in now.

But what danger could that be? Jason asked himself.

As if on cue, his favorite elevator car arrived to pick him up. Jason approached the open doors with more hesitation than he had on his previous few trips combined, then visually inspected the familiar interior of the car from the safety of the foyer. There was no sign of foul play, no indication that Marcus Jr. or anyone else had recently befallen victim to this mechanical death trap, but Jason was unnerved nonetheless. He reminded himself that, aside from a prolonged entrapment that was likely the result of his own doing, this elevator car hadn't actually done anything to hurt Jason, either. He swallowed hard and stepped into the car.

Jason reached for the ground floor button, but stopped himself from pressing it, and instead examined the control panel with which he had become so familiar. If Marcus Jr. really was in trouble, he wouldn't be in the hotel restaurant. In fact, there was only one place in the Chance Hotel where he would likely be, one place where Jason felt truly unsafe, where no guests were allowed for supposedly good reason. Jason eyed the unlabeled button that served as a placeholder for the thirteenth floor. It hadn't worked when Jason pressed it earlier, leading him to think it was just a dummy button that served no purpose other than to maintain symmetry on the control panel. But what if that wasn't really the case? What if the button could be activated, and what if Marcus Jr. had done just that? It didn't look any different from the last time Jason tried it, but looks could be deceiving.

Jason raised a finger toward the button. If this worked, there might be no going back. How much did Jason really want to risk re-entering the thirteenth floor? Was he willing to put his life on the line? Or his daughter's money should something happen to him? Were the secrets of the thirteenth floor really worth it? No, Jason decided adamantly, the secrets weren't worth it... but the life of an innocent boy who Jason might have inadvertently put in harm's way was. With that clear, he pressed the button.

Chapter Thirty
Temperature Anomaly Detected

Jason reminded himself that the informal definition of insanity was doing the same thing over and over again while expecting different results. It was a fitting reminder, for just after Jason pressed the unlabeled thirteenth floor placeholder button, the elevator car did exactly what it had done the previous times he pressed it: absolutely nothing. To rule out the elevator's unresponsiveness being due to a mistake on his part- and to secure his permanent residence in the local looney bin- Jason tapped the button several more times before giving up on it. Well, Jason thought, if Marcus Jr. found a way to get onto the thirteenth floor, this didn't appear to be it.

It was possible the kid had accessed the thirteenth floor the same way Jason had: by stealing a staff member's master keycard. But that would have also entailed Marcus Jr. locating the secret keycard reader on the thirteenth floor stairwell landing, which was unlikely, and a member of the staff being careless with their keycard, which was even more unlikely given the recency of Jason's thievery. Maybe Marcus Jr. really had gotten hungry and gone in search of food. If so, the vending machine on his own floor should have been sufficient to meet his needs. Then again, most vending machines these days accepted credit cards and even NFC payments... not those of the Chance Hotel, though. Maybe Marcus Jr. didn't carry cash and coins on him. Or maybe he was one of those weird new-age kids that prefers flavorless health food over delicious junk. Either way, there was a decent probability he had gone to the hotel restaurant after all.

Jason punched the button for the ground floor, resuming the path he had originally started down, only several wasted minutes later. The elevator doors closed, and the car began its descent. Just past the fourteenth floor, the usual electric light show began. Jason had grown accustomed to ignoring the phenomenon, but right now he was on edge, his nerves a misfiring mess from the lack of good sleep, the pounding wake-up call to start his day, the guilt of potentially playing a part in Marcus Jr.'s disappearance, and the very real possibility that the dangers of the Chance Hotel were more than a figment of his paranoid imagination. The flickering elevator lights seemed brighter than usual, to the point where they made Jason squint. And the popping sounds-

Thwomp!

The noise came from beyond the sealed elevator doors, but it was strong enough to rattle both the elevator car and Jason's nerves. What the hell was that? Jason thought wildly as the elevator descended past the twelfth floor, effectively pulling the plug on his unwanted entertainment. Jason braced himself for another impact from the unfamiliar noise, but just like the flickering light show, its reach didn't seem to extend beyond the thirteenth floor corridor. The rest of his trip was uneventful as always, and soon the elevator doors opened to release Jason to the presumed safety of the first floor.

"Hello?" Jason called out into the darkness.

Receiving no response, he stepped out of the elevator and made his way to the empty hotel lobby, where an odd sense of déjà vu washed over Jason. Yeah, he thought, his inner awareness in a heightened state, the déjà vu had washed over him just like the sea water had washed over that athletic man Jason saw get attacked in the courtyard. Maybe this was how it happened. One minute, he was strolling around the lobby in the middle of the night; the next minute, he was being snagged by a giant sea monster. As terrifying as the thought was, Jason had to remind himself that it worked out all right for the athletic man in the end; wet luggage aside, anyway.

Jason paused and looked around in all directions. There wasn't a staff member or guest in sight, not even Katie and her ever-present clipboard racing through the shadows to scare the shit out of him. Jason was going to have to complete this journey on his own. He found his way to the restaurant hallway, which was exceptionally dark relative to the rest of the lobby, passed the hostess stand where he uttered a fearful hello to the space where Marie typically stood, and entered the restaurant itself, which was downright eerie compared to the same space Jason had eaten in only hours before. There was no candlelight to give the tables and bar a warm and welcoming glow. Instead, it was replaced by the cool reflection of moonlight filtering through the swaying trees of the forest beyond the exterior facing windows. There was no piano music to relax guests as they ate, and instead the piano had been shielded with a large, dull dust cover that gave the performance space an abandoned feel. A distant wind howled beyond the walls of the room, and aside from that, it was deathly silent.

"Okie dokie," Jason whispered to himself in a falsely positive tone. "You checked the restaurant. Job well done. Time to go back to your room."

As he turned away from the arrangement of dining room tables, a loud clattering sounded from the direction of the kitchen. Jason's arm hairs stood on end as he looked at the swinging doors that stood between him and Fish Head Bay. Did he want to know what was on the other side of those doors? Nope. Of that, Jason was one hundred percent certain. But could he look Judy and Marcus Sr. in the eyes and tell them he had given the search for their son his best effort if he didn't at least take a peek? Jason scolded his conscience for chiming in at the worst times.

He tiptoed to the swinging doors and listened for additional noises. There was another light clang, then the sound of something sliding along the ground or across a table. Finally, there was a muted thud... and then silence. Jason continued listening for at least two to three more minutes, but no other noises presented themselves. Maybe the kitchen had a rat problem, Jason lied to himself. Maybe a rat had knocked over some pots and pans, tried to drag a bag of sugar or flour or whatever back to its nest, and then gave up when it scared itself by knocking something heavy over. Yeah, it must have been a rat or a mouse or a guest's escaped pet... or something.

It was no use. Jason's conscience wouldn't let him ignore the fact that the source of the noises could just as well be Marcus Jr. He was going to have to confront the *or something* whether he liked it or not. He steeled himself and pushed through the swinging kitchen doors. On the other side, Jason found the same cold emptiness as he had in the dining area. Only the kitchen was mostly darker, due to the lack of exterior windows, save for a single fluorescent light hanging over a far prep table. Jason followed the light, keeping his eyes peeled for any dangers along the way, and reached it without incident. Whatever the *or something* was, it didn't seem to pose a threat... at least not yet, anyway. Illuminated below the prep table light was a plate with a half-made sandwich and a handful of potato chips. The tools and toppings to complete the sandwich were scattered across the prep table, yet the preparer- and presumably consumer- of the meal was nowhere to be found.

Jason thought about the noises he had heard from the dining area. The clattering and clang had likely come from the items on the prep table; no great mystery there. But what about the sliding and the thud? Nothing on the prep table or in the immediate vicinity seemed a likely candidate for those noises. Jason tried looking around, but his eyes had already adjusted to the nearby prep table light, making peering into the surrounding darkness nearly impossible. For all Jason knew, the *or something* was lurking in that darkness, waiting for the right moment to pounce and make Jason the final ingredient of its otherwise normal meal. On second thought, maybe Jason was the only ingredient in the meal, and the food on the prep table had been nothing more than a lure to get him right where the *or something* wanted him to be... an elaborate mouse trap, so to speak. Jason heard his heart pounding.

Thump. Thump. Thump.

He tried to calm himself. He told himself that his fears of the Chance Hotel were overblown, that there was nothing waiting in that darkness other than whatever his imagination placed there.

Thump. Thump. Thump. Thump.

Wait a minute, Jason thought. That sound wasn't coming from his chest. His heart was beating loudly, but it was a separate beat from the thumping that Jason now pinpointed as coming from somewhere to his left. He ventured into the darkness, following the thumping sounds as his eyes adjusted to the dimmer reach of the prep table light. Soon Jason hit a dead end at one of Chef Terrance's industrial grade walk-in freezers. Outside the freezer door, most certainly not where it belonged, was a heavy-duty trash can- the source of the sliding, Jason deduced. He looked at the thick, insulated freezer door- the source of the thud, most likely when the trash can slipped out of position while propping it open. But why was it propped open? Jason's answer came in the form of a familiar series of sounds.

Thump... Thump... Thump.

"Oh shit," Jason mumbled under his breath.

Someone was in the freezer, someone who had accidentally trapped themselves inside and was banging to get the attention of anyone who might hear and help rescue them. Marcus Jr., who, just as his parents predicted, had been out and about in search of a snack. Jason shoved the garbage can aside and pulled on the freezer door handle. It released its tension in response to Jason's pull, and yet the door didn't open. Instead, a digital readout to the side of the door beeped angrily as it lit up with an explanatory message:

Temperature anomaly detected
Lockdown and deep freeze initiated
Time to preset temp: 11:34

The timer was counting down. Apparently the prolonged presence of Marcus Jr.'s body heat had triggered an emergency fail-safe in the freezer. It would let the boy out in just over eleven minutes, once the freezer achieved its targeted deep freeze state. A sudden realization sent chills through Jason's body: the freezer would open in eleven minutes... once Marcus Jr. also reached a deep freeze state. Jason yanked on the door handle even harder, but it was no use.

"Hang on, Marcus!" He yelled, unsure if his words would pierce the door's thick insulation.

Jason raced around the kitchen, turning on every light he could, hoping to spot something that would help get the freezer door open. Ideally he wanted a crowbar, but after a minute or two the closest he had found to that was a wooden-handled mop. A minute or two- time Marcus Jr. didn't have to spare. Jason began emptying the contents of storage cabinets onto the floor, the clattering of pots and pans so loud he hoped it would wake someone to come assist in the rescue effort. Still empty-handed, and another two minutes later, Jason tried to think of some other way to get the freezer door open other than brute force. He assumed the computer initiating the lockdown could be overridden, but he didn't know how to do that and he didn't have enough time to find someone who did before little Marcus Jr. turned into a popsicle.

"Think!" Jason scolded himself aloud.

Then his eyes landed on something. It was a red fire alarm

mounted against a nearby wall. Jason considered pulling it, but he knew it wouldn't do any good. By the time anyone figured out the source of the alarm, the deep freeze would be complete and all Jason would have accomplished was creating panic while still failing to save the boy. No, the fire alarm wouldn't help... but the fire axe encased in glass next to it might. Jason used the tool attached to the case to shatter the glass and gripped the axe with both hands. He returned to the freezer door and swung, the blade of the axe slicing through its exterior and embedding itself a few inches deep. Jason withdrew the axe and swung again, missing his original impact point by less than an inch, creating a second gash in the door.

Jason checked the digital readout: 4:53 to go, and that was assuming Marcus Jr. could even stay alive until the countdown completed. He swung the axe once more, putting even more force behind it than before, but his progress was simply too slow. Jason knew there was no way he could chop through the door in time. He instead wedged the blade of the axe in the minuscule crevice between the freezer door and its adjacent wall. Jason then used his body weight to put perpendicular pressure on the door, just as he would have done with a proper crowbar. The door didn't budge, and the timer was nearing three minutes.

Use your brain, Jason told himself inwardly, not your brawn. He didn't know how to override the freezer's computer, but he knew from its actions that it was designed with fail-safes in mind. A temperature anomaly inside the freezer was just one risk it had to be ready to address, which it effectively did by locking down the door and cranking up its cooling mechanism. But an equally likely risk was a failure in the cooling mechanism itself, in which case ensuring the ability for someone to transfer the contents of the freezer somewhere else was a better fail-safe than locking the freezer down. Jason just needed to convince the computer that its cooling mechanism could no longer operate properly.

He glued his eyes to the floor, following the perimeter of the freezer until he found what he was looking for snaking out from under its side panel. It was a thick, black electrical cord, and it ran somewhere behind a nearby set of built-in cabinets Jason wouldn't be able to budge. That didn't matter, though, for Jason didn't need to unplug the cord to stop its flow of power. He positioned his feet around the portion of the cord he could see and raised the fire axe high above his head. If all went according to plan, the moment Jason cut the power, a mechanical fail-safe would trigger within the freezer and unlock the door. Alternatively, if all went how things usually went for Jason, the power failure would instantly cripple the computer system, sealing Marcus Jr.'s fate. Unfortunately, there was no time left to come up with a better plan, so Jason swung the axe down as hard as he could.

Chapter Thirty-One
You Weren't Supposed To Interfere

Jason couldn't be sure whether it was the blast of electricity as the axe sliced through the freezer's thick power cable or the force of the blade rebounding off the hard floor beneath, but one or the other knocked him square on his ass. Dazed, Jason watched as a shower of sparks shot out of the live end of the power cable and danced across the floor. He then heard a loud click from the front of the freezer, and the sound reminded Jason that his mission wasn't yet complete. He pushed himself to his feet and ran to the freezer door, saying a silent prayer that cutting the cord had worked before yanking once more on the door's handle.

Jason felt the same tension as he had when previously pulling on the handle... only this time there was follow-through! The latch disengaged and the freezer door swung open, spilling Marcus Jr.'s pale body onto the kitchen floor. Jason wasted no time dragging the boy to the closest oven, which he cranked to its highest setting and opened to allow the heat to escape. Marcus Jr. let out a weak groan and shivered.

Well, at least the kid's alive, Jason thought. He then thought of a new nickname for himself considering these events: Jason Chance, Superhero. Yup, that had a nice ring to it.

"Marcus?!" Judy's voice called out from the dining room.

"We're in here!" Jason yelled in response.

A moment later, Judy and Marcus Sr. pushed their way through the swinging doors that separated the kitchen from the dining room and raced to Jason's side. Judy whispered motherly comforts and cradled her son's head while Marcus Sr. inquired about what happened. By the time Jason finished relaying the story, Marcus Jr. had regained consciousness. The three adults helped him to his feet, and Judy smothered him with a tearful hug. She then looked at Jason and expressed immense gratitude.

All in a day's work, ma'am, Jason thought, but in hindsight thankfully didn't vocalize. He even began to strike a chin up, chest out, hands on his hips pose before stopping himself.

"We're in your debt," Marcus Sr. told Jason with a firm handshake. "I don't know how we can repay you."

Jason considered asking Marcus Sr. for a hundred thirty thousand dollars to make up for his daughter's losses, but that wasn't the superhero way. "Don't worry about it. I'm just glad your boy's okay."

The Roberts family composed themselves, said a few parting words, and then began the return trip to their room, with little Marcus Jr. flanked by a parent on each side, their comforting hands firmly on his shoulders. At first, Jason thought nothing odd of their behavior. After all, the entire family had just gone through a traumatic experience. Who wouldn't want the physical touch of a loved one to make them feel safe in the aftermath? Apparently Marcus Jr., that's who... at least when it came to the physical touch of his dad. As they walked away, Jason spotted Marcus Jr. trying to pry his dad's hand loose from his shoulder and, in response, Marcus Sr. appeared to tighten his grip. Then, as the family passed through the swinging doors to the dining room, Jason heard Marcus Sr. scold his son with greater contempt than one might expect from a truly worried parent.

And then they were gone, leaving Jason to fill in the rest of their exchange with his imagination. Jason thought back to the events of the morning. When he first opened his door to the Roberts, it had been Judy that raced over to get his assistance. When the parents arrived at the kitchen, it had been Judy that rushed to her son's aid. When Marcus Jr. awoke, it had been Judy that hugged him as if she would never let him go. And when the family walked away, it had been Judy's hand that Marcus Jr. allowed to rest peacefully on his shoulder.

What had Marcus Sr. done in all that time? Jason couldn't remember him doing much of anything, and maybe that was the problem. Sure, Marcus Sr. had acted panicked that his boy was gone, and he even showed gratitude for Jason's rescue efforts. But had he done anything to let Marcus Jr. know that he cared? Heck, had he done anything at all other than feign civility for the kindness of a stranger?

"You idiot."

The words were harsh and deliberate. For a moment, Jason thought his subconscious thoughts had found a way to vocalize themselves. Then he realized those thoughts sounded a heck of a lot like Marvin, and when the manager popped up from behind a prep table about twenty feet away, Jason concluded his mental powers had not actually exceeded the limits of human ability.

"Marvin?" Jason asked, bewildered at the manager's presence. "What are you-"

Before Jason could finish the question, Richard popped up at another table just a few feet from Marvin. Then Leila emerged from a small, shadowed space behind a row of built-in cabinets to his right. She was followed shortly thereafter by Katie, who was shaking her head with vigorous disappointment as she scratched lines across the top sheet of her clipboard.

"I told you this was too uncontrolled," Katie said sternly in what appeared to be Marvin's direction. "You left too much to chance."

"Yeah," Richard chimed in, a noticeable sneer to his words. "That Chance."

Richard pointed at Jason, who, despite his superhero actions, was starting to suspect that he had done something wrong. Jason looked to Marvin for confirmation- as if getting called an idiot wasn't confirmation enough- but Marvin turned

230

away, a walkie-talkie visible in his hand.

"Sam?" He called into the walkie-talkie. "Give me an update."

"It's not looking good, boss," a female voice responded. "They just got on the elevator, but I'm not exactly feeling the love over here. If anything, the dad is being even harder on the kid than before."

Marvin lowered the walkie-talkie in obvious frustration.

"Maybe we could fall back to my original plan," Richard offered.

"Absolutely not!" Katie stated adamantly. "We'd have even less control than we did of this. Not to mention a significantly greater chance of someone getting hurt."

"But-"

Marvin cut Richard off. "No, she's right. Besides, it would look too suspicious for more harm to come to the boy so soon after this incident. We need to regroup." He raised the walkie-talkie to his mouth again. "Okay, Sam, abandon your post. Olga, are you on?"

"With eyes on the target," Jason heard the familiar European accent reply. She was far too comfortable referring to an innocent family as 'the target.'

"You stand down too. Everyone meet in the break room in twenty minutes." Marvin turned and glared at Jason. "Giorgio?" He said into his walkie-talkie.

"Right here, boss," an oddly familiar voice replied, though Jason couldn't quite pinpoint where he had heard it before.

"I need you and Reggie to take care of that thing we discussed earlier."

"You got it, boss."

Marvin slipped the walkie-talkie into his coat pocket and addressed Jason directly. "Well, Mr. Chance, once again your insufferable curiosity has landed you in hot water. I just don't understand why you can't stay in your room through the night like everyone else."

"Now wait a minute!" Jason exclaimed. "The Roberts woke me up and dragged me into this... this... whatever the hell this is!" Jason had remained quiet and attuned to the conversations taking place among the hotel staff since their appearance. From what he could gather, they had intentionally endangered Marcus Jr.'s life. For what purpose, Jason didn't know, but it clearly had something to do with Marcus Sr., on who Sam- whoever she was- was secretly spying. Marvin had told Jason he was in hot water... but Jason was pretty sure he was the only person here standing on moral ground. "You owe me an explanation," he told Marvin. "And it had better be a good one. Otherwise, I'm running straight to Judy and Marcus Sr. to let them know that the four of you were willing to watch their son freeze to death."

"You'll do no such thing," Marvin challenged.

Katie scratched her pen against the top sheet of her clipboard nervously. "No, no, no, no. That would be disastrous. The number of variables... the chain reaction... I just can't-" She crumpled the marked-up sheet and threw it aside before planting her face in her palms.

Uh-oh, Jason thought, I just broke Katie. Hope there's not a fine print exception in the 'no charges' policy for that...

Leila gripped Katie's arm and assured her that everything would be okay. Jason recognized his opportunity to get to the bottom of this situation. "Leila?" He asked, turning his attention to the consoling concierge. "Would you care to explain? We agreed there'd be no lies between us, remember?"

All other eyes fell on Leila as her gaze met Jason's. Apparently, the rest of the staff hadn't been privy to their honesty pledge, and they looked uneasy about what secrets Leila might divulge. Leila stared at Jason for nearly a minute, her face etched with concern as she tried to choose her words carefully.

When she finally spoke, her message was direct, but vague.

"You weren't supposed to interfere."

Jason wasn't sure what he had expected her to say, but it definitely wasn't that. He remained quiet as he tried to process what Leila meant.

"That's right," Marvin spoke up next. "You weren't supposed to interfere, Mr. Chance. But that ship has sailed, hasn't it?"

"Interfere?" Jason asked. "But I just saved that kid's life!"

"And you weren't supposed to," Marvin retorted. "That was his father's job."

Suddenly the pieces were falling into place. The hotel staff weren't upset that Marcus Jr. had been saved from their elaborate freezer death trap; they were upset that Jason was the one who had saved him. "You never intended to hurt that boy, did you?"

"Of course not, Mr. Chance," Marvin said. "We were trying to help him."

Once again, Marvin had a funny way of trying to help others. Jason thought about the way Marcus Jr. and Marcus Sr. had interacted as they left the kitchen, the unusual animosity displayed between a father and the son he had almost lost. "It was a setup," Jason deduced as he considered the chain of events that had unfolded since the Roberts first showed up at his door. "You set a trap for Marcus Jr., something that would endanger his life, so that his dad would have to rescue him." It was a batshit crazy accusation- at least outside of the Chance Hotel. Here, it seemed perfectly reasonable. "But what then?" Jason asked. "They just live happily ever after?"

"That's the idea," Richard commented.

"When a bond between a father and son is deeply fractured," Marvin explained, "sometimes it takes a father seeing just how much his son needs him to begin the healing process." The manager softened his tone, as if his own hostility toward Jason was healing as well. "Sometimes, it takes an extreme circumstance to open that father's eyes. Sometimes it requires a deadly circumstance." Marvin turned his attention to his head of quality control. "Katie, would you please elaborate?"

Katie closed her eyes and gritted her teeth in an expression that meant one of two things: either she felt it was too much of a bother to provide Jason with additional details, or she didn't agree with Marvin's decision to do so. Regardless, she did as asked. "At 8:03pm last night, the Roberts family got into an argument over dinner in the hotel restaurant. Marcus Jr. had been indecisive about what he wanted, so Marcus Sr. refused the meal Chef Terrance had sent to the table and made Marcus Jr. sit in silence while his parent ate. At 8:47pm, the Roberts returned to their room, with Marcus Jr. complaining that he was still hungry."

Katie referenced a sheet of notes on her clipboard. "Based on Marcus Jr.'s personality profile and caloric intake for the day, we calculated an eighty-three percent probability that he would sneak out of his room to find food during the night. We disabled the vending machines on all floors to incentivize Marcus Jr. to head to the restaurant, and strategically placed sandwich ingredients in and around the freezer that was rigged to trap him, resulting in a ninety-eight percent probability of capture. After giving Marcus Jr. a ten-minute head start, we slammed a door in the room next to the Roberts, resulting in a sixty-seven percent probability that they would awaken and notice their son was missing. We were prepared to slam additional doors if necessary, essentially ensuring that we would eventually get their attention."

As Katie spouted out figure after figure, Jason looked to Leila with a *is this for real?* kind of expression, to which Leila responded with a confirmatory shrug.

"We rigged the freezer to begin the deep freeze process as

soon as the door handle was pulled," Katie continued. "There was a ninety-eight percent probability that Marcus Jr. would have been perfectly fine in the freezer until then. Once awakened, there was also a ninety-eight percent probability that Judy and Marcus Sr. would be the ones to pull the handle."

"Which makes you Mr. Two Percent," Richard snarked at Jason.

"If Judy and Marcus Sr. initiated the deep freeze," Katie said, ignoring Richard's comment, "there was an eighty-three percent probability that they would spot the fire axe, and a ninety-nine percent probability that Marcus Sr., being the stronger of the two, would wield the axe and save their son. Based on Marcus Sr.'s personality profile, there was a seventy-six percent probability that saving his son from certain death would trigger a lasting emotional reaction that would ultimately repair their relationship." Katie consulted her notes with a worrisome frown. "Also based on Marcus Sr.'s personality profile, there was a ninety-seven percent probability that the relationship between him and his son would fracture further should anyone else step in to fulfill the 'rescuing father' role instead."

No one spoke for several moments, letting Katie's final statistic hang over all of them. Jason knew deep down that he wasn't to blame for the current predicament. He didn't ask to get drawn into this crazy plan of probabilities and child endangerment. He had no idea about the poor relationship between Marcus Sr. and Marcus Jr. and, as far as he was concerned, he had done the right thing by saving Marcus Jr. from what appeared to be- an in reality was- a life-threatening situation. And yet Jason felt as though he had committed a real no no, as his daughter would say. He felt oddly responsible for denying Marcus Jr. a better relationship with his father, a relationship that, if Katie's insane probabilities were to be believed, had a high likelihood of being turned around... that is, if Jason hadn't interfered. Jason looked at Marvin with unnecessarily guilty eyes.

"So, what do we do now?"

Chapter Thirty-Two
There Is No We

"We?" Marvin asked skeptically. "There is no 'we,' Mr. Chance. You aren't a member of this staff. You are a guest, and I think it's in your best interest to promptly return to your room."

Jason should've known to expect such a response from Marvin. The manager had tried to steer Jason clear of hotel business at every turn, and this was no different. Jason looked to Leila in protest, hoping she might join the debate as his ally, but she lowered her gaze, sending Jason a clear message that she was Marvin's inferior and bound by his decisions.

"How do you expect me to return to my room as if none of this ever happened?"

"With your feet," Marvin said without a hint of sarcasm.

Jason opened his mouth, intending to make a snappy comeback, but Chef Terrance's booming voice preempted him: "What... the... hell?"

The chef was standing in the doorway between the kitchen and dining room. He had his chef coat tossed casually over his shoulder and a rollable knife case tucked under his arm. Jason noticed that the other members of the staff, Marvin included, seemed to shrink a few inches, as if they were misbehaving kids caught in the act by their strict parent.

"Now, Chef-" Marvin started.

"What have I told you about holding these little interventions of yours in my kitchen?" Chef Terrance asked rhetorically as he walked past the cookware Jason had tossed haphazardly around the floor when searching for a way to rescue Marcus Jr. "As if I have time to clean this up before the breakfast rush!"

"We'll have one of the maids come clean it up," Marvin assured him. "We didn't have a choice. We needed food and a containment space on short notice."

"Containment space?" Chef Terrance asked. He paused as he reached the freezer door and examined the gashes the fire axe had left in its surface. "You turned my meat locker into a containment space?" Chef Terrance touched one of the gashes, then looked at Jason, who wondered where the heat of that stare had been when Marcus Jr. needed thawing out. "I'm guessing you did this?"

Jason gulped, but remained silent, because really, what was the point of answering? If Jason lied and said no, Chef Terrance would be pissed at him for withholding the truth. If he was truthful and said yes, Chef Terrance would be pissed at him for ruining the freezer. One way or another, Jason was getting piss in his mouth, so he kept it shut.

"Since when do you involve other guests in these things, anyway?" Chef Terrance asked, redirecting his inquiry to Marvin.

"Mr. Chance involved himself," Marvin replied.

"Big shock there."

Jason was getting the sense he had lost some brownie points with Chef Terrance. The hulking man examined the door gashes further, then gave the blank digital readout to the side of the door a few flicks with his finger to confirm it was as dead as it appeared to be.

"We'll have you back up and running in no time, Chef," Marvin said with false confidence. "It looks worse than it is." As Marvin continued to speak, Chef Terrance walked the perimeter of the freezer, his eyes glued to the floor as Jason's had been only twenty minutes earlier. "We tried to think of another way-"

"Some of us did think of another way," Richard muttered.

"We just couldn't take the risk..." Marvin trailed off as Chef Terrance found the severed power cable and held it up for everyone's view.

Chef Terrance glared again at Jason. He didn't ask this time if Jason had been responsible for the additional damage to his freezer; it was pretty obvious by this point. Instead, he grunted unhappily before tossing the severed cord back to the floor and setting his coat and knife case on a nearby table.

"Get out," Chef Terrance said without looking at anyone in particular. "All of you."

The subordinate staff members glanced at Marvin, who made a *wrap it up* motion with his index finger and started a procession to the swinging doors.

Not wanting to exit on an unpleasant note, Jason approached Chef Terrance to explain himself. "Chef, I just wanted to say-" Chef Terrance pulled a shiny twelve-inch knife from his case as his eyes fell upon Jason. "You know what? Never mind."

Chef Terrance grunted again, and Jason made his way to the dining room without looking back. By the time he got there, Marvin and the other staff members were already gone, the sons of bitches having ditched Jason for their secret break room, wherever that was. Jason could only hope that he would one day overcome the emotional scarring of their exclusion. On a more serious note, he considered for a moment whether he should seek the break room out, but if there was one thing Marvin had made clear, it was that his curiosity was severely under-appreciated at the Chance Hotel. So Jason decided to do exactly what he had been told to do: he was going to return to his room.

He followed his steps back to the main elevator bays and pushed the call button. A few moments later, his usual elevator car opened for him, only this time it wasn't empty. Two staff members in what appeared to be maintenance outfits stood within it with large, greasy tool bags in tow.

"Pardon us, Mr. Chance," one of the maintenance staff said.

Jason recognized the man's voice for the second time that

morning. It was the voice of someone Marvin had referred to as Giorgio when barking orders over his walkie-talkie. "Marvin's got y'all working pretty early today, huh?" Jason asked as the men exited the elevator and stepped past him.

"Maintenance work waits for no one, Mr. Chance," Giorgio answered.

"Yep," the other one- Reggie, Jason assumed based on his recollection of the walkie-talkie conversation- said. "Those fixer-uppers aren't going to take care of themselves."

Giorgio and Reggie shared a hearty laugh that Jason thought might be at his expense since nothing either man had said was particularly funny. Nonetheless, the men were cordial as they excused themselves and continued to the hotel lobby. Jason thought about following them, for they might head to Marvin's break room powwow, but he told himself that his curiosity would only get him in further trouble. Jason stepped onto the elevator and pressed the button for his floor.

When the lights began to flicker just past the twelfth floor, Jason remembered the unexpected impact the elevator had taken on his trip down, so he quickly braced himself. The thought then occurred to him that bracing was great for preventing an immediate injury should the impact land again, but it wouldn't do anything to prevent the elevator from stalling out should the impact be strong enough to dislodge it from its rigging. Why hadn't he just taken the stairs?

Luckily for Jason, there was no impact on the trip back up. The light show and popping sounds- which for some reason were still more intense than before- faded away upon reaching floor fourteen, and Jason breathed a sigh of relief that he wouldn't get trapped in the elevator again. Then it hit him.

"Giorgio!" Jason exclaimed to the empty elevator car. "That's where..."

He looked at the seams of the hidden emergency panel on

the elevator wall. Behind it was the phone that had served as Jason's lifeline upon getting stuck. On the other end of that phone had been a gruff, aggravated, yet in the end helpful voice... Giorgio, Jason now realized. If he had put it together sooner, he would've thanked the maintenance man for getting him loose. Maybe next time.

The elevator dinged and released Jason to the twenty-first floor hallway, where he immediately noticed that something was different. Jason's ghostly opponent had played another chess move in his absence, bringing Jason one step closer to defeat. Jason took joy in playing a quick responding move, however, for despite the disappointing trajectory this game was on, his opponent's move provided Jason with additional information he could add to the mental evidence locker he had created for the chess mystery.

Marcus Jr. was in no condition to sneak away from his parents again following the freezer incident, which meant Jason could reasonably scratch him off of his opponent suspect list. Leila was already in the clear, and Marvin, Richard, and Katie had all been with her in the kitchen both during and after the incident- or intervention, as Chef Terrance called it. They had left the area ahead of Jason, so he couldn't scratch their names off the suspect list completely, but he could definitely lower their positions in terms of probable perps.

Speaking of Chef Terrance, he hadn't been involved in the intervention, only showing up once it was over. He had also visited Jason's floor before to bring him lunch following his vending machine raid. Maybe he was a friendly adversary to Jason in more ways than one... Of course, now there were some new entries to the suspect list as well: Giorgio and Reggie, two members of the staff that Jason hadn't even been aware of, but who had the time to play in his absence and, as maintenance workers, surely had the access to move clandestinely around the hotel. By that logic, Sam needed to be a suspect too, for she was so clandestine Jason wasn't even sure who she was. And finally there was Olga. Jason hadn't really pinned her as the chess-playing type, but then again, he hadn't pinned her for the innocent family targeting type either... so, add her to the list.

Jason was proud of his methodical thinking. Maybe this detective thing could work out after all. Also, the chess opponent mystery was one he could solve without leaving his own floor, so it earned bonus points for keeping him out of other trouble. The question now was, among the higher probability suspects, who was at the top of the list? Jason's initial instinct was that it should be Chef Terrance, and yet, he also felt sneaking around wasn't really the chef's way of doing things. He was definitely much more of a bang-on-your-door, get-in-your-face, and make-you-feel-puny kind of adversary. No, it was looking increasingly more likely that Giorgio and/or Reggie might be the ghostly opponent. After all, they had even come off of Jason's elevator following his absence during the intervention. Maybe joking about fixer-uppers was just their way of-

Jason felt the blood drain from his face. Giorgio and Reggie had laughed about those fixer-uppers as though they had been done at Jason's expense. Now, as Jason thought about the falsely named list he had created on his phone, the same phone that had strangely begun malfunctioning during his stay at the Chance Hotel, Jason feared that expense tallied about seventy thousand dollars. He raced to his room as fast as he could, flung the door open, and ran to the closest depot from Operation Cash Stash. It was empty.

Jason checked the next closest hiding spot, then five others, all with the same result. Giorgio and Reggie had cleaned him out. Jason's head felt heavy as the room began to spin. He stumbled, catching himself on one of the kitchen island chairs, and fought to keep the contents of his stomach down. Why?

Jason asked himself. Why would two complete strangers steal his daughter's money? Jason didn't need to think very hard before the answer came to him, the words Marvin spoke into his walkie-talkie following the intervention repeating over and over in Jason's head. Giorgio and Reggie might have done the deed, but they had done so under orders from the man who apparently pulled all the strings in this hotel, the seemingly innocent manager who kept insisting he was trying to help, yet whose help constantly carried an air of moral ambiguity.

Jason's nausea lifted, and in its place rose intense anger. Marvin had tricked Jason into staying at this hotel by preventing Jason's early departure through passive aggressive actions and threats. He had intercepted Jason's curiosities whenever they got too close to unraveling the truth. And, despite Leila's claims, he was obviously willing to use Jason's daughter's money as a bargaining chip, or for blackmail, *or something*. But, as the ringleader of this insane circus, the one thing Marvin couldn't do was hide, at least not for very long... and now Jason was coming for him.

Chapter Thirty-Three
Incidentals, Mr. Chance

Jason barged off the elevator at ground level like a bull seeking a matador's flowing cape. The hotel was still in darkness, and the hotel staff was still in hiding. Jason marched to the check-in counter, behind which he spotted a brown wooden door. He had paid no attention to the door on his other trips to the counter, but now it became his sole focus, as he assumed the unseen break room was somewhere beyond it. Jason didn't care if Marvin or any of the other staff heard him coming- after all, he had no intention of being discrete- so he told himself to screw being stealthy and plowed through the door as if it were his own.

On the other side of the door was a fairly plain hallway, decorated in the same style as the rest of the hotel, but without the finishing touches reserved for guest-facing corridors. To Jason's immediate left was another door with a placard that read 'office' on it. The door was slightly ajar, giving Jason a mostly obstructed view of a desk, chair, and filing cabinet in a small room that was illuminated only by the cool glow of a computer monitor. A small part of Jason was tempted to root around the office while he had the opportunity to do so, but the larger part of him was a man on a very particular mission, so he proceeded down the hall.

Soon Jason heard voices. The first was male, most likely Marvin. The second was female, and it was followed by a different male voice than the first. Jason couldn't understand what the voices were saying yet, but they were getting louder as he approached another slightly ajar door coming up on the right. As Jason neared, he could make out Marvin saying something about only having twenty-four hours. His voice was distressed, as if the mysteriously looming deadline carried Earth-shattering consequences. Jason heard one of the females trying to console him. He guessed it was Sam, but couldn't be certain given the brief sampling of her voice to which he had been previously exposed. Olga was the next to speak- her voice was unmistakable- and she proposed something along the lines of extending the twenty-four-hour deadline. Jason couldn't be certain given her accent, but he thought the proposal involved breaking kneecaps or drinking nightcaps... he hoped it was the latter.

Jason arrived at the door. He could have stood there listening further, but he cared more about retrieving his daughter's money than any wack-a-doo schemes the hotel staff might be cooking up. He pushed the door open and stood in the entryway, bringing the conversation within to an immediate halt. Marvin, Leila, Richard, Katie, and the staff member who had brought Leila a balloon that morning- Sam, Jason now pieced together- were spaced around the break room table like military officials mapping out their battle plan. Olga and Heinrich were seated off to the side. Giorgio and Reggie were huddled in the far corner, and Jason was pretty sure he caught them snickering before they turned their faces away. All other eyes were now upon him, all with a look of puzzlement at his arrival... all except Marvin, that is.

Marvin stared at Jason as if he knew exactly why his curious guest had interrupted their break room staff meeting... and it wasn't to request room service. "Mr. Chance, this area is reserved for hotel staff only. I must kindly ask you to remove yourself."

That was all it took to set Jason off. He unleashed his inner defensive lineman and charged at Marvin, knocking the manager off his feet and slamming him down on the tabletop. "Where is it?" Jason demanded. "I know you took it, and I want it back this instant!"

For good measure, Jason briefly lifted Marvin's weight before slamming the manager back against the table once more. Surprisingly, the other staff members made no effort to interfere, not even Olga, who Jason was sure could incapacitate him in the blink of an eye.

"If you'd like to discuss this civilly," Marvin choked, "then let's go to my office. But if brute force is your preferred method of communication, then by all means, continue."

Don't tempt me, Jason thought, his muscles tense and his anger fully flared. He lifted Marvin's weight again, but then stopped, the manager's unwillingness to fight back making this a less-than-satisfactory conquest. Jason glanced around at the other staff. They still hadn't interfered, and instead were watching with intense curiosity themselves, as if they had as much of a stake in Jason's next actions as Jason did. Jason had played out this scenario in his head at least five times on the journey down from his room, and it had always ended with him being the hero who beat Marvin to a bloody pulp in retribution for stealing his daughter's money. And yet, the longer Jason stood there under the watchful eyes of the hotel staff, the more he inexplicably felt like the villain of this story. Jason didn't want to be the villain, so he released Marvin and stepped back from the table to signal an end to his physical aggression.

Sam reached out to give Marvin a hand, but he waved her off and pushed himself up. He then straightened his shirt and coat before motioning Jason toward the hallway. "Shall we?"

Jason followed Marvin to the office he had passed earlier. The manager invited him in and cordially offered him a seat as if they were about to sit down for a job interview. Jason wondered whether Marvin had planned these actions in advance, anticipating Jason's rage and specifically crafting a response that would subvert it. If so, it was working.

"What do you say we cut right to the chase, Mr. Chance?"

Marvin suggested.

Sure thing, asshole. "Where's my daughter's money?"

"It's in the hotel vault," Marvin answered. "All seventy thousand. Giorgio and Reggie have... let's just call it sticky fingers, so I had Katie verify the amount before we locked it up."

Oh, well that's a relief, Jason thought sarcastically. "I want it back. Now."

"I'm afraid I can't do that."

"Why not?"

"Incidentals, Mr. Chance, that's why." Marvin opened a desk drawer and removed a single sheet of typed paper from inside. "When you checked in, you asked me why you didn't need to put a credit card on file. I told you there were no charges, and that's still true, but there have to be some limits to our generosity."

"You never said anything about limits," Jason countered.

"I didn't think I needed to," Marvin replied firmly. "I gave you the benefit of the doubt that you would have a little decency, treat this property and the people who work here with respect. But you've proved me wrong time and time again, and in the process, you've racked up quite a debt in incidental costs."

"Bullshit," Jason told him. "You're just trying to swindle me out of my daughter's money... again." He emphasized the *again* to make sure Marvin remembered the last time he tried to saddle Jason with unexpected charges.

Marvin lifted the typed sheet of paper and cleared his throat before reading. "One broken elevator following user abuse: ten thousand dollars. One vandalized vending machine: fifteen hundred dollars."

"I thought you said teenagers did that," Jason interjected.

Marvin gave him a look that screamed *oh please* before continuing. "Recoding of all master keycards following unauthorized use: seven hundred dollars. Detailed inspection of the thirteenth floor following a trespassing incident: three hundred and fifty dollars."

"Again, you never told me not to enter it."

Marvin ignored him. "And then there's the matter of the spoiled intervention. Do you have any idea the amount of time and effort that goes into something like that?"

"I'm guessing not seventy-thousand dollars' worth."

"Not by itself," Marvin admitted, "but factor in the repair costs for Chef Terrance's freezer and the fact that now we have to plan a second intervention on short notice, and you're getting pretty close."

Jason could feel his blood boiling again. "So you're just going to steal my daughter's money then? Is that what you're telling me?"

"Not at all," Marvin replied, momentarily cooling Jason's fire. "I'm willing to let all of those charges go. After all, you were under the impression that you had carte blanche around here, so I suppose it's only fair."

Careful, Marvin, Jason thought with contempt. That generosity is supposed to have limits.

"I asked Katie to run the numbers and her calculations predict that, left unchecked, there's a ninety-three percent probability you will continue to treat this hotel like your own personal funhouse." Marvin put the sheet of Jason's offenses back in his drawer. "And since we don't know how much more damage that will lead to by the time you check out, we're holding your daughter's money as collateral." Marvin folded his hands matter-of-factly. "From what I've gathered, you care about her more than anything else in this world. Perhaps the threat of losing the rest of her education savings is enough motivation to keep you on a leash until tomorrow."

Jason's emotions were pulling him in a hundred different directions. He still felt intense anger, so much so that the testosterone-driven part of his brain was trying to convince him to resume playing things out as he had originally imagined. But Jason's gut told him to stand down, reminding him that Leila vouched for Marvin's willingness to keep his word about the 'no charges' policy. If Jason *stayed on his leash*, then maybe he would still walk out of here none the poorer for his actions. Of course, that entire string of logic rested on Jason's ability to trust Leila, and while she'd done nothing to explicitly call that trust into question, Jason was curious how Marvin knew that the money had originally been withdrawn from his daughter's education savings, a secret he had only divulged to Leila as far as he could remember. Maybe Leila wasn't as trustworthy as she had led Jason to believe...

"To be clear," Jason said, wanting to make sure he and Marvin were on the same page, "if I hunker down in my room until my scheduled check-out tomorrow, and during that time stay completely out of hotel business, you'll return my daughter's money. Correct?"

"I'll not only return it," Marvin told him, "but I'll even add one percent interest. Think of it as a return on investment, a highly competitive overnight borrowing rate, if you will."

The insanity never stopped at the Chance Hotel. Marvin had flipped from stealing all of Jason's daughter's money to giving it back with interest in a matter of minutes. Jason wondered how much the Chance Hotel paid its accountant, because whatever it was couldn't possibly be enough to deal with this fiscal idiocy on a regular basis.

"Fine," Jason agreed.

It wasn't like seven hundred dollars of interest was going to suddenly make Jason rich enough to live the sweet life, but it was seven hundred dollars more of his daughter's money than what he had now, and that made the deal worth it. Jason had nothing further to say, but before he could get up, he noticed Marvin's eyes dart to the office door. When Jason turned, he saw Leila standing there, an inquisitive purse to her lips.

"Sorry to interrupt," she said, her words aimed at Marvin, "but the staff have a question for you."

Marvin squinted at her with a look of hesitant intrigue.

"Earlier tonight, when the intervention went south," Leila said, "Mr. Chance asked what we were going to do now. You told him there was no *we*."

"That's right," Marvin confirmed.

Leila inhaled deeply, clearly nervous about how Marvin would react to what she was going to say next. "Well, the staff have been bouncing some ideas around, and we were wondering: what if there was?"

Chapter Thirty-Four
Testosterone Infused Nut Job

Marvin stared at Leila, motionless save for the periodic blinking of his eyes. Uh oh, Jason thought, Leila broke Marvin. She was going to be in as much trouble as him now. The air was thick with tension, yet Jason held his tongue, both curious to see how Marvin would react to his subordinate's challenge, and baffled at what Leila could possibly mean by her suggestion. When Marvin finally spoke, he did so with solemn consideration.

"It's highly unusual to involve a guest in hotel business. What exactly did you and the rest of the staff have in mind?"

"Well..." Leila started as she took advantage of Marvin's opening to meander into the office. "We need to be cautious about conducting a second intervention because it would be too suspicious for Marcus Jr. to have two bouts of bad luck in a twenty-four span, right?"

Marvin didn't respond, the question clearly rhetorical.

"But Mr. Chance here," Leila indicated Jason, "he has a prior relationship with the Roberts. He saved Marcus Jr., and he wasn't fairly compensated for his efforts. He's down on his luck, short on cash, and mad at the world- not the type of person to stiff for doing a good deed."

Jason looked around the office to see who Leila was talking about. Nope, it was just the three of them.

"Maybe," Leila continued, "he's even a little crazy. Maybe he's crazy enough to threaten Marcus Jr.'s life if Marcus Sr. and Judy don't make him whole. And let's face it, if a testosterone infused nut job threatening his only child can't bring out the paternal heroism in Marcus Sr., then I don't know what can."

Um, this testosterone infused nut job is in the room, Jason thought about informing Leila before she continued badmouthing him as if he weren't there.

"So you want to modify Richard's original plan, but with Mr. Chance here in the leading role?" Marvin bit his lip as he mulled over the idea. "What does Katie have to say about this?"

Yeah, what does Katie have to say about this? From what Jason could remember, she was pretty adamant about Richard's plan likely getting someone hurt.

"She thinks it's a great idea."

Jason did a double-take.

"She said it should decrease suspicion to an acceptable level and has a ninety-one percent probability of success, which is about the best we can hope for given the circumstances." Leila passed Marvin a sheet of scribbled paper that appeared to have come from Katie's clipboard. "She was extra thrilled that this new approach wouldn't put any of the staff in mortal danger."

Wait, Jason processed, if it wouldn't put the staff in mortal danger, did that mean-

"These numbers look good," Marvin said as he scanned the paper. He then set the sheet down on his desk and eyed Jason. "What do you say, Mr. Chance? Would you care to help us right your wrong?"

Ummmm... Jason looked at Leila, who gave him a discrete nod of encouragement. Either she was secretly trying to help him or she truly believed he was a testosterone infused nut job that needed to die. Good thing nothing bad could come from either of those possibilities...

"Not to sound too selfish here," Jason said to Marvin, "but what's in it for me?"

"You need a reward to do a good deed?" Marvin asked dubiously. "Just a little while ago, you were ready to volunteer without hesitation."

"That was before you took my daughter's money," Jason reminded him. "That kind of thing can change a person's willingness to play nice."

Marvin eyed him as if he wasn't buying it.

"Look," Jason then said. "I don't need a reward from the Roberts for helping them out. I didn't like what I saw between Marcus Jr. and his old man. If I can make that better, I'm all in. What I would like is a reward from you for helping you out of the pickle you're in." Jason noticed Leila's eyes drop. Apparently, he had made a wrong turn somewhere in this conversation. "I'm not asking for anything I'm not already entitled to," Jason clarified, hoping to steer back in the right direction. "Just my daughter's money- you can even keep your interest- and the ability to check out free of charge... only later today instead of tomorrow."

Marvin didn't look pleased. "You aren't enjoying your stay in the Chance Hotel thus far?"

Was he serious? Jason thought with an audible chuckle. "We both know I don't belong here. The end result is the same for you either way- I get out of your hair and whatever secrets you and this hotel are keeping stay safe from my prying eyes. For me, I get home to my daughter and start fixing my life one day sooner. It doesn't sound like much, but it's worth a lot to me."

Leila was still looking down, and Jason even thought he saw her lip quiver. Was she really that upset at the thought of him leaving, or was there something more going on that Jason hadn't figured out yet?

"The only problem with your request," Marvin said as if he too was disappointed by the prospect of Jason's departure, "is that it means going back on your word."

"My word to stay for three nights?" Jason asked. "Marvin, it's just a reservation agreement. People change reservations all the time."

"A person's willingness to keep their word is a reflection of their inner character."

Well hot damn, Jason thought, now Marvin was channeling Confucius too! "Don't think of it as breaking my word," Jason suggested. "Think of it as renegotiating the terms of our agreement."

"Call it what you will, Mr. Chance," Marvin replied, "but no deal. Your reservation stands and the terms of your checkout remain unchanged. I will keep *my word* to return your daughter's money with interest when you leave here... tomorrow."

Jason was caught off-guard. He had honestly expected Marvin to take him up on his offer and now had to think quickly to keep their negotiations alive. "But... you need me to hit your ninety-one percent success probability!" Jason snatched Katie's clipboard paper to use as supporting evidence. "You need-" He quickly realized he couldn't make heads or tails of her calculations and tossed the paper back on Marvin's desk in frustration. "You're on a timeline," Jason then said, changing tactics. "You've got twenty-four hours to pull off a successful intervention, but you've only got about twelve before I become indifferent between checking out early and riding out the rest of my sentence. So..." Jason stood to leave. "You know where my room is and what my price is. I'll be there- staying out of trouble, per your request- if you change your mind."

Jason began walking toward the hallway. In reality, his exit performance was just a giant bluff. He wasn't so much of an ass that he would refuse to help an innocent boy, but there was no harm in getting some concessions out of Marvin for his efforts if he could. Luckily, Jason was so deep into his performance that it felt real, which meant it might actually look real to Marvin.

"Wait," the hotel manager said quickly, confirming Jason's suspicion. "You're right, Mr. Chance. We need you to have the greatest probability of success. And without you, the fracture between little Marcus Jr. and his father will likely never heal."

Jason could feel the concessions coming, so he waited for Marvin to continue. But oddly, the manager went silent. "And?" Jason asked.

"And nothing," Marvin clarified. "I just wanted to make sure you can't claim ignorance when our second intervention fails. I wanted to make sure you know that you could have made a difference in Marcus Jr.'s life, had you chosen to put someone else's needs ahead of your own."

Wow, just when Jason thought extortion was the limit to which Marvin would go to get what he wanted, the manager pulled out the ultimate manipulation technique: the guilt trip. And it was so much more than a guilt trip, too. Jason's bluff at being an ass had been so good that Marvin's words solidified him as the ass he was only pretending to be. Jason wouldn't have cared if it had only been him and Marvin in the office, but... Jason looked to Leila to get a read on her feelings, but her eyes were still lowered. She was staying out of it, leaving Jason to make his own decisions, regardless of where those decisions might lead. Jason thought about how good he had felt after rescuing Marcus Jr. from the freezer. Superhero Chance, he had called himself. Some superhero he was being now...

"I'll do it," Jason said softly, attempting to hide the shame in his voice.

"Why?" Marvin asked.

"What does it matter?" Jason shot back. "I'll do it. That's what you want."

"But is it what you want?" Marvin asked, his words an eery reminder of similar words spoken by Chef Terrance on the night of Jason's arrival. "If you're going to help, it needs to be for the right reasons. It needs to be because you want to do it, because you're willing to sacrifice a piece of yourself to help a complete stranger. It can't be because we forced you or because you expect something in return. If that's the case, your help is meaningless and bound to fail." Marvin gave Jason a minute to consider his words, then continued in a sincere tone. "So, moment of truth, Mr. Chance. Do you *want* to help us give Marcus Jr. a better life?"

Jason had always wanted to help, and now he suspected Marvin knew that despite the question currently hanging between them. The manager had played him, as usual, using Jason's own bluff against him and making him look like an ass in front of Leila so he would have no choice but to go along with their plan, receiving nothing in return.

"I want to help," Jason said dejectedly. He wished he had just said it from the beginning instead of trying to garner favors for his participation.

"What was that?"

Jason took a breath of confidence and spoke louder. "I want to help."

Leila lifted her glistening eyes and smiled at him. It was that warm smile Jason couldn't get enough of, and upon seeing it, Jason couldn't help but smile back. Out of the corner of his eye, Jason even thought he caught Marvin smiling too, though the manager was quick to hide it when Jason turned back his way.

"Okay then," Marvin said with renewed energy. "Let's do this."

He led Jason and Leila back to the break room, where the other staff members seemed to light up upon seeing Jason's continued presence. Jason struggled to understand the ever changing signals the employees of the Chance Hotel gave him. Upon initial arrival, he could've sworn they thought he was the Antichrist come to kick off Armageddon. Jason had sensed apprehension, distrust, and unwarranted dislike, among other unspoken emotions. Those emotions manifested in multiple instances of deception, subterfuge, and hostile confrontation. And yet, throughout it all, the staff of the Chance Hotel had taken care of Jason, ensuring he ate well, providing him a comfortable room to sleep in, offering him transport to Mackey and Sons, cleaning up his messes, and rescuing him from death by old age in an elevator that had no business remaining in operation. And now... now it was as if the staff wanted him there- no, not just wanted him there; they were actually happy he was there. It was as if they had come to terms with whatever problem they had with him and were now embracing his temporary residence with glee.

Well, that, or they were happy because they expected him to die soon.

Jason stepped into the break room and stood awkwardly at the head of the table as the staff members watched his every move. "So..." he said timidly, "how can I help?"

Chapter Thirty-Five
You Need To Be The Bad Guy

"You can get lost," Richard mumbled in a low, but clearly audible voice.

It wasn't the first response Jason had expected, but leave it to Richard to be the one dissenting attitude in the room. Luckily, Leila came to Jason's defense, planting a firm fist into Richard's shoulder, and drawing chuckles from the other staff members as Richard yelped in surprise. She then shot Jason a supportive wink.

"Since Richard isn't interested in relaying the details of his plan," Marvin cut in, "maybe Katie could do the honors."

"Sure," Katie replied with unusual chirpiness. "As you already know, Mr. Chance, our goal is to seal the growing rift between Marcus Jr. and his father, and doing so requires manipulating the Roberts family into a situation where Marcus Sr. will feel compelled to save his son from a potentially lethal situation. We want you to be that lethal situation."

Jason looked to Leila for guidance, but she signaled for him to keep listening.

"We already know you declined any gratuity for saving Marcus Jr. from the kitchen freezer," Katie continued. "There's a seventy-three percent probability that the Roberts skip breakfast in lieu of sleep following their already eventful morning. When they get moving, there's a nearly one hundred percent probability they go straight to the restaurant for an early lunch. Marcus Jr. didn't finish his early morning snack and his father will feel guilty about his son's hunger." Katie's chirpiness took a sudden turn as she stared hard at Jason. "We want you to intercept them on their way down. Revoke your goodwill, literally, by taking Marcus Jr. hostage and threatening to finish what the freezer started if Judy and Marcus Sr. don't come up with one hundred and thirty thousand dollars cash before sundown."

"Excuse me?" Jason asked.

The amount of money Katie specified wasn't lost on Jason, leading him to wonder just how many members of the staff had been looped in on his predicament. More pressing, though, was the fact that it sounded like Katie had just instructed Jason to become a full-fledged kidnapper. It occurred to Jason in that moment that he might still be getting played. After all, Katie was setting him up to commit a felony, the motive for the felony was tied to a sum of money Jason had recently lost, and the only people who knew his actions would be just for show were members of the staff... all of who could simply deny any advance knowledge of the crime and corroborate each other's stories. If true, it was a brilliant plan that would undoubtedly land Jason in prison while his daughter's money compensated the staff for their cleverness. Jason hoped it was nothing more than a product of his paranoia.

"You want to me to just take the kid," Jason reiterated for good measure. "How do you expect me to do that, exactly?"

A large, shiny knife jutted into Jason's field of view. It must have been about nine inches long and looked sharp enough to lob off Jason's head in a single swipe. The knife's grip was secured tightly in Olga's right hand.

"This should do," the European housekeeper said.

Jason stared at the blade with wide eyes, the thought of putting it anywhere near Marcus Jr. about as unappealing as slitting his own throat. "No, I don't think so."

Olga retracted the blade, a bewildered frown across her lips. A moment later, she thrusted a new knife into Jason's view, this one over twice as long as the previous. "This one, then?" She asked.

"What- no!" Jason exclaimed as he pushed her arm away. "I don't want any knife!"

"A gun perhaps?" Olga suggested with a look of unmeasurable glee. "I have a teensy one you could hide in your pocket-"

"I don't want any weapon!" Jason exclaimed further. "I don't want to threaten Marcus Jr." Jason looked around the room wildly, but the staff members stood their ground as if these sorts of activities were par for the course. "I- what the hell is wrong with you people?"

Marvin grabbed Jason's arm and forced the handle of the smaller knife into his good palm. "Unfortunately, Mr. Chance, this is the plan with the highest probability of success. Like it or not, you need to be the bad guy." He eased his grip. "For Marcus Jr.'s sake."

Jason felt his legs getting weak, so he dropped into the nearest chair.

"You haven't been to the dedicated guest wing yet," Katie continued as if Jason's outburst had never occurred. "We refer to the floors over there as Wing One through Wing Five. Wing Four is currently empty, so we'll stage a... hideout, for lack of a better word... in a room on that floor for you to take Marcus Jr. after you've grabbed him. His dad will surely follow, but we'll have mechanisms in place to slow Marcus Sr. down and allow you time to get into position."

"Mechanisms?" Jason asked.

"Sam will be the primary eyes on Marcus Sr." Katie explained. "She'll be in contact with the janitorial team and housekeeping staff, each of which will be on standby with various physical impediments to Marcus Sr.'s progress: wet floors, stalled elevators, blocked hallways... that sort of thing."

So Jason's getaway was contingent on Marcus Sr. being unwilling to get his shoes wet, unable to use the stairs, and having too few brain cells to push a housekeeping cart out of his way... this sounded like a rock solid plan.

"Once in your hideout," Katie said, "you'll need to remain close to the common area window. Giorgio and Reggie will swap it with breakaway glass... you know, the stuff they use in movies." Katie's voice cracked a bit, as if her confidence was dropping as she spoke. "Now, we're not exactly sure how things are going to play out once Marcus Sr. finds you, but you've got to be prepared to hurl yourself through the breakaway glass and over the balcony railing. Giorgio and Reggie will also install a temporary ledge just beneath the balcony. Grab onto it, pull yourself up, and squeeze out of sight."

"Sure, that sounds easy," Jason said dryly. "Assuming all of this plays out like you've said-" Jason caught himself getting ahead of more fundamental concerns. "What's the probability of that happening, by the way?"

Katie deflected. "Well, the probability of any long chain of events going exactly as predicted-"

"What's the probability that I survive?" Jason asked directly.

"Sixty-eight percent," Katie admitted reluctantly. "Forty-five if Marcus Sr. has his gun on him," she then added quietly.

"Wait, what?"

"Marcus Sr. has a concealed carry permit," Richard chimed in. "It's why Katie didn't like my plan in the first place. We know he brought his pistol into the hotel, but we haven't been able to determine whether he actually carries it on him." Richard gave Katie a snide glance. "The Queen of Quality Control over there doesn't like dealing with unknowns."

"Rightfully so!" Katie defended. "If we had more time, I would demand that Olga locate the gun and rig it to misfire. But unfortunately, our time has run short."

"So let me get this straight," Jason said. "You had a problem with Marcus Sr. potentially shooting one of the staff, but if he shoots me..." Jason shrugged, "meh?"

Katie flashed an uncaring smile. "My job is quality control, not guest satisfaction."

Jason looked to Leila and Richard, the two people in the room with jobs specifically catered to guest satisfaction. "And you two?"

"I'd prefer you not get shot," Leila said with sincerity.

"I'm indifferent," Richard added with his own brand of sincerity.

"Great," Jason replied flatly, a sickening feeling swelling in his stomach. "So back to my original question, assuming all of this plays out as predicted, won't Marcus Sr. get suspicious when he looks over the balcony and doesn't see my body plastered on the ground below?"

"*If* he doesn't see your body, yes," Katie agreed. "But Richard will be down there serving as your deceased body double. Pretending to be dead while the rest of us get actual work done is his specialty."

Richard made an agreeable shrug.

"Anyway," Katie continued, "once Marcus Sr. is convinced that you're dead and there's no continued threat to his son, Marvin will offer to cover up the incident and comp the Roberts' stay in exchange for their discretion."

"From there, it's a waiting game," Marvin told Jason. "The family is scheduled to check out tomorrow, the same day as you. By then we should have a good read on whether Marcus Sr.'s treatment of his son has improved."

"And what if all of this goes south?" Jason asked Katie. "There are a lot of moving parts here. What if Marcus Sr. ends up doing something unpredictable? Something your numbers haven't foreseen?" Jason turned his next comment to Marvin. "I know I agreed to sacrifice a piece of myself to help a complete stranger, but I kind of expected there to be some of me left."

"Don't worry," Marvin assured him with an uncharacteristically warm smile. "The staff will have your back if anything goes off the rails. We've got plenty of experience with these sorts of things."

Jason wasn't sure if that made him feel better or even more concerned that he had become an unwitting pawn to some elaborate con. He looked at the knife in his trembling hand, unsure of whether he could truly go through with this. Leila wrapped her hands around his, steadying him as she spoke in a low, soothing voice.

"Everything's going to be fine," she said. "Sam and I will be nearby for the initial encounter; Giorgio and Reggie will man the elevators; Olga will watch the hallways of the guest wing; and Benji will have his eyes on the hideout in case you can't handle Marcus Sr. yourself."

Jason was feeling better until she got to that last line. Assuring him that Benji would have his back was like promising him Casper the Friendly Ghost would come to his rescue. If Jason was going to be killed during this little escapade, it was going to be in the staged hideout... he would've felt a lot better having Olga on hand for that particular portion of the intervention.

"And if I get shot?" Jason asked.

"Well, that's what Heinrich's for," Leila said with a charming smile.

Heinrich gave Jason an affirming nod.

"And if I miss the hideaway ledge when going over the balcony?"

"Well then you're dead," Richard answered bluntly. "Just try not to land on me on your way down."

Leila shot Richard a *shut up, idiot* kind of glare.

"Sure, that'll be my first priority," Jason told the insolent concierge.

"Look," Marvin cut in with authority, "we're not going to lie to you, Mr. Chance. There's always a risk with these things that something goes wrong. And sometimes- not often, but sometimes- people get hurt." Marvin looked proudly at the other staff members. "But everyone in this room has been through more interventions than I can count, and they're all still here. Stick with the plan, trust Katie's calculations, and with a little luck, we'll all still be here tomorrow, too."

With a little luck, Jason would only be here for the first half of tomorrow. After that, he'd be on his way home and his time at the Chance Hotel would be nothing more than a quirky tale to tell during holiday gatherings. Jason summoned whatever courage he could muster and gave Marvin an accepting nod. He then turned his eyes to Leila, who squeezed his hands in support. The other staff members stepped forward in turn, patting Jason on the back and welcoming him to the team. Even Richard gave him a half-hearted pat of encouragement, solidifying Jason's respect among the staff of the Chance Hotel. It was then that Jason realized if the story of his stay was ever made into a movie, this would be the moment of dramatic inspiration heading into the film's climax. It was an uplifting thought, but one that was mildly tarnished by the uncertainty of whether that moment of inspiration would be followed by heroic conquest... or tragic downfall. Jason feared it would be the latter.

Chapter Thirty-Six
Almost Certain

The waiting game had begun. When the break room powwow ended, each hotel employee dispersed both to prepare for the Roberts' approaching intervention and to deal with the day's guest needs. Giorgio and Reggie immediately went to work on the Wing Four hideout, guaranteeing Jason that it would be ready when the time came for him to stage his death. Sam went straight to the twentieth floor- what the staff called Main Twenty, Jason had learned- to monitor the Roberts' room. Olga left to corral a team of housekeepers in the guest wing, where they would drag their feet cleaning rooms to remain nearby for when the intervention began.

Doing nothing to ease Jason's nervousness, Heinrich stayed behind to sanitize the break room and convert it into an emergency surgery room as a precautionary measure. With no advance prep to tend to, Marvin, Richard, and Leila resumed their regular job duties in the hotel lobby, where current guests had begun gathering and into which new guests trickled. Meanwhile, the Queen of the Clipboard informed everyone, including Jason, that she would be making continuous rounds to ensure each of them stayed true to the task at hand.

That left Jason with... well, nothing to do. Nothing except to reflect on how insane this plan was and to wonder exactly how he had gotten wrapped up in it. He wandered the hotel lobby aimlessly, watching Marvin work his magic at the check-in counter, observing Richard and Leila fielding guest questions as if nothing out of the ordinary was occurring. It dawned on Jason that, aside from him, every hotel guest was oblivious to the intervention activities happening behind the scenes. Maybe this was the grand secret Marvin had been trying to keep from him since his arrival. Jason recalled Chef Terrance's surprise that Jason had taken part in the freezer intervention. Clearly, guest knowledge of these events was unusual, perhaps even taboo. But not for him...

Another thought occurred to Jason. The night of his arrival, he sensed the hotel staff were apprehensive about his presence. Had they been in the middle of a different intervention then? Had they known Jason presented a threat to the way interventions were normally conducted? Jason told himself it was a silly notion; the staff of the Chance Hotel had no idea he even existed prior to him walking through that revolving front door. Or so Jason had assumed. But now, given his insight into its backroom operations, Jason couldn't help but wonder if his arrival at the Chance Hotel truly was a surprise to the staff that ran it. If it wasn't... Jason wasn't sure what to make of the thought.

He could feel his paranoia growing. Why wouldn't it? The hotel staff had somehow convinced him to kidnap a child at knifepoint. Even if Jason lived through the event, how could he be sure he wasn't going straight to jail when it was over? It really came down to trust, and Jason had given Marvin and the staff that trust, despite having so many reasons not to. An objective observer would tell him that the really insane part of this plan was Jason's willingness to go along with it.

He needed a drink to take the edge off. Well, maybe not *needed*, but wanted. And he didn't care that the sun had barely risen. Jason followed a stream of guests to the restaurant hallway, where he found them joining a fairly lengthy line at Marie's podium. Jason bypassed the line, uninterested in getting a table and having a complete meal, and instead walked directly into the dining room, where he ran into Marie returning from seating an elderly couple.

"Oh, Mr. Chance," she said with a certain morning charm.

"Did you want some breakfast before, um, well... you know?"

"No thanks," Jason told her. "I'm just going to grab a seat at the bar, if that's okay."

"Of course!" Marie said without hesitation. "Sit wherever you'd like. And thank you for everything you're doing to help us out. These interventions mean a lot. To see one fail, especially when a child is involved..." A barely noticeable frown peeked from Marie's lips. "Well, we're just glad to have you on board."

Jason debated who the 'we' actually included, but there was no point in arguing the issue with Marie. "No problem," he said instead.

Marie excused herself to tend to the next family waiting at the podium. Jason continued to the bar, where he had his choice of seats given that no other guest wanted to look like an alcoholic so early in the day. As he waited for someone to take his drink order, Jason glanced around the lively dining room. A few hours and a handful of warm bodies made all the difference in this place, its current atmosphere in stark contrast to that when Jason rescued Marcus Jr. Aside from the growing sunlight streaming in through exterior windows, one of the most noticeable differences was the piano. Its dust cover had been removed, and the pianist was tapping away energetically, projecting a relaxing, yet upbeat, tune through the dining room. As Jason looked his way, the pianist briefly glanced up from his performance to communicate a grateful nod.

Jason's eyes drifted over the rest of the room and the guests seated throughout. Waiters hustled from one table to the next, taking orders, delivering drinks and food, and chit-chatting if encouraged. The guests they served all seemed pleased with their service, and Jason was more than confident they were pleased with their food. As one waiter passed by Jason, he gave a silent nod of acknowledgement, similar to that given by the pianist. The other waiters then did the same, each taking a moment to catch Jason's eye and express their gratuity. Jason's cynical side told him the special attention was just another hotel manipulation intended to guilt him from backing out of the intervention. The more reasonable side of Jason sensed a certain sincerity to the gestures, as if even these tangential staff members truly appreciated his potential sacrifice.

"The axe man returns," Chef Terrance said from behind the bar.

Jason turned and flashed the gruff chef an apologetic *that's me* smile.

"What can I get for you, Mr. Chance?" Terrance then asked. "I assume you don't want a menu."

"No," Jason said. "I'll just have a glass of whatever's strongest back there." He pointed to the rows of liquor bottles that decorated the bar wall.

Terrance looked at the bottles, then looked back at Jason, his face puckered in that challenging way of his. "Nah, you don't want that."

This again? Jason asked silently. Thinking quickly, he then turned Chef Terrance's tactics against him. "It may not be what I want, but it's what I need."

"If you say so," Terrance replied a little too easily. He perused the rows of liquor until he settled on a rather ornate bottle of skillfully etched glass that contained a deep amber liquid inside. Terrance retrieved a tumbler from behind the bar and filled it halfway with the liquid. "Our strongest... per your request," he said, passing the tumbler to Jason.

As Jason lifted the glass to his mouth, he noticed the liquor had a surprisingly sweet smell. He wasn't typically fond of sweeter drinks, but strength took precedence over personal preference right now, so he held his breath and downed it. The amber liquid wasn't even halfway down his esophagus when it sent Jason into a coughing fit that sent part of the drink spraying across the bar surface. Chef Terrance bellowed with laughter.

"What the hell was that?!" Jason exclaimed.

"That," Terrance said as he showed off the ornate bottle of liquid, "is an extremely rare, unusually expensive, and unmistakably potent vanilla extract. You just gagged on about five hundred dollars' worth."

"Tell Marvin to add it to my bill," Jason choked. "Who would want to drink that, anyway?"

"It's not for drinking," Terrance explained. "It's for garnishing. I sprinkle a few drops on my bananas foster and a handful of other desserts."

A waiter arrived with a damp towel for Jason and a handful of rags for the counter.

"Then what the hell is it doing in your liquor selection?" Jason asked.

"The same thing the rest of the extracts and flavorings are doing there." Terrance waved his hand at the variety of decorative bottles and colorful contents that lined the walls of the bar. "If you wanted liquor, you should've said so. We keep the hard stuff in the back."

Of course you do, Jason thought silently. It made too much sense for the Chance Hotel to display hard liquor *at the bar*, where patrons were most likely to consume it. "I'm going to move a few seats down," he told Chef Terrance after wiping his face and sliding out of the waiter's way. "Can you just bring me a glass of a *drinkable* alcohol, preferably something on the stronger side?"

"I'm going to bring you a glass of orange juice and a plate of breakfast," Terrance replied resolutely. "Just telling you now so you don't get your hopes up for something different."

How kind of you, Jason thought sarcastically. He shook his head in frustration and proceeded down the bar, where he plopped onto a clean seat and laid his head on folded arms. All he wanted was a little liquor to settle his nerves before marching into a potentially deadly situation. Was a last request prior to execution too much to ask? If it was, put it up there next to solitude, for it hadn't been two minutes before Jason felt another body take the seat next to him.

"Unless you've got a bottle of vodka, go away," Jason mumbled from his arm pillow.

"I've never actually had vodka," Leila said. "Am I missing out on something?"

Jason lifted his weary head to look at her. Leila was her normal, vibrant self, a presence of warmth and comfort that was seemingly unfazed by the events that were about to unfold. How was she keeping her cool? Had she simply been through so many of these interventions that they no longer unnerved her? Or was she taking it in stride because her role in the coming intervention was a largely passive one that wouldn't put her in harm's way?

"Well you look like shit," Leila said bluntly.

And you look gorgeous, Jason thought, pressing his lips tightly together to ensure the words didn't slip out unexpectedly. "My stomach is in knots," Jason said once the thought had left him. "I'm light-headed, my pulse is all over the place... I don't know how you do this stuff."

"Well, they aren't all as dangerous as this one," Leila explained. "Some are quite easy, believe or not. But even the dangerous ones... I guess you get used to them after a while."

"So you've been in my position before?"

"Minus the alcohol cravings," Leila said with a warm smile, "yes. But trust me when I tell you that you're going to be okay. And tomorrow, when you see Marcus Jr. and Marcus Sr. walk out of this hotel with a newly forged loving bond between them, you'll discover it was all worth it."

Jason hoped so. Chef Terrance returned from the kitchen and delivered a glass of freshly squeezed orange juice and a breakfast platter as promised. He set the plate down forcefully, his unspoken way of telling Jason to eat up and *tough shit about the liquor*. Jason glared at Terrance unhappily before begrudgingly picking up a piece of perfectly crisped bacon and taking a bite. It wasn't a stiff drink, but it would do.

"There you are, Mr. Chance," Jason then heard Marvin say from somewhere behind him. The manager soon stepped into view next to Leila. "How are you doing?" Jason continued to eat his bacon without responding. "That good, huh? Well, you'll be happy to know that Giorgio and Reggie have finished their preparations. You'll be holding up in room W414." Marvin paused and bit his lip. "Or was it W415?"

It's a kind of important detail, Jason thought as he stared at Marvin with wide eyes.

"No, definitely W414... I'm almost certain."

Jason wondered how many percentage points 'almost certain' had just knocked off his probability of survival.

"Anyway," Marvin continued as if it didn't matter, "you'll need a key to get in." He produced a room keycard from his jacket pocket and set it next to Jason's plate. "Given the... latitude, let's say... in how this intervention plays out, I haven't coded it to a particular door. That way, you have the freedom to move about the hotel as needed to keep you safe."

Jason raised his brow. Did that mean-

"Yes," Marvin confirmed before Jason could ask the question aloud. "That's a master keycard. I assume by now you know the responsibility that comes with having one in your possession." Marvin's voice grew stern. "I also assume that I can trust you not to abuse the power it gives you. No thirteenth floor, no deviations from the plan we've laid out, unless absolutely vital to your survival."

Jason picked up the keycard and turned it between his fingers to confirm it was real. To think of all the effort he had gone through to steal a master keycard and sneak onto the thirteenth floor... when all along Marvin was willing to give him one if he simply played ball with the demands of the hotel. "I'll behave," Jason assured the manager.

"Good," Marvin said, his jolliness returning.

The walkie-talkie buried in Marvin's pocket squealed, the noise followed by Sam's garbled voice. "Boss? Boss, come in." She sounded panicked as Marvin brought the walkie-talkie to his mouth.

"Yes, Sam," Marvin acknowledged. "What's going on?"

"Katie might want to rerun her numbers!" Sam exclaimed. "The Roberts? They're on their way down... right now!"

Chapter Thirty-Seven
Hulk No Care About Logic

Jason felt his stomach perform a somersault. "What did she just say?"

"You heard her," Marvin replied as he returned the walkie-talkie to his jacket pocket. "Do you have the knife?"

"It's right here." Jason patted the sheath hidden beneath his shirt. Olga had given him one to help conceal the blade after Katie raised concerns that other guests may not react well to a random stranger carrying an exposed weapon through the hotel lobby. The sheath itself didn't bother Jason, but he wasn't sure what to make of the fact that it had already been modified to strap clandestinely to a person's body. Then again, it had come from Olga, so-

"The keycard?" Marvin asked, breaking Jason's thoughts.

Jason held it up proudly, then tucked it into his pants pocket for safekeeping. "Check."

"Okay. Now remember, room W415."

"I thought it was W414."

"Right," Marvin said, brushing off his mistake.

Jason was already on edge about this whole intervention thing, and Marvin's wishy-washy memory wasn't doing much to bolster his confidence. He wanted to slow Marvin down and have him confirm which room Giorgio and Reggie had truly prepped. That one would contain breakaway glass and a safety ledge on which Jason could hide. The other would contain a real balcony window and pretty much certain death, regardless of whether Jason managed to leap through it. It was too late to put his mind at ease, however, for Marvin was already on the move.

"Let's go," the manager said as he guided Jason and Leila toward the restaurant entrance. His eyes frequently checked

with Marie, who was keeping a lookout on the restaurant hallway and feeding Marvin silent signals to proceed. "Richard should be running interference at the elevators," Marvin explained as they walked. "Leila will join him and steer the Roberts so that their backs are to you. That'll be your opportunity."

Jason's legs were getting weaker with every step. His heart felt like it would leap out of his throat at any moment. "I'm not sure I can go through with this."

"If you don't," Marvin said plainly, "Marcus Jr.'s relationship with his father will forever be a loveless one. It may not sound like a big deal to you, but the negative repercussions to Marcus Jr.'s life will be unmeasurable."

Jason wondered whether those were Katie's probabilities or Marvin's own assumptions talking. Then again, he supposed either could be based on pure bullshit, so at this point he had no choice but to take Marvin at his word. After the group passed Marie, Marvin held up a hand to slow their progression. They didn't have another staff member ahead to feed them intel. Instead, they had to hope that Richard was doing his job properly for a change. In a moment of distracted thought, Jason wondered what the probably of that actually was. He quickly decided he was better off not knowing.

"Stop," Marvin said, bringing the group to a halt near the end of the restaurant hallway. "I'll go ahead and make sure we're clear to proceed. On my signal, Leila will join Richard. After that, the ball's in your court, Mr. Chance."

Marvin didn't wait for Jason or Leila to acknowledge his plan before charging forward. At least, Jason thought he charged forward. The world was spinning, so for all Jason knew, Marvin had floated skyward and vanished through the ceiling like he assumed his chess-playing apparition tended to do. Jason felt the single piece of bacon he had eaten start working its way back up. What the hell had he been thinking agreeing to this? If he could get a moment to focus, maybe he could devise another way to help Marcus Jr., one that didn't involve criminal acts and the threat of death. Maybe-

"Hey," Leila said as she placed a steadying hand on his arm. "It's going to be okay. Remember, just stick with what we discussed. The hotel staff will be there every step of the way to keep things on track." Leila's eyes glanced up at Marvin, who signaled her forward. She released her grip on Jason's arm and proceeded into the lobby, tossing off her next set of words like a casual farewell: "Oh, and try to not get killed."

Such wonderful words of encouragement. Well, this was it. Jason was alone and the next step of this cockamamy plan was on him. He spotted Richard entertaining the Roberts family as Marvin said he would be. He then watched as Leila joined them and so sneakily used friendly conversation and touches of her hand here and there to angle each member of the Roberts family so that their backs were to both Jason and the hallway that led to the hotel's guest wing. Jason looked around to ensure no other guests were paying attention to him, then lifted his shirt and removed Olga's knife from its sheath. His hand was sweaty on the grip, and the splint from his previous day's injury was interfering with his leverage. Jason questioned whether he would be able to hold on to the knife through the action to come. He also feared that, even if he could maintain possession, he may not have enough control over the blade to prevent accidental injury to Marcus Jr., which he definitely didn't want. Jason's eyes drifted to Marvin, who was cautiously observing the exchange between the Roberts and his concierges. A moment later, Marvin turned his gaze to Jason and gave a firm nod.

Oh God, Jason said inwardly, just get me through this and I promise I'll be a changed man. He wiped his sweaty hand on his shirt, adjusted his grip on the knife to better accommodate the splint, and jogged forward from the hallway. Jason was three-quarters of the way to Marcus Jr. when something peculiar caught his eye: a bulge in the side of Marcus Sr.'s right pant leg, just around the ankle... a holster, likely containing a very real gun. Jason's legs were moving faster than his brain, and unfortunately by the time he realized the implications of that bulge, he was already to Marcus Jr., his hand bringing the knife around the young boy's chest.

"Hey!" Marcus Jr. yelled, not fully aware of the gravity of the situation.

He elbowed Jason in the groin, causing him to drop the knife. Jason tried to go for it, but Marcus Jr. started pulling away, and it required both of Jason's hands to restrain him. Jason fought through the pain between his legs as he tightened one arm around the boy's chest and the other around his throat, applying just enough pressure to keep him from squirming away.

"What the hell?!" Marcus Sr. shouted as he turned toward the commotion. "You! What are you-" His eyes drifted to the knife on the floor, and in that moment Jason was pretty sure Marcus Sr.'s inner Hulk had been unleashed.

"I uh... I-"

Jason watched as a wide-eyed, red-faced Marcus Sr. quickly reached for his right ankle. Yup, he thought, the time for explanations and empty threats was over. He turned on his heels to run. Jason heard Judy yelling shrilly and Marcus Sr. swearing like a sailor as he dragged Marcus Jr. down the hallway to the guest wing. The little boy refused to go easily, kicking and screaming the entire way, forcing Jason to tighten his hold. The hallway wasn't overly long, and Jason knew it should take only ten or fifteen seconds to reach the end of it, even with a feisty kid in tow. Yet, the glass doors that led to his destination seemed so far away... too far, given the immediacy of the danger behind him. The first gunshot rang out. Jason wasn't hit, but he definitely felt the displacement of air as the bullet whizzed closely by before burying itself in a wall.

"Are you out of your mind?!" Jason yelled as he repositioned Marcus Jr. between himself and the barrel of Marcus Sr.'s gun. "You could hit your own kid!"

Jason assumed the argument was logical enough to buy him a temporary reprieve from gunfire. But, as he looked at the rage-fueled mass that was Marcus Sr., Jason realized that assumption was wrong. *Hulk no care about logic.* The second gunshot rang out. This time, the bullet grazed Jason's ear before shattering the glass doors to the guest wing. Jason hunkered down behind Marcus Jr. and pedaled backwards toward the now-open doorway, the tip of his ear searing with pain and the warmth of blood spreading down his neck. A third gunshot sounded, but this time the bullet ricocheted several feet away from Jason.

Jason felt the crunch of broken glass beneath his shoes, then the blast of outside air as he transitioned to a covered walkway that connected the hotel's main building to its guest wing. Marcus Sr.'s eyes must have had trouble adjusting from the dim interior lighting of the hotel to the bright exterior in which Jason now stood, for he stopped shooting and instead began following. Jason knew this would be his only opportunity to escape without getting shot, so he turned his back to his pursuer and darted toward the guest wing entrance. Five seconds later, he was through the next set of doors, Marcus Jr. still firmly in his grasp as he entered a miniature version of the main building's lobby.

Giorgio was waiting just beyond the threshold, rapidly pointing for Jason to proceed. "Elevators, that way!"

Jason was on autopilot now, doing as he was told and trusting that it would get him safely to his destination. He ran past a pair of janitors who dumped buckets of soapy water on the floor in his wake. He then reached the elevators, where Reggie was holding one open for him.

"I'll shut them down as soon as you reach your floor," the maintenance worker assured him.

Jason got on and jammed the button for the fourth floor. He looked out to discover that Giorgio and the janitors had slipped into hiding. He suspected Reggie would do the same as soon as his role in this sort-of-real, sort-of-not kidnapping was complete. Then Jason saw the harbinger of doom: a hulking silhouette at the entrance to the guest wing, dark against the backdrop of sunlight outside. Jason wasn't sure why the silhouette had stopped moving, but a loud crack followed by a bullet bouncing around the interior walls of the elevator car put that mystery to rest quickly. Luckily, neither Jason nor Marcus Jr. were hit, though the gunfire sent Reggie ducking for cover. So much for shutting down the elevators...

The silhouette marched forward, its blackness giving way to Marcus Sr.'s enraged features. Why hadn't the elevator doors shut? Jason tapped the button for the fourth floor rapidly as Marcus Sr. lifted his gun. With his pupils re-adjusted to indoor lighting and Jason confined to what was essentially a tiny shooting gallery, it was unlikely Marcus Sr. would miss again. Jason saw the barrel of the gun aimed directly at him. He saw Marcus Sr.'s finger tighten around the trigger. And as another shot rang out, he saw the welcoming silver sheen of the elevator doors, which intercepted the incoming bullet as they slid shut.

Chapter Thirty-Eight
The Hitman Housekeeper

Jason released his grip on Marcus Jr. since both he and the boy were currently confined to an unescapable space. Jason then fell against the rear wall of the elevator car, his body weak from tension and stress. He realized he had been holding his breath in anticipation of being shot, so Jason let out a series of unsteady gasps. He looked down at his own body, then over to that of his unwilling hostage, to confirm both were free of any life-threatening injuries.

"Why are you doing this?" Marcus Jr. asked. "Weren't you the guy who saved me last night?"

Jason looked at the boy with weary eyes. The next few phases of this plan would go so much smoother if Marcus Jr. was in on it. But was Jason allowed to spill the beans to his fake hostage? What would that do to the probability of fixing Marcus Jr.'s relationship with his father? Ah, screw it, Jason thought. This entire plan was falling apart quicker than a Jenga tower. What was the harm in calling an audible now?

"Listen," he told Marcus Jr., "I'm not going to hurt you. I know that's not what it looks like, but you need to trust me."

"Yeah, right."

Jason swallowed hard as he tried to think on his feet. "You and your old man... you've got problems, right? He hasn't exactly been father-of-the-year?"

"Years," Marcus Jr. mumbled. "Plural."

Jason could see he was getting through to the boy. "I want to help make that better. And... I know what's happening right now may seem batshit crazy- believe me, it's crazier than you can probably imagine- but it's going to make things better." Jason saw Marcus Jr. look at him doubtfully, and he knew time was ticking, so he laid it all out in the open as plainly as he could. "You need to let me be your bad guy, and you need to let your dad be your hero. It's the only way he'll realize just how much you truly mean to him."

The elevator dinged as its doors opened to Wing Four. Jason ignored their arrival, and instead waited for Marcus Jr. to make the first move, somehow subconsciously aware that he wouldn't succeed without the boy's willing participation.

"Okay," Marcus Jr. said softly after a tense half minute of silence.

"Okay," Jason repeated with a relieved smile.

He led Marcus Jr. out of the elevator and down the fourth floor hallway. A handful of housekeepers were at the ready, emerging from rooms at both ends of the hall and pushing their carts into the most inconvenient positions possible, essentially barricading Jason and Marcus Jr. between them. Jason spotted room W414 and removed the keycard from his pocket. He waved it over the room's card reader, which responded with a negative buzz.

"Shit," Jason said under his breath.

He tried the card reader again, but received the same response. Maybe Marvin really had the rooms mixed up? Jason turned to the opposite door, room W415, and tried the keycard there. That one refused him entry as well.

"Shit," Jason repeated. "Shit shit shit."

"What's wrong?" Marcus Jr. asked.

Jason ignored him and returned to room W414. He tried the door handle, but it was locked. He tried the keycard once more, but to no avail. Jason looked up and down the hallway, but the housekeepers had ditched their posts after positioning their carts, creating what was essentially a makeshift kill box. So this was the actual plan all along, Jason quickly surmised. There was no hideout, no breakaway glass, and no Richard to pretend to be

Jason's body on the ground below. There was only this hallway, a carefully designed mousetrap full of locks to which Jason had been led to believe he had the key. Now all that remained was for Marcus Sr. to arrive and put the mouse out of its misery. Then the Roberts could live happily ever after and the Chance Hotel could go on doing business, with no one the wiser about its staff's role in the crimes that had taken place.

Jason buckled over, his hands propped against his thighs. How could he have been so stupid? He had always been gullible when it came to finances, but never when it came to his life. But that was the past. In the present, his gullibility was about to cost him the one thing he could never earn back.

"What's that?" Marcus Jr. asked, pointing to a credit card sized object pressing against Jason's tightened pant fabric.

Jason followed Marcus Jr.'s finger. "That's just my room key." Then it hit him. "My key..."

Dumbass Chance was at it again. In his haste, he had slipped the master keycard Marvin had given him into the same pocket as his room key. Maybe he wasn't the victim of a long con after all. Maybe he was just the victim of his own carelessness. Jason swapped the keycards and tried room W414 again. The card reader beeped acceptingly, and the door unlatched, revealing a rather simple hotel room on the other side. Hot damn, Jason thought with relief.

The common area was empty, with most of the furniture pushed slightly aside in a manner that wasn't immediately obvious to the random onlooker, but noticeable to Jason. The window curtains had been drawn, revealing a large pane of what Jason hoped truly was breakaway glass. On the couch was a white box that reminded Jason of a shirt box, and beside it was a small envelope. Jason ushered Marcus Jr. into the room, shut and bolted the door, and grabbed the envelope. Inside was a folded note:

A little protection from your naughty ways. -O

Jason had no idea what was in the box, but if it had come from the Hitman Housekeeper herself, he definitely wanted it. Jason tore its lid off, revealing a thick kevlar vest nestled like a gift in tissue paper. As he removed the vest from the box, Jason heard shouting and the crash of housekeeping carts being toppled over in the distance. Those noises were followed by a loud crack as a guest room door was kicked open.

"I think you're running out of time," Marcus Jr. said.

No kidding, Jason thought. There was another crack, this time closer, as he took off his shirt, slipped on the kevlar vest, and replaced his shirt to cover it. Jason directed Marcus Jr. to the open floor in front of the breakaway glass, where they assumed the positions of hostage taker and victim.

"Now, when your father comes in, I want you to elbow me like you did in the lobby," Jason instructed. "Then get out of the way so he has a clean shot at my vest."

"Okay," Marcus Jr. replied. Then, innocently, he asked: "What if he shoots you in the head?"

Jason hadn't considered that, but it was too late anyway. The door to the room shuddered violently as a force slammed into it from the hallway. Jason could hear Marcus Sr. shouting to someone that he had found them. Then the door shuddered again, this time splintering at the hinges. Jason felt his heart pounding as his probability of survival tanked like the stock market during a recession. One more hit was all it took, then the door hinges broke free of their frame, and Marcus Sr. pushed the slab of wood aside as he raised his gun in Jason's direction.

Marcus Jr. did as instructed, elbowing Jason in the groin once more and then diving aside. Jason doubled over in pain; he had expected Marcus Jr. to take it easy on him this time, but apparently the boy wanted to make sure it looked real. Jason supposed he deserved the tear-inducing groin strike, all things considered. The only problem was that his subsequent reaction had left Jason's eyes level with the barrel of Marcus Sr.'s gun. Jason quickly rocked backwards as the gun discharged. He felt the bullet slam into the upper portion of his kevlar vest, the force of the impact thrusting him backwards, through the breakaway glass, which shattered in full action movie fashion.

Jason landed on his ass on the balcony, his body aching and the world a blur. Was it over? He asked himself. No, wait... he hadn't gone over the balcony railing. He had been too low to the ground when the bullet knocked him backwards, which meant he was still in Marcus Sr.'s crosshairs. Jason used the balcony rail posts for leverage as he pulled himself to his feet. Another blast of gunfire rang through the air as Jason felt a bullet plant itself into the back of his kevlar vest. He fell against the balcony railing, his head hanging over the edge, where he caught a cathartic glimpse of a dead body below. *His* dead body... or rather Richard pretending to be his dead body. Jason needed to act quickly to prevent the facade from becoming a reality. Under the guise of trying to keep his footing, he pulled himself further over the railing, nearly all of his torso suspended in the air as Marcus Jr. fired a third bullet into him.

Jason didn't know for certain where that bullet had landed, but something about it was different. The pain was greater, sending a shock through the left half of Jason's body unlike anything he had felt before. Luckily, its impact had also been just what Jason needed to complete his morbid performance, tipping the balance in Jason's body to the other side of the balcony railing, where gravity greeted him with an unspoken *I've got it from here.*

The last thing Jason remembered before free falling was the upside down sight of Marcus Sr. still in Hulk mode and ready to shoot again, Marcus Jr. safely off to the side, and Marvin and Sam watching with a strange combination of joy and worry from the busted doorway. Then the exterior of the hotel overtook Jason's view, so he reached out blindly, remembering that he still had one final task to do. It was perhaps the most important task: to catch the secret ledge and pull himself to safety instead of going splat on the concrete below. Jason didn't know where the ledge was, and he had only a second to find and grab it, but against all odds he did just that, one flailing hand finding itself gripping the edge of a plank of solid wood that didn't belong among the hotel's decor.

Unfortunately, the hand that found that plank was the same hand Jason had beaten black and blue against a concrete wall the day before, and after everything Jason had put it through, it seemed eager to return the favor. As he felt his fingers slip, Jason tried to swing his other arm up to the ledge. He missed on the first attempt, the momentum wriggling him violently as he hung precariously to the only thing standing between him and a forty-foot nosedive to the afterlife. With no other choice, Jason then made a second attempt, and this time he overshot the ledge, the momentum of his swing so great that it ripped him free of his makeshift life raft altogether. The last thing Jason thought as his free fall resumed was *well, this is a real shitty way to go out.*

Chapter Thirty-Nine
Luckily

Jason recalled the saying 'when you die, your life flashes before for your eyes.' If that was true, then Jason's life consisted of nothing but concrete and wood, for that's all he saw as he fell from the ledge that was supposed to be his saving grace. Strictly speaking, little of this intervention had gone according to plan, and yet somehow the end result was tracking just as it should. Well, with the exception of Jason's early departure- from both the Chance Hotel and life itself- that was. He had played his part and the hotel staff had been there for the assist, and Marcus Jr.'s life would be the better for it. That's what Jason was going to tell himself just before getting up close and personal with the ground below, anyway. That way he could end life on a good note.

An excruciating pain shot through Jason's body. He felt as though his left side had split open as that same side's arm ripped from its socket. Jason's weight slammed against a vertical slab of concrete before bouncing a few inches and then coming to a rest. His feet were still dangling in midair, the ground nearly as far below as it had been when Jason first toppled over the balcony of room W414. He was also upright... a very odd position for someone who had just taken a four-story nosedive into solid pavement.

"What the hell?" Jason gasped.

He felt a painful cinching of his left hand- somehow there was still feeling left- and looked up to find Sam hanging over a balcony railing, both of her hands clasped tightly around his. Sam's face was taut with strain and her body was shaking as if it would give out at any moment, sending Sam careening over the edge with Jason. Leila popped into view beside Sam and put her finger to her lips, indicating for Jason to keep quiet. She then stretched over the balcony railing and motioned for Jason to swing his loose hand up to hers. Jason recalled how swinging his loose hand had gotten him into this situation to begin with, but it wasn't like he had another choice. He would just need to make sure the first try counted.

Jason tried to take a deep breath to ready himself, but a sharp pain in his lower chest halted his inhale. Oh well, he thought. Ready or not, here he came! Jason mustered every bit of energy he had left and swung his free arm as high as he could. Leila's hands made contact around his own. Jason's weight retracted with gravity, yanking her a few inches further into space, but Leila held both her ground and Jason. Sam and Leila then made eye contact and nodded off a silent count: one, two... they both reared back as hard as they could, leveraging their feet against the balcony posts to lift Jason onto the railing. From there, he flopped forward, crashing face first into the balcony floor as Leila and Sam landed hard on their butts. It wasn't graceful, but it was better than the alternative.

"How-"

Leila shushed Jason before he could continue. She pointed up as if to say *he's right above us, dumbass*. Sam rose quietly and stepped into the adjacent hotel room. Leila immediately followed and signaled for Jason to do the same. Before he could move, however, he heard Marcus Sr.'s voice on the balcony just ten feet over his head.

"That's what happens when you mess with my boy."

Jason rolled his eyes at the cheesiness of the line. If only Marcus Sr. knew...

"I don't know what would possess someone to do such a thing," Marvin chimed in from overhead. "He must have been a truly deranged man. I'm just glad you were prepared to do what was necessary. Things might have gone quite differently if it had been any other guest." Marvin was laying the butter on pretty thick in anticipation of his coming request. "You know, I don't think getting the police involved would benefit anyone in this situation. In fact, I'm thinking it might be best if we keep this incident just between us. Wouldn't you agree?"

"What?" Marcus Sr. asked as if the suggestion had caught him off guard. "Well, yeah, I suppose... but what about him?"

"Don't worry," Marvin said, his voice louder, as if he was looking down over the balcony edge. "My staff can take care of him."

Jason wondered just how many times Marvin had said that phrase since his arrival at the Chance Hotel, and why the manager seemed so comfortable saying it.

"Of course we would comp your stay..." Marvin continued.

"What?" Marcus Sr. sounded distracted again. "Yeah, yeah sure." Jason heard Marcus Sr.'s footsteps travel back into room W414. "Marcus? Are you okay? I would've shot that man dead sooner, but I had to aim wide so I wouldn't hit you. He didn't hurt you, did he?"

Sam tapped Jason on the shoulder and waved him in. Despite the pain radiating from every part of his body, Jason actually wanted to hear how the conversation upstairs played out. However, he couldn't hear Marcus Jr.'s response to his father and even Marcus Sr.'s voice was becoming difficult to understand as he moved further away, so Jason did as he was instructed and joined Sam and Leila in the hotel room, crawling on all fours to get there.

"Where are we?" Jason asked as Sam shut the balcony doors.

"Room W314," Leila replied. "When Katie realized the odds weren't swinging in your favor, she decided we should implement some redundancies to bolster the probability of your survival. Luckily for you, this room was vacant."

"Luckily?" Jason asked weakly. He wasn't sure he wanted to

know how his luck would have fared if the room had been occupied. "I guess I should be grateful... though I suspect death would be a lot less painful right about now."

"We'll sneak you out to Heinrich as soon as we can," Sam told him. "You did good up there."

Jason looked to Leila, who gave him a reaffirming nod and smile. That didn't help with the pain, but it sure did make him feel better. A few moments later, the door to the room emitted a beep and Olga slipped inside carrying an arm full of towels and washcloths. She went straight to Jason and dropped the towels on the ground next to him before crouching to examine his wounds.

"You look like livestock waiting to be put out of its misery," Olga said in her unique accent as she assessed Jason's injured ear. She produced a bottle of water from her pocket, soaked a washcloth, and pressed it where the bullet had clipped away some cartilage. "Hold that," Olga instructed as she guided Jason's hand to the washcloth. Olga then proceeded down Jason's face, then his neck, and to his chest, where she fingered one of the bullet holes in his kevlar vest. "I see your package came in handy."

"Yeah, thanks for that."

Olga continued down to Jason's side, the side that had seared ever since Marcus Sr. fired that final bullet. "Tsk, tsk, tsk... not too pretty over here." Olga grabbed one of the larger towels and wet a section. "This is going to hurt," she said in her sing-song way before slapping the towel against Jason's side.

Jason howled as a shock wave of pain shot through him. Sam dashed to his side and cupped a hand over his mouth, while Leila took his good hand and patted it for comfort. Jason contorted his head to see why his left side was causing him so much pain. With Olga's towel in the way, he couldn't see the wound itself, but he could see a growing stain of deep red seeping across the carpet.

"Oh God. Is that all from me?"

"Don't you worry about that," Olga told him. "Olga knows how to clean a little blood."

That hadn't been Jason's primary concern, and yet he took comfort in the fact. The door beeped again, and this time a bruised and bloodied figure strolled in. For a moment, Jason thought the blood loss was starting to take its toll, for the grotesque arrival looked sort of like himself. Had he died in Olga's care and was now seeing the room from the third-person viewpoint of his spiritual form? That didn't explain how he had left the room, or how his body had returned as a zombie...

"Well that was fun," Richard said with his usual undertone of sarcasm.

"What are you doing here?" Leila asked alarmingly. "And why are you still wearing that?"

"I thought it looked good on me," Richard said as he pulled a mask of expandable fabric over his head, revealing his face. "Besides, the boss man took the Roberts back to the lobby."

"Someone else could have seen you," Sam told him.

"Wrong. Someone else *saw* me. Some punk kid roaming the stairwell. He told me I looked sick and asked what comic convention I was heading to."

Leila looked away from Richard, clearly aggravated. The second concierge approached Jason, and it was only then that Jason got a good look at the bodysuit he was wearing. It appeared to be some sort of high-tech spandex. It clung tightly to Richard's body, and its surface glowed softly with the digital image of a splattered body. Up close, the image was highly pixelated, but from afar, those pixels meshed together to create a very convincing facade.

"Pretty cool, huh?" Richard asked Jason. "We keep a pair of them on hand for special situations like this. They're hot as hell to wear, and as you can see, they don't do shit if you get too close to someone. But from a decent enough distance, they get the job done." Richard's suit flickered and went dark, the pixelated glow giving way to unassuming black fabric. "Oh yeah, the battery life sucks."

Jason wondered what such an advanced piece of technology was doing in a place like the Chance Hotel. The notion was fleeting, however, Jason's mind lacking the energy to hold on to any one thought for too long. The door beeped again, and this time Marie entered. It was turning into quite the party in room W314. A party... or a wake, Jason considered. Either way, everyone but him was in store for a load of fun.

"How is he?" Marie asked.

Jason's vision was getting a bit hazy, but he was pretty sure both Leila and Sam responded with questionable shrugs.

"Well, it might please you to know that things are going as smooth as can be expected down in the lobby," Marie informed everyone. "The Roberts have agreed to keep things quiet and Marvin is currently working to put other guests at ease. There were significantly more witnesses than we had hoped..." Marie trailed off, as if she had more to say about that, but didn't want to harp on the negatives. "Anyway," she then continued cheerfully, "Katie has reassessed the situation and puts our chances for success at eighty-nine percent."

"Why only eighty-nine?" Jason asked. He was going to be really pissed if there was a one-in-ten chance he had risked his life for nothing.

"Katie always leaves a percent off to account for unpredictable outcomes," Marie explained. Her voice then turned timid. "The other ten percent is because she doesn't trust you to stay out of trouble before the Roberts depart."

In any other circumstance, Jason would be mad at the assumption. But given his actions since arriving at the Chance

Hotel... "That's fair," he said.

Marie turned her attention to the other staff members. "So, we're just waiting for the Roberts to clear the lobby. After that, we'll get Mr. Chance here back to the break room-" She stopped mid-sentence. "Mr. Chance? Mr. Chance, are you all right?"

Marie's voice had grown distant and the world around Jason had turned dreamy, blurring and pixelating like Richard's bodysuit as the members of the staff drifted out of focus. The washcloth Jason had been holding to his ear grew too heavy to support, so he let it and his arm fall to his side. Then he felt his body toppling over, only there was no floor to catch him. Instead, there was only air, and then darkness.

Chapter Forty
You're One Of Us Now

Jason's eyes fluttered open. He was lying on a soft mattress, staring at the ceiling of his hotel bedroom. No, not his room... but definitely a room in the Chance Hotel. Maybe W314? But then, why was he in bed? Jason's body provided the answer to that question as a dull ache radiated through it. There was also an odd ringing in his ears, as if someone had tapped a tuning fork and it refused to quit. Jason heard someone scurrying about nearby, barely audible footsteps moving from one side of the bed to the other, then the sound of rummaging through a bag. Jason could tell by the sound that it must have been a thick bag, maybe leather or canvas, rather than a thin plastic bag like the ones used for groceries. He tried to turn his head to see, but discovered it had been restrained by some sort of brace.

"Ah, you're awake," Jason heard Heinrich say. "Things were a little rough early on, but I think I've got you stable now. My apologies for the unsanitary conditions, but you were too far gone to move you to the break room."

"How long have I been out?"

"About six hours."

The doctor's wrinkled face floated into view. He hovered inches from Jason's nose while performing a perfunctory visual examination of his patient. He then unbuckled a strap to each side of Jason's head and removed the brace that had been limiting Jason's movements. Jason slowly rotated his stiff neck to loosen its joints, then sat up straight, wincing in pain as an invisible knife sliced into his left side.

"Easy," Heinrich instructed. "If you rip your stitches, it will set back your recovery by another half day."

Jason looked down at his shirtless chest, which was marked

by a deep bruise larger than a grapefruit. The bullet that left the bruise would have likely killed him had it not been for the kevlar vest. And if that bullet hadn't gotten the job done, the one that slammed into his back definitely would have. Though he couldn't see it, Jason assumed an equally ugly bruise was on display there. Jason's eyes traveled down to his injured side. Heinrich had taped a thick stack of gauze about the size of a standard piece of paper over what Jason could only presume was a pretty serious wound. The gauze was bright white, suggesting Heinrich had recently replaced it. Jason looked to the nightstand, where Heinrich had piled used, blood-soaked gauze into a collection bin.

"I lost that much blood?" Jason asked.

"That?" Heinrich nodded toward the bin. "No. You lost that in the past two hours. You lost about ten times that before I got you stabilized."

That would explain the light-headedness Jason had been feeling since waking. He checked his injured ear and found that Heinrich had heavily bandaged it. Heinrich had also replaced the splint on Jason's bruised hand, which, in light of everything, seemed like the least of his bodily concerns.

"Three times per day," Heinrich grumbled as he gathered medical tools from whatever procedures he had performed on Jason.

"What?"

"Three times per day," Heinrich repeated sternly. "I told you to ice that hand three times per day. How many times have you iced it?"

"Ummm…"

"Exactly." Heinrich shoved a handful of tools into his leather bag. "Typical patient. Thinks he knows everything. What's the point of having a doctor if you aren't going to listen to what he has to say?"

"I was... busy?" Jason offered as a half-ass excuse.

"That's what they all say," Heinrich replied. "But what would've happened to you if I had been too busy to race over here before you bled out?" Heinrich waved a dismissive hand. "Ah, never mind. It's a waste of breath giving you orders."

Wow, Jason thought, Heinrich's infinite wisdom knew no bounds. Despite it being a waste of breath, however, Heinrich dutifully relayed a set of wound care protocols to Jason as he finished collecting his tools. Just as he was wrapping up, the bedroom door opened, revealing Marie carrying a covered room service tray.

"How's our hotel hero doing?" She asked cheerfully.

Jason forced a smile. "I thought I was the villain in this little scenario."

"Well, I guess sometimes they're one and the same," Marie replied. She showed off the room service tray. "Chef Terrance asked me to bring this over. He figured you'd be hungry after being unconscious for so long."

Wait... how did Chef Terrance and Marie know that Jason had woken up? Jason was pretty sure Heinrich hadn't called or messaged anyone. He looked around for a camera or some other monitoring device, but a throbbing sensation pulsed on one side of Jason's head, halting his search. His brain was telling him *slow down, cowboy; you've done enough speculating for one hotel stay.* Heinrich closed his bag and excused himself, taking the bucket of bloody gauze with him to make room on the nightstand for Jason's meal.

"Chef apologizes that this may not be up to his usual standards," Marie said as she set the tray down. "He's under strict orders from Heinrich to provide you with a more medically friendly diet today."

"I'm sure it'll be the best damn hospital food I've ever eaten," Jason told her. He had intended sarcasm, but deep down, he knew it was probably true.

Marie smiled and unpacked the contents of the tray, which contained a spring mix salad topped with grilled chicken, sliced almonds, and strawberries. Accompanying it was a small container of vinaigrette, barely a tablespoon by Jason's estimate. Chef Terrance had also sent a whole grain roll- no butter- and a glass of freshly squeezed lemonade that Jason assumed contained no added sweetener. Jason checked that he was still wearing pants before swinging his legs around to angle toward the food. He hadn't heard the door to the hallway open over Marie's preparations and was surprised when Leila walked in a moment later. Marie turned her face away from Jason so he couldn't see the expression she made to Leila, but whatever it was caused Leila's face to lightly blush.

"You look like you're recovering well," Leila said in what appeared to be a distraction from her physical reaction. "Want an update on what you've missed?"

"Sure," Jason said as he dug into his salad.

"Marvin got the Roberts to agree to keep your little incident hush hush. Once they calmed down, they grabbed a late breakfast. From what we saw, there appears to be a change in the way Marcus Sr. treats his son already. Katie says it's still too early to know for sure. Apparently, she's still concerned that you're going to find a way to screw things up."

Jason swallowed. "Get Heinrich to lift his healthy food order, and I promise not to leave this room."

"Oh please," Leila shot back with a dubious glare. "I eat that salad all the time. It's amazing."

She had him there. It was an excellent salad.

"Anyway," Leila continued, "it turns out gunshots are kind of loud, so Marvin's been glad-handing the rest of the guests with room comps and assurances that the hotel is safe."

"No one called the cops?" Jason asked.

Leila squinted as if he had landed on a touchy issue. "We have ways of cutting off communication with the outside world when needed."

Jason thought about his own troubles contacting his wife and daughter. Had the staff of the hotel intervened in his attempts to communicate as well? Jason's head throbbed again... probably best not to think too hard about it.

"So," Leila said, "aside from you turning out to be the most expensive guest this hotel has ever had, I'd say all is going pretty well."

"I bet Marvin wishes he had just let me check out yesterday when I asked."

Leila shrugged with one of those famous Chance Hotel non-answer gestures. She then joined Jason on the bed, sitting closer than he had expected her to. "You sure you're doing okay?"

"Physically or mentally?" Jason asked with a chuckle.

"The former. I think I have a pretty good sense of the latter already."

Jason feigned hurt. "Hey hey, I'm in the room." He then looked down at his beaten body. "Don't get me wrong; the pain isn't pleasant. But, if Marcus Jr.'s life is the better for it, then I guess it was worth it." Jason caught Leila staring, and she quickly averted her eyes. "I do have one question for you," he said, letting her off the hook for the stare. "Benji was supposed to be on standby to intervene if things got out of hand in room W414. Given how things played out..." he motioned to the gauze on his side. "Where the hell was he?"

"It's not a good look, is it?" Leila replied. "In Benji's defense, he felt you had everything under control right up to that moment, and by then you were falling over the railing, so there wasn't much he could do."

Jason eyed her suspiciously. "It's okay to admit Benji doesn't exist."

Leila laughed, but it was a defensive laugh. "He exists! I swear. And if you had really needed him, he would have been there to save you."

"Mm-hmm."

"Okay, look," Leila said with determination, "maybe you can meet him tonight."

"Tonight?"

"Yeah, we're having a party in the courtyard after we shut down for the evening, remember? Hotel staff and friends of staff only." She gave him a sly smile. "You're technically both, so I guess that means you're invited."

"Both, huh?" Jason questioned.

"Well, you're part of the inner circle on what we do around here, and you did just risk your life helping us complete a difficult intervention. So when you think about it, you're one of us now... unofficially, anyway." Leila shot him a wink.

"Obviously," Jason agreed with a teasing smile. "I was questioning the 'friend of the staff' status. Does it need to be a majority of the staff? Because if so..."

"It only needs to be one member of the staff," Leila clarified. "And in your case, it happens to be the only staff member who counts."

Jason raised his brows. "Why is that?"

"Because it's my party," Leila replied. "Today's my birthday."

"No shit?" Leila caught Jason off-guard with the revelation. He had assumed the party was a celebration of the successful intervention. Then again, he should've known better since preparations were already underway the night before and Katie still hadn't made a call on the intervention's outcome. "Well happy birthday!" Jason said, trying not to sound like an uninformed jackass. "Sorry you had to spend it dealing with..." He waved his hand over his injured body. "This."

"It wasn't so bad," Leila admitted. "I mean, I was supposed

to have the day off, but *someone* had to go and interfere with our original intervention..."

"Sorry about that," Jason said sheepishly.

Leila giggled. "I'm just giving you a hard time. No one takes days off at the Chance Hotel. We've got nothing better to do."

"Nothing better?" Jason asked. "What about having a social life?"

"This hotel *is* my life," Leila countered.

"Well, what about spending time with family?"

"The people that work here are my family."

"Relaxing?" Jason tried.

"We have a spa if I need it." Leila had a response for everything.

Jason took a sip of his lemonade to buy time to think before presenting his next argument. What was something the Chance Hotel didn't have? Good food? Check. Comfortable beds? Check. Lively people? Check. Chess-playing ghosts? Check. The occasional shootout? Check. Then it hit him.

"What about travel?" He challenged. "What about seeing new places, outside of this hotel?"

Leila was quick to respond again. "I sometimes watch the travel channel during my lunch break."

"That's not the same thing," Jason countered.

Leila smiled, but it wasn't a happy smile. Behind it hid some sort of remorse, or hesitation, or- Jason couldn't put his finger on it. He didn't want to upset Leila today, on her birthday of all days, so he gave her an out.

"Maybe we can talk about it some other time."

"Maybe so," Leila said, the tension in her face instantly easing. "So, the party starts at ten. Luckily for you, Katie calculated a ninety-nine percent probability that the Roberts will retire early tonight to get rest before they hit the road tomorrow, so you should be clear to leave this room by then."

"And between now and then?" Jason asked.

Leila stood and retrieved the television remote. "We have over one hundred channels. I'm sure there's something on that you'll enjoy." She tossed Jason the remote and headed toward the door. "Stay inside and away from the windows. Oh, and don't even think about hitting up the vending machine down the hall. I'll make sure we send up room service around dinnertime."

"Another salad?"

"Or grilled salmon and steamed veggies," Leila countered playfully. "I'm sure Chef will shake it up for you." She reached into her jacket pocket and pulled out a deck of playing cards. "I also brought you these, in case you get really bored." She tossed the deck onto Jason's bed and flipped on her heels. "See you tonight!"

Jason watched Leila walk away. Yup, he thought with an uncontrollably stupid smile, he would see her tonight.

Chapter Forty-One
One Percent

To say Jason spent the remainder of the afternoon and early evening on the verge of going stir crazy would be an understatement. His television might have had access to over a hundred channels, but weekday afternoons weren't exactly prime programming hours. Game shows, soap operas, and nature documentaries were the highlights among a crowd of syndicated reruns and twenty-year-old movies. There were also only so many games of solitaire one person could take before going a little loopy. Jason considered sneaking back to his own room, but it wasn't like his entertainment options were any different there. He also considered making a clandestine trip to the twenty-first floor foyer to continue his chess game. *What's the harm?* The miniature devil on his shoulder asked. *Getting caught by Marcus Sr., that's what,* the miniature angel on his other shoulder replied. *Or worse, proving Katie right about you screwing things up.*

It was the latter argument that kept Jason at bay. He found a channel marathoning black and white episodes of *Maverick* and used the deck of cards Leila had left him to host an imaginary poker game. Jason secretly hoped that whatever ghosts resided in the hotel might join him for a hand or two, but they were no-shows, so Jason wound up playing each imaginary opponent's hand in turn. Luckily, he got several breaks from the monotony of his solitude. The first was when Heinrich stopped back in to check his wound and vitals. He uttered a few grumbles about Jason having no business dealing playing cards with his injured hand, then gave Jason the okay to be discharged for Leila's birthday party.

Whew, Jason thought. To think he might have had to disobey

an order if Heinrich hadn't signed off on his release...

The second break from monotony came in the form of Olga, who, aware that Jason was forbidden from visiting the vending machine, brought the vending machine to him. She had retrieved one of everything so Jason could choose his favorites. Jason picked three items: a roll of mini donuts, a bag of salted peanuts, and a soda. He asked whether Heinrich approved Olga's delivery, but she shushed him and insisted that no one else needed to know. Jason then offered to reimburse Olga for the snacks, reminding her that the 'no charges' rule was between him and the hotel, not him and her personal funds. But Olga shushed him on that as well, waving a hand over her collection of goodies and insisting that no else needed to know about them, either.

Jason tore through the donuts and chugged the soda shortly after Olga left. He saved the peanuts in case he got the munchies later. At first, he almost felt guilty about eating the junk food, certain that Heinrich would spank him with a tongue depressor if he ever found out. But then Jason's third interruption arrived. This time it was one of the waiters from the restaurant, sent by Chef Terrance to deliver Jason's dinner. True to Leila's prediction, the dinner comprised sautéed catfish, a side of steamed carrots, and a soup that appeared to be ninety percent broth. Like all other dishes Chef Terrance prepared, it was delicious, even despite its low salt content. It also alleviated Jason of any guilt he felt about gorging junk food for an appetizer.

Jason's final break from going stir crazy was Richard, who knocked on the door, waited for Jason to hobble out of bed to answer it, tossed a hangar of clothes with an attached bag of shoes to him, and continued on his way without muttering more than three words. As with everything else Richard-related, Jason had to settle for being grateful for the thought.

The bathroom of room W314 was stocked with everything Jason needed to make himself presentable. He showered as best he could, brushed his teeth, combed his hair, a put on the clothes Richard had so kindly delivered. They were a perfect fit, which on the one hand surprised Jason, and on the other came as no surprise at all given the Chance Hotel's knack for knowing things about people it had no business knowing. Getting ready took Jason over twice as long as it would have had he not been injured, but he still finished with time to spare before the phone in his bedroom rang.

"Hello?" Jason answered.

"Good evening, Mr. Chance." It was Katie, sounding about as chipper as a dead squirrel. "The Roberts have gone to bed. There's a ninety-nine percent probability that you can leave your room without causing serious harm."

Jason wasn't sure what she expected him to take from that. "So... does that mean I can come to the party now?"

"That depends," Katie replied. "How much risk do you place on the one percent differential between coming out and staying in for the night?"

"Umm... one percent of risk?"

The phone was silent, but Jason could hear the disdain oozing out of Katie following his response. It took her nearly a minute to continue speaking.

"Just be extra careful on your way down," Katie finally said. "Maybe stick to the stairwell. You seem to like those."

"I'll do my utmost," Jason said mockingly.

Again, silence. Then a click and a dial tone. Jason winced at the sound, wondering with what probability Katie could rescind his invitation to the party. He wouldn't wait around to find out. Jason turned off the television, pocketed the deck of playing cards as a souvenir, and bid farewell to his criminal hideout. He silently prayed never to see it again. Jason did as Katie suggested, taking the stairwell to ground level, and was cautious as he made his way from the guest wing back to the main building.

Jason noticed that Giorgio and Reggie had already replaced the door glass that had shattered under the impact of one of Marcus Sr.'s bullets. Apparently fixing that was a higher priority than fixing a broken sprinkler head. Jason also spotted several new paintings mounted to the walls of the hallway down which he had initially dragged Marcus Jr. Jason suspected they had been hung to hide bullet holes, but he wasn't going to waste time confirming the suspicion. The lobby was dark and empty, just as it had been on Jason's first night in the hotel, though there was one stream of light angling in from the restaurant hallway.

Jason ignored it and proceeded to the courtyard door. So far, so good, he told himself, reaching the door without encountering any other guest. Jason then exited into the courtyard, where his ears were met with casual party music and his eyes spotted colored lights beyond the trees of the winding path. Jason followed the lights and sound until he reached the patio, which had been resurrected from its dormant state and now pulsed with the energy of at least fifty people. Some were mingling or eating around the umbrellaed tables, whose umbrellas were now open and whose tops had been draped with royal blue and white tablecloths. Some were plating food at the stone island, which had been adorned with a feast of meats, cheeses, fruit, chips, dips, and desserts. The rest were bopping to the beat of the music on the deck overlooking the woods. Colored spotlights and floodlights swung over their bodies, making their shadows dance across the trees.

Jason tried to blend in as he searched for the birthday girl. It wasn't overly difficult, for most of the party attendees appeared to be hotel guests. Luckily, that meant he fit right in. Unfortunately, it also increased the likelihood that someone would recognize him as an armed assailant. Had Katie already factored that in to her one percent screw-up probability? Jason tried not to think about it, for the more he did, the more he felt like he was being stared at by every guest he passed. Paranoia feeds paranoia, he reminded himself. Just let it go.

Jason spotted Richard meandering near the dance floor. The concierge wouldn't have been Jason's first choice to mingle with, but he was the only staff member Jason had seen so far, so Jason headed his way. More stares greeted Jason as he pushed through a roadblock of guests near the island buffet. Jason told himself that this was a dumb idea, that he should just go back to his room and hunker down until he was certain the Roberts were long gone from the Chance Hotel. What was the point of coming to the party, anyway? It wasn't like Leila was going to swoon over someone she had just met two nights earlier. Even if she did, it wasn't like Jason had a life near the Chance Hotel. His life was hundreds of miles away, near his daughter. What did he expect to come of this course of action? What-

"Mr. Chance!" Jason heard a female voice yell over the music. "Mr. Chance, over here!"

Jason peered through the ever-flowing sea of people and spotted Marie near the door to the event hall. She was bouncing on her toes and waving to get Jason's attention. Standing near her were Marvin, Katie, Sam, the valet with the happy pill addiction, Giles, Richard- wait, Jason caught himself. He turned back to the dance floor, but there was nothing but empty air in the space where Richard had previously stood. Jason then swung his gaze back to the group of staff near the event hall to confirm Richard was indeed among them. How the hell had he moved so fast? Richard supposedly never moved fast.

"Mr. Chance!" Marie yelled again, as if unsure whether Jason had heard her.

She looked like she might pee herself if Jason didn't get over there, so he shrugged off the mystery of Richard's superhuman speed and made his way to the group of familiar faces. Marie ran up to Jason as he approached and greeted him with an exaggerated hug. Despite having referred to him by his formal name, her actions made it clear that this was a social, rather than professional, event. Marie escorted Jason to the rest of the group, most of which greeted him with smiles.

"Glad to see you made it, Mr. Chance," Marvin said sincerely, unclear whether he was referring to Jason's arrival at the party or survival of the day's events. "Heinrich tells me you're healing well. Is there anything we can do for you?"

Jason figured it was pointless to ask for an early checkout now, so he kept his response simple. "Nope. I'm good."

Marvin patted his shoulder. "Glad to hear it."

Jason made eye contact with Katie, who was standing next to Marvin. "I trust your walk over was uneventful?" She asked with forced casualness.

"Completely," Jason assured her.

Even though Katie had dressed down for the evening and was clipboard-free, Jason could see her checking off a box in her head and updating her mental math for Jason's successful departure from the guest wing. He decided to let her be.

"So, where's the birthday girl?" Jason asked Marie.

Marie pointed toward the dance floor, where Leila and Olga were boogieing with one another among the dancing guests. Leila looked stunning, her body wrapped in a tight black dress that sparkled subtly when the light hit it just right, her hair down and flowing as freely as her spirit. Olga looked... like Olga, just with an added dose of uncharacteristic fun. Jason smiled as he watched the two of them letting loose, something inside sparking a sense of happiness and belonging, though he didn't know why.

"They're something, aren't they?" Marvin asked as he joined

Jason's side.

Jason quickly rolled his drooling tongue back into his mouth. "Y-yeah," he stammered. "They're fun to watch."

"Mmm," Marvin replied with an air of knowing that he let simmer for nearly a minute. Then he said, "Little Leila there is the crown jewel of this hotel. She gives this place energy. She motivates us to be the best people we can be." Marvin turned toward Jason to steal his attention from the dance floor. "I don't know why she's taken to you the way she has, but you're scheduled to check out of here tomorrow. Please don't do anything to hurt her... before or after. We're very protective of our jewelry at the Chance Hotel."

So there it was. Marvin had confirmed what Jason had suspected since his arrival, that Leila was giving him special treatment, and that his attraction to her wasn't one-sided. Like Marvin, Jason didn't understand why he and Leila had developed such a bond, either. All he knew was that it was real, and that it was powerful. That also made it dangerous. Jason was still a married man, even if by legality only. And he was checking out tomorrow, going home to his daughter miles away from the Chance Hotel and its crown jewel. What had Marvin called her? Little Leila? That was the first time Jason had heard the nickname. He wondered whether he'd ever learn the story behind it.

Jason looked back at Leila on the dance floor, at her warmth and radiant beauty, so close, yet so far away. "I won't." He promised Marvin. As a gesture of good faith, Jason retrieved the master keycard from his pocket. "Speaking of protection," he said as he held the keycard out for Marvin to take, "I guess I no longer have a need for this."

Marvin eyed the keycard, then Jason, an odd smile inching across his lips. "You keep it for now. I'm off duty. You can turn it in when you check out tomorrow."

And with that, Marvin walked away. What game was he playing now? Jason wondered. Was this the same man that had wrestled him for possession of Richard's keycard on the thirteenth floor? Why would he suddenly entrust Jason with so much power? Was it to tempt him into breaking more hotel rules? No, Jason told himself. He had misjudged Marvin. The manager wasn't malicious, as Jason once thought. He was, as he always claimed to be, just someone trying to help, even if that help was offered in the strangest of ways. But if that was true, what help would the master keycard serve Jason now?

A loud sizzle distracted him from his thoughts. Jason's eyes darted to the lighting truss above the dance floor, where one of the mechanical spotlights had begun spewing blue sparks as something within it shorted out. A moment later, the light emitted an enormous pop and went dark. Though it had startled everyone nearby, the light didn't appear to have caused any damage. But, as the party resumed, Jason's eyes remained fixated on its burned metal shell, which hovered twelve feet over Leila and Olga's heads. Jason had seen that flickering blue-ish light before, only from twenty-one floors away, on the night that started it all. It was the night of his arrival, the night he may or may not have witnessed a giant sea creature attack another guest in this very courtyard. Maybe it meant nothing. Maybe it was just a coincidence that the lights looked so similar. And yet, as Jason returned his gaze to the master keycard in his hand, he couldn't shake the feeling that something ominous was still waiting for him- no, still *standing between* him and his imminent departure from the Chance Hotel.

Chapter Forty-Two
There Were No Transformers

"Can I get everyone's attention, please?" Marvin's amplified voice asked as feedback squealed from the courtyard speaker system.

It had been over an hour since the spotlight malfunctioned, but to Jason, it felt like it had barely been twenty minutes. He had opted to tuck his foreboding feelings away and to instead enjoy the evening. Marie hadn't eaten yet, so she provided a pleasant distraction by asking Jason to escort her to the island buffet. While there, he prepared a plate of finger food for himself, which incited scolding eyes from Heinrich upon returning to the congregation of staff. Then the evening proceeded like a typical party. The staff included Jason in their conversations, which ranged from absurd- Richard and Giorgio arguing about whether it took seventeen or eighteen strides for guests to traverse from the front door to the main elevator bays stood out among these- to comical- apparently Olga had walked in on a couple engaged in much naughtier activity that raiding a vending machine earlier that day.

In true party fashion, the conversations were anything but serious. There was no talk of day-to-day business, nor interventions, nor Jason's situation, nor his observations about chess-playing ghosts, sea monsters, and the thirteenth floor. In fact, if he didn't already know better, Jason would have thought the staff of the Chance Hotel were completely normal people. The strange thing was that he actually enjoyed hanging out with them. Leila had told Jason he was one of them, and she and the rest of the staff were doing their part to support that claim, even if his honorary membership was unofficial.

"I'd like to say a few words," Marvin continued. He was

speaking into a microphone at the front of the dance deck. "I hope everyone is having fun this evening. I don't know about the rest of you, but we at the Chance Hotel have been quite busy these past few days. A night of great food and even better company was exactly what we needed." A handful of guests clapped and whooped to show their agreement. "Speaking of my staff, could I get a round of applause for the excellent job they do around here?"

Marvin waved his hand toward the congregation of staff, and a spotlight swung to illuminate them. The rest of the attendees erupted in genuine cheer, as if Marvin had opened the door to hands that would have joined in synchronized clapping even without his prompting. Jason was inadvertently caught in the spotlight, and it would have been too awkward to try to slink out of it, so he stood among the staff, receiving cheers meant for them, hoping that the bright light would wash out the redness that had filled his cheeks.

"And that brings me to our birthday girl," Marvin said. "Leila, can you come up here for a moment?"

As great as the evening had been, the one aspect that had fallen short of Jason's hopes was his interaction with Leila. He had wanted to spend more time with her, if not in private, then at least in one-on-one conversation. But she was the birthday girl, and the other guests were here for her, so when she wasn't out on the dance floor with Olga, she was bouncing around the crowd, mingling as the star of the show was wont to do. Now she emerged from that crowd and joined Marvin on the deck, an uncharacteristic shyness about her, as if she would have been happy to remain out of the spotlight.

"Leila," Marvin said once she was by his side, "We couldn't do the things we do around here if it wasn't for you. You're our lighthouse in the dark, guiding us to shore when the waters get stormy. You're an inspiration, bringing joy to so many people's lives. Most of all, you're part of this family, and we wouldn't have it any other way." Marvin paused as Leila wiped fresh tears from her eyes. Then he spread his arms as if to conduct the orchestra of guests. "So, without further adieu..."

Marvin kicked off the first few words to Happy Birthday, and everyone joined in, guests, staff, and Jason alike. The crowd parted mid-song, creating an aisle down which Chef Terrance rolled a decorative food cart containing a five-tier birthday cake that could rival even the most elaborate of wedding cakes. The cake was a fondant and buttercream caricature of the Chance Hotel, and atop it were three dazzling sparklers burning so brightly they left streaks across Jason's vision. Chef Terrance parked the cake near the island buffet and Leila came down from the deck to give him a bear hug. When the singing concluded, Leila picked the sparklers from the top of the cake, closed her eyes to make a wish, and dunked them in a tall glass of water. The crowd cheered, and Leila nodded and waved in gratitude.

"I hope everyone saved room," Marvin said over the speakers. "Dig in!"

A couple of waiters joined Chef Terrance. The three of them surrounded the cake, carefully cut out slices, then topped them with colorful syrups from a handful of Chef Terrance's fraudulent liquor bottles. Terrance gave Leila the first slice. Then it became a free-for-all, with him and the waiters passing out subsequent slices indiscriminately. The staff initially stayed back while hotel guests lined up for their shares of cake, but apparently expectations for the dessert were so high that two minutes was all the head start they would give before joining the line too. Between his junk food appetizer, dinner, and finger food, Jason thought it was best not to indulge further, so he held down the congregation spot along with Katie and Giles.

"You're full too?" He asked Giles to avoid making chitchat

with his other best friend.

"No," the older man said with a peaceful smile. "I've just been around long enough to know there's always some left. I'll get my piece once the crowd thins a little."

Jason could identify with that. He wasn't the type that enjoyed rubbing shoulders with others, though probably for different reasons than Giles. He watched the guests who had received their cake. They were so happy to be here, almost as if they weren't customers and this wasn't a business...

"Giles?" Jason asked. "What's the deal with these people?"

"What do you mean?"

"Leila told me the party was for hotel staff and friends of staff," Jason explained. "But these are just... guests. They're people who have paid money to stay here between destinations. Where are the friends of the staff? Hell, where are Leila's friends?"

Giles smiled wisely. "Mr. Chance, are you a guest of this hotel?"

"Well, yeah, but-"

"And do you consider yourself Leila's friend?"

Jason stammered. "I- I'd like to think so."

"So then, the two aren't mutually exclusive, are they?"

Of course they weren't, Jason thought. But his was a unique situation. "I've seen behind the curtain," he reminded Giles. "I took part in one of your interventions. From what I understand, that's not common for a guest to do. I don't think you're making an apples-to-apples comparison."

Giles patted Jason's back the way a parent might pat a proud but naïve child. "You only peeked behind *one* curtain of the Chance Hotel. Besides, there are other ways to take part in an intervention other than being a willing participant."

Jason wasn't sure which of those two pieces of information his brain wanted to process more. Had Giles just admitted that interventions weren't the only secret Marvin and the staff had been keeping from him? It sure sounded like it, but what did that mean? Which of Jason's other suspicions were closer to the truth than he realized? Or did the other secrets have nothing to do with him? Was Giles just making a generic statement to clue Jason in that he might not be as special as he thought? But that led to the second piece of information. Jason had been a willing participant in the Roberts' intervention. So had the staff. The only people who had taken part in the intervention without being willing participants were...

Jason looked at the crowd of guests again. He had already noted how happy they appeared to be here. Now he noticed how happy they appeared to be in general. There wasn't a scowl, frown, or other look of sadness among them. It was as if the valet had slipped them some of his stash. That, or-

"All of these guests went through interventions?" Jason asked.

Giles nodded affirmatively.

"But I thought the guests had to be kept in the dark."

"Did you keep Marcus Jr. in the dark?" Giles asked in response. "It's true. Some guests need to be shielded from the fact that we've interfered with their lives. Take Marcus Jr.'s parents, for example. But others need to be looped in for the intervention to succeed. And even when they don't need to be looped in, some figure it out on their own after the fact."

"But wouldn't that just piss them off?" Jason argued. "I know I wouldn't be too happy to find out someone interfered with my life."

"Even if you knew that interference was for the better?"

There was something about the way he asked the question... Jason couldn't put his finger on it, but it was as if Giles wasn't speaking in a purely hypothetical sense. "I just- I think I would feel manipulated."

"Oh they do," Giles confirmed. "It's a natural human reaction. But then they realize we did it with their best interest in mind. Eventually they see the positive results from our interference, and those feelings of manipulation change into feelings of gratitude."

"So everyone here tonight..."

"Has had their lives changed for the better as a result of a past stay at the Chance Hotel," Giles finished for him. "More specifically, as a result of Leila's part in their interventions. It's why they come back to celebrate her birthday. It's why they consider her their friend."

Jason's eyes found Leila. She was finishing her piece of cake as she chatted with an elderly couple and a younger man Jason guessed was their son. She was so graceful in her movements, so beaming with energy, and yet so gentle in her interactions. Jason felt like he could watch her forever and never get bored. But his brain wasn't willing to let him do that, at least not tonight.

"Giles? Am I the target of one of your interventions?"

The old chauffeur stared at him with those solemn, sunken eyes. "That's something you'll have to determine for yourself, Mr. Chance."

Jason appreciated Giles' honesty, even if that honesty delivered another quintessential Chance Hotel non-answer. "Tell me this then," Jason said, taking advantage of the honesty while he had it. "Are there really a bunch of overloading transformers near the hotel?"

Giles looked at him inquisitively. "Not that I'm aware of." The chauffeur's eyes then traveled to the cake cart, where the line of waiting guests had dwindled. "Ah, that's my cue. It's been nice speaking with you, Mr. Chance."

"Likewise," Jason told him.

As Giles left to claim his piece of cake, Jason meandered to the now empty deck. He paused under the lighting truss and stared up at the blown-out spotlight. So the transformers weren't real... which meant the loud cracking sounds Jason heard his first night there weren't real either. He had simply dreamed them while asleep in the tub. But if that was the case, why did Katie lie to cover them up? Unless the cracking sounds were real, but the source was something she wanted to keep hidden. The source of the sound... the source of the blue light... the source of the water that dripped from the athletic couple's luggage... they were all pieces of a jigsaw puzzle Jason couldn't quite fit together.

The party would be winding down soon, but while the hotel staff were distracted, there was something Jason wanted to check. He quietly slipped through the crowd and back to the winding courtyard path. Jason headed to the end of the path where he had seen Richard or Benji or whoever the hell it was mopping the concrete. He kneeled and examined the first sprinkler head. Jason was no landscaper or groundskeeper, but he had common sense and a decent dose of logic to go with it. If Giorgio or Reggie had swapped out a broken head in the past forty-eight hours, there should be some way to tell it apart from the others. Or so Jason thought. As far as he could tell, every sprinkler head from the start to the halfway point of the path looked the same. Not just the same, in fact, but dirty, with caked-on soil and debris as if they had been there for a long time. There were no transformers. There was no broken sprinkler head. But there were thunderous cracks, and there was water, and unless Jason truly was dreaming, there was that blue light.

What was he missing? Why didn't the pieces fit? Marvin and his underlings certainly weren't going to tell Jason. The only other people who possibly knew the truth were the athletic man and Sarah. Jason had already accepted he'd never be able to hack the hotel computers to locate their contact information, but he also remembered the invoice Marvin asked him to sign when he tried to check out the previous day. Maybe there were other physical records maintained by the Chance Hotel. Maybe there were records he could access with nothing more than a master keycard, a master keycard like the one Marvin had entrusted him with for the night. Maybe Jason could get his hands on the athletic couple's contact info after all. Of course, that meant taking a one percent risk. One percent that he might stumble across Marcus Sr. or Judy. One percent that he would screw up everything he and the staff had sweat and bled to accomplish that day. Jason looked down the winding path, back toward the party, where every administrative staff member would remain occupied for at least another five to ten minutes. One percent... versus an opportunity Jason might never get again. The devil on his shoulder materialized in a puff of smoke. *What's the harm?*

Chapter Forty-Three
Chance, Jason

The lobby was dark except for the glow of dying flames in the great room fireplace. Jason hadn't recalled seeing a fire when he came down for Leila's party, so he scanned the lobby from end to end to ensure no guests, especially not Marcus Sr. and Judy, were loitering in the shadows. Seeing no one, he then crept toward the check-in counter, wincing with every step as his new shoes squeaked against the freshly polished floor. The thought crossed Jason's mind that Richard had purposely given him squeaky shoes to prevent the very type of sneaking around in which he was engaged right now. But that was crazy, right? The hotel staff couldn't have predicted a spotlight would malfunction during the party, nor that the malfunction would reignite Jason's curiosity about the sea creature he dreamed of nights earlier. Then again, there was a reason the Princess of Probabilities expressed concern that Jason would end up undoing all the good they had accomplished that day. Maybe she hadn't predicted the specific series of events that had occurred that evening, but predicted that, at a minimum, *something* was likely to unfold that would entice Jason back to his naughty ways.

It was too late to worry about that now. Jason cleared the main floor and made his way to the employee side of the check-in counter. He tapped the keyboard of Marvin's computer and was greeted by a password prompt. For the hell of it, Jason typed 'password123' into the prompt and pressed enter. The computer responded with a red letter warning about five attempts remaining before it would trigger a time lock. For the fun of it, Jason typed 'Marvin is an asshole' into the prompt. The computer informed him that his five attempts had just been reduced to four. Jason could have continued until the computer locked itself down, but he knew he had a better chance of getting struck by lightning before guessing the correct password. Besides, his inner child had already gotten its laugh, so Jason abandoned the computer.

Trying to make as little noise as possible, Jason thumbed through the random stacks of paperwork that sat nearby. Most of it was hotel business unrelated to guests' personal information: inventory counts of supplies, room cleaning schedules, sign-up sheets for a spa Jason hadn't taken advantage of, and so on. One stack was entirely devoted to Katie's checklists, which apparently varied by day of the week and time of day. Another contained a series of unsigned invoices with tomorrow's date on them. Were these the guests scheduled to check out? If so, Jason's invoice should be among them. He wondered if it carried a zero balance as Marvin had promised...

"Hey, it's the vending machine guy again!" A teenage voice yelled from across the lobby.

Jason looked up and spotted a silhouette of a head sticking up from the couch opposite the fireplace. Two more silhouetted heads popped up to flank it. Though Jason couldn't make out their features, he knew from their number and their designation of him as 'the vending machine guy' that it must be his favorite teenage trio. They had caught him red-handed.

"What are you doing back there?" The girl of the group asked. "That area's for employees."

"I-" Jason dug deep for an excuse, and the words Leila spoke to him in room W314 rose to the forefront of his mind. "I am an employee," he said, then added, "unofficially, anyway."

The teenagers slithered off the couch like a pack of vipers moving in for the strike. Their features were still shadowed against the flickering flames of the fireplace, yet Jason could feel the suspicion in their stares.

"If you work here, then why'd you need our help with the vending machine?" The pretzel boy asked. "You some kind of pervert?"

Yes, Jason thought. Yes, I am, if that's what it takes for you to leave me alone. He kept the thought to himself, however. "I just wanted a second opinion. You were the first people I saw."

"I think he's lying," the bubble gum bandit said. "You lying, mister? If you're not lying, show us some ID."

The trio was close enough to Jason that he could finally see them clearly. They looked ready to pounce at the first wrong word, and Jason was relieved that the check-in counter still stood between him and them. What did they think they were? Marvin's undercover security detail? Actually, Jason considered, it wasn't all that crazy of a possibility... He patted himself down, pretending to search for the employee identification he knew he wouldn't find while formulating his next excuse.

"Ah!" Jason exclaimed when he felt the master keycard in his pocket. He took it out and held it high for the teenagers to see. "Is this good enough ID for you?"

The teenagers looked at him as if he was the biggest moron they'd ever encountered. They then held their own keycards up for Jason to see.

"We've got those too," the girl told him. "Just like every other guest."

Right, Jason thought. The master keycards and guest keycards looked identical. He glanced around and spotted the brown door that led to Marvin's office and the break room. Did Marvin's office have a digital lock on it? Jason couldn't remember, but it was worth the risk.

"Fine," he told the teenagers. "Check this out."

Jason opened the door to the employee hallway and waved the teenagers forward. They followed, but maintained a noticeable distance. Probably just enough to prevent Jason from grabbing them and dragging them into his pervert sex dungeon, Jason thought. He saw that Marvin's office door was closed, and yes, there was a digital card reader next to it. Jason showed off his master keycard again as if he were a magician telling them to keep their eyes on the trick. He then said a silent prayer that Marvin hadn't coded any special exemptions into his master keycard and passed it over the reader. The reader beeped positively, and the door to Marvin's office unlatched. Jason breathed a sigh of relief and pushed it open.

"Whoa…" the pretzel boy said. "He really does work here."

"He doesn't just work here," the bubble gum bandit said as he pointed to the 'office' placard above the door. "He's the manager!"

The girl elbowed him. "He's not the manager, stupid. That other old guy is the manager."

"Well, maybe they're both managers," the bubble gum bandit argued.

Jason saw a golden opportunity. "That's right. We're both managers. And unless you want me to charge your room for the time you've wasted tonight, I suggest you get out of here."

The teenagers stopped bickering.

"Not cool," the girl said before dramatically exiting the hallway.

"Yeah," the bubble gum bandit agreed. "Not cool, vending machine manager pervert guy." He left in a slightly less dramatic fashion.

The pretzel boy lingered for a moment. "I'm kind of hungry. You think I could get another dollar for some snacks?"

"Out," Jason told him, pointing a rigid finger.

The boy groaned and followed his friends, closing the hallway door behind him. Jason shook his head in silent disbelief, then looked into Marvin's open office. Not much had changed since Jason had been in there earlier, aside from a handful of hotel documents spread across Marvin's desk. Jason flipped on the office light and glanced at the documents. They were uninteresting, mostly signed invoices waiting to be filed and a handful of customer comment cards praising the service they received during their stays. The praise was a little too glowing, so Jason made a mental note to fill out one of his own to bring balance to the force once he was finally free of this hellhole.

Jason moved to Marvin's side of the desk, and his eyes immediately fell to a steel safe nestled under the right-hand drawer. It was about the size of a microwave and looked to be protected by biometrics, most likely a fingerprint, based on the interface mounted to its door. Jason wondered if his daughter's money was in that safe. He also wondered whether it was easier to ride out the night in the Chance Hotel or to manufacture an unfortunate accident that would separate Marvin's hand from its thumb. Or was it his index finger? Hell, maybe Jason should take the entire hand just in case.

Jason chuckled at the notion, then let it drop. He and Marvin were on good terms for now. Jason had to trust the manager would come through on his promise about the money. He moved on from the safe and opened the drawer that hung just above it. Inside was a series of hanging folders, each with a tab that displayed the last name, then first name, of what Jason presumed were hotel guests. He opened a few folders, flipped through the contents within, and put them back. Each was similar, containing a photocopy of the guest's driver's license or other identification, some basic contact info, a list of preferences regarding room, food, activities, etc. It was the homework Leila had told Jason the hotel performed on its guests, only there was one guest whose folder was notably missing. Jason checked in the clusters of names beginning with both C and J, but he still couldn't find his own.

Jason shut the drawer and looked around again. He hadn't come here seeking information about himself. He wanted to get in touch with the athletic couple, and there was a strong possibility that Jason could do just that if he took the time to flip through each of the folders in Marvin's drawer. But he didn't know if he had that much time before the party wrapped. More importantly, he really wanted to know why his folder wasn't among the rest. Leila had already admitted he had one, so it wasn't simply an omission of non-existence. Jason thought back to his office conversation with Marvin earlier. Marvin had produced a list of incidental charges during their chat. Only that list hadn't come from the drawer of folders through which he just finished rummaging.

Jason yanked open the drawer on the other side of Marvin's desk. The list of charges was laying right where Marvin had put it, and beneath the list was a folder that had been segregated from the rest. Jason checked the tab:

Chance, Jason

Bingo, he thought. He grabbed the folder and the first thing he noticed when lifting it onto Marvin's desk was that it was about ten times the thickness of any other folder he had seen. Jason flipped it open and, just like every other folder, found a photocopy of his current driver's license right on top. The strange thing was, Jason didn't recall giving Marvin his driver's license, much less allowing the manager to copy it. Behind the photocopy was Jason's contact info, including his correct cell phone number and home address. After that was a sheet labeled 'Known Relatives,' which contained the names, current addresses, current phone numbers, and relation to Jason of every living and deceased family member he had.

"What the hell?" Jason muttered aloud.

Behind the list of relatives was a paper-clipped stack of bank and investment statements, the foremost ones showing the nearly two hundred thousand dollar reduction in his daughter's savings balance. After that were medical records, an education and employment history, a series of recent photographs taken God-knows-when, and a mathematical assessment from Katie that was mostly gibberish, but ended in a bold '96%.' This wasn't basic homework, Jason thought with an angry shiver. It was a goddamned dossier of someone who'd been targeted. But for what purpose?

"Please put that back," Katie said from the open office doorway.

Jason broke from his immersion in the documents and glared at the Queen of Quality Control. "What the hell is this?"

"It's hotel property," Katie said calmly. "Now please return it where you found it."

"This isn't property!" Jason screamed, flailing a stack of pages in front of her. "This is my life!"

If Katie was shaken, she didn't show it. "Yes, it is, Mr. Chance. It's everything you were before you arrived at our hotel. And it's everything you'll be when you leave here tomorrow. It's a collection of facts. Nothing more, nothing less."

Jason swapped the pages in his hand for Katie's gibberish calculation. "Yeah, well, what about this? This isn't fact. This is speculation. *Your* speculation. What's ninety-six percent?"

"I'm afraid I can't tell you that," Katie replied robotically. "The moment I do, that number plummets significantly."

"Why?" Jason inquired. "Am I the target of one of your little interventions? Is this the probability that you can successfully turn my life around? If so, I've got news for you. Nothing you people do to me here will change my life. You think I don't already know how much I screwed it up? You think I don't know that it's on me to fix it?"

Katie remained silent, which made it hard for Jason to keep yelling at her.

"I don't need any of you to fix me," he said defeatedly as he set the calculation down. "I just need to go home to my little girl." He dropped into Marvin's chair and closed his eyes.

"You will," Katie told him. "At eleven o'clock tomorrow morning, you can sign your zero-dollar invoice, collect your daughter's money and whatever interest Marvin promised you, and be on your way. No one here is going to stop you." Katie collected the documents from Jason's dossier and stacked them neatly before returning them to Marvin's drawer. "You've come so far, Mr. Chance," she then said in an uncharacteristically sincere tone. "And you're so close to the end. You knew we did our homework on you; you just didn't know the extent. But ask yourself, what difference does that make now? What does it change?"

"Nothing," Jason said, though inside he felt like it had changed everything.

"That's right," Katie told him. "So maybe you should just get some rest and put what you saw in here behind you. Tomorrow, it won't make any difference."

"You aren't going to tell Marvin about this?" Jason asked dubiously.

"Of course I am," Katie snapped. "You just cost me half an hour of sleep while I file a formal incident report." She paused and forced herself to loosen up. "But I'll note in my recommendations that no follow-up action is necessary. That is, *if* you can behave and spend the rest of your night in your room."

Jason considered her offer. He had already been physically exhausted; now he was emotionally exhausted, too. And he certainly wasn't looking to screw up his scheduled departure. "It's a deal."

Katie let a pleased smile slip from her lips. She then escorted Jason out of Marvin's office, back to the lobby, and all the way to the main elevator bays. Apparently, she wasn't taking any chances. Jason's usual elevator arrived within seconds of calling it, and Jason obediently stepped on for the ride back to his floor.

"When I leave tomorrow," he asked, holding the elevator doors from closing, "will you tell me what the ninety-six percent was about?"

Katie blinked as if she were debating whether to respond, then spoke with carefully chosen words. "When you leave tomorrow, the uncertainty will have already resolved itself." She then added "Goodnight, Mr. Chance."

Katie had signaled that she was done with their conversation, so Jason let the elevator doors shut for what he hoped would be one of the last rides he ever took.

Chapter Forty-Four
If You Say So

When Jason arrived at the twenty-first floor, he immediately examined the chessboard to see what move his ghostly opponent had played during Jason's lengthy absence. Sure, Jason had promised Katie he would stick out the rest of the night in his room, but considering he seemed to be the only guest staying on the twenty-first floor, Jason felt he had a strong argument for the entire floor being his true room. What was the harm in trying to salvage his chess game while everyone else got some shut eye?

His opponent had shifted its queen, and Jason felt the walls of checkmate closing in. If he continued to play recklessly, he would soon lose. If he played too safely, he would probably still lose. Jason needed to do what he did best: introduce a little risk into the situation. He could move one of his pawns into a strategically beneficial position, but doing so would open his own queen for the taking. Jason didn't want to sacrifice his queen while already in a losing position, but he needed to advance that pawn to have any shot at pulling off a win. He considered heading back downstairs to ask Katie to run a probability assessment on the move, but tabled the idea in the interest of keeping the peace and preserving her sanity. Jason slid the pawn forward.

"Your move," he told the inanimate opposing army.

His ghostly opponent had yet to apparate with Jason present during his stay, and Jason had no reason to suspect it would change its behavior now. He made Katie proud and returned to his room. It was the first time Jason had stepped foot in his home-away-from-home since discovering Giorgio and Reggie had 'borrowed' his daughter's money, and boy, it felt good to be back. Room W314 might have been his salvation from death, but room 2101 was his salvation from all of life's other troubles. Jason loosened his shirt, kicked off his shoes, and fell back on his bed, sinking into the cool mattress as every muscle in his body relaxed. He told himself not to fall asleep yet, that he needed to conclude his chess game before morning so he could check out without leaving his opponent hanging. But it was late and Jason's eyes were heavy. The wounds he had sustained during the day's events throbbed, but Jason's mind tuned them out as it drifted to another world...

A knock on the door jolted Jason from his half-asleep state. Who the hell was looking for him right now? Probably Katie making sure he was holding up his end of the deal, Jason deduced. But what if it wasn't? What if it was Marcus Sr. and Judy again? What if they had returned to Jason's room to confirm his undead corpse wasn't shuffling around inside, mindlessly plotting another attack on their boy? That was silly, Jason knew, and yet not impossible in this looney bin of a hotel. Jason waited for the knock to repeat, but it didn't. He sat up, slipped on his shoes, and quietly made his way to the door.

Jason put his ear to the slab of wood, but heard no sounds coming from the other side. He cracked the door open and saw no one waiting to greet him. Jason then peered up and down the hallway, but it was empty. Curious, Jason strolled back to the elevator foyer, and sure enough, his ghostly opponent had already played a responding move. But was it really a ghostly opponent? Jason now wondered. After all, what kind of ghost knocked on your door to get your attention? Then again, this ghost could freely move chess pieces, so it was only logical that it could make physical contact with Jason's door, too.

Jason analyzed the move. Surprisingly, the ghost hadn't taken Jason's queen. Instead, it had moved its remaining bishop to a square that, on the surface, seemed to hold little tactical advantage. Even better, the move left an opening to the ghost's king. Had Jason just caught a break? He considered every possible play he could make. It made no sense for Jason to check his opponent right now; the ghost could easily slip out of any checking move and more than likely take one of Jason's pieces in the process. But...

Jason slid his queen to a position just past center-board. One move. That's all he needed now. Survive one more move, and he could checkmate his ghostly competitor. Jason had gone from underdog to favorite-to-win in a span of about ten minutes. Adrenaline pumped through him, so he returned to his room unafraid of falling asleep, then sat on the living area couch and waited for the next knock. It took less than five minutes. Jason hurried to the door and flung it open, ready to seize his victory, and nearly ran over Leila, who was waiting in the hallway with a covered dinner tray and teapot.

"Whoa!" He exclaimed, both catching himself and steadying the objects in Leila's hands. "Sorry about that. I- I thought you were someone else."

Leila squinted at him. "You were expecting company?"

"N-No," Jason stammered, "I was- I mean-" He pointed toward the hallway, but his words failed him. "You know what? Never mind." He shook his head with a chuckle and cleared the way for Leila to enter the room. "Come in."

Leila walked past Jason and set the tray and teapot on the coffee table. "I noticed you didn't have any cake at the party," she said as she revealed a piece of the moist dessert, "so I brought you a slice."

Jason shut the door and smiled. Leila had been so busy being a social butterfly, he wondered how she even noticed what he had or hadn't eaten. Somewhere inside, he also wondered *why* she had noticed. "You're not supposed to be on the clock on your birthday."

"It's after midnight," Leila told him. "Birthday's over." She staged the cake with utensils and a napkin, then poured Jason a cup of tea. "I assume you're getting antsy about checking out tomorrow. This will help you sleep."

"I've heard about the sleep benefits of sugar and caffeine before," Jason said dryly. "One out of like... every thousand doctors highly recommends them."

Leila laughed, nearly spilling the tea as she poured her own cup. "Okay," she said. "You've got me there. Maybe I was just looking for an excuse to come talk. I don't know how much time we'll have in the morning." She sat on the couch and patted the seat next to her. "Katie told me you found your file."

"Yeah," Jason said as he joined her. "Can't say I was too happy about that."

"If it makes you feel better, neither was Katie," Leila said with a friendly grin. "You've created a lot of paperwork for her these past couple of days."

"Good."

Leila sipped her tea nervously. "I supposed you haven't been too happy about a lot of things around here since you arrived. I just want you to know that we never meant to hurt you... in any way. We really are good people, if a bit unconventional. I guess-" She took a deep breath. "I guess I just don't want you to think ill of us once you're gone."

Jason nodded. "As long as Marvin comes through tomorrow, I won't."

"He'll come through," Leila confirmed. "He was never going to keep your daughter's money. He just needed leverage to get you to hang around for another day."

"So he could use me for your intervention?"

"I don't think so," Leila said. "The staff came up with that plan, not Marvin."

"Then why?" Jason asked. "None of you wanted me here. I

saw it on your faces the night I arrived. And it certainly didn't make financial sense to keep me here, so what's his game?"

Leila's eyes sunk at Jason's accusation, as if he had nailed their feelings to a tee, but also as if those feelings had changed between his arrival and now. "I think..." She hesitated as she searched for the words that could ride that fine line between honesty and secrecy. "I think maybe he wanted you to give the hotel a chance. To see what we were all about."

Jason considered her theory. It made sense in light of all that had transpired. Marvin had given Jason significant leeway to explore the hotel, even those parts of the hotel that were off-limits, despite Katie having predicted the trouble Jason doing so would cause. Then Marvin allowed Jason to save Marcus Jr. from that freezer, effectively ruining their intervention, even though he could have stopped Jason at any point to salvage their operation. Marvin also permitted Jason to participate in the replacement intervention, despite it being a rarity to involve hotel guests. And now Marvin had entrusted Jason with a master keycard, the golden ticket that gave Jason unfettered access to the candy factory known as the Chance Hotel. In hindsight, it was as if everything Marvin had done contributed to some grander test Jason was unknowingly expected to complete.

He looked at Leila and asked her directly: "Am I the target of an intervention?"

Leila shook her head. "No."

"We made a deal not to lie."

"It's not a lie," she said, staring at him with those warm and caring eyes. "Maybe you will be one day. Who knows? But today, I can tell you with no uncertainty that your life is not being intervened with. Not by us, anyway."

Well, that shot down that suspicion, Jason thought. And yet, he couldn't shake the nagging feeling that something more was at play. He just couldn't figure out what that something was. "I appreciate you telling me the truth." Jason took a bite of Leila's birthday cake and moaned in ecstasy at the explosion of fruity flavor in his mouth. "Oh, God. Chef Terrance made this?"

"Every year," Leila said.

Jason took another bite. "This is the best cake I've ever eaten."

"I know, right?"

Jason moaned his way through several more bites as Leila watched with a giant grin. When he finished, Jason wiped icing and crumbs from his lips with the napkin, then looked at Leila, the sugar rush energizing him to nail her with another question. "By the way, you told me I was going to meet Benji at the party. Guess who didn't show?"

Leila cocked her head as if to say *this again?* "He was there. Apparently, you didn't make an effort to find him."

"I saw guests. I saw staff. I *did not* see Benji."

"I saw Benji about two minutes before you arrived," Leila told him. "You're blind."

"That's a really nice way to talk to a gunshot victim," Jason said, feigning a frown as he placed a hand on his wounded side.

Leila wouldn't bite. "If you're such a victim, then maybe you should stick around another week so Heinrich can look after you. I could even arrange for Benji to deliver balloons to your room so you can stop claiming ignorance about him."

"I'll pass."

Those words cooled the back-and-forth between them.

"So you're really going to check out tomorrow, huh?" Leila asked with a hint of repressed sadness.

"I have to get back to my daughter," Jason told her. "If it wasn't for her... I don't know."

Leila forced a smile and took his hand. "You'll figure it out." She then stood. "Well, I should get some sleep. Not everyone around here had the luxury of a six-hour nap today." She winked playfully at Jason. "Besides, I don't want to accidentally sleep through check-out time tomorrow. You never know what might happen."

So many thoughts flew through Jason's mind. The inquisitive part of him wondered what Leila had meant by her check-out comment, but the more emotional parts of him overshadowed it. Especially the part of him that wanted to grab Leila and pull her into his arms, to do whatever it took to keep her with him until sunrise. Jason felt ninety-six percent sure she would resist him, but that four percent just might be worth it. However, another part of Jason knew Leila had to go for that very same reason. Maybe they would cross paths again, in this life or the next, but now wasn't the appropriate time. A true gentleman at heart, Jason walked Leila to the elevator. He caught her glancing at the chessboard as they passed, but she didn't say anything until she was in the elevator car waiting for the doors to close.

"It's not looking too good over there."

Knowing he only needed one move to win, Jason replied confidently. "I've got it under control."

Leila shrugged with doubt. "If you say so." Then, as the elevator doors shut, "See you tomorrow, Mr. Chance."

Jason didn't have time to reply. For all the wrongs that elevator had done to him since his arrival, cutting off his final late-night goodbye with Leila was, without a doubt, the worst. Luckily, it sounded as though his ghostly opponent had made its next play, which meant Jason was a single rook move away from at least one hotel happy ending. He returned to the board and put a hand on his conquering rook, then paused as his opponent's previous play set in. One move. One move was all Jason needed, and now his ghostly opposition had denied him even that. Jason had been checkmated. He had been so caught up in achieving victory that he had left his king vulnerable to attack, and now the game was over.

Jason supposed it was only fitting. In the morning, his time at the Chance Hotel would be over, too. All games were coming to an end. But what if there was more to Jason's loss than that? What if his loss on the chessboard was a premonition of one more loss yet to come? What if it was confirmation that, yes, something ominous did stand between Jason and his planned departure? Maybe it was a giant sea creature that glowed with blue light. Maybe it was a member of the staff, or a guest. Maybe it was nothing at all. One way or another, Jason thought as he toppled over his king in admission of defeat, he would find out soon enough.

Chapter Forty-Five
It Was Never About My Name

Jason woke with an odd sense of peace and calm. The sun was shining, there wasn't a giant sea creature attacking guests outside his window, and there wasn't even a hint of panicked shouting or gunfire outside his door. Jason took his time showering and shaving, then packed what few belongings he had removed from his suitcase, and bid farewell one last time to room 2101. He headed to the elevator foyer and checked on the chessboard. The pieces of both armies had been reset to opening positions, Jason's ghostly opponent readying the board for its next victim. Jason briefly thought about initiating a rematch, but decided against it. He didn't need one more temptation to keep him in the Chance Hotel.

His elevator arrived, and Jason gave it a friendly hello before boarding with his bags. The ride down was strangely uneventful. There was no flickering light show, and there were no electrical pops. There was also no random impact from an unseen force, for which Jason was extremely grateful. Jason wondered why the elevator's behavior had suddenly changed, but as with the chessboard, he decided to let it go. Jason Chance, Amateur Detective, was officially retired. He arrived at ground level and exited, turning to give his favorite death trap a departing salute. Then Jason's eyes drifted upward to the metallic gold 'no charges' slogan affixed to the wall. Something struck him about the slogan, something he hadn't considered before now, but Jason couldn't quite put his finger on it.

"Mr. Chance!" A cold, stern voice yelled from across the lobby. "Mr. Chance, what are you thinking?!" Katie stomped toward him like a schoolteacher about to take the paddle to a misbehaving student. "You can't be out in the open like this!"

"He's fine," Richard said lazily from a half-slouched position at the concierge podium. "Sam's got eyes on the Roberts' room. She'll warn us when they're on their way down."

"I don't care," Katie snapped before turning her focus back to Jason. "Chef Terrance left a breakfast platter for you in the break room. I expect you to stay there until the Roberts have left this building!"

"Yes, ma'am," Jason said with an exaggerated schoolboy grin.

He rolled his luggage toward the employee hallway behind the check-in counter. The doorman, who Jason still had yet to meet, intercepted him and offered to bring the luggage to Jason's car. Apparently, Marvin really was planning to let him check out today. All this time, Jason had been thinking it was a coin flip.

"Good morning, Mr. Chance," the manager said as Jason passed. "I trust you slept well?"

"Best night ever," Jason replied.

He proceeded through the brown door behind the check-in counter, followed the hallway to the break room, and sat before a warm plate of bacon, eggs, and hash browns. If there was one thing Jason would miss about this place- aside from Leila- it was Chef Terrance's food. He wiped the plate clean, downed a glass of orange juice, and nursed a cup of coffee as he waited for Her Highness to give him the all clear.

"Pssst."

Jason turned to find Leila standing in the break room doorway. She looked radiant as always, though Jason noticed a bit of red puffiness around her eyes, a rare crack in her joyful exterior. Regardless, seeing her made Jason's heart flutter, and for a moment he second guessed whether checking out was truly the right thing to do.

"The Roberts are leaving," Leila said in a hushed voice.

"Come see."

She led him to the lobby door and gently cracked it open. Ten feet away, Jason saw Marcus Sr., Judy, and Marcus Jr. chatting with Marvin at the check-in counter. Marvin was expressing his repeated apologies for the trauma the Roberts endured during their stay, and both parents were being receptive to his gesture. Jason tried to get a read on the relationship between Marcus Jr. and his dad, but the family was so focused on Marvin that there wasn't much to go on. Then-

Jason's breath caught in his throat. Marcus Sr. had placed a hand on Marcus Jr.'s shoulder. Marcus Jr. reached up, just as he had the morning of the first intervention, as if ready to pry the hand away... only he didn't. Instead, Marcus Jr. placed his hand on top of his father's and gave it a loving squeeze.

"Holy shit, it worked," Jason whispered.

His words caught Marcus Jr.'s attention, but the boy maintained Jason's secret presence. Judy signed the Roberts' zero-balance invoice. All three family members shared friendly words of departure with Marvin, and then they walked away from the counter and toward the revolving front door. Marcus Jr. still had one hand wrapped around his father's, and with the other, he snuck Jason a thankful wave. Jason smiled and waved back, then let the lobby door close.

"You were right," he said to Leila as he fought back unexplainable tears. "It was totally worth it, bullet wounds and all."

Leila smiled proudly. "I know."

"You can come out now, Mr. Chance," Marvin called from the other side of the door.

Jason and Leila emerged into the lobby, where Marvin waited at the check-in counter and Katie stood nearby, scribbling ferociously on her clipboard.

"Well?" Jason asked.

Katie scribbled for another moment, then circled something at the bottom of her page and clicked her pen. "There's a ninety-eight percent probability that Marcus Jr. and his father will go on to live much happier lives. It would have been ninety-nine if you hadn't clued Marcus Jr. in on our plan."

Sure, but then Jason might be dead. He felt his life was worth the one percent cost. "You couldn't just... I don't know, round up for us? You had to leave a small possibility of failure in there?"

"It's called the Chance Hotel," Katie replied firmly, "not the Guarantee Hotel. There's always a possibility of failure."

She stormed off. Jason assumed it was so she wouldn't have to humor additional comments or arguments from him. Or maybe she just really needed to use the bathroom. She was exhibiting signs of grumpiness often associated with constipation. Oh well, it was *probably* the last time Jason would ever see her... though he figured he needed to leave some leeway for failure in his calculus.

"So," Marvin said, "are you ready to check out?"

Jason moved to the customer side of the counter and Marvin presented him with a detailed invoice. It contained an itemization of every charge Jason had racked up during his stay, both for normal hotel usage and for his mischievous incidentals. But every price had a line struck through it, and the total at the bottom read zero dollars.

"No charges, as promised," Marvin said.

"No charges..." Jason repeated under his breath. He thought about the slogan above the elevator, then about what Katie had said about the hotel name, and suddenly his revelation from earlier became clear. "It was never about my name, was it?"

"Excuse me?"

"No charges for the chances," Jason said. "It was never about my name." Jason looked at Leila. "You told me. The night we had dinner. You told me that there were no charges for the chances here. I didn't put it together at the time… you weren't talking about me. You were talking about the opportunities you give people, the second chances to make their lives better."

Leila smiled warmly. "Chef said you were a fast learner."

Jason turned back to Marvin. "This is why you made me stay."

Marvin nodded. "I wanted you to see that we weren't just some run-of-the-mill hotel. I wanted you to see that we have a purpose; that we serve the greater good."

"Why?"

Marvin took a nervous breath. "Because you're a Chance. And I know you don't understand the significance of that right now. Maybe you never will. Then again, maybe…" He shrugged.

Jason studied Marvin's face. "That's all the explanation I'm going to get out of you, isn't it?"

"You are a fast learner," Marvin replied. "Now, if you'd kindly turn in your key…"

Jason debated pressing Marvin for more information, but he knew it wouldn't lead anywhere, so he dug his room key from his pocket and set it on the counter.

"And your other key?" Marvin asked.

Jason smiled. He had hoped Marvin would forget about that one. He pulled out the master keycard and set it next to the other.

"Great, now all that's left is for you to sign your invoice and to be on you way." Marvin motioned toward the front door. "Bobby has your car out front. It's freshly waxed and has a full tank of gas."

"Who?" Jason asked.

"Bobby," Marvin repeated, drawing Jason's attention to the overly friendly valet that greeted him on the night of his arrival.

"Oh!" Jason said as the valet waved to him ecstatically. "You know, I never got his name. I've just been referring to him as the happy pill guy."

Marvin chuckled. "I believe I had a similar nickname for him when I first arrived here."

Something about Marvin's words struck Jason as odd. Bobby seemed so young, and Marvin seemed so much older. There was no way Bobby was already working here whenever Marvin was hired. Maybe the manager was just humoring Jason.

"Your suitcase is in the trunk and your shoulder bag is on the passenger seat," Marvin said. "Feel free to count it when you get out there, but all of your daughter's money is inside. Plus the interest I promised, and another twenty thousand dollars I threw in for the physical toll we put you through."

"I thought your generosity had limits," Jason poked.

"And I'm pretty sure I told you that management has some discretion," Marvin jostled back. He handed Jason a pen. "Unless there's anything else..."

Nope, Jason thought, there is definitely nothing else. Or was there? He looked at the invoice awaiting his signature, then at Marvin, who was playing it cool, but Jason suspected was actually quite nervous to see what he would do. Then Jason looked at Leila, at the tears streaming down her cheeks. Why did this feel like it would be goodbye forever? He could come back, right? He could return once his life was in order and give this thing with Leila a fair chance... Only Jason knew that wasn't true. He didn't know how he knew, but deep down, a voice told him that his signature on that invoice would signify the last time he ever saw the Chance Hotel.

"Is something wrong?" Marvin asked.

"No, I-"

Thwomp!

Jason heard the distant noise, and it instantly triggered an unforgettable memory. His eyes darted to the elevator bays.

Thwomp!

The doors to his usual elevator shook with the noise. Richard, who was the closest staff member, bolted upright and looked at Marvin with obvious concern.

Thwomp!

Jason saw the same concern wash over the faces of Marvin and Leila.

Thwomp!

Marvin's walkie-talkie squealed from his pocket. "Boss?" Sam said with alarm. "Boss, we have a problem!"

Marvin lifted the walkie-talkie to his mouth. "What is it, Sam?"

Thwomp!

"Something's gone wrong on thirteen," she replied. "You'd better get up here!"

A shrill screech filled the lobby, forcing Jason, the staff, and the other guests to cover their ears. The screech had come from the elevator bays, yet was loud enough to pierce eardrums. When it subsided, there was silence.

Marvin looked back and forth between Leila and Richard. "Go. Now!" He then turned to Jason. "Unfortunately, Mr. Chance, this is where our goodbye must come to an abrupt end. Safe travels, and... I do hope you'll visit us again one day. When you're ready."

With that, he raced after Leila and Richard. Jason watched the three of them gather at the elevator bays and push the call button. Marvin continued his conversation with Sam over the walkie-talkie, and though Jason couldn't make out their words, both sounded frantic. It's not your problem, Jason told himself. Just sign the damn invoice and get out of here.

Thwomp!

That sound... that sound was Jason's problem. It had come for him on the very elevator Marvin, Leila, and Richard were about to board. What the hell was it?

Thwomp!

Jason looked down at the invoice and at the pen shaking uncontrollably in his hand. Just sign it, he told himself. Just sign it and go home. Your daughter's waiting for you. Let the hotel staff deal with whatever craziness they've got locked up on the thirteenth floor. It doesn't matter anymore.

Thwomp!

The sound jolted Jason's eyes away from the invoice. He saw Katie watching him from the far end of the check-in counter, her own pen and clipboard at the ready. Jason recalled her words: *When you leave tomorrow, the uncertainty will have already resolved itself.* Ninety-six percent, Jason reminded himself. Ninety-six percent probability... of what?

Thwomp!

And what was causing that noise? Why did the lights in the elevator flicker? Why did they make electrical pops? What exactly was on the thirteenth floor?! Jason closed his eyes tight. Ninety-six percent...

Thwomp!

There were too many unanswered questions. Jason Chance, Amateur Detective, doesn't leave unanswered questions. And Superhero Chance doesn't let his friends run toward danger while he turns tail in ignorance. Jason dropped the pen without signing the invoice, swiped his keys from the countertop, and dashed toward the elevator bays. He caught the doors just before they closed, forcing them back open, and was met by the confused stares of Marvin and his concierges. Jason half-expected Marvin to tell him to take a hike, that he wasn't welcome on their adventure to the thirteenth floor. Instead, Marvin nodded his head toward the space in front of him.

"Well, get in if you're coming."

Jason hopped aboard. He could feel his chest about to

explode, and he knew pools of fear-driven sweat were collecting on his exposed skin. He wanted to keep it together better than this. He wanted to put on a brave face, to head toward danger with confidence and gusto. But the truth was, he was about ready to shit himself.

Chapter Forty-Six
This Is So Much Worse

Inside the elevator, Marvin waved his master keycard over the blank placeholder button for the thirteenth floor. In response, the button illuminated, ready to be pressed. So that's how that works, Jason thought. He watched, as he had done so many times before, the number on the elevator's digital floor reader tick higher. Only this time, the number would actually stop at thirteen instead of bypassing it altogether. Jason felt honored to witness such a rare sight.

Thwomp!

The car shuddered with the impact of the unseen force.

"You don't think that's-" Richard started to ask.

"No," Marvin cut him off.

"It really sounded like-"

"It's not," Marvin cut him off again. "It can't be."

As firm as Marvin's words had been, Jason sensed uncertainty in his voice. He glanced at Leila, and she motioned for him to let it go. It made sense. If Marvin wouldn't entertain Richard's comments about the source of the noise, he certainly wouldn't entertain Jason's, either. Jason checked the floor reader. Nine... ten... They were almost there. Since Jason had been last to get on the elevator, he was naturally first in line to get off. It occurred to him that Marvin may have been so agreeable to invite him on their journey because the manager wanted a human shield between him and whatever waited on floor thirteen. Jason told himself that was just his nervousness talking, but then again, the idea had merit...

Ding.

They had arrived. The elevator doors opened to a dark foyer. It reminded Jason of his own, only this one contained no chessboard, nor any comfy recliners. It did have quite a collection of cobwebs, though, and Jason was pretty sure he spotted movement on several of them. He stepped out of the elevator and made room for the others to disembark. Then Jason's eyes fell to the adjacent hallway, that oddly twisted take on a regular hotel floor. Its crooked lanterns flickered just the way he remembered, and for a moment Jason thought he could hear them whisper his name, its syllables floating from the hallway on a light breeze.

Jason's trance was broken by another eardrum-piercing shriek that forced him and the hotel crew to their knees as they tried to muffle the noise. When it passed, Marvin was the first to rise, his face determined as he stepped into the twisted hallway.

"Sam?" Marvin called out.

"We're down here," she responded from the other end of the hall. "By the stairwell!"

Marvin set off into the darkness. Leila and Richard helped Jason back to his feet, and the three of them followed. Jason had almost forgotten about the weird spacing between doors on this floor. It threw off his sense of distance as he proceeded farther and farther from the elevator foyer, which his brain unhelpfully reminded him was also farther and farther from a hasty retreat.

Thwomp!

Jason felt a violent vibration shoot through the walls and floor of the hallway. He also developed a better idea from where the sound was originating. Coming on to the thirteenth floor, Jason had assumed that whatever threat they were going to face would lurk behind the door to room 1301. After all, it was the source of Marvin's fear when Jason almost opened it two days earlier. But the impact noise was being generated from significantly farther down the hallway. Sure enough, a moment later, Jason and Marvin's crew were passing room 1301, which sat dormant, with Leila's vase of yellow flowers still out front.

343

The room was no more a threat than the darkness itself.

Thwomp!

They continued on their way, and soon Jason saw the glow of the run-down vending machine room. He was on familiar turf now, the secret stairwell entrance to the thirteenth floor still far away, but definitely closer than the elevator if he needed a quick escape. The only problem was, according to Sam, and corroborated by his own ears, whatever problem existed on this floor stood between here and there.

Thwomp!

They were close now. The vibrations were getting worse, their shock waves causing support beams within the hotel walls to creak and moan. Soon, Sam came into view. She and Olga were standing near the end of the hallway, nervously watching a rather benign hotel room door. Oddly, Jason's presence seemed to momentarily distract them from their primary concern, with both women shooting him curious looks.

"Fill me in," Marvin said, redirecting their attention.

"We don't know when it started happening," Sam told him. "A guest on fourteen told Olga she couldn't sleep last night because of a repetitive pounding coming from a room below. Obviously, it didn't take us long to locate the source."

Thwomp!

Jason flinched, not only because the sound had startled him, but because it was so much louder now that he was right on top of it. The benign door bowed slightly outward, as if something had rammed it from the inside. Jason looked around at the faces of the hotel staff, whose nerves seemed just as rattled as his.

"I called Giorgio and Reggie up here to inspect," Sam continued. "They said the door's seal had been compromised. They're downstairs looking for supplies to reinforce it, but I don't know if it'll hold until they get back."

Leila approached the warped door and ran her hand along its

surface, as if she had an emotional connection to the faltering slab of wood. "Who would've done this?"

Marvin instinctually shook his head, as if he had no idea who would've vandalized the door. But then he froze and lowered his eyes. Jason could tell Marvin's gears were turning. He was piecing together a puzzle, and when Marvin turned his gaze toward Jason, Jason knew exactly what that puzzle looked like. The day he had trespassed on the thirteenth floor, he and Marvin had gotten into a scuffle at this end of the hallway. When the two men crashed into a door- a very specific door, Jason now realized- Jason had heard a sharp crack. He had assumed the noise came from something in his body. But now...

"Shit," Jason said aloud.

"Yeah," Marvin agreed. "Shit."

Sam looked confused. "Is there something you two need to share with the rest of us?"

Thwomp!

The door bowed again, its surface splintering as it flexed beyond its limits.

Marvin kicked into leader mode. "Olga, get downstairs and round up all the seasoned staff. Tell them to hide until I give the all-clear. That includes you."

"You think it'll come after us?" Olga asked.

"I know it will. That thing doesn't let go of grudges."

Olga nodded and headed into the secret stairwell corridor. Well, Jason thought pessimistically, there goes our best chance of survival against... whatever's coming for us. Richard must have felt the same way, for he slinked in Olga's footsteps.

"Where are you going?" Marvin asked.

"Into hiding," Richard replied in his usual carefree tone. "You know, seasoned staff, don't want to die... all that jazz."

Marvin shook his head. "You're a concierge. You don't get that privilege."

Richard snapped his fingers in disappointment and returned to Leila's side.

Thwomp!

Jason looked back to the not-so-benign-after-all door as more splinters broke away from its surface. He wondered what was in there. It had the hotel staff spooked, so maybe it was a ghost of some sort. Maybe it was his chess playing ghost, and it was just a little cranky because its opponent was checking out. Yeah, right, Jason admitted to himself. The thing behind that door was no more a ghost than he. It had substance. It had strength. It- Jason paused mid-thought. He had witnessed something else with substance and strength during his time at the Chance Hotel. He had witnessed something scary, something violent, something he had convinced himself was a product of Richard's suggestion and his own vivid imagination.

"The sea monster," Jason uttered.

"What?" Richard asked.

"The sea monster," Jason repeated. "That's what's behind the door."

"Don't be ridiculous," Richard said with an eye roll. He then added, "the sea monster is farther down the hall. This... this is so much worse."

"Shut up, both of you," Marvin barked before Jason could process Richard's words.

Thwomp!

This time, much larger splinters of wood shot loose from the door. One of its hinges broke free of the doorframe, and a thin trail of black smoke rose from an exposed corner. Jason watched the smoke twist and curl playfully through the air, never expanding far from its origin, but never dissipating, either. Marvin backed away.

"The maintenance crew isn't going to make it," he said with a quivering voice. "Everyone run!"

The hotel staff complied immediately. Jason was the only dumbass to linger for a moment, still unclear what Marvin was so scared of. Before he could turn to follow the others, he found out, for the compromised door burst open, flinging scraps of wood and metal in all directions as a wall of black smoke poured out of the freshly opened doorway. The monster inside the smoke released another piercing shriek. Jason dropped, his hands to his ears not enough to stop the pain of the noise from stabbing his brain.

When the shriek subsided, Jason saw a bulky, spiked claw emerge from the smoke. It slammed into the hotel carpet, the flooring beneath no match for its sharpness. Strangely, the claw wasn't attached to an appendage. Instead, it seemed like it was attached to a string of thick, gray mist. More claws shot forward, latching onto the walls and ceiling. They were guided by tentacles of mist too, and as the black smoke retracted back into the room from which it had come, Jason saw that those misty tentacles all connected to a misshapen gray cloud hovering less than five feet away from him. Inside the cloud bobbed a collection of bloodshot eyes, and beneath them, several rows of razor-sharp teeth.

"What the fu-"

"Jason, run!" Leila shouted from somewhere behind him.

This time, he got the message. Jason turned and raced down the twisted hallway as fast as he could. The misty monster let loose a deep guttural roar and chased after him. Jason could hear each of its spikes slamming through fabric, linoleum, and wood as it gained ground on him. He could see the glow of the vending machine room ahead. Sam and Marvin were leaning out into the hallway with their hands extended, waiting to pull Jason to safety. Jason just needed to make it about thirty more feet, but his body simply wasn't up to the task. Jason had abused it too much over the past few days, and it didn't have enough gas left in the tank to outrun a supernatural creature.

Marvin and Sam must have seen that Jason was losing momentum, for they withdrew into the vending machine room before he was close enough for them to grab. The next thing Jason knew, he was tumbling forward. No, check that. He was flying forward, having been swept off his feet and thrown down the hallway by the misty monster. Jason crashed into a wall and tumbled to the floor. He then saw a spiked claw smash through the carpet just inches from his face. He smelled what he could only assume was the scent of death as the misty cloud hovered over him. And then, all went dark.

Chapter Forty-Seven
You Can't Stop The Ghoul

"Hey," Jason heard a distant male voice say. "Hey, come on."

He felt something... well, more than one something, to be exact. He felt his body aching from head to toe, complaining about the continued abuse Jason had subjected it to. He also felt a sharp pain in one of his cheeks, and a wetness below that cheek. Had that thing stabbed him in the face? Was he bleeding out on the carpet of the thirteenth floor? If so, Jason hoped the stain would set in quickly, a permanent reminder to Marvin and the staff of his sacrifice in the name of... well, of absolutely nothing. Jason had accomplished jack squat by coming to the thirteenth floor when he could have simply signed his check-out paperwork and been on his merry way. What a way to go...

"Mr. Chance?" Jason heard the distant voice repeat.

This time, the voice was accompanied by a series of light pats on his dry cheek. Afterwards, Jason heard additional voices, each muffled and engaged in heated debate. Then he heard something that sounded like 'we don't have time for this.' A hard slap that stung enough to jolt Jason from his delirium followed. Jason's eyes fluttered open to the sight of Richard, who looked exceptionally pleased with his slapping prowess.

"Am I dead?" Jason asked half-heartedly.

"Not yet," Richard said with a 'welcome back to the party' grin.

He and Marvin helped Jason to his feet. Disappointment washed over Jason as he discovered they were still on the thirteenth floor, surrounded by its disturbing decor and the damage that misty thing had left in its wake. Jason winced as something shifted in his cheek, sending another sharp pain through his face. He reached up and found a smooth and angular object wedged into his skin. Jason grit his teeth and yanked the object free. It turned out to be a bloody piece of broken glass, which Jason quickly connected to the shattered vase of yellow flowers near his feet.

Sam examined Jason's wound. "It'll heal," she said matter-of-factly. "We need to get moving."

Marvin and his staff turned on their heels and started toward the elevator. Jason stood there watching them, his continued curiosities and his desire for self-preservation waging war in his mind. It took less than ten seconds for self-preservation to win.

"I think I'm out," Jason called to the crew.

Marvin froze and looked back. "Excuse me?"

"You heard me," Jason said. "I'm out. You do whatever it is you do around here. But, to put it in words that you'll understand: there is no 'we.' At least, I'm not part of the 'we' anymore. I'm checking out."

Marvin eyed Jason as if he didn't believe the claim. "You had a chance to check out earlier. You chose to come with us instead. What did you think you were going to see up here? Did you think fairies and rainbows were shaking the hotel to its core and blowing everyone's eardrums?"

"I didn't think I was going to see a supernatural creature!" Jason hollered. "I didn't think I was going to see- to see- what the hell was that thing, anyway?!"

"We call it the Ghoul," Richard chimed in nonchalantly, as if sharing the name of a cuddly pet instead of a horrendous otherworldly creature.

"The Ghoul?" Jason asked. "What kind of name is that?"

"Um, didn't you see it close up? Body made of mist, claws that'll punch your heart out, teeth that'll tear your throat open, way too many eyes... it sounds kind of ghoulish, right? What would you have called it?"

"A delusion brought on by hysteria." Jason started for the

stairwell end of the hallway. "At least that's what I'm going to tell my therapist when I get home. Bye!"

The truth was, Jason didn't have a therapist. He had never seen the benefit of unloading his life's troubles into another person's ears. But his stay at the Chance Hotel had certainly changed that mentality. He hustled down the twelve flights of stairs between him and ground level as fast as his body would allow. He emerged from the stairwell in the tucked-away hallway that led to the great room. Jason could hear the noise of distant objects being tossed around by the Ghoul- what a stupid name- much the way it had tossed him. The sounds, and the fleeting screams that accompanied them, seemed farther away than the great room, so Jason crept forward and peaked out.

Sure enough, it looked as if the Ghoul had already passed through this area of the hotel. The floors were pocked with ragged holes where its claws had slammed through the surface. Some furniture was scattered in pieces across the lobby, and the furniture that was still intact was overturned and out of place. There were no guests or hotel staff in sight, but there was no immediate danger, either, so Jason stepped into the open and crossed to the check-in counter. Marvin had been explicit that Jason needed to sign his invoice to complete the check-out process. It seemed silly to worry about such inconsequential things when Jason's entire view of life had just been swept up into supernatural chaos. But Jason feared if he didn't follow the rules, he would never truly rid himself of the Chance Hotel and its never-ending insanity.

The check-in counter had been decimated. Large chunks of wood and granite were completely missing and several sections of the remaining structure were cracked or pocked with claw holes. Electronics, keycards, and shredded paperwork littered the surrounding lobby floor, and Jason quickly realized he would never find his invoice in the mess. He heard muffled conversation growing louder from the hallway to Marvin's office and the break room. It was probably Marvin and the rest of the crew from the thirteenth floor, who would have arrived at ground level before Jason since they took the elevator down. Jason had little desire to get wrapped up in another debate with them about staying versus leaving, so he beelined it for the revolving front door.

Once outside, Jason spotted his car waiting for him, just as Marvin had promised. Also as Marvin had promised, Jason's suitcase and shoulder bag were inside, and in the shoulder bag was significantly more money than Jason had arrived with. He didn't waste time counting it on the spot. It was better for Marvin to have shorted Jason a few dollars than for the Ghoul to show up and shred it the way he had shredded that paperwork inside. Jason went to start the car's engine, then realized he didn't have the key.

"Shit," he mumbled.

Jason looked under his butt and on the passenger seat. He dug through the glove compartment and his messenger bag, then checked behind the sun visor. His keys weren't there. It was possible Marvin had instructed one of the staff to hide Jason's keys to prevent him from leaving. But it was much more likely that Bobby had been so excited to flash Jason his pearly whites one last time that he had the keys when the Ghoul broke loose. Which begged the question: where was Bobby now? As if in response, one of the rear doors opened and Leila climbed in the car. She slammed the door behind her, then leaned forward to stare at Jason with disappointed eyes.

"What?" Jason asked.

"You know what," Leila said sternly. "You told me you wanted to get your life straight. You told me you wanted to stop being an idiot and do right by your daughter."

"That's what I'm trying to do!" Jason replied.

"By running?"

"By going home," Jason said. "By getting away from this place before my daughter doesn't even have a daddy anymore."

"Then why haven't you left?"

"No keys," Jason told her. "Mr. Happy-Go-Lucky must have them." Jason wasn't sure, but he thought he caught Leila stifle a grin. "I don't suppose you know where he is?"

"Bobby?" Leila asked. "Olga probably grabbed him. I'm actually not sure where they're hiding out. Maybe in the basement."

"Olga grabbed Bobby?" Jason asked doubtfully. "What's your definition of senior staff around here? Two months?"

Leila bit her lip, as if debating whether to respond. She then spoke with a *screw it* kind of attitude empowering her words. "Not that it's any of your business, but Bobby has been this hotel's valet for nearly forty years."

Jason waited for the punchline, but after a minute, he realized there wasn't one. "You see that?" He said. "That's the reason I'm getting the hell out of here. Something's not right with this place, Leila."

"What clued you in?" Leila snarked.

Jason flung open his door and climbed out of the car. "I'm going to find Bobby."

He was only halfway to the front door when Leila climbed out after him. "You could help us, you know."

Jason froze. This was precisely the conversation he had raced to his car to avoid. "How?" He asked, turning to face her. "You want me to call the Ghostbusters for you? I can't. My phone magically broke when I got here. Also, they're fictional characters, unless there's something else you want to tell me about this place."

"Yeah, I like Ghostbusters, too," Leila said. "And of course they're fictional. I didn't say you could *call* help for us. I said you could help us. You can be a part of the team, just like you were for the intervention. Look how well that worked out!"

Jason's eyes bulged. He pointed at the bullet would in his side.

"I meant for Marcus Jr.," Leila clarified. "You helped change that boy's life. You gave him another chance to have a loving relationship with his father. And I know it touched you." She stepped toward Jason, her eyes pleading. "Maybe what's happening now is your next chance to be touched again. Maybe by helping us, you're really helping yourself."

Jason felt Leila reeling him in. He knew if he let her keep talking, he'd end up caving to her wishes. It wasn't a risk he could take. "I draw the line at supernatural monsters."

Jason turned away from her to continue his search for Bobby, but he found Marvin, Richard, Katie, and Sam blocking the entrance to the hotel. At first, Jason expected an Old West standoff like in those ancient movies the hotel televisions showed all day. It was Showdown at the Chance Hotel, where Jason Chance and the Marvin gang would shoot it out over a prized set of car keys guaranteed to the last person standing. But Marvin quickly subverted Jason's expectations by tossing his keys to him. What a letdown.

"You've done plenty, Mr. Chance," Marvin said. "Get home to your daughter safely."

Jason felt he should say something, but he really just wanted to leave and never think about what he had witnessed that morning again. He gripped his keys tightly and turned his back to Marvin and his staff. Jason walked toward his car, each step feeling like he was fighting through quicksand, his legs bogged down by the conflicting feelings swirling through his body. When Jason passed Leila, he uttered a quiet apology while keeping his eyes low, and when he got to his car, he opened the driver's side door without looking back.

Then Jason paused, a last nagging thought pushing through his conflict and confusion to once again take center stage at the forefront of his mind. He looked at Katie. "Is this the ninety-six percent outcome or the four percent outcome?"

Katie looked at Marvin, who gave her a go-ahead shrug. "Four percent," Katie told Jason, her lips curling into a frown. "Sometimes life defies the odds."

Jason stewed on her answer. He still didn't know which outcome was supposed to be the good outcome, if there was such a thing. But four percent sure didn't feel like a good outcome. "Hypothetically, let's say I'm willing to help," Jason suggested. "How do we stop that thing?"

"Oh you can't stop the Ghoul," Richard answered so casually it might have been common knowledge. "That thing's a giant mass of mist, teeth, and claws. Anything you throw at it passes right through. Anything it throws at you... well-" He sliced his finger across his throat.

Marvin shot Richard a glare that silenced him immediately.

"So what then?" Jason asked.

"We trap it," Marvin replied. "We get it back to the thirteenth floor and we lock it up."

Jason shifted his gaze to Leila, who shot him a silly smile. "What do you know? It's kind of like Ghostbusters, after all."

Jason couldn't help chuckling. He took a deep breath and looked at his car keys. He could leave Marvin and his team in suspense. He could get in his car, maybe even start the engine, heck, even drive a few feet before backing up. But Jason already knew he wasn't going to leave. He wasn't going to go back to his little girl and tell her that her daddy was a four-percenter. He was going to go back with a fantastical story about how he fought a supernatural creature to save the day at this weird place called the Chance Hotel. He was going to go home a hero... assuming he survived, anyway. Leila and Marvin must have

355

figured out what was going through Jason's mind, for they both looked as though they were bottling a celebratory cheer. Jason saved them the suspense and closed his car door.

"Okay," he said, his brain both blissfully ignorant of the danger ahead and still in denial about the next words that would leave his lips. "Let's go get the Ghoul."

Chapter Forty-Eight
Live Bait

The Ghoul team was assembled around the table in the employee break room: Jason, Marvin, Katie, Richard, Leila, and Sam. Now that his daydreams of grandeur had had time to subside, Jason questioned what he was thinking when he agreed to stay. Or rather, he questioned which organ had done the thinking for him, for surely his brain hadn't concluded that this was the smart decision.

The absence of most of the other staff didn't help, so Jason inquired why they weren't participating too. Marvin assured him they would if necessary, but for now, he preferred to keep them tucked away because they were either too critical to the hotel's continued operations, too seasoned to risk losing, or too inexperienced to send into battle. Jason already knew that Olga and Bobby had been labeled 'too seasoned,' and surmised that Giles fit that bill as well. Of course, anyone could have worn that label, Jason reminded himself, since apparently age was deceptive in the Chance Hotel.

Leila informed Jason that most of the day-to-day maids and janitors, as well as the more mild-mannered members of the staff, such as Marie, the doorman, and the pianist, hadn't dealt with supernatural threats like the Ghoul in the past. When Jason asked about more capable staff members, such as Chef Terrance, Marvin told him that only a fool would put his cook and doctor on the front line of a deadly engagement. Jason interpreted Marvin's words to imply Chef Terrance and Heinrich were part of the 'too critical' classification of staff. Richard added his two cents, but instead of bringing anything new to the conversation, he berated Jason's ineptitude in strategic thinking until Leila elbowed him to stop.

"What about Benji?" Jason asked last. "Is he in the too inexperienced or too seasoned group?" Jason felt comfortable not offering 'too critical' as an option.

Leila rolled her eyes.

"He's too seasoned," Sam replied. "But when I last spoke to Olga, she hadn't found him yet."

"Don't worry," Richard chimed in. "Benji will be there if we need him."

Jason had heard that one before, and he had the bullet wounds to prove otherwise. Oh well, there were bigger concerns hanging over them right now. Like, how to stop a monstrous supernatural creature from running amuck through the hotel and not get killed in the process.

"Okay," Jason said, shifting gears. "Tell me about the thirteenth floor. You said we need to get the Ghoul back there to trap it. Why the thirteenth floor and not any other floor of this looney bin?"

The staff looked to Marvin for the answer. "You might have noticed the thirteenth floor isn't like the other floors of the hotel," he said.

"You mean aside from the haunted mansion decor?" Jason asked sarcastically. "Nah, hadn't noticed a thing."

Marvin didn't humor him. "Behind each of those tightly spaced guest room doors is a portal into what we can best describe as limbo. For obvious reasons, none of us have been inside to see for ourselves. But the hotel archives speak of those rooms as containers of non-existence, pockets between life and death where physical and spiritual beings exist in perpetuity, and yet don't exist at all."

Jason opened his mouth to speak, then thought better of it. At this point, he was probably best just going along for the ride.

"The first time a limbo room was used, it was to capture a saber-toothed tiger that was terrorizing a village of primitive men. The room was more of a cave back then, and there really wasn't a hotel to speak of, but when those Neanderthals saw it could save them from becoming a predator's dinner, they knew they had something special on their hands. They built a neighboring structure to the cave, the first Chance Hotel, though it was really more of a hut, I suppose."

Jason glanced at Leila with an *is he serious?* kind of look. Apparently he was.

"Over time, the hut grew into a series of huts," Marvin continued. "Then a fortified structure, then a structure encompassing the very cave that gave rise to its existence. As threats to humanity shifted from predatory animals to humanity itself, a team of ancient architects discovered they could build prison cells around the cave, then demolish the cave to transfer the portal within to those cells, essentially creating pocket portals where one larger portal to limbo once stood. They used those pocket portals to contain supernatural human threats: witches, vampires, werewolves... those sorts of thing."

Jason rubbed his aching head. His bullshit meter was off the charts. If he hadn't seen the Ghoul with his own eyes, he'd be dialing the psychiatric hotline for assistance. Then again, Jason was starting to question whether he could even trust his own eyes in this place.

Marvin ignored Jason's dramatics. "Eventually, the prison became a castle, the castle became an oversized inn, and the inn became a modern hotel... with hundreds of years of evolution between them, of course. The limbo pockets had begun at ground level, were transferred to an underground dungeon area during the castle years, and then transferred again to the upper floor of the inn after that. They were masked as guest rooms to avoid suspicion about their true purpose. As more threats arose, more limbo rooms were sectioned off to contain those threats."

"Why couldn't the threats just be tossed into the same

section of limbo?" Jason asked. "I assume beings trapped in oblivion don't have a personal bubble requirement."

"It's a safety mechanism," Sam spoke up. "So if one of these otherworldly beings ever escapes, it doesn't release all the others with it."

"Precisely," Marvin added. "Our ancestors learned that one the hard way. Anyway, as the inn grew taller, the limbo rooms shifted to higher and higher floors. That is, until the inn became a hotel and an architect with a particularly odd sense of humor decided to leave the limbo rooms on a superstitious floor while building additional normal guest rooms above them."

"And here we are today," Jason said. "Does anyone actually believe this shit when you tell them about it?"

"The few people that get told don't need convincing," Marvin replied. "They've seen enough for themselves by then. As have you."

Jason thought back to his encounter with the Ghoul. "So that black smoke that poured out of the Ghoul's room... that's the portal to limbo?"

"Yep."

"And it can move from one location to another?"

"You've got it."

"So why didn't it fill the hallway when the Ghoul broke loose?" Jason asked. "Why didn't it just whisk us all away to limbo?"

Marvin smiled, almost as if he was proud of Jason's logical reasoning. "Unfortunately, that's not something we have a complete answer to. The limbo smoke will transfer from one contained space to another, but only at the will of whomever is in charge of the hotel at the time. Otherwise, it remains in whatever confinement it's been allocated to, even if no physical barrier keeps it there. The physical barriers are for keeping things in limbo, not for keeping limbo out."

"So when the Ghoul got loose..."

"I could have let the limbo smoke consume the hallway," Marvin confirmed. "And none of us would be standing here right now discussing it. Obviously, that wasn't an ideal solution."

Jason couldn't argue with that. "So, how do we get it back in the room?" He looked at Richard. "How'd you get the sea monster back in its room?"

Sam seemed confused. "The what?"

"He still thinks he saw a giant sea monster a couple of nights ago," Richard snickered, eliciting chuckles from Leila and Katie.

"You told me it was real!" Jason said. "Right before the Ghoul escaped, you said it was just down the hall!"

"Well yeah," Richard huffed. "It was right down the hall. Behind a door. In limbo. You don't think we let supernatural creatures out around here willy-nilly, do you?"

Jason shook his head. "W-what?!"

"What Richard isn't telling you," Leila said, stepping in to clear the air, "is that what you saw was an elaborate electronics show based on the sea creature locked up on thirteen. It wasn't the actual creature itself. Have you ever seen the stage production of Little Shop of Horrors?"

Jason nodded.

"Same idea, larger scale. Also, remember the LED suit Richard wore to look like you during the Roberts' intervention? He wore one to look like Adam- the man with the wet luggage you saw check out the next day- and I wore one to look like his fiancé, Sarah. We arranged an intervention where Adam and Sarah *witnessed* each other's tragic sea creature deaths. Then we drugged them, put them back into bed, and soaked all of their belongings with salt water so they couldn't be certain about what was real and what was a dream when they woke up the next morning."

"What the hell good did that do?" Jason asked.

"It made them realize how much they loved one another," Leila told him. "Before they came to the Chance Hotel, Sarah was debating calling off the engagement and Adam was on the verge of getting into a sexual tryst with a co-worker. Neither was what they really wanted; they were both just caught up in whirlwinds of external pressures. Job troubles, family troubles... you know how that can go."

Jason shrugged. He did indeed know how that could go.

"When Adam and Sarah woke, they didn't care about explaining what they had just experienced or what was real and what wasn't. All they cared about was how they felt at the prospect of losing one other. And now they'll stay together for life."

Katie cleared her throat obnoxiously.

"Excuse me," Leila apologized. "There's a ninety-nine percent probability that they'll stay together for life."

Katie smiled.

There was one thing that still wasn't connecting for Jason. "I thought I dreamed of seeing Adam and the sea creature. I even woke up in my bathtub with Richard's stupid sea monster novel."

"That was always the plan," Marvin said, "to introduce a credible degree of doubt in your mind. I had Olga on standby to knock you out, but you saved her the effort. She put you in the tub and restored your room to its undisturbed condition." Marvin gave him a mischievous smile. "For what it's worth, she commended you on your physique." His eyes flashed to Jason's crotch for a half-second.

Jason's cheeks flushed. He tried to ignore Marvin's comment as he looked at Richard again. "So that really was you mopping the courtyard, not this mythical Benji guy?"

This time, almost the entire staff groaned. Apparently, they were tiring of Jason's questions about Benji.

"Nope," Richard said. "I was playing poker, just like I told you. The game started as soon as the intervention ended. It's our way of decompressing." Richard bit his lip in thought. "In hindsight, I should have mopped the courtyard. I'd have a lot more money in my pocket right now."

Stonewalled about Benji once more, Jason course-corrected their conversation. "Okay, forget the sea creature. How'd you trap the Ghoul the first time around?"

"Richard?" Marvin redirected. "You were around back then."

Richard shrugged. "The usual. Live bait."

"Live bait?" Jason asked. "As in... worms *or something*?"

"Eh," Richard muttered. "Or humans... or just anything it's really angry at. The Ghoul has quite a temper."

As if on cue, the Ghoul released one of its ear-piercing shrieks in the distance. Sam excused herself to check on its status.

"That's why you sent the seasoned staff into hiding," Jason said to Marvin.

"Of course," Marvin replied. "But it's also why I kept Richard here. He'll make fine bait."

Jason released a nervous laugh. "For a moment, I thought you were going to peg me with that job... again."

Marvin smiled. "Nah. The Ghoul couldn't care less about you. That's why it ran past you instead of slaughtering you on the thirteenth floor. From what I've read, that thing's surprisingly smart."

Sam returned from her scouting exercise with an update. "Well, if you thought Chef was mad about his freezer door, you won't want to be around when he sees what the Ghoul has done to his kitchen. What's left of it, anyway."

"Time?" Marvin asked.

"Not long," Sam replied with a headshake. "Maybe another two or three minutes. It's already scoured the restaurant and lobby, so best guess is it'll either come here or head to the guest wing next. It knows we won't leave the premises, so it likely won't either until it's found the seasoned staff."

Marvin sprang back into action. "Okay, we don't want that thing to spend any more time near the guests. The Ghoul won't target them directly, but it also won't care if they become collateral damage, either. Richard, you need to keep it distracted long enough for us to implement The Old Switcheroo."

Jason interrupted. "I'm sorry, did you just say The Old Switcheroo?"

"Yes, I did."

"And that is...?"

"We locate an empty room on thirteen that aligns with an empty room on twelve," Leila explained. "We set a small charge to blow the ceiling between them and trigger it as soon as the Ghoul is secure in the twelfth floor room. The limbo portal expands..." she made a poof motion with her hands "and no more Ghoul."

Jason's eyes darted back and forth from Leila to Marvin. "You've done this before?"

"Once or twice," Marvin said. "It comes in handy when the creature we're after is too smart to be tricked into a thirteenth floor room directly."

"Riiiiight... so when we-"

"Shh!" Sam whispered. "Everyone shut up!"

Jason and the rest of the Ghoul team did as they were told. Sam held still for a moment, listening, then repositioned her head and listened for a moment more. Jason tried hard to hear whatever it was she was hearing, but only silence reached his ears.

"I don't hear anything," he whispered to Sam.

"Exactly."

It only took Jason a second to realize her concern. The Ghoul had been making so much consistent racket that he all but tuned it out as background noise. Silence meant the Ghoul was done with his kitchen destruction, which also meant it was on the move. Jason eyed the open doorway to the break room hallway. He really didn't want to look out there, but he was the closest to the door and figured seeing the empty hall could put his mind at ease. He tiptoed to the doorway and looked out. There, at the far end of the hall, already through the lobby door, was the Ghoul, its misty body swirling around its bloodshot eyes as they scanned their surroundings. Suddenly, each eye swung forward, honing in on Jason. The Ghoul gnarled its razor-sharp teeth.

"Um, guys?" Jason called into the break room. "We might want to run."

Chapter Forty-Nine
It Is Now

"No!" Marvin whispered loudly. "Don't move a muscle. Remember, the Ghoul doesn't want you."

Jason continued watching the creature, which stared him down as if they were in a contest to see who would blink first. The Ghoul didn't have eyelids, though, so Jason was pretty much screwed. "It sure looks like it wants me," he told Marvin.

"It doesn't," Marvin insisted. "Just be still."

Sure enough, the Ghoul's eyes broke contact a moment later. It plowed forward, its spiking claws punching holes in the hallway walls as it made its way to the door to Marvin's office. The Ghoul punched the door open and maneuvered its way inside.

"He went into your office," Jason relayed as he stepped back inside the break room.

"Good," Marvin replied. "That gives us a chance to get out of here." He turned to the group and spoke with authority. "We're out of time, so here's the deal. I'll go first in case the Ghoul lashes out unexpectedly as we pass the office. Leila and Katie, you follow. We need to get a lobby computer up and running to locate our target rooms for The Old Switcheroo."

Jason felt his eyes involuntarily roll at the ridiculous name.

"Sam, you need to get to the seasoned staff. Tell Giorgio to prepare a Switcheroo ceiling charge. Then help Reggie grab a containment door from the basement. We'll need it in place before we lure the Ghoul in."

"You got it, boss," Sam replied.

"Mr. Chance," Marvin continued, "you're our wildcard. Stay close to me and be prepared to step in wherever you're needed."

Jason nodded.

"Richard," Marvin said as he turned to his insolent concierge, "you come out last. The Ghoul won't hesitate to kill you, so you need to keep moving. Use the parking lot, the stairwells, the thirteenth floor... just keep that thing away from the guests. Understood?"

"I'll be the finest bait I can be," Richard replied flatly.

"Um?" Katie chimed in. "Does anyone else see a problem with this plan? I mean, Richard, he's... well, he's not exactly a world-class sprinter."

Marvin grinned at her. "I suspect Richard places a slightly higher priority on his life than on doing your bidding."

Richard nodded dumbly.

"He'll move," Marvin assured Katie.

A loud boom emitted from Marvin's office.

"Well, there goes my filing cabinet," the manager said. "Okay, what do you say we get this over with?"

He led the group into the hallway, the other members filing behind him in the order Marvin dictated. Marvin stepped slowly toward his office. For all his talk about the Ghoul only being interested in the most seasoned staff, Marvin sure seemed hesitant about walking openly past it. He paused just before the office door, took a deep breath, then proceeded forward. Jason watched from his place in line, and just as Marvin predicted, the manager bypassed the office without incident and made it to the lobby door.

Leila and Katie followed Marvin, and they too bypassed the office without drawing the Ghoul's attention. Sam turned to Jason and Richard to wish them good luck before she did the same. Now it was Jason's turn. He told himself not to worry. The Ghoul had already shown him twice that it wasn't interested in him. He just needed to walk by that office as if there wasn't a deadly supernatural creature inside. Just treat it like a stroll in the park, Jason told himself. He stepped one foot forward, then the other, creeping along for fear of startling the Ghoul. As Jason passed the open office door, he saw the Ghoul knock Marvin's computer to the ground with one of its misty tentacles. Then Jason saw it fling Marvin's desk drawers open, nearly ripping them from their tracks.

Jason took his eyes off of the Ghoul and fixed them on his destination, the door to the lobby, which Katie was holding open for him. Sam was already racing across the Ghoul's destruction, no doubt on her way to find Giorgio and Reggie, while Marvin and Leila were checking overturned computer screens near the check-in counter to determine whether any system was still functional.

Jason was at the office window now. He glanced back at the Ghoul, which was motionless except for its eyes. Those were darting up and down and side to side, as if reading something in Marvin's left-hand desk drawer. Jason paused, mesmerized by the Ghoul's apparent display of reading skills. Marvin had said the creature was smart, but Jason hadn't expected it to understand human language. A moment later, one of the Ghoul's eyes turned toward Jason, causing his heart to leap. Jason remained still, hoping that, just as before, the Ghoul would analyze him and then ignore him, so he could be on his way.

"Mr. Chance!" Katie whispered.

Jason held up a hand to silence her. The Ghoul's eye turned back down toward the reading material in Marvin's drawer, then it swung back up toward Jason. *Something's changed*, Jason's inner voice told him. The eye swung down again, but quickly returned, bringing all the Ghoul's other eyes with it. The creature growled. *Something's definitely changed*, Jason's inner voice repeated. Then his brain reminded him of what had been in that drawer. It was his dossier, the one the hotel staff had assembled in secret. Something about that dossier had triggered a response in the Ghoul... and Jason was ninety-nine percent sure it wasn't a happy response.

"Run!" He yelled to Katie as he took his own advice.

The Ghoul came crashing out of Marvin's office. It didn't even notice Richard, who was still awaiting his turn to exit the hallway. Instead, its full attention was firmly planted on Jason, who stumbled into the lobby and backed away from the employee door.

"Mr. Chance," Marvin said as he ran to Jason's side. "What happened?"

Jason pointed. The Ghoul pushed open the employee door and clawed its way into the lobby. Katie was barely three feet away, petrified, but the Ghoul showed no interest in her. Leila looked to Marvin for silent advice, but he motioned for her to continue her assessment of the computer terminals. The Ghoul slammed its claws forward as it approached Jason, who, along with Marvin, slowly backed away.

"What the hell happened?" Marvin asked again. "It wasn't interested in you."

"It is now," Jason informed him.

Half of the Ghoul's eyes swung to Marvin. It growled again.

"And apparently it's interested in you as well," Jason added.

The Ghoul reared back and released an ear-piercing shriek. Everyone dropped with their hands clasped around their ears. As soon as the shriek subsided, the Ghoul charged. Marvin was the first to his feet, and he tackled Jason just in time to prevent Jason from being skewered by one of the Ghoul's claws. But now both men were on the floor, and the Ghoul was already rotating toward them. It slammed a pair of claws into the ground at their feet, then lifted several others. Jason recognized a kill strike when he saw one, and all he wished at that moment was that he had gotten in his car and gone home when he had the chance.

"Hey!" Richard yelled from the other end of the lobby.

The Ghoul swung all but two eyes in his direction. It kept the remaining two planted on Marvin and Jason.

"Remember me?" Richard asked to an affirming growl. "Yeah, remember how- oh, shit!"

The Ghoul charged at Richard. Richard bolted toward the courtyard door and made it through just as the Ghoul swung and missed with one of its tentacles. The Ghoul's momentum carried it past the door and into the nearest wall. The creature didn't stay down long, though, for it quickly emerged from the dent it had created in the wall and followed Richard.

"There's no way he can outrun that thing long enough for us to get it back in limbo," Jason told Marvin.

"You're probably right," Marvin agreed. "But we have three pieces of bait now. Maybe between us..."

"I thought you weren't going to put me in that position again."

Marvin shrugged. "I didn't. The Ghoul did." He turned to Katie and Leila. "Find those rooms and coordinate with the maintenance crew. We'll keep Richard alive until you're ready."

"Coming through!" Richard hollered as he tore through the hotel's revolving front door.

He shot past Marvin and Jason, who joined the sprint. The Ghoul started pushing through the front door, but its misty tentacles got jammed in the revolving mechanism. Richard, Marvin, and Jason stopped near the concierge podium.

"Where to?" Jason asked.

Marvin assessed their surroundings. "Richard, double back to the courtyard and take a different route this time. Mr. Chance, you're familiar with the stairwell. Take it to thirteen. I'll try to lure the Ghoul onto the elevator and do the same."

There was no time to argue, so Jason did as he was told. Out of the corner of his eye, he saw Richard return to the courtyard door. He also glanced back to see Marvin summoning the elevator. Three pieces of bait. Three different directions. Jason performed some simplified Katie math and told himself he had a sixty-seven percent chance the Ghoul chased someone else. He performed some simplified Jason math and told himself that meant he had a thirty-three percent chance he would become the Ghoul's next meal. Jason liked Katie's math better.

The Ghoul squeezed its body into the lobby and yanked at its last remaining trapped tentacle. That was the last Jason saw of it before rounding the corner into the stairwell hallway. He reached the stairwell door and climbed to the next floor. His body protested at the amount of effort Jason was demanding of it, but Jason ignored its pleas and willed his adrenal glands into overdrive.

He made it to the third floor, then the fourth, before the stairwell door at ground level flung off of its hinges. Jason didn't bother looking down. He knew the Ghoul was coming after him, and he knew it would eventually catch him. The thirteenth floor was his only possible salvation. If the Ghoul really was as smart as it appeared to be, it would think twice before going near its limbo room. Jason reached the seventh floor. He heard the Ghoul's claws clacking against the concrete corridor below him. Luckily, it still sounded far behind. Jason made it to the tenth floor. He reached into his pocket and readied his master keycard, knowing he wouldn't have much time to activate the hidden keycard reader once he reached the thirteenth floor landing.

The Ghoul's claw clacks grew louder. The creature must have caught sight of Jason as he rounded floor twelve, for it let out another guttural roar and its clacking hastened. Jason reached the thirteenth floor. He found the hidden card reader, activated it with his master keycard, and ran through the secret doorway. As Jason passed the heavily hinged concrete facade, he realized he didn't need to make it to the Ghoul's limbo room to be safe.

He just needed to lock it out of the thirteenth floor altogether! The Ghoul appeared at the top of the stairs to the thirteenth floor landing. It launched itself at Jason, slipping a misty tentacle through the secret door's partial opening before Jason could shove it shut.

The claw at the end of the tentacle swung wildly, but Jason stretched his neck as far back as he could to avoid making contact. The Ghoul retracted the claw, likely to regain leverage, but that gave Jason the opportunity to close the secret doorway completely, putting a thick slab of concrete between himself and his pursuer. He breathed a momentary sigh of relief as he listened to the Ghoul roar with rage and slam its claws repeatedly against the other side of the door. Confident it would hold, Jason then composed himself and headed into the thirteenth floor hallway. Unfortunately, he knew this was far from over.

Chapter Fifty
Conscience And Oblivion

Jason saw that the thirteenth floor was still a disaster. And he didn't mean 'disaster' in the usual sense, with the thirteenth floor's twisted architecture, half functioning electricity, and generally dilapidated condition. No, it was still a wreck from the Ghoul's escape; even more so than Jason had initially realized. The splintered remains of the Ghoul's door littered the carpet and walls outside its room. A trail of those remains then led down the hallway where the Ghoul had tracked them while chasing Jason. Large punctures marked the hallway's surfaces every few feet, exposing old sheetrock, wood, and wiring. With their tight spacing, Jason wondered if the Ghoul had inadvertently punctured any other doors- any other containment doors, Jason recalled Marvin calling them. If so, how much time did they have before other supernatural creatures escaped and escalated their current situation?

Jason supposed he couldn't worry about that right now. One supernatural creature was all his brain could handle at any given time, and his one creature was still in the stairwell behind him. It was pounding against the concrete facade of the hidden landing door, trying against all odds to force its way in. Jason wondered why the Ghoul suddenly wanted him so badly. What was in the dossier that triggered such a quick change in its mentality? If Jason died here today, he'd never have the chance to find out. Then again, even if Jason lived, Marvin might not share this newest secret of the Chance Hotel with him.

Jason stopped in front of the doorway to the Ghoul's room. The black smoke to limbo swirled beyond its border, filling the entire frame and blocking Jason's view of anything else in that room. The smoke was majestic, almost ballerina-like in the way it twirled and wisped and folded into itself, ever looking to expand beyond its confined space but never actually doing so. For a moment, Jason pondered what it must be like to live- or rather exist- inside of that smoke. He wondered what sort of magic and mystery the realm of limbo held. Was it merely an otherworldly cage meant to contain the dangerous anomalies of the world? Or was it an alternate plane of reality, completely different from his, with its own potential for fascination and discovery? Jason felt himself drawn to the smoke, attracted to the idea of that newness, of that escape from the turmoil of his current life. He reached his hand toward the swirling mass-

"Mr. Chance, stop!" Marvin yelled from down the hallway.

Jason broke from his mesmerized state. What the hell had he been thinking? He didn't want to go to limbo, no matter what supernatural discoveries awaited him there. He wanted to get back home to his daughter, and to do that, he needed to get the Ghoul back into containment. Speaking of... Jason listened, but he no longer heard the Ghoul pounding on the stairwell wall. All he heard were his own heavy breaths and Marvin's voice.

"I know it's tempting," Marvin said as he joined Jason outside the doorway to limbo, "but there's nothing in there worth sacrificing your life over. According to the hotel archives, it's a void, emptiness, nothing but conscience and oblivion merged into one."

Nope, that didn't sound inviting at all. "I wasn't trying to-"

"I know," Marvin assured him. "It's like a black hole. It tries to suck in anything that gets too close." He looked past Jason. "I take it the Ghoul is still in the stairwell?"

"He was," Jason said. "But I don't hear him anymore."

"Then we'd better get back to Richard. He might need our help."

Marvin led Jason to the far end of the hallway. Since the hotel guests had either run away scared or hunkered down in their rooms, the elevator car Marvin had taken up- Jason's usual elevator car- was still waiting for them. The two men stepped inside, and Marvin pushed the button for the ground floor. Jason felt an odd wetness on his side and discovered that his stitches had ripped.

"That can't be good," he said, displaying the freshly opened wound.

Marvin gave it a brief inspection. "The bleeding's minor. We'll get Heinrich to patch you up as soon as the coast is clear." Marvin bit his lip as if restraining his next thought, then added, "try not to die before then."

Oh, sure, Jason thought sarcastically, he would give it his best effort. Though Marvin had assured him otherwise, this was like the Roberts' intervention all over again. At least this time, it wasn't just Jason's life on the line. He glanced at the elevator's digital floor reader. It flipped from ten to nine. It was ironic, Jason considered, that he had spent so much of his time at the Chance Hotel trying to get out of this elevator car, when right now all he wanted was for it to get stuck and never reach ground level. Jason felt a sense of security in his formerly adversarial steel box of death. He felt safe- slowly bleeding to death aside- and didn't want the elevator to release him into the lobby, into the open, where he was fair game for the Ghoul's next meal.

Jason heard two loud thuds beyond the elevator car's walls. He then heard a tearing of metal, first close, but then trailing into the distance as the elevator continued its descent. Was the hotel answering his silent prayers? Was something going wrong with the elevator's cabling or track or some other crucial system? Jason braced himself, hopeful that the car would suddenly grind to a halt, but instead it shuddered violently as something landed with a heavy *thwomp* on its roof.

"Oh no," Jason said aloud.

One of the Ghoul's spiked claws shot down through the roof

of the car, nearly taking Jason's head off. He ducked into a corner, and saw that Marvin had done the same, as the first claw retracted and two more punched their ways through. Jason checked the floor reader: six stories to go. He felt confident he and Marvin could dodge the Ghoul's random attempts to stab them for the rest of the ride. He felt less confident that the roof of the elevator car would withstand those stab attempts and keep the Ghoul out. The second two claws retracted, and this time three more shot down right through the center of the roof. Instead of flailing for Jason or Marvin, the tentacles holding those claws pressed outward, ripping open a basketball sized hole in the metal, against which the Ghoul pressed its misty body. Its swarm of eyes rotated downward to peer inside the elevator. Jason could feel the intense rage they projected just before the Ghoul reared back and shrieked.

The sound wasn't only close, but amplified by the metallic elevator shaft. Jason dropped to the floor and covered his ears, but the pain was excruciating anyway. When the Ghoul stopped shrieking, it left Jason with an uncomfortable ringing sensation throbbing through his eardrums. Marvin didn't appear any better off. The Ghoul channeled its energy back into tearing the elevator car apart. It punctured hole after hole in the roof as Jason watched the numbers on the floor reader decline slower than he remembered them ever declining before.

Soon, the Ghoul had enough of a gap to squeeze half of its misty mass through. It brought half of its tentacles with it and used those to swipe at Jason and Marvin. Its other tentacles continued their assault on the roof, focusing on the area around the existing gap. It wouldn't take them long to grow the hole large enough for the Ghoul to squeeze completely through. Jason bobbed and weaved his body in ways he hadn't done since playing dodgeball in school. Whatever hold the stitches still had on his skin was torn loose, and Jason could feel the warm wetness of blood spreading across his shirt. He knew time wasn't on his side.

The elevator dinged as it reached the ground floor. The doors opened, and Jason and Marvin tumbled into the lobby. Before either could get to their feet, the roof of the elevator car collapsed, shooting a puff of dust and sparks behind them. Within the cloud of dust, the Ghoul rose from a heap of torn metal and severed wires. It fixed its eyes on Jason and Marvin, then growled, its rows of razor-sharp teeth ready for the kill. In his peripheral vision, Jason saw a male hand turn an oddly shaped key in a slot just to the side of the elevator shaft. The elevator doors slammed shut, trapping the Ghoul inside, the car's locking mechanism emitting two loud clunks as it activated. Relieved, Jason followed the hand of his savior to its owner, who turned out to be Richard, smiling proudly at his good deed.

"Whew!" A panting voice said from the other end of the lobby. "I don't know about you two, but I'm taking a break from the gym for at least a month. My legs are killing me!"

Jason looked for the source of the voice, which turned out to be... Richard? Jason looked back at the man at the elevator. Definitely Richard. He looked back at the man panting his way to them. Yup, also Richard.

"Two Richards?" Jason asked. His blood loss must have been worse than he thought.

The two Richards laughed, as did Marvin as he helped Jason to his feet.

"Jason Chance," Marvin said in an introductory fashion, "meet Benji."

The man at the elevator waved. "How ya doing?"

"Twins," Jason said under his breath. Then, to the real Richard, "You couldn't just tell me that Benji was your twin?!"

Richard shrugged. "You never asked."

377

"I-" Jason caught himself before going apeshit on Richard. He didn't have the time or energy to let the insolent concierge know how he felt. So many questions, so much paranoia, could have been avoided if someone had simply explained that Benji was Richard's twin brother. "I'm filing a complaint with Katie about your communication skills when this is over."

Richard rolled his eyes.

"Thanks for the assist, Benji," Marvin told the twin. "Get down to safety with the rest of the seasoned staff. We've got it from here."

Benji gave him a comical salute and jogged away.

Thwomp!

Jason's eyes darted to the elevator doors. He thought he saw an unusual refraction of light on one of their surfaces.

Thwomp!

Another refraction appeared as the Ghoul's strike left an outward dent in the surface metal.

Thwomp! Thwomp! Thwomp!

The Ghoul pounded fiercely, the dents in the elevator doors multiplying exponentially as it tried to once again free itself from captivity. Jason felt his side. Blood has soaked through his shirt, leaving a sticky layer on the outer fabric that clung to Jason's fingertips as he pulled them away. He wasn't sure how much more of this he could take.

Thwomp! Thwomp! Thwomp!

Jason saw that Marvin and Richard were staring at the faltering elevator doors, too. Marvin appeared worried, as if he also questioned how much more of the Ghoul they could take before they succumbed to the deadly embrace of its claws and teeth. Richard appeared... well, as indifferent as ever, like he just wanted to get this over with. In that moment, Jason realized that he also wanted- no, needed- to get this over with. That, or he was going to need a full body blood transfusion. He grabbed

Marvin's attention.

"So, what now?"

Chapter Fifty-One
The Old Switcheroo

In response to Jason's question, Marvin's eyes shifted to the check-in counter. Jason followed his gaze, but saw that no one was there. Where had Katie and Leila gone? More importantly, had they found a room that could be used to trap the Ghoul before they left? The brown door to the employee hallway opened and Sam emerged. She spotted Marvin, Richard, and Jason, then watched the warped elevator doors fearfully as she joined them near the concierge podium.

Thwomp! Thwomp! Thwomp!

"Those won't hold much longer," Sam assessed. She handed Marvin a small metal box with exposed wires and a red button protected by a flip top- the charge detonator, Jason presumed. "I sent Katie and Leila into hiding in case the Ghoul changes its mind again about who it wants for dinner. Room 1214 is ready. The charges are primed and the containment door is in place. Now you just need to get the Ghoul inside."

"Thanks, Sam," Marvin said before turning to Jason and Richard. "Okay, no more splitting up the bait. We'll take the stairs together to the twelfth floor, lure the Ghoul to room 1214, and commence the Old Switcheroo."

Jason raised his hand. "Since I might die doing this, can we at least give it a cooler name? I don't want my tombstone to read 'here lies Jason Chance, killed during the Old Switcheroo.'"

Marvin put a reassuring hand on his shoulder. "Don't worry, Mr. Chance. If the Ghoul gets you, there won't be anything left to bury."

Real comforting, Jason thought.

"Um, boss?" Richard asked. "Just to be clear, when we reach room 1214, how exactly are we going to get the Ghoul inside?"

Marvin stared at him as if it was obvious, so Richard reworded the question. "I guess what I'm really asking is, how are we going to get the bait back out before blowing the charges?"

"Leave that to me," Marvin replied. "When we get to the room, you and Mr. Chance keep running. Don't go inside. I'll make sure the Ghoul gets back where it belongs."

Richard looked dumbfounded. "Yeah, but... how are *you* going to get out before blowing the charges?"

Marvin smiled as if to say *don't worry about it*. Richard may not have been getting the hint, but Jason sure was. Maybe Marvin had some elaborate escape plan to escape the clutches of the Ghoul before unleashing limbo from the floor above. Or maybe he planned to leap from the twelfth floor balcony and take his chances with the ground below. Then again, maybe Jason's initial instincts were correct. Maybe Marvin had already accepted this might be a one-way trip, that, as the game warden of this supernatural zoo, he had a duty to get the monster back in its cage, no matter the cost.

Jason felt he should say something. "Marvin, I-"

"Look out!" Sam yelled.

She launched herself into Jason, sending them both crashing to the floor. As Jason fell, he saw the elevator doors finally give, one bending in half while the other launched across the lobby like an oversized murderous frisbee. Richard landed hard on the lobby floor next to Jason, unconscious, with a bloody gash in his forehead. The detonator landed with a clatter on the other side of Jason. He looked around for Marvin, and eventually spotted the manager pinned between the projectile door and an overturned couch. Marvin appeared alive, but just barely.

Sam climbed off of Jason and helped him up. The Ghoul growled as it lurched over the bent elevator door and slammed its claws into the shiny lobby floor. Its collection of eyes looked at Richard, then at Marvin, and finally at Jason, the only bait it had yet to immobilize. Deep down, Jason knew what he had to do. Worried that any sudden movement would trigger an attack, he slowly bent for the detonator. The Ghoul took a step forward, as if unsure what to make of Jason's actions. Sam put herself between them.

"Do you have it?" She whispered over her shoulder.

"Not yet." Jason was too scared to take his eyes off the Ghoul, so he missed in his first attempt to grab the detonator. He was successful with his second attempt, however. "Got it."

"Okay," she whispered. "Then run!"

She didn't have to ask Jason twice. He took off toward the stairwell as the Ghoul charged forward. Sam must have tried standing her ground, for the next thing Jason knew, her body flew past him and landed in a pile of rubble in the pseudo-great room. Jason heard the Ghoul inhale as it reared back for one of its ear-piercing shrieks. He braced himself for the pain that would follow, knowing if he stopped to cover his ears, he was as good as dead. The shriek came as Jason rounded the corner to the stairwell hallway. If it hadn't been for the adrenaline in his system, the sharp noise would have likely incapacitated him instantly. But Jason stayed the course and ran through the broken stairwell doorway, even as he felt trickles of blood running down his earlobes.

He took the steps two at a time, knowing he would need every inch of lead possible to make it to the twelfth floor before the Ghoul caught him. This time, Jason reached the fifth floor before the Ghoul plowed into the stairwell beneath him. Jason ran some quick mental math. The Ghoul had reached him just as he had entered the thirteenth floor when they last did this dance. Now Jason had a one floor lead and one less floor until his destination. That should give him just enough time to get the door to room 1214 open and then... then... well, Jason honestly didn't know what he was going to do then. He would have to figure it out when he got there.

The Ghoul quickly closed the gap between it and Jason as they ascended. When Jason reached the twelfth floor landing, the Ghoul was less than two flights beneath him and advancing quickly. Jason charged through the door to the twelfth floor hallway, then scanned room numbers as he pushed his legs with what little energy he had left: 1222, 1220, 1218... at least he was headed in the right direction. Then, there it was: room 1214. Jason pulled his keycard from his pocket and waved it over the reader next to the door. It buzzed at him negatively.

"Oh, come on!" Jason shouted.

He waved the keycard again, but received the same feedback. The stairwell door flung open, and the Ghoul stepped into the twelfth floor hallway with the air of a predator that had just cornered its prey. Jason waved the keycard again, but the door wouldn't open. Had Reggie screwed up the door's installation? Had the door been specially coded just for Marvin? Jason tried again, but was met with the same negative buzz. The Ghoul marched toward him, and Jason could almost see its razor teeth mold into a victorious smile.

Wait! Jason's subconscious yelled. *You still have two keys, remember?* In his haste fleeing the Ghoul earlier, Jason has shoved his master keycard into the same pocket as his room key. Had he really made the same mistake again?! Jason swapped the keycard in his hand with the one in his pocket. He waved the new keycard over the digital reader and the door clicked open. The Ghoul leaped forward, two claws pointed straight ahead and its teeth spread to take a chomp out of whichever part of Jason they hit first. Jason charged into room 1214, narrowly escaping the Ghoul's attack, and stumbled over his own feet as he toppled onto the entryway carpet.

By the time Jason stood, the Ghoul was already in the doorway. Jason backed away to entice it into the room. The

Ghoul hesitated, then, apparently sensing no threat, proceeded across the threshold. Jason watched the Ghoul advance, then shifted his gaze to the open doorway behind it. How was he going to get back through it? Jason tried to think of something clever, but the only thing his brain would give him was a replay of the scene in Back to the Future where Marty tricks Biff into looking away before sucker punching him. The Ghoul understood English, or at least Jason thought it did, so it was worth a shot.

"Hey, what's that?!" He yelled, pointing to the Ghoul's left.

As if following the script, the Ghoul's eyes swung to its left in search of the source of the exclamation. Amazed that such a stupid gag had worked, Jason ran past the blind side of the Ghoul and through the open doorway. He thought he was in the clear, but the Ghoul must have caught onto his ruse quickly, for a misty tentacle suddenly latched around Jason's leg. The tentacle yanked him backwards, causing Jason to lose his balance and face plant against the hallway floor. Another tentacle latched around Jason's other leg, and together, they dragged him back into the room. Jason flailed his arms for anything he could use for leverage, and in doing so, accidentally knocked the containment door shut, sealing him inside.

"Shiiiiiiit!" Jason hollered as the Ghoul lifted him into the air. He was hanging upside down, suspended by two misty tentacles that pulled him closer to the Ghoul's central mass. Something caught Jason's eye on the ceiling. It was a series of small, clay-like blocks, wired together and topped with a thin antenna. Jason looked down at his hands. Somehow, through all the scuffle, he had maintained a grip on the detonator. Jason felt an odd charge to the air as the Ghoul pulled him within inches of its teeth. Those teeth represented certain death, but the alternative- pushing the detonator button- represented nothing better. Jason's eyes darted back and forth between the explosives rigged to the ceiling and the teeth approaching his face. Certain death. Limbo. Certain death. Limbo. Neither was a wonderful option, but on second thought, Jason supposed anything was better than death, even if by a small margin. As he felt the Ghoul's first tooth press into his cheek, he flipped the protective cap off of the detonator with his thumb and jammed down on the button.

The force of the explosion knocked Jason loose from the Ghoul's grasp. He fell to the carpet as black limbo smoke flowed down from the newly created hole in the ceiling and enveloped the Ghoul. The creature shrieked in a combination of horror and rage as it realized the trap into which it had fallen. It tried lashing out at Jason, but the black smoke restrained its tentacles, firmly suffocating the Ghoul with its otherworldly grasp. Then the Ghoul's shrieks faded as its physical presence did the same.

Jason stood and spun toward the containment door, thinking he still had time to make a quick escape, but it was too late. The smoke had already flowed across his feet and connected with another lake of smoke spreading across the ceiling, walling off Jason's only way out. Then the smoke at his feet climbed up Jason's ankles, swirled over his knees, and encased his torso. Jason's chest and arms were the next to go, followed by his neck. His head was all that remained, and soon the darkness engulfed that too. The last thought Jason had before fading away from this mortal plane was that he suddenly felt as weightless as air.

Chapter Fifty-Two
That Looks Familiar

Jason floated slowly through the vastness of space. He was amazed at how vivid and crisp it was, its sea of bright stars and colorful gases unobstructed by the artificial lighting and celestial congestion of mankind. Jason watched a comet streak across a stream of purple haze. It left sparkling dust in its wake that spread in all directions like a glitter bomb unconcerned with the nuance of gravity. To Jason's right, a heavenly body exploded in the distance, creating a blinding sphere of light that emitted rings of energy as it pulsed with successive fusion reactions.

Jason instinctually covered his eyes, then felt foolish for thinking he still had eyes, or a hand to cover them with, for that matter. Jason no longer had a corporal form in the traditional sense. He existed, and as part of that existence, he associated himself with a physical presence. Yet, he suspected that physical presence was nothing more than a mental coping mechanism, a tool to help his conscious being come to terms with the otherworldly state into which it had been thrust. Jason thought about Dave Bowman's final transmission in 2001: A Space Odyssey...

My God, it's full of stars.

Maybe the famous monolith from that story had been a portal to limbo as well. Maybe Arthur C. Clarke had stayed a night or two at whatever iteration of the Chance Hotel graced his time on Earth, influencing what would become one of his most famous works. Or maybe Jason was connecting dots that were never meant to be connected. He saw another comet blast by, this one depositing small chunks of ice and rock into the blackness of space as it plowed through smaller objects that were no match for its might.

As fascinating as this was, Jason knew he would go mad if it was all he had to look at for the rest of eternity. He needed to find... something... anything that he could latch onto. He needed a source of purpose, something to encourage his mind to hang on to whatever sanity it had left. Jason tried flapping his non-existent arms, but found they provided no propulsion through his new celestial home. He told himself to focus on mental action, on the thought of propulsion, rather than on the physical act of actual movement.

Soon Jason was floating faster. He wasn't just floating, either; he was directing himself, willing his non-corporal being through space like an extraterrestrial on the hunt for a new home. For a moment, Jason wondered whether he would encounter any extraterrestrials during his time here, but then he reminded himself that this was not really outer space. It was simply the environment that limbo manifested in his mind. Did that mean Jason would find nothing beyond that which his own mind could conjure? Did it mean his search for purpose, for a reason to continue existing in this plane of nonexistence, was as futile as setting fire to rain? If it did, was there even a way for Jason to end his existence, or was he trapped in this state for all eternity?

Jason opted not to think about that for now, but he knew the thought wouldn't remain on the back burner for long. Jason felt the vacuum around him vibrating. Suddenly, the entire field of view beneath his nonexistent feet filled with a dark, rocky surface. It spewed gases and debris as it rolled by at lightning speed, and then it finished passing Jason and continued into the void. Jason watched the asteroid with awe. Maybe he shouldn't be so concerned with finding a purpose; maybe he should be happy with the endless sights other men could only dream of seeing. Only, he knew that was impossible. Jason needed to be with his daughter to be truly happy, and she didn't exist in this celestial wonderland. Jason stopped floating, a sense of hopelessness killing any motivation he had previously mustered.

A familiar shriek ripped through the veil of hopelessness. Jason looked around. The shriek had come from far away, yet it was close enough that Jason had no doubt as to its source. It was the Ghoul, trapped somewhere in this limbo with him, likely looking for its own purpose. Jason put himself in the Ghoul's mindset and quickly realized that purpose could only take one form given the current situation: revenge.

Jason willed his being in what he thought was the opposite direction from the noise. Soon the Ghoul shrieked again, and this time the sound echoed all around Jason, making triangulating its origin impossible. Jason wondered whether there was truly anything to fear. Could the Ghoul harm him in their dual existent, yet nonexistent states? Should he try to stop it even if it could? Jason had already chosen limbo over death, but now he questioned whether that had been the right decision. Maybe he should take advantage of the looming threat of the Ghoul to end what would otherwise be an eternity of isolation and nothingness.

Snap out of it, dumbass, his inner voice told him. Maybe there was renewed life on the other side of death, or maybe death simply represented another eternity of nothingness. At least Jason knew the eternity of nothingness he was in now had a hell of a view. He also knew, from his own experience with the Ghoul, that the barrier between the one he was in now and life as he formerly knew it was not impenetrable. Maybe Jason would find a way out. Maybe Marvin would find a way to get him out. Both scenarios were unlikely, but as Katie had told him, sometimes life defies the odds.

Jason felt something large moving behind him. As in the real world, Jason knew he couldn't outrun the Ghoul. If it was on his tail, it was going to catch him eventually. Jason felt it was better to face his threat head-on to give himself a fighting chance of avoiding whatever attacks were coming, so he spun his phantom being around, prepared to face the Ghoul's swarm of bloodshot eyes and razor teeth once more.

Nothing was there. Well, except for a million stars and the wide colored rings of a planet-like object that hadn't been there a moment ago. Jason stared at the planet-like object and wondered how long it would take to push his consciousness to its surface. He also wondered whether it was habitable, whether it might be home to the other beings that had been trapped in limbo since the dawn of time. On second thought, given the nature of those beings, Jason decided the planet-like object was probably the last place he wanted to go. He turned back in his original direction.

The Ghoul was waiting for him. As soon as Jason turned, it lashed out with four of its claws, aiming straight for Jason's chest. The attack came so quickly there was nothing Jason could do to avoid it. But it turned out he didn't need to, for the Ghoul's claws passed right through the artificial physical form Jason had imagined for himself. It was then that Jason noticed something odd, but in hindsight completely logical. The Ghoul wasn't there either, at least not physically. Its claws, tentacles, and even its central mass were a transparent manifestation, an image of what the Ghoul perceived itself to be, and not a true body in which its consciousness resided.

The Ghoul seemed confused by its inability to touch Jason. It swiped a tentacle through Jason's manifested head, then through his torso. Then it pressed its phantom eyes and mouth against Jason's equally phantom head and growled. Jason held his ground, no longer afraid of the beast that had nearly killed him. The Ghoul reared back in frustration and shrieked louder than Jason had ever heard it before, yet the shriek was not bothersome. Jason had no physical ears, nor physical eardrums.

They were both a manifestation of his mind, and they couldn't be hurt by a sound that may or may not be a manifestation of the Ghoul's mind itself.

The Ghoul must have come to this same realization, for it slumped before Jason as if finally accepting defeat. Then, with one final grumble, it floated away, until moments later it was too far for Jason to see any longer. Jason wondered whether he would ever encounter the Ghoul again. He even wondered whether, given an eternity to work out their issues, the two might one day become friends. The Ghoul already understood English. Maybe if Jason learned to understand shrieks and growls, they could start having civil conversations. Maybe he didn't have to spend eternity alone...

A glint of light caught Jason's metaphysical eye. He scanned the emptiness ahead, but nothing seemed out of the ordinary. Jason pushed forward, and the light flickered again. No, Jason thought, it wasn't a flicker. It was more of a reflection. He had a sense of the general area from which the light emitted, so Jason headed toward it. Soon, an object floated into view. Jason couldn't make out its specifics, but it was small, rectangular, and made of some type of metal, for now the light reflected off of its surfaces constantly is it spun through the void. Jason willed his being toward the object, and within minutes was upon it. He reached out with his phantom hands and grabbed the metal prism, which up close was about the size of two gallons of milk stacked on end. Jason didn't know how he could touch this object when nothing else in limbo seemed tangible, but he supposed there were many things he wouldn't understand until he had an eternity to figure them out.

Jason rotated the prism until he found a pull-tab on one of its shorter edges. He applied mental pressure, and the tabbed side of the metal prism swung down on a pair of hinges. Inside the hollow object was a glowing sign that read:

USE IN CASE OF EMERGENCY

"Well I'll be damned," Jason said aloud, the memory of a similar box in his favorite Chance Hotel elevator rising to the forefront of his mind. "That looks familiar."

Jason looked beneath the sign, where in his former life there had been a red phone he used to call Giorgio for help. Only there was no phone in this emergency box. Instead, there was a heavy-duty flashlight. Jason took the flashlight in his manifested grip and willed pressure upon the power button. The flashlight emitted an intense beam that reminded Jason of his headlights the night he had first come to the Chance Hotel. Just like his headlights, the beam cut off only ten feet ahead. Only, it disappeared against a wall of transparent space rather than a road sign guiding him to his final destination.

Jason swung the beam through the void, unsure how it was supposed to help him, until he caught a glimmer of light along its edge as he passed it beneath his feet. Jason redirected the beam toward the glimmer, which he could only describe as stardust, a collection of glittering speckles floating among the dark. When Jason moved the beam, the stardust faded. When he directed the beam back toward it, it glowed with an aura of golden light, the same golden light that filled the hallways of the Chance Hotel.

There was something else, Jason then realized. The stardust wasn't limited to a single patch at Jason's feet. That patch was just the beginning of a longer trail that extended as far as Jason's flashlight beam could stretch. Curious, Jason followed the trail, using his flashlight to identify the otherwise invisible speckles as they twisted and turned through the void, forming a scenic route past comets and stars and distant planets. Soon, Jason spotted another object ahead. This one was also rectangular, but larger, and it didn't reflect light the way the metal prism had. The stardust road led Jason straight to the object, which turned out to be a hotel room door. The door had no handle, nor any other means by which Jason could see to open it. But Jason strongly suspected if he could get through it, then maybe, just maybe, he could return to the life he left behind.

He pointed his light at the door, thinking it might be a secret key, but that did nothing. Jason then shined his light around its perimeter, hoping to find a crack or gap in the seal between the door and its frame, thinking that maybe he could mimic the Ghoul's method of escape. But the door was solid. Trying to think of another solution, Jason tapped the flashlight against his metaphysical chin, and that's when he saw it: a digital card reader, made of invisible stardust just like the trail that had led him here, floating next to the waiting door.

Jason kept his flashlight trained on the card reader so it would remain illuminated while he reached for his nonexistent master keycard in his nonexistent pocket. Hmm, Jason considered, that wasn't going to work. He stared at the speckles of stardust that formed the card reader, and that's when it dawned on him. The card reader wasn't real; it was just another manifestation of the reality with which Jason's mind was familiar. It wasn't a physical object waiting for a physical key to enter its proximity. But that didn't mean it was any less of a mechanism for opening what appeared to be a very real door.

Jason held his transparent hand in front of him and concentrated, willing the manifestation of a master keycard into existence between his metaphysical fingertips. "Please God, let this work," he said before waving the manifested object before the sparkling reader.

The stardust card reader beeped in acceptance, and the door clicked as a crack of white light appeared between its edge and frame. Jason pushed the door all the way open and the now blinding light washed over him, spilling out from an unclear destination, pushing away the darkness of the void which had become Jason's new home. Jason hesitated. For all he knew, whatever lay beyond that door was even worse than the limbo he found himself in now. But something told him he would be all right. Something told him that, despite going through an experience beyond the comprehension of man, this was not the end of his journey. He still had a purpose, and that purpose was through the open door before him. Jason took a deep, metaphysical breath and willed himself forward. The light enveloped his very essence as he passed through the doorway, and he suddenly felt the weight of his mortal form return.

Chapter Fifty-Three
Tomato, Tomahto

Jason felt himself tumble forward, his mind and body not quite back in sync yet. He landed on a soft surface and heard a door slam shut behind him. Jason's vision was impeded by a wall of black spots, the remnants of the blinding white light he had just stepped through. Unsure of where he was or what terrors might await him there, Jason lied still and waited for the spots to dissipate. When they finally did, he found himself staring at a crystalline pattern of interconnected, reflective angles. The angles glowed with a soft golden color reminiscent of the stardust path, and beyond them was a blurry splotch of green.

For a moment, Jason thought he had passed from limbo into an equally unfathomable plane of existence, one where the endless void had been replaced with an endless lattice of cut crystal and subtle coloring. Jason rolled onto his back, and the subsequent pain that shot through his body confirmed that he was no longer beyond the boundaries of mortality. Jason saw the ceiling of a Chance Hotel hallway come into focus. The ceiling was dark and littered with cobwebs. Flickering light cast an occasional yellow glow into its shadows.

Wonderful, Jason thought. He was back on the thirteenth floor, the one place that might actually be worse than limbo. Jason fought through his body aches and sat up to look around. The condition of the thirteenth floor was similar to how he left it before journeying into limbo. The damage from the Ghoul's escape was still evident, but repair efforts were clearly underway. Wall patches covered the punctures made by the Ghoul's claws. The carpet was free of splintered wood, and even the door the Ghoul had busted down had been replaced. But the general decrepit state of the thirteenth floor remained unchanged. Unfortunately, so had the decrepit state of Jason's body. His torn stitches were still bleeding through his shirt, and he felt a sharp pain where the Ghoul had taken a taste of his cheek before Jason blew the explosives that freed him from its grasp.

Jason wasn't sure how long he had been in limbo, but he guessed it was long enough that no one was coming to look for him. He needed to get to Heinrich before he bled out. Jason rolled onto his knees, and that's when he noticed the crystalline object that had filled his vision upon first emerging from the void. It was a decorative vase, positioned just outside of the door he assumed he had come through, and inside was a single red rose. Jason smiled. With renewed energy, he pushed himself to his feet and staggered down the thirteenth floor hallway.

Jason reached the elevator bays and pushed the call button. Less than a minute later, a set of elevator doors opened, revealing the teenager girl, pretzel boy, and bubble gum bandit, each on their phones with rolling luggage at their sides.

"Hey, it's the vending machine guy again!" The pretzel boy said.

"Whoa, you don't look so good, vending machine manager dude," the girl added.

Jason smiled weakly and limped into the tiny amount of empty space still left in the elevator car. The teenagers had already pressed the button for the ground floor, and they hadn't seemed to notice they just made a stop on a floor that didn't exist, so without a word, Jason waited for the doors to shut and the elevator to descend. When the elevator arrived at ground level, Jason staggered out and stepped to the side so the teenager trio could be on their way.

"Later, vending machine guy," the bubble gum bandit told him.

All three teenagers gave a brief wave, then beelined it for a

395

group of adults waiting with luggage near the revolving front door. Jason thought about following through on his manager act by yelling for them to come visit again, but he didn't have the energy. In fact, what little energy had replenished his tank on the thirteenth floor had been exhausted simply by making it to the elevator. Jason fell back against the elevator bay wall and slid onto his butt. He thought for a moment he was back on the thirteenth floor, for the lights dimmed and his vision went hazy once more.

"Mr. Chance?" Jason heard Richard's voice say from far away.

Then he heard Leila yell. "Marvin!"

And all went quiet.

When Jason woke, he was lying in a hotel bed surrounded by IV poles and medical monitors. He heard the rhythmic beeping of his pulse as the green blip of an LED display spiked and fell. Jason saw bags of fluid dripping into at least three different hoses that ended with needles in his arms. He also heard a familiar shuffling as Heinrich passed back and forth between the various pieces of equipment, checking readings and confirming all were operating as they should.

"Ah, you're awake," the doctor's gravely voice said upon seeing Jason move. He was suddenly hovering over Jason with a bright penlight, which he shined in each of Jason's eyes without warning. "And alert, I see. Very good."

"How long have I been out?" Jason asked as Heinrich grabbed a pair of pillows and helped him prop up.

"Since you collapsed in the lobby? About three hours. Since you disappeared from existence? Four days."

"Four days?" Jason was sure he hadn't been in limbo for more than an hour. If he had been in there for as long as Heinrich suggested, how had he not bled to death before escaping? Then again, the repairs to the thirteenth floor were consistent with Heinrich's claim, as was Leila's rose, and the teenage trio checking out as if it was a normal day at the Chance Hotel. Jason's brain hurt trying to resolve the discrepancy.

"Who's to say how time works outside of the world we know?" Heinrich said with a gentle pat to Jason's shoulder. "Don't worry. All troubles eventually pass." The old doctor's eyes shifted to the bedroom door, where Leila stood waiting. "I'll leave you be," Heinrich said in an abrupt but sincere manner.

Jason thanked him and turned his attention to Leila, whose eyes were puffy and red, and whose hair was disheveled and clothes wrinkled. None of that mattered, though, for Leila was still the most gorgeous person Jason had ever seen. Heinrich collected his wrinkled bag and gave Leila a friendly nod on his way out. Jason scooted over as best he could to make room for her to sit.

"I thought I'd lost you," Leila said, her voice cracking. "I thought-" She couldn't finish.

Jason smiled and brushed a finger across her cheek. "I'm still here. Four days past checkout, apparently. What are the odds Marvin slaps me with seventy thousand dollars' worth of late fees to keep me from leaving?"

"Oh, one hundred percent," Leila said with tearful laughter. She placed her hand over Jason's and pressed it against her warm face. "I'm so glad you're safe. I didn't know if I could take losing two people to that wretched floor."

"This is what happened to your friend?" Jason asked. "The one in 1301?"

"Something similar," Leila told him, apparently still uncomfortable elaborating further. "Only, she never got out." Leila's grip on Jason's hand tensed. "No one has ever gotten out," she added. "Not without an opening from the hotel side, like what happened with the Ghoul."

Jason could sense Leila's trepidation. "What does that

mean?"

Leila shrugged. "Marvin's been hunkered down in the hotel archives for the past three hours trying to figure that out. I think he has his suspicions about what's going on, but he hasn't shared them with the rest of us yet."

"Can I be a part of that conversation when he does?" Jason asked, half-jokingly. "As an honorary member of the staff?"

Leila chuckled. "Of course."

Jason looked at the collection of tubes and wires protruding from his skin. "You might have to hold the meeting in here, I'm afraid. A half-naked man who looks like he escaped a psych ward might scare off whatever guests the Ghoul didn't."

That one got both a chuckle and a snort out of Leila, which made Jason smile so hard he felt the tug of fresh stitches in his cheek.

"Don't worry," Leila said once she settled down, "it looks worse than it is. Heinrich was just being overcautious given everything you've been through. He expects to have you out of this room by mid-afternoon."

"Mid-afternoon?" Jason asked as if it was years away. "I don't suppose anyone's told Chef Terrance that I'm awake yet? Technically speaking, I haven't eaten in four days."

"I've got you covered," Leila assured him. "Once Heinrich told me you'd be waking soon, I asked Chef to prepare both of our lunches for room service. They should be here any minute."

"And after that?" Jason asked with puppy dog eyes. "I mean, it's a long time until mid-afternoon."

Leila held up a fresh deck of playing cards in one hand. "I figured you could challenge yourself to a solitaire rematch." She held up the television remote in her other hand. "I also heard there's a Hitchcock marathon on channel thirteen."

Jason took the remote and tossed it haphazardly across the room. "No thanks. I've had enough of the number thirteen for one lifetime." He then took the deck of playing cards and tugged at its cellophane wrapper. "You know," he said mischievously, "I heard the staff likes to play poker to decompress after stressful situations."

Leila nodded.

"I also heard that some jackass ruined your time off for your birthday."

Leila nodded again, this time with a grin. "Some jackass might have done that... though I believe I told you that no one really takes time off around here."

"Tomato, *tomahto*," Jason said, rolling his eyes. "The way I see it, you're owed both some decompression and some time off. Oh, and lookie here! I just happen to have time to kill and a brand new deck of playing cards." Jason raised his eyebrows at Leila as if to say *well?*

Leila huffed playfully. "Under one condition: you have to deal. I hate breaking in new decks."

Jason held up his bruised hand, on which Marvin had fashioned a new splint while he slept.

Leila groaned and snatched the deck of cards. "Fine. I'll deal. But you owe me."

Jason smiled warmly. "Anytime."

Chapter Fifty-Four
A Good Manager

By mid-afternoon, Jason had lost nearly thirty-thousand pretend dollars to Leila. She offered to forgive his imaginary debt if he conceded she was the superior poker player, and he agreed to her condition. Heinrich returned to do a final check on Jason's vitals shortly thereafter. He gave Jason the all-clear to check out as long as Jason promised not to get into a fistfight with any more concrete walls, not to purposely throw himself off of any more balconies, and not to release any more bloodthirsty supernatural creatures from oblivion. Jason agreed to Heinrich's conditions as well. He thanked the doctor for keeping him alive through his numerous ordeals, then Leila escorted him downstairs. She made Jason promise to tell her goodbye before he left and handed him over to Marvin, who was waiting at the concierge podium with Richard.

"Welcome back, Mr. Chance," Marvin said warmly. He reached for Jason's uninjured hand, then shook it firmly with a nod of gratitude and respect. "I truly feared we'd never see you again."

"Trust me," Jason told him, "it's good to be seen." He then looked around the lobby with more alert eyes than when he had first escaped from limbo. Aside from a ding here and a dent there, the lobby looked pretty much back to normal. "You guys fixed this place fast."

"Of course," Marvin said. "We have to maintain appearances if we're going to keep the guests flowing."

Jason recalled the repairs still in progress on the thirteenth floor. "It's less of a concern in *less traveled* areas of the hotel, I take it?"

"Those *less traveled* areas of the hotel don't exist,

remember?" Marvin said with a wink. "Besides, we have to be a little more cautious with those repairs… given the importance of structural integrity up there." Marvin motioned toward the check-in counter. "Shall we?"

Jason followed Marvin across the lobby, feeling disoriented by the normalcy with which the hotel was operating. Some guests were arriving; others were leaving. Children ran around the lobby playing games while a line formed outside the restaurant. Katie was summoning janitorial staff with magical snaps to clean barely visible blemishes off the floor and walls, and the maids, doorman, Richard, and now Leila were going about their jobs as if it were any other day. No one acted as though a supernatural mist monster had rampaged through here only four days earlier, nor as if it could happen again under less than optimal circumstances.

"What about the twelfth floor?" Jason asked, his curiosity peaked about the hotel's return to form. "Does it *not exist* now, too?" He made air quotes around the words 'not exist.'

Marvin bellowed in a manner reminiscent of Jason's first days in the hotel. "No, Mr. Chance. We haven't erased the twelfth floor's existence. There was no need. Once you trapped the Ghoul in limbo, I redirected the limbo smoke back into the room above 1214. Giorgio and Reggie repaired the hole in the ceiling and performed any necessary touch-ups to the walls, floor, and furniture. Then Olga and her crew performed a deep clean, and room 1214 was ready for business. There's a young couple staying in there now, if I'm not mistaken."

"Just like that, huh?" Jason asked. "You've got innocent people sleeping ten feet under a portal to a world beyond this world, where any number of supernatural monsters lie waiting."

Marvin stopped at the check-in counter. "First of all, the couple appeared to be newlyweds, so I'm not sure how much sleeping they're actually doing."

Jason rolled his eyes.

"Second," Marvin continued, "the intent of the Old Switcheroo was never to leave the portal to limbo in room 1214."

"Oh God, you're still calling it that? Seriously, you've got to come up with a cooler name."

"The point is," Marvin said, ignoring Jason's unsolicited advice, "people sleep just below and just above the thirteenth floor all the time in this hotel. And few are ever the wiser for it. It only seems strange to you because you're part of the inner circle now. You know what really happens on the thirteenth floor... better than most of us, I'm afraid."

"Speaking of," Jason said. "Leila told me you were digging into how I escaped limbo when most people haven't. Did you find anything?"

"Yes and no," Marvin replied. "It's not *most* people who haven't escaped limbo, Mr. Chance. It's *all* people. I went through every record this hotel has on the thirteenth floor. Despite a number of tragic instances when an innocent person was accidentally trapped in limbo, the only times any have gotten back out is when the portal was re-opened from the hotel side. And even then, it was only if the trapped victim happened to be near the portal on the limbo side when the door opened. More often than not, something less desirable made it out before the innocent victim did."

"Less desirable? As in the Ghoul?"

"Or any of the other dangerous creatures that reside in limbo," Marvin confirmed. "And now you know why we didn't open the door when you got trapped. There was no guarantee we'd get you back, and there was a greater risk we'd get something other than you instead."

Jason shot Marvin a curious look. "So you never opened the door?"

Marvin shook his head. "No. And that leads to my next

finding. This hotel's purpose is to help people, to give them second chances to make their lives better. Over time, many employees have questioned why, if that's the case, the hotel would let an innocent person remain in limbo for all eternity, rather than helping them escape."

"And that is... what?"

"No one knows for sure," Marvin admitted. "But the general consensus is that interference must come at a high cost. The hotel is a vessel, not a participant, in this game of life we play. Managers who were much wiser than me believed that interference in the game would be like crossing a line that could never be uncrossed. The hotel can't do it, no matter how much someone deserves it, without putting its own status as limbo's protective vessel at risk."

"Then why did it save me?" Jason asked. "I'm nobody, Marvin. I'm a failure of a husband, a failure of a father, and pretty much a failure at life in general. I wasn't worth saving at any cost."

Marvin nodded and placed a gentle hand on Jason's shoulder. He then spoke solemnly, with great care behind his words. "You weren't a failure *here*."

Jason opened his mouth to speak, but no words came. What could he say to that? Sure, he had been a pain in Marvin's ass, and he had stuck his nose where it didn't belong, and he had lost a chess game, and then later a poker game, but for the things that mattered, he had succeeded for a change. He gave Marcus Jr. a chance at fatherly love. He stopped the Ghoul- something no one would ever believe and that he might eventually wind up in a psych ward over- but he stopped it nonetheless. He was even the first to escape limbo on his own... well, almost on his own, anyway. And now he had earned his ticket home, the thing that mattered most of all. In the grand scheme of things, Jason realized he hadn't failed one bit during his time at the Chance

Hotel.

Marvin moved to the employee side of the check-in counter and ruffled through a stack of paperwork. He removed a crumpled piece of paper that had been flattened as best as crumpled paper can be and presented it to Jason along with a pen.

"Your invoice, unchanged from when you last saw it, give or take some Ghoul damage," Marvin said. "Don't worry, we're comping the last four days, especially considering you weren't corporally present for most of it."

Jason chuckled. "How generous of you."

He took the pen and looked at the line awaiting his signature. Jason half-expected something to interrupt him, another ear-piercing shriek from the elevator shaft or a national emergency on the thirteenth floor, but there would be no interruption this time. Nothing stood between Jason and checking out other than his own hand scribbling a messy signature it had scribbled thousands of times before. Jason inhaled deeply to clear his head, then pressed the point of the pen to the crumpled paper.

"Before you sign," Marvin said, "would you mind humoring some thoughts of a hotel manager far past his prime?"

Though he couldn't explain why, Jason actually felt relieved that Marvin had lifted the burden of an immediate signature from him. He smiled and set the pen on the check-in counter. "I'm all ears."

"The night of your arrival, you asked me whether we were related and whether I owned the hotel," Marvin said. "Do you remember that?"

Jason nodded.

"Do you remember what I told you?"

Jason thought for a moment before answering. "Something about us not being the only two people with the name Chance to

404

have stepped foot in this hotel."

Marvin smiled. "That's right. As a matter of fact, the Chances have run this hotel from its very first incarnation hundreds of years ago. William Chance was the inaugural manager, then Richard Chance, then Frederick Chance, Collin Chance, Elizabeth Chance, Arthur Chance, Penelope Chance, and many, many years down the line, a meager old man named Marvin Chance. Do you know what these managers had in common, except for their last names?"

Jason shook his head.

"They were the right person for the job when the hotel needed them." Marvin looked down and bit his lip, as if trying to build up the courage to continue. "When a manager is no longer needed, their time in charge comes to an end, and another Chance comes along to take their place. I never saw the end of my time coming, but then you walked in and gave me your name." Marvin shook his head, and Jason was certain he saw tears swelling in the older man's eyes. "I didn't want to believe it. I had run this place so well for so many years. I couldn't understand why my time was over. And then you started snooping around, and you found the thirteenth floor... and suddenly it hit me. Change is unavoidable, Mr. Chance, and whether I like it or not, it's coming. Admittedly, I may not be the best person to deal with that change when it arrives."

Jason remained silent. Part of his brain heard what Marvin was saying and had already processed the implications. Another part of his brain was building a solid brick wall of denial and hanging petitions on that wall for Jason to sign his invoice and run.

"A good manager does his job to the absolute best of his ability," Marvin continued. "And a great manager recognizes when it's time to pass that job to someone else." Marvin mustered the strength to look into Jason's eyes. "When I took over this job, I vowed to be nothing short of a great manager."

Jason's warring thoughts were creating a tornado of emotions within him. "What are you saying?" He asked with more aggression than intended. "That you get to walk out of here while I get forced to stay in your place?"

"No, of course not," Marvin said calmly. "No one is going to force you to stay."

Jason's lip quivered. "Funny, I recall you doing exactly that for the past seven days."

"Only the first three," Marvin clarified. "And that was only because I needed to know whether you were worthy of being my successor. Please understand, Mr. Chance, not all previous managers have been good people. I couldn't pass the reins to someone else without knowing that they would take proper care of this place and the staff who work here. You proved that with your actions. You protected this hotel. You protected the people who work here. And you were willing to sacrifice your life to do it. I couldn't ask for a better replacement than you."

Jason shook his head and grabbed the pen from the counter. He pressed it against the signature line of his invoice, but before he could sign, Marvin slapped another paper down next to it. "What's this?"

"It's the employment contract that's been sitting in my office since you arrived," Marvin said. "It's the contract I've been too afraid to show you, so I left it sitting in my desk drawer along with the dossier we'd prepared on you."

Jason tried to ignore the new document, but he couldn't help himself. He didn't release the pen, but he did move it away from the invoice as his eyes skimmed over the contract Marvin had presented. It named Jason as the new manager of the Chance Hotel, effective upon the old manager's departure, and valid until an unspecified future time when his services were no longer needed. Beyond that, the document contained an official

Chance Hotel seal and a signature line to indicate acceptance.

"I thought for sure you saw it the night Katie caught you rummaging through my desk," Marvin said. "But I guess you overlooked it. Unfortunately, I don't think the Ghoul did."

Jason made the connection. "The Ghoul came after me because it discovered I was going to be the next hotel manager?"

Marvin nodded. "And when it realized I was the current manager, it saw an opportunity to sever the chain of succession for good. Eliminate the wardens, and you no longer have a viable prison."

"Holy shit," Jason muttered. "You said it was smart..."

Marvin's eyes narrowed. "It's not the only danger, Mr. Chance. Whatever price the hotel paid to retrieve you from limbo, it did so because the benefit of you being here to face the threats that lie ahead outweighs that cost." Marvin straightened the two pieces of paper on the counter before Jason. "Of course, the choice to stay ultimately lies," Marvin shrugged, "with you."

Chapter Fifty-Five
I Know This Place

Jason looked back and forth between the check-out invoice and employment contract. For all the craziness he had experienced in the Chance Hotel, this might have been the most subdued, yet craziest, experience of all. Jason had no business managing a hotel; especially not a hotel inhabited by supernatural creatures and whose primary goal involved strategic meddling in other people's lives. Jason could barely get his own life straight, and he certainly had no desire to face down another creature like the Ghoul any time soon. Besides, he still needed to get home to his daughter, and home wasn't exactly within acceptable commuting distance.

Then again, Jason didn't have a rich man's paycheck or a place to live. He suspected the hotel would provide the latter and alleviate him of most desires for the former. And Marvin had made a good point about Jason's ability to find success within the Chance Hotel, something he sorely lacked outside of its walls. There was also the matter of Leila. Jason could feel her watching him as he contemplated his choice. He forced himself to avoid looking in her direction to abstain from biasing his decision.

"I'm sorry, Marvin," Jason said after a few minutes of deep thought. "I just don't see how I could make it work with my daughter being so far away."

Marvin closed his eyes as if Jason had touched upon a pain point. When he opened them again, he spoke with a strange sadness in his voice. "That's actually something we need to talk about."

Jason could feel a deal-breaker coming. "What?"

"Managing this hotel requires a level of dedication that could never be achieved by someone with strong emotional ties to their previous life. When you checked in, you asked me if we were related. The truth is, I wouldn't know, because I have no memories of the life I lived before signing my contract. I don't know if I was a garbage man or tycoon billionaire. I don't know who my friends were. I don't know if I was married or at least had a significant other." Marvin stared at Jason hard. "I don't know if I had kids. The hotel locked those memories away the day I took the job."

"You can't be serious," Jason said, unwilling to accept Marvin's claim. "Nothing can take your memories away like that. If you had someone you loved in your life, you would know. If you had a child, you would know!"

Marvin replied with calm patience. "Mr. Chance, in your short time here, you battled a supernatural creature straight out of tales of fiction, and you spent the last four days in a state of corporal non-existence, in an oblivion the average person could only dream of. Do you really think it's beyond this hotel's capability to strip a person of a handful of memories?"

No, Jason told himself. If he was being honest, he already knew Marvin was telling him the truth. He slid the contract back toward Marvin, unsigned. "I can't. What you're asking is too much. I'm sorry."

Marvin smiled acceptingly. "It's okay, Mr. Chance. That's why it's a choice. Not everyone who's been presented with a contract like that has accepted it. Another Chance will come along eventually. Until then, I'll continue being the best manager I can be."

Jason was thankful Marvin hadn't tried to pressure him further. He pressed the tip of the pen above the signature line of the check-out invoice, but then found himself unable to write his name. He wasn't physically unable; something just didn't feel right about the decision. Jason dropped the pen and slumped his head into his hands with a heavy sigh.

"Maybe it would help if we took a walk," Marvin suggested. "It's a lovely day outside."

That sounded like a fantastic idea. Jason stood straight and smiled at Marvin, who proceeded around the check-in counter and started for the front door. Jason watched the guests coming and going around him as he followed. They seemed so happy to be here, as if the Chance Hotel had some magical ability to bring out the best in people. Maybe it does, Jason considered. Maybe that was the true gift of this place. It had brought out the best in him, after all. It had brought out the best in Marcus Sr., too, and the athletic couple who had been so thankful for the traumatic experience that pulled them closer together. In its own quirky way, the Chance Hotel was a place for redemption, for second chances, for new beginnings...

Marvin and Jason emerged into bright afternoon sunlight and a crisp, cool breeze. The fresh air instantly cleared Jason's mind, and the warm sunlight made him feel more alive than he had felt in days. Jason saw Bobby waiting with his car keys, and his car parked directly out front, just as it had been before he agreed to help trap the Ghoul. Marvin waved Bobby off and led Jason down the tree-lined sidewalk that bordered the hotel's entrance street.

"Taking away someone's cherished memories may sound cruel at first," Marvin said as they walked, "but it's actually in the best interest of everyone involved. Imagine if I had someone special in my previous life. What would I have done when the Ghoul escaped? Would I have put my life on the line, knowing the impact my death might have on that other person? What if that other person fell sick, or experienced some other life-derailing event? Would I continue serving the hotel while knowing that the person I care about needs me? By taking my memories, the hotel ensured I would serve it faithfully. But it also ensured I had no regrets, because you can't regret what you don't know."

Jason and Marvin reached the end of the street and turned the corner. Instead of the adjacent road Jason recalled taking into the Chance Hotel the night of his arrival and when returning from the bank with Giles, he now saw the fringes of a quaint neighborhood where parents pushed strollers down the sidewalks and older kids biked in the street.

"What the hell?" Jason asked.

Marvin laughed. "The Chance Hotel serves far more people than will ever come across it off a random highway exit," he explained. "It has access points wherever it needs to, whenever it needs to, so that its doors can be open to the people who deserve a little help in their lives. It's a little disorienting at first, but you get used to it. Come on."

Marvin led Jason down one of the neighborhood sidewalks, past freshly mowed lawns and neighbors socializing in their driveways. Something felt oddly familiar to Jason about these new surroundings.

"Where are we?" He asked.

"We'll get to that," Marvin replied coyly. "For now, let's just keep walking and talking."

Jason could tell Marvin was up to something, but the outing was a pleasant escape from the troubles of the past week, so he played along.

"Have you given any thought to what you'll do when you go home?" Marvin asked. "From a long-term perspective?"

"I've been a little busy to think about it," Jason replied with a sarcastic smile. Then, more seriously, he said, "Like I told Leila, I've got to make things right for my daughter. I'll need to find a higher paying job- one where I don't forget my daughter exists- and hunt for a cheap apartment until I can afford something better."

"Well, you know there's always a free room for you at the hotel if you need it," Marvin said. "As a guest, of course, not the manager."

"I appreciate that, Marvin," Jason said with subdued sincerity. "But I suspect I won't be seeing the hotel again after today."

"Why is that?"

Jason stopped walking. "How long had you been at that highway exit before I arrived?"

"What do you mean?"

"You said the hotel has access points wherever needed." Jason waved his arms over their neighborhood surroundings. "I'm inclined to believe you. So, how long had it had an access point at that particular highway exit?"

"Just for the day," Marvin admitted.

Jason shrugged as if to say *see?*

"You think the hotel opened an access point there specifically to lure you in," Marvin said, reading Jason's mind. "And now that you're declining the manager job, you think it'll close that access point."

"And probably any others I might come across," Jason added as he resumed walking. "When I tried to check out the first time, I had this odd feeling that it was permanent, like I would never see any of you again. I think now I understand why. The hotel brought me here for a purpose, and if I opt not to fulfill that purpose, it's going to have to reallocate its resources into finding someone who will."

Marvin raised his brow. "That's an interesting theory. Unfortunately, there's only one way to test it." He glanced across the street. "Ah, we're here."

As Marvin crossed the street, Jason followed his trajectory to a large playground littered with kids and their parents. Some kids were climbing through the towers of a wooden fortress.

Others were crawling over a giant rope spiderweb. Some were playing tag in the open green space and more were taking turns on slides and swings.

"Wait," Jason said, the entirety of the scene triggering something deep in his brain. "I know this place."

Marvin stopped on the opposite sidewalk. "Well, of course you do. It's where your wife takes your daughter to play almost every week." He nudged his head. "Come on."

Marvin was right. This was the playground his daughter frequented. They had a similar one in their own neighborhood, but a handful of her good friends from school lived closer to this one, so his wife would take her there to play instead. Jason had only gone a few times, usually because his wife was sick or had a last-minute business meeting. So why had Marvin brought him here now? Unless...

Jason raced across the street, his eyes scanning the faces of the kids on the playground. His heart pounded as his vision shifted from child to child, hoping against all hope that his daughter was somewhere in the crowd. And then he saw her. She was being chased by a group of girls Jason recognized as her friends. She dodged one member of the group, then ducked under a slide to dodge another. But as she neared one pillar of the fortress, a third girl caught her and both went tumbling to the ground. The rest of the girls piled on top and all giggled happily.

Marvin held out a hand to keep Jason at a distance. "I think we should stop here."

"But she's right there," Jason said excitedly. "Couldn't I just-"

"You could," Marvin said, "but that's not why we're here. I want you to watch."

Jason's daughter and her friends clambered from their pile and ran to a picnic table where Jason's wife and the other moms waited with juice boxes. Jason watched his little girl sipping at her drink while she recounted the details of their playground game to her mother. She was so full of energy and happiness. It was just as Jason remembered her. He lingered for a moment, then looked away.

"What is it?" Marvin asked.

Jason didn't know how to put it into words. He thought his daughter looked just as he remembered her, but after watching for only a few moments, he realized he was wrong. She was *happier* than he remembered. She was more energetic, more lively than he remembered. She was a strong, independent little girl who knew her father loved her no matter where he might be. She didn't need him to be physically present. If anything, his physical presence had dampened the bright flame within her. His constant bickering with his wife, his constant stressing over their financial situation... those things had detracted Jason's attention from the one thing he loved most. And somehow, he hadn't recognized it until this moment. If he returned home, could he honestly say those things would stop? Could he truly give his daughter what she needed? Or was this whole crusade to check out more about himself and what he needed?

"You've put the pieces together," Marvin said after analyzing Jason's face. "Katie ran the math. She told me I should just let you know that there was a ninety-nine percent probability your daughter would turn out okay if you didn't go home, versus the fifty-four percent probability if you did. But, knowing your stubbornness, I thought it best to let you reach that conclusion on your own."

Jason looked up, his eyes red and flush with tears. "How can you do that? How can you casually tell a father that his daughter will be better off without him? Huh? You said Katie ran the numbers. Why? Is this some sort of last-minute intervention? A trick to get me to take your job so you can finally unshackle yourself from the hotel?"

"It's no trick," Marvin said without emotion. "And I haven't told you anything you didn't already figure out for yourself." He tried putting a consoling hand on Jason's shoulder, but Jason swiped it away, eliciting a frown. "You're correct," Marvin then admitted. "This is your intervention, Jason Chance. I hoped it wouldn't be necessary. These things can be rather painful, especially when that pain comes from the heart. But as long as I'm still the hotel's manager, it's my duty to give people second chances to make better choices with their lives. Now, I'm not telling you that you have to take the manager job. We can go back to the hotel, you can check out, and you can go wherever you'd like to give yourself a fresh start. I'll even throw in some extra starter money to help you get back on your feet. All I'm trying to show you is that you *shouldn't* return home, not if you really care for your daughter as much as I believe you do."

Jason stared hard at Marvin, his eyes burning with a combination of sadness and rage. He wanted to hate the manager for bringing him here, for showing him the truth about his absence from his daughter's life, and in turn, the truth about his presence in it as well. But Jason had no one to blame for that truth but himself. Marvin had fabricated nothing. He had simply opened Jason's eyes before Jason made another in a long series of life's mistakes. Despite the anger, Jason knew he should be grateful. He just couldn't show it right now.

He looked back to the playground, where his daughter and her friends were packing their stuff and their parents were exchanging parting words. Jason stared at his daughter's face, burning her image into his mind, on the one hand never wanting to forget it, and on the other not knowing how he could live with himself if he didn't. One of his daughter's friends gave her a hug before strolling away.

"Goodbye!" Jason heard the friend yell.

"Yeah, goodbye!" Two more friends yelled along with waves.

"Goodbye!" Jason's daughter called back to them with that sweet and innocent voice.

Jason raised his own hand halfway, never taking his eyes off of his daughter's vibrant smile, and gave a suppressed wave of his own. He whispered, his voice cracking under the strain of heartbreak. "Goodbye."

Chapter Fifty-Six
You Never Know

Jason was a shell of a person on the walk back to the Chance Hotel. He didn't speak a single word, and Marvin kindly didn't try to force one out of him. When Jason walked back through the revolving front door, Leila was waiting to catch him in her arms. He sobbed into her shoulder uncontrollably, and she held him so tightly she may as well have been trying to squeeze the sadness from him. After a few minutes, Jason regained his composure and proceed back to the check-in counter, where his decision still awaited him. He picked up the pen and looked at the employment contract, then turned his swollen red eyes to Marvin.

"No memories of her?" Jason asked.

"None whatsoever," Marvin confirmed.

Jason hesitated for only the briefest second before signing on the acceptance line. He closed his eyes and waited for the magical respite that would sweep his pain away, but a minute later, the pain still lingered. Jason opened his eyes and looked questionably at Marvin.

"It doesn't take effect until I leave," Marvin clarified with a sad smile. He then tapped the check-out invoice. "I still need you to sign this, too. You can't be the manager and a guest at the same time."

"You made it seem like a choice between the two," Jason said as he eyeballed the competing documents.

Marvin shrugged. "Yeah, well, I thought it'd be more dramatic that way."

His words eliciting a weak, but relieving chuckle from Jason. Jason felt Leila's comforting hand rub his shoulder as he signed the zero-balance invoice and returned both documents to

417

Marvin. Marvin reviewed and approved both signatures with a nod, then instructed Jason to follow him to the manager's office.

The office was in better shape than Jason imagined it would be following the Ghoul's rampage. A new computer had been installed atop the desk, the filing cabinet had been returned to its original location, papers had been picked up, and the only visible evidence of the Ghoul's intrusion was a random assortment of scratches across metal and wooden surfaces alike. Marvin directed Jason to the manager's side of the desk, where he kneeled down before the biometric safe Jason had seen during his own intrusion into the office.

Marvin placed his thumb on the biometric reader and the safe unlatched. Jason noticed Marvin hesitating, as if scared to look inside. The manager closed his eyes and took a deep breath. He then swung the safe door open, revealing a shelf containing a wallet, a photograph, a set of keys, and an old-fashioned gold watch. Marvin picked up the wallet first. Inside was a Nebraska driver's license with Marvin's picture on it. Surprisingly, though the license appeared quite old, Marvin didn't look any younger. Apparently, he had been an old man most of his life. Inside the wallet was also an assortment of wrinkled dollar bills and a business card that indicated Marvin had been in farm equipment sales in his previous life.

Without a word, Marvin closed the wallet and slipped it into his pocket. He grabbed the keys next. There were five in total, and there was nothing notable about any of them. Marvin put them in a pocket as well and reached for the watch. He analyzed its face and an inscription on the back that was too small for Jason to read from his distance. Marvin then slipped the watch over his left hand and clasped it around his wrist.

"What do you know?" He said as if he were someone trying on the watch for the first time. "A perfect fit. And it still works too."

Lastly, Marvin picked up the photograph. It was black and white, and showed a lovely woman a little younger than Marvin smiling at the camera from beneath an oversized sunhat. Marvin stared at the photograph for several minutes, as if making a connection that would conjure distant memories. The manager remained silent for so long that Jason wondered if those memories hadn't triggered a brain aneurism.

"Marvin, are you-"

"Yep," Marvin replied hastily as he tucked the photograph into the same pocket as his wallet. "I'm totally fine."

"Do you remember who she is?" Jason asked, curiously.

Marvin pursed his lips. "No." He then smiled at Jason. "But I'm sure it'll come back to me once I leave. Okie dokie, Mr. Chance. Now it's your turn." Marvin stepped aside to give Jason access to the empty safe. "Just place anything of personal significance inside."

A part of Jason considered how insane this whole procedure sounded. He would put his personal effects in the safe, lock it, and then magically forget about them and the memories attached to them. Just like always having room, it sounded like total bullshit. And yet, from everything Jason had seen and experienced during his time at the Chance Hotel, he knew it wasn't bullshit. He knew this was the point of no return, when he gave himself completely in service of the hotel. He kneeled down in front of the safe.

Jason removed his wallet from his back pocket and placed it on the shelf where Marvin's had been. He didn't have any jewelry to add to the safe, for the only meaningful jewelry Jason ever wore was his wedding ring. But now there was just a pale circle around his finger where it had hidden his skin from the sun for so many years before he ripped it off during *the fight* with his wife. Jason took out his busted cell phone, powered it down, and placed it where Marvin's photo had been. He then stood and patted himself down, confirming he had nothing else to add to the safe.

"We have just a few more things," Marvin said.

As if on cue, Bobby appeared in the open office doorway. He was carrying Jason's messenger bag and car keys, which he sat carefully on the desk.

"Thank you, Bobby," Marvin said. He removed the cash and handed Jason's bag back to the valet. "Can you please ensure this and the rest of Mr. Chance's belongings get back to room 2101?"

Bobby flashed his pearly whites. "Sure thing, boss!"

And then he was gone. Marvin motioned to the newly arrived objects, which Jason obediently added to the safe. Marvin also collected Jason's dossier from his desk and passed it to Jason for inclusion. He then showed Jason how to seal the door and asked him to press his thumb against the biometric reader. Jason heard the reader hum as it recorded his fingerprint, then felt a thud as the safe secured itself with a heavy deadbolt.

"That's it," Marvin said when the procedure was complete. "You can retrieve your belongings once another Chance takes your place. When that time comes, walk him or her through this process just as I walked you through it. It's the final task of every manager."

Jason nodded that he understood.

"Well," Marvin then said. "I've got to pack my clothes. I'm waiting to leave until after we shut down for the night so I can give the staff a proper goodbye, but feel free to hang out here and get familiar with things. It may not be official yet, but you're the boss now."

Marvin held out his hand, and Jason shook it firmly. The two men understood each other in a way no one else could. Jason was filled with the sorrow of knowing the life he left behind was better off without him, and the Chance Hotel was his future refuge from that sorrow. Marvin was filled with the sorrow of leaving that refuge to return to a life he no longer remembered. Jason wondered whether Marvin's previous life mirrored his own. If so, would Marvin's return be the same as if he had remained in that life from the start? Or would his return take a different course, one shaped by his tenure at the Chance Hotel? Jason supposed he would find the answer when it was his turn to pass the mantle to the next in line... someday.

Jason spent the next several hours rummaging through Marvin's office- he still thought of it as Marvin's office as long as the former manager was still on the property- and trying his best to grasp how operations at the Chance Hotel worked. Leila, Sam, and Benji popped in around dinnertime and invited Jason to join them in the restaurant. Chef Terrance prepared a remarkable meal as always, and Jason felt relaxation finally setting in as he and his new coworkers dined and laughed together, though most of the laughter was at Jason's expense over his insistence that Benji didn't exist. After dinner, Jason walked the hotel grounds for a little over an hour, familiarizing himself with its layout and amenities from a manager's point of view, until finally the time came.

Sam found Jason in the courtyard and escorted him to the main building stairwell. Instead of going up, Sam led Jason down into the hotel basement, which was dim and made of exposed stone walls and flooring that Jason suspected might be a remnant of the hotel's early days as a castle. The basement contained a centralized space beneath the hotel lobby, with multiple hallways branching out like spokes from a bike wheel.

Sam directed Jason to a hallway illuminated by flickering lanterns. There, the hotel staff lined each side of the hallway, from its opening at the basement's central room to a closed door at the far end. Above the door glowed an out-of-place neon sign that read:

Sam joined the other staff along the hallway edges as Jason felt a tap on his shoulder. It was Marvin, standing behind Jason with two old suitcases in hand. The doorman rushed forward and took Marvin's suitcases, then dropped them off near the exit door and resumed his place among the staff.

"So, this is it," Marvin told Jason. "Any last-minute questions for me?"

Jason gave it a moment of serious thought, then asked the one thing that came to mind. "Yeah. Was it worth it?"

Marvin smiled reassuringly. "You bet."

Marvin proceeded down the rows of staff, giving each a personal, heartfelt goodbye. He encouraged Sam to keep the hotel safe once he was gone. He also encouraged Olga to keep Jason out of trouble. Marvin thanked Katie for her years of advice and Chef Terrance for his years of great meals and even better friendship. He shared brief words with Giles, Bobby, the doorman, Benji, and Heinrich. He gave Marie a caring hug and wished her the best, then instructed Giorgio and Reggie to take it easy on their new boss. Marvin exchanged friendly farewells with the restaurant pianist and the assortment of maids, janitors, waiters, and miscellaneous employees to who Jason would soon have to introduce himself.

At the end of the hallway, closest to the exit door, were Leila and Richard. Marvin shook Richard's hand and instructed him to try a little harder because Jason was going to need all the help he could get. Katie stifled a laugh, and Jason wondered which part of Marvin's words had tickled her funny bone. Probably the part about Richard needing to try harder, Jason told himself. Then Marvin turned to Leila, who embraced him in a tight hug. Marvin told her that everything was going to be okay, and Jason saw a tear streak down her cheek. Marvin planted a gentle kiss on Leila's forehead and closed the last gap to the exit door. He took a deep breath and pushed it open.

Blinding white light flooded the hallway. It was so bright that it shielded whatever was beyond the door from view. Jason recalled his time in limbo, and the door of white light that served as his exit from it, and he couldn't help but notice the similarities.

"What the hell is that?" He asked Sam, who was still close by.

"It's the exit door," she replied, aware she was stating the obvious. "It's what we all have to eventually pass through to sever our connection to the hotel."

"What's on the other side?"

"No one knows," Sam said, her eyes focused on Marvin's silhouette against the white light. "It's a one-way trip. Once you retire from the hotel, you can never return."

Jason supposed it made sense. A clean break gives the next regime the opportunity to do what it deems best, without scrutiny from those who came before. But that didn't explain the uncomfortable pit in Jason's stomach. Maybe the restriction on returning was benign, or maybe it was a fairytale to hide what retirement truly represented. Jason looked at Marvin and the white light that awaited him. The light would take Marvin home, wherever home happened to be, right? Jason wanted that to be true, for deep down, he felt as if Marvin's departure was somehow his fault. But what if it wasn't true? What if-

"Hey Marvin!" Jason called out. Marvin turned to look at him, but Jason wasn't sure what he should say next. So he swallowed hard and said the first thing that came to mind. "Maybe I'll see you around someday."

Through the shadows that hid Marvin's face, Jason could see an appreciative smile. "I guess you never know." The manager picked up his suitcases. "Best of luck, Mr. Chance."

Jason nodded acceptingly. "You too, Mr. Chance."

And with that, Marvin stepped into the light and made his

final exit from the Chance Hotel.

Chapter Fifty-Seven
I Hope You Enjoy Your Stay

The next morning, Jason woke up in room 2101 with a renewed energy he hadn't felt since first checking in to the Chance Hotel. By the time the staff had dispersed following Marvin's departure, and Jason had unpacked his suitcases upon returning to his room, it was nearly two o'clock in the morning. Katie informed Jason that the manager was usually expected to be on duty by six, but that it would be acceptable for him to sleep in this one time, given everything he'd been through. Jason thanked her for her leniency and took the opportunity to sleep until eight-thirty. Despite getting only six and a half hours of sleep, Jason felt fully refreshed. His mind was clear of exhaustion. His body, while still banged up from his accumulation of injuries, was free of any debilitating pain.

Jason strolled into his bathroom with an extra pep to his step. He showered and brushed his teeth, made himself as professionally presentable as possible, and grabbed a suit from the closet. Jason had discovered the suits when unpacking his clothes the previous night. There were ten of them in total, each perfectly fitted, crisp and free of wrinkles, and accompanied by dress shirts and ties. In a baggie hanging near the suits was a collection of identical nameplates bearing Jason's name. Jason grabbed one nameplate, clasped it to his right jacket pocket, and returned to the bathroom to examine himself in the mirror. His normal conceitedness aside, Jason thought he looked pretty damn good.

It was almost nine-thirty by the time he left his room. Jason walked to the elevator foyer and reached for his usual call button when something caught his eye. It was the chessboard, sitting just as he had last seen it, with all pieces back in their starting positions. Part of Jason was surprised his ghostly opponent hadn't tempted him with a new move now that he was a permanent resident of the Chance Hotel. Another part of Jason wondered if his ghostly opponent wasn't so ghostly after all, and had simply checked out, or perhaps retired, during the past few days. And yet, a voice inside of Jason told him that wasn't the case. Maybe his opponent was just being kind, giving him the chance to move first after his previous loss. Well, Jason told himself, there was only one way to find out. He advanced a white pawn two spaces.

"It's your move," Jason said with a smile.

He pressed the elevator call button and his usual car arrived moments later. Jason stepped aboard, confident he was in store for a smooth ride now that the Ghoul issue had been resolved. But Jason had forgotten that the strange elevator phenomena he repeatedly witnessed had begun well before his and Marvin's wrestling match compromised the Ghoul's containment door. That memory returned along with the flickering lights and electrical pops that greeted him after passing the fourteenth floor. Jason made a mental note to talk to Giorgio and Reggie about fixing the problem... whatever it was.

The elevator dropped Jason off at ground level. The first person he saw was Richard, who was doing his best lazy scarecrow impersonation at the concierge podium. Guests were already abound in the lobby, most headed to breakfast, others already checking in, and the usual lobby staff members- other than Richard- were already hard at work.

"Good morning, boss," Richard said as Jason approached the podium. "Ready for your first day on the job?"

"As ready as I'm going to be," Jason told him. "Is there anywhere particular I should start?"

"Marvin liked to work the check-in counter, but Leila's got that covered for now." Richard pointed discreetly to a middle-aged couple seated in the pseudo-great room. "That's our next intervention target right there. I guess you could start planning for that."

"Okay," Jason said. "Where can I find their file?"

"File?"

"Yeah, you know, their dossier." Jason noticed Richard's blank stare. "Like the one you had on me? Contains all their personal information?"

"Oh, their background research!" Richard said, as if that wasn't the same thing as a dossier. "Yeah... sometimes we get those, sometimes we don't. It's kind of a crapshoot."

"Did we get one for this couple?"

"Not that I'm aware of."

Really helpful, Jason thought. "So, how do we plan an intervention if we don't have their background information?"

Richard shrugged. "I dunno. I'm just a concierge. You're the boss. You're going to have to figure that out."

If this was Richard's way of trying a little harder, Jason hated to see how hard he tried under Marvin's tenure. "Thanks, Richard." Jason said flatly as he moved on.

"No problem!" Richard replied happily.

Jason spotted Katie observing a child with a coloring book on one of the great room couches. He could feel her twitching every time the child got close to the edge of the paper. Heaven help that poor kid if he got crayon on the couch cushion. No, wait, heaven help the janitor who gets snapped at to clean it up.

Jason started toward Katie, but stopped after his brain told him that something wasn't quite the same about the lobby today. He tried convincing himself it was just Marvin's absence, but his inner voice argued that wasn't it. Jason scanned the lobby for anything unusual, but all looked as it always did. He shrugged off the odd feeling and resumed his march toward Katie, then stopped again after only two steps, the source of his uneasy feeling entering his vision directly ahead.

It was a watercolor painting of a young girl posing against a sunset. The girl had wide eyes and bright cheeks and a lively smile. Her painting had been mounted just above the great room fireplace, where it was visible to all as they passed through the lobby. Jason stared at the painting for nearly two minutes. He was certain it hadn't been there for the duration of his trip, and he was fairly confident it hadn't even been there the day before when he returned from limbo. Whoever picked out the painting for its lobby placement had done a great job, though. The featured girl emanated warmth and happiness that inexplicably made Jason feel a serene sense of inner peace. Odd, Jason thought, that it would affect him so much, considering he had no idea who the girl in the painting was.

"It's beautiful, isn't it?" Katie asked, snapping Jason from his trance.

"She is," Jason replied. "I mean, *it* is. When did it go up?"

"This morning. It was a special delivery, though the return address was blank and the delivery man didn't have the sender's info. We assumed you ordered it."

Jason shook his head. "Wasn't me."

Katie shrugged. "Ah, well, maybe it was a parting gift from Marvin." She rifled through her clipboard and removed a piece of paper from the back. "Today's calculations," she said, handing the paper to Jason.

Jason looked over the document, which was filled with scribble he couldn't make heads or tails of, except for the bold '83%' circled at the bottom. "You know I don't have a clue what this means, right?"

Katie smirked at him. She knew. "I guess you'll have to figure that out. You're the boss now."

"So I've been told."

Katie fluttered away, presumably to resume her quality

control duties for the day. But as she left, she turned back to Jason with a cryptic, off-the-cuff remark. "I guess life doesn't defy the odds that often after all." She raised her brow as if to add *hmph*, and then continued on her way.

Jason added a second mental note to have a communication skills training session with his staff. He meandered to the check-in counter and waited patiently while Leila finished with her last awaiting guest. She appeared to be as much a natural with check-in duties as she was with concierge duties. Maybe if Jason didn't like the front desk role, Leila would be willing to shake things up.

"Good morning, Mr. Chance," she said as she organized a stack of paperwork.

The formality was like nails on a chalkboard to Jason's ears. "Since I'm not a guest anymore, maybe we could try *Jason* on for size."

Leila's mouth dropped open dramatically. "You're not a guest anymore?! I would have never known! Unless, oh wait... I've been back here doing *your* job all morning!"

"Ha ha, smartass."

Leila giggled and batted those charming eyes at him. "Why don't come back here and I'll show you the ropes?"

For the next hour, Leila walked Jason through the basics of the hotel's reservation system. She made him watch as she checked a few guests in and out, then observed and corrected as he tried a few on his own. The system wasn't overly difficult, and luckily there were failsafes in place to prevent most major screw-ups, such as double-booking a room, forgetting to issue an invoice, or, God forbid, assigning an innocent person to a room on the thirteenth floor. By the time Leila was done with him, Jason felt he had a competent grasp on the process.

"Thank you," he told her. "You've been a bigger help than Tweedle Dee and the Quality Queen over there." Jason motioned to Richard and Katie.

"Hey!" Leila feigned hurt. "If he's Tweedle Dee, then what does that make me?"

Jason was quick on his feet. "The best employee in this place."

"Damn straight," Leila told him. "And don't you forget it." She stared at him for more than a lingering moment, as if there was something more she wanted to say. But then Jason saw her face shift back into professional mode. "Check-out time is nearing. That should give you a good chance to practice everything we covered. If you run into any problems, you know where to find me."

"Whipping Richard into shape?"

"If only that were possible," Leila said with a roll of her eyes. "Anyway, if you'll excuse me, *Mr. Chance-*"

She said the name with so much emphasis, Jason knew it had been on purpose. "Leila, my name is Jason. I know you can say it, because I heard you do it when the Ghoul busted out of containment."

"Oh, you mean when you were just standing there like an idiot waiting to be slaughtered?" Leila leaned in and whispered, "Life and death situations can make people do and say crazy things."

"Crazy or not, you did say it," Jason challenged. "And I liked the way it sounded."

Leila dismissed him with an *oh please* kind of glare. "You were too busy shaking in your shoes to like the way it sounded."

"To be fair, it was my first encounter with a homicidal supernatural monster," Jason argued.

"I suppose there's that," Leila agreed with a flirtatious smile. "Personally, I thought for sure you were a goner, even if you survived the Ghoul. I mean, what kind of idiot actually sticks around after something like that?"

"I'm pretty sure I've been accused of being an idiot at least once in my life," Jason said, recalling a hazy memory of a conversation he and Leila had over dinner several days earlier.

Leila leaned in and whispered again. "For what it's worth, I'm glad you stuck around." She planted a light peck on Jason's cheek. "*Boss.*"

Jason's heart skipped a beat as Leila pranced away playfully. Once he had his wits about him again, Jason returned his computer to its home screen to prepare for his first solo guest. He then straightened a stack of invoices he and Leila had collected and transferred them to a temporary hanging file in a drawer below the computer. It was then that Jason noticed something he hadn't seen before. It was the corner of an envelope, sticking out ever so slightly from beneath his keyboard. Jason retrieved the envelope, which he discovered had his name typed across the front, and removed a single sheet of paper from within. The paper was Chance Hotel letterhead, and in the middle was a single sentence:

I hope you enjoy your stay. -CH

Jason's mind churned. Who the hell was CH? He examined the letter once more, and then a sudden realization dawned on him as his eyes fell across the name in the header. No... Jason told himself. It couldn't be. Jason looked up at the busy lobby, at all the guests who had come to stay, and at the quirky employees who were there to serve them. This was his new home, this magical, crazy place called the Chance Hotel. And it was clear from the letter that despite everything Jason had seen and gone through, despite his trip beyond the limits of mortality and his new role as the manager of the hotel, he still had a lot to learn.

Author's Note

I hope you enjoyed your visit to the Chance Hotel! As you've probably guessed, Jason's tenure in this magical place has only just begun. He and the rest of the staff will return for more mysteries, fun, and maybe even a new monster or two in *Chance Hotel: Under New Management*, launching on Kindle Vella in the fall of 2022 and releasing as an ebook in 2023. If you're a fan of science fiction, please check out my debut novel, *Shortcake*, the first in a technothriller trilogy that will continue with *Shortcake: Impulse Reborn* in late 2022 and conclude with *Shortcake: Prophecy Fulfilled* in 2023. If you're a fan of action/adventure, please check out my ongoing Kindle Vella series *Pendant of God*, which will also be available as an ebook when it concludes in 2023.

I appreciate all feedback, so please consider leaving an honest rating and review on Amazon. Doing so will help other readers discover the world of *Chance Hotel*. Thank you for supporting my work, and I hope you'll join me for another story in the future!

- Christopher Gorham Calvin

Made in the USA
Columbia, SC
26 September 2022

67579216R00237